*the*
# BOOK
*of*
# EVERLASTING
# THINGS

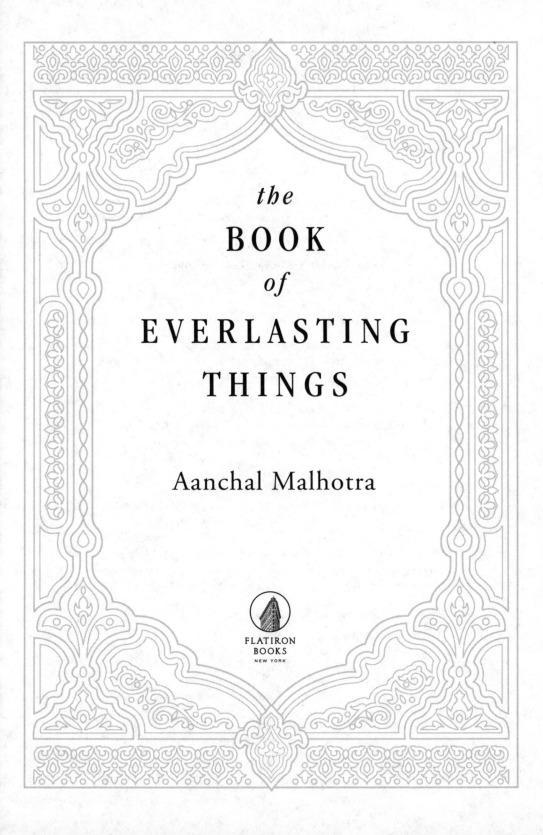

*the*
# BOOK
*of*
# EVERLASTING
# THINGS

Aanchal Malhotra

FLATIRON
BOOKS
NEW YORK

THE BOOK OF EVERLASTING THINGS. Copyright © 2022 by Aanchal Malhotra. All rights reserved.
Printed in the United States of America. For information, address Flatiron Books,
120 Broadway, New York, NY 10271.

www.flatironbooks.com

Designed by Michelle McMillian

Library of Congress Cataloging-in-Publication Data

Names: Malhotra, Aanchal, author.
Title: The book of everlasting things : a novel / Aanchal Malhotra.
Description: First edition. | New York : Flatiron Books, 2022.
Identifiers: LCCN 2022019620 | ISBN 9781250802026 (hardcover) |
ISBN 9781250802019 (ebook)
Subjects: LCGFT: Romance fiction. | Novels.
Classification: LCC PR9499.4.M353 B66 2022 | DDC 823/.92—dc23/eng/20220609
LC record available at https://lccn.loc.gov/2022019620

Our books may be purchased in bulk for promotional, educational, or business use.
Please contact your local bookseller or the Macmillan Corporate and Premium Sales Department
at 1-800-221-7945, extension 5442, or by email at MacmillanSpecialMarkets@macmillan.com.

First Edition: 2022

10   9   8   7   6   5   4   3   2   1

*For my grandfather Vishwa,*
*and in memory of my grandmother Amrit,*
*who had to leave Lahore behind*

A place belongs forever to whoever claims it hardest, remembers it most obsessively, wrenches it from itself, shapes it, renders it, loves it so radically that he remakes it in his own image.

—Joan Didion, *The White Album*

# PART ONE

# The Inheritance

His nose woke up first.

It shook Samir from his slumber, and he sat upright in bed, sniffing out the storm before it began. Sliding out from underneath the mosquito net covering his four-poster bed, he walked up to his window and opened its shutters. Ominous clouds had begun collecting, the moon camouflaged. Staring up at the firmament, he cupped his chin with both hands, resting his elbows upon the windowsill. It would arrive shortly, he could smell it; it would materialize out of nowhere with a crack of bright light and thunder. So he waited, for it was impossible to sleep through an imminent storm.

Ten years earlier, when he had opened his mouth for the first time—a crying, breathing, living being—the bedroom window had flung open and a gust of wind had swept into the room, where it was swallowed completely by the newborn. Samir, his parents would name him. *Samir*, meaning a gust of wind. Samir, the boy who'd swallowed the monsoon.

Now, as the dark skies parted, he welcomed the rain shower that had unfailingly graced his birthday each year since his birth.

"Hello, friend," he spoke into the night.

If asked, he might not have been able to explain how he knew of a storm approaching before it actually did. Water was an odorless substance, and so rain had no smell of its own. It married odors everywhere, smelling eventually of the land where it fell. In Lahore that morning, the rain smelled predictably dusty yet fresh. But Samir, eager to smell past the curtain of precipitation, held out his perceptive nose and followed its aquiline slope down his neighborhood, meandering through streets and homes.

There were many ways to smell. The seat of smell was located in the nose, and so, naturally, he smelled first and foremost from there. But the way that gave him most pleasure, how he felt most physically and intimately connected to any smell, fragrant or foul, was by smelling it through his gut.

With his gut, then, the boy pressed against the open window frame, smelling musty moisture-soaked walls, moss and algae, dung cakes, damp wood, lemongrass, and lotus flowers. Assembling this bouquet within his atlas of smells, Samir returned to bed one year older and many smells richer.

⚜

Like clockwork, at 5:30 a.m., fragrant smoke drifted into Samir's room from underneath the door, and he knew that his uncle was awake in the next room, ritualistically lighting the morning agarbatti. The rain had subsided and the world resumed its calm. Samir got out of bed and dressed in a pair of brown shorts and a blue shirt. He quietly opened the door and walked down the corridor to the tall earthenware pot placed at the end. He splashed cold water on his eyes and wiped down his face. When he looked up into the mirror hung on the wall, his uncle was standing behind him, smiling. Samir turned around and touched his feet.

"Taya ji," he addressed his father's elder brother.

"*Jinde raho, mere puttar,*" Vivek replied in Punjabi, placing his hand affectionately on his nephew's head. "May you live a long life. Ten years old today, how time flies." He laughed.

Together they climbed down the stairs to find the rest of the family preoccupied with the morning routine. Samir walked across the stone aangan to where his grandfather sat, an old man of seventy. Som Nath was hunched over the day's newspaper with a magnifying glass as well as his spectacles comically positioned at the very tip of his nose. Upon seeing Samir, his face broke into a smile and he hugged his grandson. Samir's mother, Savitri, came out from the kitchen, an opal-pink sari tied around her frame, covering her head. She was holding a tray with four tall metal tumblers of lassi, and, handing one to Samir, she kissed him on the forehead.

"*Saalgirah mubarak,* my child," she wished him, before placing two glasses down for Som Nath and Vivek and calling out to her husband. Mohan emerged from the room and took a seat beside his father. In the wake of the early-morning storm, the daylight seemed crisper and bluer than usual. Raindrops clung to the bright green leaves of tulsi planted at the center of the courtyard, and the jasmine lining both sides had thrived in the midnight shower, swathing the entire house in their fragrance.

"Tayyar, ready?" Mohan asked the birthday boy. "Shall we leave?"

Samir gulped down the last sip of frothy milk. "Yes, Baba." He took his father's hand.

⚘

The Vij family lived deep in the heart of the Walled City of Lahore. Though the city had existed for centuries prior, it was under the reign of Emperor Akbar in the sixteenth century that it truly gained prominence. The emperor ordered the building of a palace, around which a defensive wall was constructed, built with thirteen imposing gates, each unique in its design. Over the centuries, many of these majestic gates were destroyed, though the Shahalmi Gate had survived, and it was in its neighborhood that the Vij family built a home.

Their two-story brick house, Vij Bhawan, its name proudly engraved on a stone plaque, stood on the corner of the wide Shahalmi Bazaar Road and the narrow kucha Reshmiya. The silky, delicate, gossamer word *Reshmiya* never failed to make Samir giggle as it slid off his tongue. His grandfather would often tell him the story of how the family had once dealt in the textile trade and how their work in ittar had begun just a few years before Samir was born. Som Nath would extract an embroidered handkerchief from the pocket of his crisply ironed kurta and offer it to the boy as a sample of their once well-established familial craft.

"Back in our day, this is how neighborhoods were formed." Som Nath would gesture with his frail hands, taking his grandson on a journey. "Why, you can trace communities, religions, clans, and people through the names of the streets they live on. Like us, on kucha Reshmiya, named after the silky resham cloth we traded, or gali Dhobiyan, after the washermen. There is a gali Kabootarbaaz, lords of the pigeons, and kucha Faqir Khana, named after the Faqir family, gali Achariyan, the picklers, and my favorite"—he would clap his hands together—"the gali Kababiyan, on which live the makers of delicious kebabs!" Grandfather and grandson would both burst into laughter, and this became a ritual between them, for no matter how many times Som Nath narrated the tale of the entwined streets of their ancient metropolis, Samir loved to hear it.

"Where do the perfumers of Lahore live, Dadu?" Samir would ask. "Why don't we live with them?"

"Well, puttar, there is a community of perfume-sellers who live and work in a neighborhood called Dabbi Bazaar, not far from here. Their shops are clustered around Sunehri Masjid. And you know you're near even before you spot them because the entire street is bathed in extraordinary scents. You can always visit them"—he paused—"but remember, this is the home that your ancestors built. Whatever you do, Samir puttar, whoever you become, however life changes, this is the place where you belong. This is home."

⚜

As Vivek, Mohan, and Samir walked through Shahalmi, smells of the first chai being brewed—tea leaves, cardamom, ginger, tulsi, milk, and sugar—

wafted out of windows, sounds of morning prayer and daily chores rang out, and men and children emerged from winding lanes onto the main street, all making their way to the eastern edge of the old city. Some were dressed in straight pajamas with knee-length cotton kurtas; some wore dhotis with the folds of cloth secured tightly at their waists, reaching down to mid-calf length; and a few, like Vivek, were dressed in the more Western pant-and-shirt combination. Most men donned turbans of varying heights and styles, leaving a tail of fluttering fabric.

In silence, the Vij men walked through the city to its outskirts, not speaking until their destination was in sight, until the mighty, legendary Ravi greeted them. The wild, mischievous river had, in the last many years, changed its direction as it willed and broken its banks open in flood when it desired, indifferent to those who resided close to it. That August morning, people strolled around it in pairs or groups; some sat at its edge, some bathed in its depths, while others devotedly performed their prayers and salutations.

As the waters of the Ravi rose and fell, relaying thousands of years of memory and myth, the Vij men settled down on its sandy banks. It was on these very banks that many saints and holy men had prayed to the mighty gods for enlightenment. It was here that the Sikh Guru Arjan, after five days of torture by the Mughal Emperor Jahangir, had bathed his last, disappearing completely into its stream and passing on to the next world. It was here that the remains of Leelawati, the grandmother Samir never knew, were once scattered. It was here, just a few years ago, that Jawaharlal Nehru had declared purna swaraj, the demand for complete independence from the British Raj. And it was here, on the banks of the historic river, on what would prove to be no mere weekend excursion, that the tides of ten-year-old Samir's days would be altered forever.

Through the long walk, a vial had sat safe in Vivek's front pocket, and now that they were seated, staring ahead at the river that nourished their city, he extracted it and placed it on the ground before his nephew. A small glass vial with an oval bottom and a thick neck, secured shut with a glass stopper. Against the sand it sat, a deep ruby. Samir observed it for a few seconds until his father gently nudged it closer.

Smiling, the boy picked it up and uncorked it, and even before he had a chance to bring it up to his nose, the fragrance struck him. It was absolutely extraordinary, more evocative that anything else he'd ever smelled. During the course of his short life, his eager nose had smelled many things—flowers, leaves, the barks of trees, an assortment of kitchen spices from sweet to spicy, dry stones, wet stones, mossy stones, small insects and domestic animals, and even some of the ittar bottles from the shop if no one was watching. But never had his nose felt so arrested as it did now; never had it come into contact with anything so divine. He'd never smelled it before, and yet for the briefest of moments, he felt as if he were being reintroduced to something long forgotten, as if he'd once been enveloped by this magnificent smell, its memory emanating from deep within.

As the childish smile disappeared from his lips, Samir realized that some smells would affect him in ways different from others. When he was five years old, his uncle had formally introduced him to his first real ingredient, khuss, the essence of vetiver. The deep emerald liquid had instantly reminded Samir of the fragrant grass woven into the curtains of their haveli during summertime. Even at that age, he'd been able to recognize the smell of vetiver from memory, but was never drawn to it in quite the same way that this new aroma invited him in.

His gut was aroused. Desperate, yearning, hungry. Tightening his grasp on the glass stopper in his left hand, he closed his eyes and deeply inhaled the contents of the bottle. Uninhibited, untrained, he concentrated only on smell, as far as his gut would take him. Everything else could wait, had to wait. All that surrounded him—the river, the legends, the sand, the breeze, the morning light, even his family—dissolved. Everything solid melted into air. What remained was a canvas of velvety opulence. It was creamy, fresh, intoxicating, honey-like, yet sharp and dark altogether.

When he opened his eyes, they were lined with tears. And even before he had consciously connected all the dots, the tears began trickling down his face. Unsettled and almost embarrassed, he placed the bottle down and reached up to wipe his eyes. But Vivek held his arm tightly.

"Don't," he began. "You will need those."

Samir looked at his father, the pools of tears now moistening his eyelashes.

Mohan brought his hand to his chin, rubbing it pensively. "How strange it is," he contemplated, "that you should somehow inherit an organ from a man who acquired it completely from his environment. That the nose of your uncle and all its talents be bequeathed to you . . ." He paused. "Incredible."

Vivek smiled knowingly. Since the day he was born, the boy had smelled just about everything he could extend his nose to, making it clear that his destiny was entwined with perfume. But what fascinated Vivek was that someone so young could be provoked so deeply. For a moment, he felt a twinge of jealousy, a wish that his nose would have dictated his decisions earlier than it did.

Clearing his throat then, he inquired about the tears.

Samir shrugged. "I–I don't know, Taya ji. They just appeared." He didn't understand how and couldn't explain why, but felt certain he shared a history with this smell.

"What did you smell?"

"I didn't expect it to be so . . ." He paused, trying to find the words.

"But puttar, what did you smell?" Mohan repeated the question.

"The night," he began softly. "I smelled a beautiful, endless night." Though this was an accurate description, Samir felt the words fall utterly flat when compared with the smell itself. Was it meant to be reduced this way, described in words at all?

Vivek pointed to the vial. "This is the essence of tuberose, or rajnigandha. It blooms at night, and is incredibly precious and difficult to extract. Tell me, what did you *feel?*"

Samir felt almost silly as he said, "Safe, the smell made me feel safe. Like I was lying in a bed of stars."

Mohan shot a look at his older brother, and the perfumer smiled. "Smells can produce visceral, physical reactions in our body—pleasant, unpleasant, or simply intriguing."

"Like the tears, you mean?" Samir asked, eyes wide.

Vivek pursed his lips and nodded.

"It was like a storm erupted in my heart." The child's voice was painted with an ache unnatural for someone his age. "I felt the smell in my heart. Yahaan, here." He placed his palm on his chest.

"But remember, you don't smell with your heart, you smell with another organ." Vivek touched his forefinger to the tip of his nose.

Samir's eyebrows knit together. Surely one could smell from the heart. He *had*, he *did*—from his heart, his gut, his nose, even his fingertips. From his whole body, in fact. But these thoughts were interrupted by his uncle's pragmatism.

"Whatever effect a smell has on your heart is simply one prescribed by memory. When you smell something beautiful, you feel awash. You are taken in by its tide. It's so powerful that you can't explain it and allow yourself to . . ." His voice trailed off.

". . . to drift within it?" Samir completed.

"Exactly. For all those who are afflicted with a keen sense of smell, fragrances no longer remain static liquids, but rather"—Vivek paused, his hands midair in explanation—"become living, breathing, growing, evolving forms. You, it appears, are capable of *experiencing* smell."

*Afflicted,* his uncle had said.

After a few seconds of silence, Samir picked up the glass vial and handed it back to his father.

"No, now this is yours. A birthday present, a welcome gift. It is time." Mohan enclosed the bottle within the palm of Samir's hand, amazed still at the likeness between his young son and his older brother. "From today, you are a perfumer's apprentice."

# 2

# A Brief History of Belonging

The story of Samir Vij and his nose could be traced back to long before his birth. It was, in fact, born in the dreams of his uncle, Vivek, in a field of the Great War, far removed from Lahore, as a product of impossibly cold nights, a desperate longing for home, and a desire for beauty. Over time, this gift of smell was bequeathed to Samir, who, unaware of its origins, wielded it to create a world of his own.

Since 1830, the Vij family had been successful traders of luxury cloth, catering mostly to aristocracy, the courts of maharajas or officers of the Raj. They imported silk from Kashmir, Bengal, and even as far as Central Asia and the Far East. Whether it was Japanese brocade for a dress, pure Chinese silk for a sari, or soft Dhaka mulmul for a kurta, they stocked it all. The family lived in a two-storied haveli in the Shahalmi area, and had rented a shop close by to sell their wares. However, over several decades, as the city developed around them, so did their enterprise. In the late 1800s, to accommodate their growing trade, they purchased a large shop in the famous Anarkali Bazaar, which had transformed from British military barracks, to the city's first lunatic asylum, to a bustling marketplace frequented by the British and Indian elite.

The market was named Anarkali, after the blossom of the bittersweet pomegranate plant, and also a title given to Sharif-un-Nisa, the common courtesan from Lahore who was famously rumored to have captured the attention of Mughal Prince Salim and, thus, had been entombed alive by his father. Salim, upon becoming the Emperor Jahangir, had a beautiful mausoleum built in her memory in the year 1615, and placed above the grave of his beloved a pure marble sarcophagus engraved with ninety-nine attributes to God, and one self-composed Persian couplet to express his undying love. As time passed, the marketplace swallowed this quiet tribute into its chaotic landscape, and stretching from Lohari Gate for one mile up to Nila Gumbad, it became a shopper's paradise.

In 1870, when Som Nath was two, his twenty-four-year-old father set up the Anarkali shop. On opening day, he proudly hung the iconic black-and-white sign passed down from his ancestors, painted in English and Urdu, at the entryway: VIJ & SONS, ESTD 1830, LAHORE. Each morning, rolling up the front curtains of the shop, his father would take a long look down the road as far as the eye could see, all the way to Lohari Gate, from where he'd walked, to this crowded, vibrant center of commerce, and know that they had finally arrived.

Som Nath was twelve when he began working at the shop. Dutifully, he'd organize the turbans and silk cummerbunds displayed in the front window. At times, he would hold the fabrics up to his cheeks, as he'd seen his father do, to discern the texture of each item they sold—the sturdiness of brocade, the smoothness of crepe, the heaviness of silk. As the years passed, his hands—baby soft, able to perceive the differences in fabric on first touch—would retain the last traces of this familial craft.

Business prospered until 1892, when Som Nath's father died suddenly of cholera after a trip to the nearby village of Mian Mir, leaving his recently married son as his sole scion. The women in every generation of the Vij family had died young, and Som Nath, too, had grown up without his mother, who had died in childbirth. Now an orphan, Som Nath took his father's place at the shop.

An outsider had never been hired to assist, and so the young man asked

Leelawati, his brown-eyed, convent-educated bride, whether she'd like to join him at work. Gaze lowered, she agreed, but an unexpected warmth coursed through her body. She remembered how, when she was young, her father had sent her away from the village to study in the city, emphasizing the importance of education for girls. A man ahead of his time. Similarly, it seemed that her new husband, either out of personal belief or sheer requirement, did not believe that one's gender should dictate one's prerogative. The marker of a truly good man, she would note that day, was his ability to treat a woman as his equal. And her husband did, for after that, the couple fell into a routine, both at home and at work.

Som Nath would leave early and open the shop, and Leela would follow around mid-morning, carrying lunch. The smell of her skin, ritualistically cleansed with sandalwood paste each day, would mix with the smells of cumin and flour, tomatoes and garlic, cardamom and potatoes. At times, the bitter turmeric she used in the food would cling to the bottom of her fingernails. All these odors would trail along with her into the shop and get lost within the starchy smell of local cotton and freshly unwrapped shipments of oriental silk. This routine gave to Som Nath healing after the death of his father, and to Leela a welcomed sense of liberation. Together, they ran the business as partners and, in a matter of years, had two sons, Vivek and Mohan. Born six years apart, their boys' childhoods seemed like their ancestors', preemptively woven into the familiar lengths of satin and silk. But little did Som Nath know that fate had other plans.

Though he dutifully helped around the shop, Vivek showed no true interest in the difference between velvet and chiffon, or the grades of fabric and their textures. The business of cloth was not for him, he'd state coolly, whenever asked. All the romance and luxury of decadent textiles that besotted Som Nath fell flat on Vivek.

Instead, he would dream about the places the fabrics had come from, weaving invisible excursions. Picking up oriental silk, he would wonder what Cheen looked like. Making a curtain with the fine Dhaka mulmul, he would dream of the eastern edge of the country, where it was woven. And what about the south of Hindustan from where they sourced remarkably decadent Kanjivaram silks? His father never told him any stories. So though he respected the successful enterprise his parents had built, Vivek couldn't imagine spending his life measuring out bales of fabric after fabric when there was a whole world waiting to be discovered.

Avoiding his chores, he would often stroll the length of Anarkali Bazaar, drinking the delicious peda lassi and gorging on samosas and imli chutney at halwai Bhagwan Das's shop, or flying kites with his friends. When he had to make deliveries outside the Walled City, he took his time by cycling through the fluffy cotton fields around Railway Colony. But what he loved the most was to spend time in Khushboo Lal's perfumery, in the company of ittars and essential oils. Vivek was less affected by perfumes than by the stories that accompanied them, for Khushboo Lal was not just a perfumer but a storyteller, indulging in everything that Som Nath would not. He drew from history and mythology, from the geography of smells, and recited anecdotes about people who distilled extraordinary perfumes from their ordinary surroundings. Sitting in Lahore, Vivek traveled the lengths of Hindustan, and ultimately the world, through smell. By way of Khushboo Lal's stories, he walked through saffron fields in Pampore and picked bright white jasmine in Madurai, gathered ambergris on the shores of oceans faraway and smelled the musk deer in Leh. He listened to sacred histories of rose and sandalwood, and learned about the fragrance of the earth.

Vivek would never understand that cloth could tell stories too, that weave and pattern could also be the stuff of legends, that with every fold, every pleat, tradition could take shape, and the *earth*, the very earth, could be woven right into fabric. No matter what Som Nath tried, there was no way of impressing the significance of family legacy on the boy. In the long line of his ancestors, an alternative profession had never once been pursued. But his firstborn saw on the horizon something vaster and more immeasurable than yards of fabric. This became more apparent as the years passed, and at the age of twenty, having passed his college examinations, Vivek Nath Vij enlisted into the army with the help of Smith sahib, an English patron who had been a regular at the shop for years.

It was unusual for an educated young man like himself, with no military relations or financial need, really, to become a soldier. The modest sum of eleven rupees a month hardly proved an incentive for someone who had grown up in relative comfort. He was Khatri, a caste of people who had, at the time of the Mughal Empire, risen to importance by holding administrative and financial positions. He did not belong to any of the preferred martial races, nor had he any desire for rank or status. Yet in the year 1913, driven not by ambition or any sense of duty but rather a hunger for adventure, Vivek officially became a part of the Indian army. Som Nath tried repeatedly to dissuade him, to no avail. He wanted to be happy for his son, but the concern for legacy refused him that luxury, and an uneasy distance grew between the two.

Then, in August 1914, when the shadow of war extended as far as Hindustan, Vivek, a soldier in the Lahore Division, was dispatched overseas as a part of the Expeditionary Forces. They were to fight alongside British soldiers on European soil for the first time. And though the Vij family had interacted closely with English men and women at the shop, the boundary between them and Indians was well-defined. The war grew in Vivek's mind as an opportunity to *feel* equal, to exist in the same world, to rise above ingrained inferiority, and to attempt to obscure—if only temporarily, for the duration of war—the difference between white and brown.

As Vivek stood at the threshold of Vij Bhawan, ready to enter the war on behalf of the angrez king, George Pancham, Leela painted a tilak onto his forehead, and the rich, earthy smell of sandalwood filled the entryway of the haveli. Through the course of Vivek's life, sandalwood had come to define his mother's presence, and during these parting moments, he inhaled the fragrant air around them, imprinting her into his very anatomy. Leela wiped her tears away with the edge of her sari and proudly hugged her elder son, running her fingers through his thick, bushy beard. She blessed him by placing one hand on his uniform turban. Mohan, only fourteen at the time, made his brother promise that he would write as often as he could about all the wonders of vilayat, the foreign land. Laughing, Vivek agreed, and then looked around the courtyard until his eyes met his father's. No words were spoken, no gestures of affection were made, and so Vivek turned around and walked out the door. Barely had he gone twenty paces from the corner of kucha Reshmiya when he heard his name being called out.

Som Nath, his pale yellow kurta fluttering, ran to him. His slippers were caked with fresh mud from puddles left by the morning rain. He wiped down the specks of wet dirt clinging to the back of his pajamas before looking up at Vivek. A rehearsed silence settled for a few moments until Som Nath conceded defeat. The brink of a long separation was no occasion to persist with old grudges, Som Nath admitted softly. Then he suddenly began patting down his kurta, digging through all his pockets, wishing to give his son something to remember home by. Unable to find anything more precious, he extracted a notebook, barely a few inches in height and width, basic brown with the words VIJ & SONS, ESTD 1830, LA-HORE embossed on its cover. He shrugged, smiled sheepishly, and held it out; this would have to do.

Vivek took the notebook from his father's hands and flipped through it. The first few pages were filled with measurements and details of orders, but apart from that it was brand-new. Tears stung his eyes as he read the cursive handwriting, and then placed the notebook in the shirt pocket closest to his heart. Of all the mementos to remind him of what he was so readily leaving behind, this was perhaps the most fitting, for within its pages wrestled a legacy fractured by the pursuit of dreams. Overwhelmed, he bent down to touch his father's feet, and Som Nath placed a gentle hand on his head and blessed him.

Then, quietly, the duo parted.

3

·───◇───·

# The War Years

At the beginning, Vivek's letters home were long and unhurried, detailing all the wonders of vilayat.

Som Nath would read aloud the Urdu passages about traveling over the dangerous black waters, about trains that sped through tunnels underground, people who looked like the sahibs but spoke a language called Francisi, and the statue of an imposing woman on a horse, reminiscent of the Hindustani Rani of Jhansi. The welcome the soldiers would receive was kingly, complete with cheering and flowers and common citizens rushing to shake their hands and take their photograph. Vivek sent home a stack of Francisi newspapers, fearing that no news was being reported at home.

Nearly a million and a half of Hindustan's young men, including Vivek, fought for the British Empire, along with its allies, in fields of war far removed from everything familiar. Vivek's letters about his regiment were full of admiration for the sepoys who, quite unlike him, carried generations of martial history in their blood. Though the letters did not detail his exact location, they were generous in their descriptions of routine and feelings of excitement. Strange as it was, Vivek's absence from Lahore allowed him to grow closer to Som Nath, their letters speaking more openly than father and son ever had in the last many years.

But by late autumn of 1914, when the colors of fabric at their shop metamorphosed from light hues and pastels to the shades of earth and shadow, Vivek's letters also grew darker. He had fought his first battle, and suddenly, like the war, his tone became distant, his letters detailing the cold weather and unending wait. Waiting was the only constant, for there passed days without activity. He wrote about the waterlogged and marshy tunnels they would crouch in during battle, the sounds of bombs and fear of the enemy. He wrote of those who had died, and many more who had been wounded and were recovering in hospitals. In rare moments of lightness, he mentioned his fellow sepoys, and that he was learning to speak the Francisi language. As a literate sepoy, Vivek had been appointed as the company scribe, a kaatib, and in addressing letters to homes and battalions deployed across the world, he had realized the sheer scale of the war.

When winter arrived, the smell of guavas permeated the air of Vij Bhawan. Soft, leathery, creamy, sweet, eaten with black salt or sugar, they were Vivek's favorite fruit, and became a reminder of his absence. His letters had become infrequent, and when he wrote in December 1914, he described how the entire battlefield had frozen under a thick bed of snow, and the temperature had become unbearable. His tone no longer read as defiant or yearning for adventure, but rather somber, suddenly mature, even plaintive. "This morning, I found the ink in my inkpot to have frozen, and had to melt the dark crystals over a fire so I may write this letter to you. All trace of green has vanished. Frost covers the earth as far as the eye can see. The clothes on our back are barely sufficient to protect us, and we have not seen the sun for months. Here, we are starved and sacrificed." These candid words left an unshakable sadness in Vij Bhawan, for before this, they hadn't quite understood what war had meant, what it *could* mean. The thought of Vivek entombed under a blanket of snow began to haunt his family.

In February 1915, they learned that Vivek had sustained a head injury but returned to the trenches shortly after. Though spare in details of physical pain, the note concluded with, "I wish not to worry you, but there is not much else to tell. There are orders against writing too much. No one knows how long the fighting will go on for, one month or three more years. On the battlefield, there is fire everywhere. When this war is over, I am certain I shall fear the sight of a burning matchstick."

In spring, the Indians had fought another major battle, and Vivek's letter described the dwindling number of soldiers, some succumbing to the cold and others to the inevitable consequence of war. Som Nath read from the page, his voice hardly louder than a whisper, the words choking in his throat: "Every moment we fear to be our last, and now it is difficult to say if I will return. These letters may be my last traces. It's become clear that many of us here will remain unremembered, unrecognized, unknown, for there is no one keeping record. Our contributions and our blood will quietly mix with the soil of this foreign land. Let me say this while I still can: we were here too."

As Som Nath finished reading, a heaviness settled into the room. Leela used the end of her sari to wipe her tears. Mohan looked out the window, unable to face his brother's words. Som Nath exhaled deeply. "We were here too," he repeated. "We were here too."

That day onward, he waited impatiently for the postman to come, desperate to see anything with a foreign postage stamp, and gradually, anxiety and fear became his constant companions. He habitually returned to the stack of Francisi newspapers, poring over the grainy monochrome images of ships and marching regiments, scanning every discernible face for a likeness of his son.

When summer began, a letter arrived addressed only to Som Nath. "You told me not to join the army, but I paid no heed to your words," Vivek admitted. "I now regret this terribly."

The cloth merchant had neither the nerve nor the courage to respond immediately, and the letter lived in his front pocket, close to his heart, for a week. Then one day in the shop, as the curtains were lowered at lunchtime, Som Nath broke down and penned three words on a postcard, instructing Mohan to run and post it to the vilayati address at once.

"*Ghar aa jao*," he wrote. "Please come home."

But weeks passed without word from Vivek, and in the lull of the Lahori summer, Leela, conscious of her childish scrawl, dictated to Mohan the contents of her first letter to the front. "My son, raja puttar, why do you not write?" she asked. "We have been waiting for weeks to hear any news. Are you still on the battlefield? There is no need to spin long yarns of your days, but do write that you are well. Your silence is far harder to endure than this long separation. The summer is upon us here. The neem tree has sprouted its branches right into the courtyard, leaving a sea of yellow seeds on the ground each day. The Chaunsa mangoes have arrived from Mintgumri early this year. Do write, my son. The house is quiet without you." With a hopeful heart, she stuck the stamps onto the envelope and sent it out.

A few weeks later, a letter confirmed that Vivek was still alive. It was an almost blank sheet upon which were written just two questions: "Did Mohan fly kites during basant? What kind of ittar is Khushboo Lal distilling this season?" Troubled and confused, Som Nath wrote back about the smell of jasmine and henna, and the two kites Mohan had won during the kite-flying festival a few months earlier.

To this, there came no reply. Many weeks passed and, in despair, Som Nath subscribed to an English daily, the *Tribune,* in hopes of reading whatever was written on the war, but the offering was scant. From those whose fathers and brothers had also enlisted, he'd gather information, but no one's letters ever mentioned his son. Then one day, while walking along Circular Road, he came across a group of people standing by the local vegetable-seller, listening intently as an elderly man read out from a newspaper. Overhearing the word *jung,* war, he, too, joined the crowd and listened. That day, Som Nath discovered that Mahbub Alam's Urdu daily, *Paisa Akhbar,* was printing news from where Vivek had been sent. The report reveled in the glory of the Indian sepoys for the invaluable service they had rendered to the Empire. "Their casualties may be heavy; but the reward is rich," it stated. Some people called it Laam, the Long War, while others described it as *Jarman di larai*, the German War, though no one knew any facts of battle. Still, some news, even if it was unpleasant, was better than no news at all, Som Nath concluded, temporarily relieved.

But rumors wafted through the old city of soldiers who had died on the battlefield, of Germans who had decapitated them, of enemy spies hiding in Lahore, of new brides whose husbands had gone to war without spending even a single night with them, of mothers who roamed the streets day and night, waiting. And slowly, much against his will, Som Nath began to lose hope. The Vij men had not been made for warfare, after all. He looked for Smith sahib, who had originally helped Vivek enlist in the army, but he, too, had been called upon during the war years. Despairingly, Som Nath would return to the last letter they'd received and read it again and again, as if searching for clues, certain that he'd missed something. *Basant,* spring. *Patang,* kites. *Ittar,* perfume. It wasn't long before he'd memorized the contents and was able to recite the letter entirely from memory.

At the end of the 1915 monsoon season, one year after Vivek had left, Leela went to visit her family in rural Punjab. Though she had been sent as a young girl to a convent school in the city, her family had always remained in the village, tending to their farmlands. She traveled escorted in a tanga, hoping to return to Lahore in two weeks' time. But during her stay, it rained all day and all night, filling her childhood village with mosquitoes and disease. When she finally returned to the city, she felt a hot fever seize her body. Alarmed, on the first night, she soaked the end of her sari in cold water and wiped her face and arms, hoping to cool the fever down. Over the next week, she remained in her room, no longer able to accompany her husband to work. Leela grew considerably weaker, but did not allow anyone to be around her, apart from bringing food or water, for fear of contamination. A panicked Som Nath wrote to Vivek, though he knew a response would not arrive anytime soon. On the tenth day, when he entered Leela's room with a glass of haldi doodh, she was gone, leaving a body covered in inflammations. The illness had consumed her.

Together with Mohan, Som Nath performed Leela's last rites. On the banks of the river Ravi, she was consigned to fire and smoke. Three hundred kilograms of ignited sandalwood, inside which was tucked the body of a beloved—washed, cleansed, and shrouded. Father and son waited for six long hours until the creamy smell of sandalwood that Leela had borne on her person entwined with the raw earthiness of the sandalwood pyre. Using a stick, Som Nath's trembling hands struck his deceased wife's skull with a startling crack—the only way to release her soul. Mohan watched in silence, unable to comprehend how abruptly his mother had departed from the world. When all was over, the aroma of sandalwood was replaced by odorless ash.

Leela's body had been reduced completely to embers, save one blackened, wood-like bone. Her death had been so swift, too swift, and yet here was a bone that refused to burn. Som Nath picked up the charred bone and pressed it discreetly into his palm. Briefly, he wondered which of Leela's bones it was—the collar jutting out from beneath her cotton blouses, that last rib visible through the sheer fabrics of her summer saris, the ankle upon which sat the silver payals he loved so much. Which part of her did he now possess? The priest handed him the ashes. Once those were immersed into the holy waters of the Ravi, Leela disappeared completely.

A heartbroken Som Nath wrote to Vivek about what had transpired, but no letter came. For months, he continued to write to the foreign address, but no letter ever came. Then a sinking thought crossed his mind. *What if his son, too, had perished?*

Alongside familial suffering, business had also suffered. During wartime, restrictions grew on imports, and with the advent of the Swadeshi movement, demand for foreign cloth diminished rapidly. Hindustanis wanted local homespun khaadi, which the Vijs had never sold, and without the luxurious silks they'd once imported from Central Asia and the

Far East, British patrons also dwindled. Mohan had turned seventeen and single-handedly took care of whatever little business remained. Meanwhile, fifty-year-old Som Nath succumbed to his sorrows. Since there was no word in his vocabulary to denote a parent who had lost a child, he accepted the other role life had meted out to him—widower. By 1916, as the war had reached its halfway mark, Som Nath was convinced he had lost half his family.

When the war ended two years later, far fewer men returned home. From time to time, Som Nath would leaf through the Francisi newspapers and discover a world of violence unfamiliar to him, a world that had claimed his son. In moments of desperation, he'd want to shred the newsprint to bits, but nostalgia prevented him, for in the pockets of grainy black and white were the last landscapes his older son had walked.

Silence descended upon the cloth merchant and his younger son. While Som Nath became overwhelmed with sadness, Mohan assumed the role of parent, caregiver, and homemaker, and continued to open the shop every day, more out of habit than because doing so brought in much money. With hardly any customers, their wealth dwindled, and he knew they wouldn't remain afloat for much longer. Some days, sitting by the wooden jharokha window, the boy would survey the large two-story house and wonder how long it would be before this physical trace of ancestry would have to be abandoned.

It was on a Friday in late August 1920 that someone knocked on the narrow side entrance of Vij Bhawan. Mohan opened the door to a slim, clean-shaven man wearing brown pants and a white shirt with suspenders. In his arms were a large suitcase, a small leather case, and a woolen coat. Mohan looked on, puzzled, until from his shirt pocket, the man extracted a brown notebook with the words VIJ & SONS, ESTD 1830, LAHORE embossed on the cover.

# 4

# The Affliction

The story of what had happened to Vivek Vij in the foreign land was never divulged, though upon his return, Som Nath's spirits lifted considerably. But the Vivek who had left Lahore was not the same man who had returned, for he refused to talk at all—about the war, about his time in vilayat, even about his returning. There was no sign of his uniform, his demeanor had become guarded and reticent, and his features angular, almost unrecognizable from the warm, full-bearded face he'd left with in 1914. The only thing Son Nath truly recognized was the large mole on his son's right cheekbone, which had thankfully remained unchanged. On his first Diwali home in six years, when the entire neighborhood was bursting celebratory firecrackers and singing festive songs, Vivek remained confined to his room, palms stiffly shutting his ears to the noise and fire outside, face buried in his chest. When Mohan found him this way, he had neither the words nor the courage to comfort his brother.

Some evenings, Som Nath would sit next to Vivek on the four-poster bed. Using Leela as a bridge, he'd try to find a way back to his son. He would recount how much she had missed him, how she had placed his photograph by her bedside, how certain she was that he would return. He would offer him memories of sandalwood and mangoes and guavas.

And all these Vivek would quietly accept, but he would not utter a word. Eventually, Som Nath deduced that encounters in battle, much like those with death, hardened the heart, for the war seemed to have rendered his son impassive.

Then one morning, as the sky was marbled in shades of blue and burned orange, Vivek sat cross-legged on the floor of his room. Outside the window, the neem tree swayed noisily, but he paid no heed. Before him lay the brown leather case he'd carried back from vilayat, covered in dust and cobwebs from being stored under the bed. Three months had passed since his return to Lahore, but the case had not once been opened. Sometimes he would bring it out and gingerly run his fingers across the weathered surface, or play with the clasp, yet he was unable to summon the courage to confront its contents. This case was not only the reason for his return, but also the reason for his silence.

The previous evening, Vivek had found a sepia photograph of a smiling couple, tucked into a book. The woman had doe eyes and an oval face, her hair styled into a bun, and the man had a dark mole on his right cheekbone. It had unsettled him, and he'd been unable to sleep all night, lying awake, staring at the ceiling, wrestling with his thoughts, repeatedly retrieving the photograph, caressing the smiling faces, and then placing it back into the book. But the discovery had stirred something in Vivek, something resolute, adamant, like ancient sand from the bottommost layer of the ocean. By dawn, he'd made his decision. It was time.

Using his hands, he wiped the dust off the surface of the case and, with a deep breath, unclasped it to reveal several rows of small glass bottles with wooden corks, secured in place by thick leather straps and thin wooden boards. Vivek's face relaxed as he placed his hands over the bottles. Each one had a label with a different name, number, chemical formula, and description. Running his fingers over them, he extracted a vial of pale yellow liquid and uncorked it. Then bringing it up to his impatient nose, he closed his eyes. *Inhale.* Whiskey, iris flower, peaches, subtle notes of patchouli, grapefruit, bergamot. *Exhale.* He opened his eyes, and again lifted it to his nose. *Inhale.* Musk, wood, leather. *Exhale.* Placing the soft cork back into the mouth of the vial, he sighed.

"Veer ji," a voice called out from the half-opened door. Elder brother, Mohan still called him, just like when he was little. "*Eh sab ki hai?* What are these bottles?"

Since his return to Lahore, Vivek would sit by the wooden windows and stare at the world outside, he would water the tulsi Leela had planted in the center of the courtyard, he would ritualistically light the incense sticks each morning, he would watch quietly as his father and brother tallied up the losses of their fading business, but he would never talk. It was as if the war had claimed his voice. But on that morning, he motioned for his brother to come sit beside him.

"Ambrette," he said, enunciating the word slowly, his accent flattening and rolling the foreign *r,* unable to reproduce its ordinarily throaty sound. "Mushk dana, it is called here. A very important base note." Vivek's eyes glimmered and he held out the bottle.

"Base note?" Mohan began, confusedly, and then shook his head into silence.

Maybe it was the fact that he hadn't heard his brother's voice in years, or perhaps it was the absurdity of smelling vials of colored liquid, but the scene brought a smile to Mohan's face. He asked not a single question—not a why or how or where from—but simply held the bottle and smelled as he'd been instructed.

"Mushk dana," he repeated, concentrating, "smells like skin or animal hide." He scrunched his nose. Vivek nodded in agreement.

That day at Vij Bhawan, satins and silks gave way to fragrances and essential oils. One year had passed since Khushboo Lal left to go back to his native Kannauj in the United Provinces, and Vivek decided that it was time a new ittar shop be opened in the bazaar.

Som Nath quietly followed his son's lead, grateful to have Vivek show an interest in *something,* even if it was something as unfamiliar as ittar. What did his son know about perfumery? How could a soldier understand scent? Why had he asked what Khushboo Lal had been distilling all those years ago in his letters? Questions multiplied in Som Nath's mind, but upon seeing the passion in his son's eyes and, most of all, the keenness in his demeanor, all doubt was cast aside. If this is what his son truly wanted to do, then the family had nothing to lose by trying. After all, everything that could have been lost had already been lost, he told himself, thinking of Leela.

For a few months, they temporarily closed the shop and disposed of any remaining textile stock. While Som Nath and Mohan built new shelves and counters inside, and an atelier in the back, Vivek began an expedition. If he were to open a perfumery, he would need a treasury of smells. Leaving the pair at work in Lahore, he traveled across the country to source ingredients, and the first person he sought out was Khushboo Lal. Spending weeks with him in Kannauj, he learned the art and mechanics of distillation in order to set up a unit in Lahore. He brought over earthy mitti ittar from Kannauj, nutty kewra from Orissa, and leathery saffron from Pampore. With the resuming of international trade, he arranged for the import of foreign ingredients, rare and unheard of in Hindustan. He compared the sweet roses of Turkey and Bulgaria to the exquisite local Hasayan rose from the Central Provinces and the Damask rose from Pattoki. He obtained not the flower but the intensely green, slightly cucumbery leaves of the violet plant from France. He procured Mediterranean orange blossom and Italian bergamot.

As expected, the sudden closing and extensive renovation of the shop sparked gossip among the other shopkeepers of the bazaar, who would sometimes peek through the newspaper-covered windows. The Sikh couple who lived above the shop had passed away, and since no new tenant occupied the space yet, Vivek promptly bought it, tore down the interior walls and roof, fortified its floor, and set up his distillery, leaving only the original carved wooden balconies at the front as they were. Needless to say, this perplexed fellow shopkeepers even more, as they watched construction materials being carried in and out of the mysterious site.

Vivek then searched for the distillers who had once created Khushboo Lal's scented empire—the masters of aromatic extraction who had learned the art from their forefathers. Three such men, Ousmann, Aarif, and Jameel, he employed to construct and work the six distillation units. They built their world using bricks, wood, copper, bamboo, clay, and rope. To enliven it, they added fire, water, and air. Finally, to infuse it with soul, they offered fragrant flowers and roots, herbs and grasses, woods and soils. Within months, this unused space became an operating perfumery, smoke ascending to the sky, and traces of rose, jasmine, or lemongrass often wafting down the staircase and cascading onto the road.

In the years following the war, Anarkali Bazaar blossomed to such new heights that by the 1920s, it emerged as the most magnificent marketplace in all of North India. The nobility arrived in their horse-drawn carriages, local women imitated the English style and fashion, while street bards sang qissas of the vanishing modesty of the times, and people from the farthest corners of the Punjab traveled to the bazaar to shop for specialty wares.

It was here, in the sprawling urban center of commerce that had fashioned the fortunes of his family for decades, that Vivek Nath Vij set up a perfumery. A house of fragrance, an ittar-kadā. And like his ancestors, he, too, on the first day of its opening, proudly hung up a black-and-white sign at the entryway, the only difference being the vocation it stated: ITTAR KADĀ, VIJ & SONS, ESTD 1921, LAHORE.

# 5

# The Perfumer's Apprentice

In 1937, after his initiation at the river Ravi, ten-year-old Samir began his apprenticeship at the ittar shop. He was in grade four at a boys' school in a large haveli at Wachowali, not far from his maternal grandparents' home. A section of the building was set apart for older Sanskrit scholars, and every morning the teachers led the students in prayer. Most boys in Samir's grade were Hindu or Sikh, with the exception of a few Muslims. Classes were held outdoors on reed mats, and in the winter, they'd move to the rooftops, where it was warmest.

Waiting for the school day to end, Samir sat impatiently, tapping his fingers on his wooden takhti, which served as a writing board. Master ji was laying great emphasis on the English language, which had been introduced into their lessons that very year. Prithvi, Sunder, Baljeet, Zahir, and Ashok all repeated the words after him, giggling as they rounded their *o*'s and extended the ends of their sentences like they'd heard the British sahibs do. Samir, too, mouthed the words distractedly, but as soon as the bell rang, he zipped out of the courtyard, takhti in hand, and ran all the way home. Sitting with Som Nath, he scarfed down his lunch and then rode his bicycle out of Shahalmi Gate to Anarkali Bazaar for his first day of work.

⚶

That afternoon, Savitri clicked a photograph of Mohan, Vivek, and Samir outside the shop, commemorating the occasion. *Two brothers and a perfumistic child,* she thought, smiling. Once developed and framed, the black-and-white image would hang proudly on the wall behind the cash counter. Samir might have been the heir to this sacred world of scent, but he had hardly been granted any formal intimacy with it until now. Even the first few months of his apprenticeship would extend only to the shop, not the distillery above or the atelier at the back, for a position at the altar of delights, even as a spectator or a student, had to be earned.

Every member of the household was engaged, in some way, within the family's fragrant foundation. From his uncle, Samir would inherit the skills of composition. From his mother, the daughter of a hakim, a traditional physician, he learned the medicinal properties of certain oils and ointments. And from his father, he came to understand the working of a business.

Young Samir had waltzed into the shop that day carrying a distinct feeling of self-importance, which quickly deflated when he learned that his task for the foreseeable future was only to run errands and become acquainted with every nook of the shop. His uncle's warmth quickly melted away as he handed Samir a rag and sent him off to dust the many, many bottles arranged along the many, many shelves. With a sigh, the boy trudged to the back.

The ittar-kadā housed hundreds of different fragrances and oils. One wall was fitted with sturdy shelves upon which sat row after row of identical dark glass bottles. Round-bodied and wide-necked with wooden corks, they were tinted to protect the delicate ingredients inside, and each one still bore the original handwritten Urdu label. Running his index finger across these dusty, peeling labels, Samir took in the order of display and the varying quantities of liquid the bottles held. Carefully climbing onto a wooden ladder, he started from the topmost shelf and made his way across, committing each name to memory. Even though the task was trivial and tedious, his closeness to the magical contents of each bottle inspired him to labor on. And for the length of the autumn season, as the perfumery above them distilled the rich subcontinental rose, the sweet smell draping itself like a tapestry on the air, the lean ten-year-old carefully lifted bottle after bottle, peering at its label, silently mouthing the words, cleaning the spot where it once sat, and then placing it back, just as carefully.

Week after week, as Samir dutifully continued on, Vivek began to delegate to him other tasks, like measuring out and pouring ittar into smaller bottles for purchase, or sticking on labels, or making deliveries across the city. One day, he handed his nephew a small notebook, similar to the one Som Nath had given him at the beginning of the war. He asked the boy to begin noting down the ingredients he smelled and what they evoked, and, delighted to have ascended in his perfumistic education, Samir began uncorking and unbottling every container and inhaling its contents. He would lift the stoppers slowly, hover his attentive nose over the bottles, and inhale the trail of scent before scribbling his observations in the notebook.

Sometimes, after a prolonged day of smelling, Samir would return home exhausted. By evening, his nose would have given up on him, unable to distinguish between even the most basic of smells, much to Samir's frustration. On days like these, Savitri would climb the stairs up to his room and sit by the foot of his bed, glass bangles clinking on her wrists, and teach her son the tricks she had acquired over the years to momentarily escape the overwhelming realm of odor.

One night, she held out her arm, rolled up the long sleeve of her sari blouse, and gestured to the inside of her elbow, the crook. Light brown skin with pulsating dark green veins visible underneath. "Hold out your arm and smell this part."

Lifting his tired self to an upright position, he held out his left arm, cradling the elbow with the right hand, inserted his nose into the crook, and inhaled. Nothing. He tried again, digging his nose deeper into the soft fold of skin, his mouth slightly ajar. *Inhale. Exhale.* This time, he only smelled his own breath, warm and recycled.

"Your nose is tired, overused, underrested. This is natural. When we constantly smell things, the glands in our nose begin to acclimatize and recognize the smells and, eventually, stop warning us of their newness. For a while, we smell nothing. If it happens again, which it will, just smell your own skin, the crook of the elbow. Imagine it to be . . ." Her voice trailed off as she tapped her forefinger on her lips, thinking. "Imagine this plot of skin as an island. Isolated from all smells, a brief interlude, a patch of renewal."

Looking at his mother, Samir smiled into his island.

One afternoon, watching his nephew sniff a bottle of woody nagarmotha essence, Vivek suggested applying it onto his skin before smelling. By absorbing into the skin, ittar mixed with the natural scent of its wearer, making the same perfume smell different depending on who was wearing it. Doing this, Samir found that on sweaty days, the lavender essence fell flat on his skin, while on other days, it bloomed to perfection. Some days, he adored the spicy ginger flower, and on others, it pierced his nose severely. If he happened to rub the eucalyptus oil onto his fingertips in the early morning, the resulting smell felt heavy and potent, but if, by chance, he happened to dab it into the depression of his collarbone close to the evening hours, then its green, medicinal, camphoraceous notes would never fail to please. At times, he would apply ittar onto his own as well as his mother's wrist and note the differences. Meandering through the collection of ingredient bottles, Samir would try to record in tangible terms the very intangible nature of scent.

*Ne-ro-lee.* He whispered the foreign name as he wrote it on the page, breaking it into its syllables after reading the Urdu label. It was refreshing, heady, and smelled similar to both orange blossom and bitter orange, placed right beside it. But the vial labeled *orange leaves,* on the other hand, emanated a woody orange. The bottle of narcissus reminded Samir of an overwhelming cluster of green.

Holding in his hands two bottles of pale yellow-green liquid, he smelled them one at a time, and deduced them to be related. The first, bergamot, was light, delicate, smooth, clean, herbal, and halfway between a lemon and an orange, but retaining the crispness of both. It was rare and exotic, unlike anything he'd smelled before, and even after he'd placed the glass stopper back on the bottle, the smell of bergamot persisted, the oil clinging to his fingertips. The second bottle contained pure citrus, reminding Samir immediately of freshly squeezed lemonade in the summertime. Zesty, astringent, bright, and vibrant, it created a familiar wetness on his tongue.

His uncle had once told him that he was capable of experiencing smell; perhaps this was what he meant—to feel it, to live it, to have a bodily reaction to it. Closing his eyes, he inhaled the citrus once again and felt his tongue reach out instinctively and touch the roof of his mouth, filling it with saliva. He pictured Savitri in the kitchen of Vij Bhawan, slicing raw lemons and squeezing out their juice with her bare hands. He thought of the totems made with lemons and green chilies hanging outside the Hindu shops of Anarkali, placed to ward off the goddess Alakshmi, known to bring poverty and misfortune. He imagined lying under the summer sun, chewing lemon and mint crushed on ice, chomping on roasted peanuts, onions, and tomatoes splashed with lemon, eating boiled white rice or salted chapatis squirted with fresh lemon juice. A mere whiff created an endless montage.

Fragrance possessed the power to provide instant, pure pleasure. Quicker than even sight or sound, it penetrated Samir's senses, transporting him simultaneously to multiple places with each whiff. He was told that true beauty was in the ingredients. They were building blocks, like the verses that constructed a poem. The essences, the soul, ruh, they were called in Urdu.

۔ـ

As winter arrived, the floral, fruity, green, light ittars, popular through the hot months of the year, gave way to the voluminous, woody, resinous, leathery ittars like musk, saffron, oudh, and the herbaceous, spicy shamama. Most patrons purchased the already filled vials lining the shelves, but some came in with demands for a bespoke fragrance—perhaps to bottle the smell of their childhood in a desert village, or of their mother's hands after she had applied henna to her hair, or of the earthy saffron they had once smelled along a valley in the mountains. These customers Vivek would lead to his atelier, and there, in the sanctum of smell, they would ideate, equal parts nostalgia and chemistry, and over the course of weeks or months, the sensory demands would be met, almost always to satisfaction.

Day after day, Samir would observe Vivek uncork each bottle and rub small quantities of viscous liquids onto the wrists of his customers, and Mohan dutifully tally up the sales of the day, balancing the books and inventory. Sometimes, when he arrived after school, the boy would stand at the foot of the stairs up to the distillery and smell the smoke that rose from the cauldrons, but his mother would sternly march him into the shop and assign stock-taking or window-cleaning duty, reminding him that he would have to earn his place at the distillery.

In the hours she spent in the shop, Savitri transformed it, much as the mother-in-law she never met had. Several decades ago, when Som Nath had found himself alone in the old family business of textiles, he'd sought the assistance of his wife, Leela—a tradition swiftly inherited by the next generation. Thus, Savitri became not just a member of the Vij family, but also a crucial part of their work, enjoying the freedom that so few other women did. She often helped the more reserved female patrons, who were bound by their modesty and reluctant to be assisted by a member of the opposite sex, discover their fragrant fancies by setting up intimate smelling sessions in their carriages outside or at the back of the shop, away from any male gaze.

Mostly, Samir observed the rise and fall of noses in the air as customers sniffed their way through memory and dreams, aided by his family. Then, at night, he would lie awake and imitate the actions of the day—the flick of a wrist as one held it up to smell the daub of perfume, or the tender closing of the eyes as one inhaled the contents of a bottle, or the rehearsed friction of a forefinger against the thumb as it rolled and prepared smelling strips made out of wicks of cotton, or the way one poured measured quantities of liquid out of a large vessel and into a smaller one, forefinger assuredly resting on the mouth of the larger bottle. He practiced these gestures repeatedly, until they had become second nature.

The hours that daunted him the most were those he spent with his father, learning the affairs of business. Every number had to be tallied, every unit of measurement understood, every order fulfilled. A few days each week, Samir sat with his father at the cash register and learned his resolute ways. At times, this routine reminded Mohan of when he was a child and the cloth shop was his classroom, Som Nath his teacher. There had been no initiation at the Ravi, as his son had had. There had been no tests. Actually, there had been no choice in the matter at all. His father's unspoken expectation had compelled him to work once his brother left for military training. Those were difficult days. Days of war, days of loneliness, days of death.

*So different from the days of now,* he reassured himself, looking around the shop.

At the same time, Mohan was acutely aware of the bond Samir shared with his uncle, an extraordinary relationship that, in some ways, surpassed the ties of father and son. Samir even dressed like his uncle, a miniature version of a local sahib in Western clothes, rather than the kurta-pajama that Mohan and Som Nath wore. Even the child's lean frame was more reminiscent of Vivek's lithe physique than Mohan's softness. He wished that twinges of jealousy didn't steal their way in from time to time when he saw them together. Perhaps that's why he deemed these lessons in business so important, for him to be able to bequeath something of consequence to his son.

# 6

# The Calligrapher

A cross the old city, ustad Altaf Hussain Khan locked up his huj-ra, one of sixteen alcove studios in the Calligrapher's Bazaar inside the Wazir Khan mosque compound, and accompanied his students to offer the zuhr prayer. Eight on either side, standing at a height of two steps above the ground, these two-story studios flanked the octagonal entrance chamber and were built with ornate arched entrances in red brick, with parrot green and ochre-yellow columns. They were divided by a short passageway running on the north-south axis, opening up into the main courtyard of the mosque. Each morning, this passage would be sprinkled with rosewater from a silver gulabdaan, dousing the bricks in a sweet, floral aroma, as an homage to the practice in Mecca.

The alcoves had been originally earmarked as the studios of select master calligraphers, who had once worked on Quranic inscriptions and Persian verses that embellished the interior and exterior of the mosque. After the construction was completed in 1641 AD, these alcoves became the shops and studios of khattatan, the calligraphers, and naqqashaan, the embellishers, of books. Scholars from Central Asia would journey to the subcontinent and, upon reaching Lahore, leave their rough manuscripts with calligraphy masters either at the mosque or the Naqqash Bazaar, before journeying on to the royal courts of Delhi. In their absence, the pages would be beautifully handwritten, illuminated, and bound, ready to be picked up by the scholars on their way back home. Successive generations of these master calligraphers had continued their trade from the studios, some transforming them into institutes of calligraphy, or baithak-e-katiban, to teach the sacred art. This was how, centuries after an ancestor from the North-West Frontier Province had traveled to Punjab to render verses on the walls of Wazir Khan mosque, Altaf found himself the inheritor of a studio as well as a revered profession.

Altaf had received his earliest education at the local madrasa, which included memorizing chapters of the Quran. He became proficient in Arabic, Farsi, and Urdu, and at age ten, under the official tutelage of his father, ustad Hafiz Hussain Khan, he began training in khattati, calligraphy, at the Wazir Khan mosque. After attaining a level of proficiency, Altaf was sent to an artist to learn the art of naqqashi, the embellishment of manuscripts.

Altaf's elder sister, Nasreen, had been deprived of this education. A sweet girl with pistachio-green eyes identical to her brother's, Nasreen was, at the age of fourteen, married off into a family from the Frontier and gave birth to a baby boy shortly after. But upon the premature death of her husband ten years later, she returned home, uneducated and disrespected, unable to provide for herself or her child. Teenage Altaf had sympathized with his sister's predicament and vowed that if he ever fathered a daughter, she would be given an education no different from his, one filled with books and texts, history and culture, vocation and occupation.

The zuhr prayer over, Altaf stood at the entrance of the mosque, enjoying the smell of roses. The winter sun shone brightly, but the air was still cool. Wrapping the Kashmiri dussa around his shoulders, the calligrapher placed his karakul topi on his head and, with a stack of papers under his arm, made his way home for lunch.

Like every day, he walked down the stairs of the mosque, along the crowded shops on the eastern facade, and into the open maidan, crossing the karwaan serais, where scholars from around the world congregated and exchanged ideas. Along the way, he greeted fellow scribes, acquaintances, shop owners, and even the bhishti carrying his goatskin bag full of water.

Altaf walked through the lanes of Kashmiri Bazaar lined with papermakers and bookbinders, making his daily visit to a longtime collaborator. Nearly at the end of the lane, he stopped in front of a middle-aged man with a salt-and-pepper beard, rubbing a dry sheet of paper with a shell in order to make its surface gleam. RAHIM KAAGZI, the sign above read in blue. Like Altaf, Rahim had been born into his trade, proclaiming, as often as he could, that centuries ago, his once-Arabic ancestors had learned the art of papermaking from skilled Chinese prisoners of war in Samarkand after their defeat in the Battle of Artlakh. Whether any of this was true, Altaf could not know for certain. All that mattered to him was that Rahim's family had been supplying high-quality material to his for decades, and so far, the romance between paper, kaagaz, and ink, siyahi, had remained nothing short of magical.

"*Salaam, Rahim mian,*" Altaf addressed the man. "How are you today?"

"Aha, ustad sahib! Like clockwork, you arrive every day at the same time!" He laughed, placing the shell back into a metallic case holding many others. He unrolled the sleeves of his kurta and stretched his tired arms.

"Habit, I suppose." Altaf smiled and began looking around the shop.

"*Aaj ki farmaaish?* What can I show you today?" Rahim asked.

"I have a special order for *Alf Layla* for a traveler from Baghdad, a precise re-creation of this, as far as it is possible." Altaf placed the pile of papers he was holding onto the table and from them extracted a whisper-like sheet of flax. It was merely half of what would have been the original page, worn and ragged at the edges, though the calligraphy upon it was still somewhat legible. In what remained of the fading border, one could see an exceptional floral pattern in dim red, speckled blue, and dustlike gold. Rahim carefully took the page from Altaf's hands and held it up to the light.

"*Alf Layla—One Thousand and One Nights.* Mashallah! How old is this document?"

"Well, the traveler claims that it once belonged to his grandfather, and the tales from it have been passed down through the generations. Now this is all that survives of the manuscript, and so he wishes to own a re-creation. Rahim mian, I'd like to make something worthy of his legacy. Show me your finest Kashmiri paper."

Rahim led the calligrapher through the shop to a stack of warm colored paper at the back, carefully maneuvering around both materials and employees. Men were tearing large sheets of fabric into smaller pieces, or fashioning objects in papier-mâché, or carefully sewing together manuscripts and books, barely looking up. Rahim's family were the keepers of the ancient art of papermaking, preparing the pulp in their homes using kai grass, and producing sheets in small batches along the banks of the Ravi.

Altaf approached the stack of paper, placed a palm over the topmost page, and gently ran it over the surface. It was opulent, glazed, often known as silken paper. He nodded approvingly, and then placed the sample page upon it, comparing the quality. With outstretched arms, he held up the sheet and watched the sunlight filter through. Meeting Rahim's eye, he nodded approvingly yet again. And then finally, bringing the sheet toward his face with eyes closed, he inhaled. Rahim watched him, ustad sahib, connoisseur of calligraphy, master of manuscripts, place the paper down and scrunch up his nose.

For a few seconds, there was silence.

"Gulab," Altaf uttered softly, the smell from the mosque creeping into a smile on his lips.

"Gulab?"

"Gulab. Ward. Jannat-e-ward, a heaven of roses. I want you to make a batch of this very paper for me, but it must smell of roses."

"Well, I do have some perfumed paper here, someone had once requested . . . mixed with ittar . . . oh, it must be here somewhere." Rahim began rummaging about in the shop, but Altaf stopped him with a click of his tongue.

"Let me bring you an ittar of roses," Altaf offered.

Rahim nodded. "And when you do, we will add it in the paper pulp just before we form the sheets. Inshallah, the result will be as heavenly as you desire."

"Inshallah, Rahim mian, I have no doubt. *Khuda hafiz.*"

And with that, Altaf collected his papers, adjusted the topi on his head, and bid his old friend goodbye. His home was not far from there, down Kashmiri Bazaar, into Dabbi Bazaar, and then a few streets over, to a house that overlooked the splendid Sunehri Masjid. That distance he crossed in leisurely strides, but happened to look down on the ground to find a deep burgundy leaf staring up at him. Elegantly almond-shaped and marvelously rare in coloring, it lay abandoned. Picking it up and wiping its dusty surface, Altaf pocketed it. A special present for a most special girl.

Minutes later, he was climbing the steps to his home where Zainab greeted him at the door. They'd been married for a decade, but the mere sight of her was still enough to make Altaf blush. His heart raced each time her gray eyes looked into his green ones, and he knew deep down that coming home for lunch, though it had become routine, was simply a ruse to spend more time around his beloved. An oasis from the many toils of the day.

"*Salaam, Khan sahib.*" Zainab smiled, reaching out for his pile of papers. "Let me take that from you." She'd never quite got around to calling him ustad; it was too formal, too distant. Khan sahib, she called her husband instead, each syllable lavishly infused with affection.

"*Salaam, Zainab jaan,*" he responded and then lifted his nose to the delicious aroma wafting out of the kitchen. "Wah!"

Laughing, she sauntered back in. "It'll still be a few minutes."

He nodded, and then asked, "Is she home yet?"

"By the window in her room."

Altaf removed his shoes and walked through the house to its most sunlit room, where no buildings interrupted the view of the golden mosque. He leaned on the door frame, watching his daughter from the back. So absorbed she was in whatever lay on her table that she hadn't even heard him come in. Smiling, he drew out the leaf from his pocket and flattened it to remove any creases. All of eight years old, she sat on the floor in front of a low wooden worktable by the window, with her kurta sleeves rolled up to the elbows and a thick khaadi dupatta draped over her shoulders to keep warm. Her hair was tied tightly into two braids. The calligrapher watched as her pale arms glided through sunlight and shadow, arranging a bottle of ink, qalams, and brushes, and then carefully rolling out a small piece of handmade paper to reveal the incomplete outlines of a delicate and ornate border.

On days like today, Altaf marveled at her fragility, comparing her to the finest, wispiest, subtlest, feather-like sheets of hand-pressed paper that he'd seen at Rahim's shop. From a large leather-bound book, she extracted a red leaf, pressed and dehydrated to perfection. He remembered the day she had found it, after a rainstorm during a monsoon, brilliant fiery red among a sea of ordinary greens and yellows. She was the keeper of her own private seasons, his silent child who sought refuge in the solitary leaf, the oddly shaped stone, anything that shrank the vastness of the world into the periphery of her palm. It was never flowers, always leaves, and within the pages of her many books lived these dried souvenirs from around the world, each carried safely across in the pockets of scholars, travelers, and acquaintances of the Khan family, who knew well of the child's curious collection. Her treasures included the rounded forest green ziziphus leaf from southern Persia, the heart-shaped velvet maple from Baku, the sharp needles of fir and pine from Jalalabad, the brilliant magenta foliage of the Judas tree from Istanbul, long slim twin olive leaves from the coastal town of Ayvalik. The newest addition was carefully cradled in Altaf's palm.

He watched as she lay the red leaf down on the page and traced its veins with her small fingers. Then she began drawing from observation, copying it into the pattern of a wreath, the soft pressure of her charcoal leaving shadowlike traces. Despite her young age, she had a surprisingly unwavering hand. Tongue slightly out, face inches away from the page, breath shallow and controlled, and eyes alternating between the leaf and the drawing, she completed a section of what would eventually grow into a border. Then, gently, she blew away any excess charcoal from the page. Perhaps the youngest apprentice of naqqashi in all of Lahore, Firdaus Khan studied her creation.

He must have been towering over her for a few minutes when, seeing that she had at last finished, Altaf gently placed one hand over her eyes. Firdaus reached up, feeling his veins, running her pale fingers over his inky, darkened ones.

"*Abba jaan,*" she said softly as he let her go, "*as-salaam-alaikum.*"

"*Wa-alaikum-salaam, beti,*" he said and held out the burgundy leaf.

Firdaus gasped. "Shukriya, Abba jaan! It's beautiful."

She placed the striking leaf onto the page and noticed immediately how pale the red one looked in comparison. Carefully, she inserted it within the thick pages of a book of poetry, certain that its weight and the parched December air would dry the leaf out evenly. As she did so, her father studied her drawing. Ever since Altaf had been commissioned the *Alf Layla,* she had expressed a desire to work on it with him. While his skill lay in khattati, hers was in the extraordinary naqqashi. He had tasked her with designing the borders, which would be filled in with pigment and gold leaf after Altaf had rendered the text. Looking closer at her drawing now, using the nib of a bamboo reed as a measuring unit, he considered its scale and balance, making corrections. Firdaus was a gifted artist, of that there was no doubt, but she was young and needed rules and direction.

Altaf had made sure that his daughter was raised no different from how a boy would have been, taught to read and write, sent to school, and inducted into the familial art. For this, he was considered far too liberal by many in the mohalla and perhaps all at the mosque.

Sometimes Altaf wondered whether he'd deprived Firdaus of the boundlessness of childhood. Whether his insistence on her partaking in his ancient, scholarly art had forced her to mature beyond her years. While most girls her age would accompany their mothers to the bazaar or learn the art of embroidery or cooking, or play with dolls and earthenware toys, she chose the company of ink and paper. She spent most afternoons with her father at Wazir Khan, where she'd settle into a corner of the hujra to practice her art. Altaf was proud of his principled child, and proud of the way he was raising her, similar to how his father had raised *him*. But too many times had he longed to hear juvenile laughter ring through the house, for his daughter to enjoy the company of others her age rather than the words of deceased poets. He would never admit this to Zainab, who had watched with disappointment as her daughter was absorbed into his world. With a sigh, he looked at the drawing one last time, took her face in his hands, and kissed her forehead, his precious child.

Zainab called out from the kitchen, and the two made their way outside for lunch. A simple spread had been laid out on the dastarkhwan, and the family ate for a while in silence. Midway through, Altaf began telling them about his idea for rose-perfumed paper, and much to everyone's surprise, his begum's eyes lit up.

"Oh, Khan sahib, there is a famous ittar-kadā in Anarkali Bazaar that everyone is talking about. Salima's brother bought her the most exquisite

vial of jasmine ittar, and the ittardaan in Rukhsana's trousseau was also
bought from there. It was a velvet box filled with six beautiful cut-glass vials of perfumes that were inspired by the different seasons . . . jasmine and
marigold and sandal and deep, deep ambers. She said they were so lush,
like wearing the flowers themselves. Vij something-or-the-other, they are
called, two Hindu ittar-saaz brothers. It is rumored that they even procure
some of their perfumes and oils from as far as vilayat, where one of the
brothers fought in the War."

Firdaus quietly chewed her rice and watched her mother.

But Altaf raised his eyebrow. A soldier. Now this caught his attention,
for his cousin Iqbal had also fought in vilayat during the War. He never
returned from the front, but a large bronze medallion, roughly the size
of an outstretched palm, did eventually make its way back to the family.
Altaf remembered it bearing his cousin's name in proud relief, along with
the images of an imposing woman and two lions, symbolic of the Empire.
A memorial plaque, it was called, and the family had wondered what to
do with it. No body had accompanied it, no record, no letters, no personal objects that could be held as the last remaining physical traces of
Iqbal. Just a cold metal plaque, immortal yet devoid of all the warmth
of mortality.

*Perhaps,* Altaf thought, distractedly looking into the distance, *perhaps
this ittar-saaz soldier would have known him.*

"Actually . . ." Zainab cleared her throat, interrupting his thoughts, re-
adjusting her dupatta so it covered her head properly. "The rose oil I use
in Firdaus's ubtan is finishing, and the poor child just pales without it.
Sometimes I think this Barkhat Ali fellow in Dabbi Bazaar sells water and
not ittar, because it never smells as rich or full or wonderful as Salima's or
Rukhsana's did. Could we not go to this shop and smell their perfumes?"
Having never ventured out into the vibrantly modern world of the famed
Anarkali Bazaar, she saw this as a perfect opportunity to make a family
outing of it.

"To Anarkali?" Altaf asked, surprised by this sudden wave of enthusiasm, not to mention the amount of information his wife had collected about the shop, having never been there before.

Zainab was quiet for a moment and then, with coquettish eyes, looked up at her husband. "Well, Khan sahib, you said yourself that you wanted the best ittar for your manuscript. The soul of the rose."

Oh, how she knew the ways to will him into submission.

# 7

# Paradise Found

As the new year began, Firdaus turned nine years old. A few days after that, in the crisp January air, the Khan family hired a tanga and drove through the old city until they reached Anarkali Bazaar. Zainab watched through the latticework eye patch of her burqa as images from the chaotic, colorful world of her dreams unfolded before her.

They turned left into the bazaar at Circular Road and Lahori Gate, and bright heaps of fruit and decorative baskets greeted her from the many open-air stalls. They crossed stores selling carpets and trunks, mithais and fruit juices. Women walked around wearing the newest fashion. Chiffon saris and georgette suits were draped on the outside facades of shops. Names like Dhunichand & Sons, Durga Das & Co., and Bombay Cloth House, which she'd only overheard of in the local markets of Delhi Gate, displayed gorgeously embroidered shawls and sweaters. English sahibs sipped on dainty cups of tea and coffee; groups of men smoked beedis and huddled around small bonfires to warm themselves. There were all kinds of sounds and languages, music and song, fruits and vegetables, smells of oily pakoras and sweet jalebis. Anarkali was nothing short of an explosion of life, a marketplace unlike anything she'd ever seen. Underneath the dark veil of her burqa, her smile belonged to her alone.

Their destination approached and the tanga came to a gradual halt. Carefully alighting first, Zainab adjusted her clothes as Altaf helped Firdaus down and paid the tanga-wallah. Zainab's gray eyes scanned the board, ITTAR KADĀ, VIJ & SONS, ESTD 1921, LAHORE, and then looked at the rows of dried flowers, leaves, and spices methodically arranged on the shelves of the front window. Excited and intrigued, she followed Altaf in. Firdaus trailed quietly behind her mother, holding her hand. Her long black hair was tied into a tight braid, her small body bundled in a warm kurta and sleeveless cardigan, a dupatta swathing her head and shoulders.

All it took was a single moment, the very first step in, for Altaf to know that this was the place. It was as if an invisible curtain separated the infinite delights of the ittar shop from the outside world, and his nose had no choice but to succumb.

"*Salaam,*" came a voice from the front of the shop. Sitting by the cash was a man in his late thirties, dressed in light blue kurta and thick khaadi jacket, the silhouette of a small round belly beginning to appear through the folds of his clothes.

"*Salaam,*" replied Altaf, and Zainab, from under her veil, gave a gentle nod. "We are looking for . . ." The calligrapher's voice trailed off as he began to look around the shop. The entire interior was an arrangement of different colored glass vials, like sacred offerings from a liquid world. There were also gilded bottles and painted flasks, displays of pendants and lockets of solid perfume, ittardaans, bronze burners and rows of incense sticks. On the ground were placed large green glass demijohn bottles and metal funnels to decant or refill them. Smells from every corner begged Altaf to come closer, to explore, to wander. Unable to employ the exactitude he demanded in his own work, he looked at the shopkeeper, overwhelmed by choice.

Mohan smiled. "Is this your first time in our shop? *Aap fikar na karein,* my brother will help you find exactly what you need." He craned his neck and called out, "Veer ji . . ."

A slim man just a few years older craned his neck out from the back of the shop. He was dressed like an English sahib: suited and booted, suspenders, cardigan, and all. Altaf took in his rigidly straight frame, chiseled clean-shaven features, and trim body, and deduced that this was the soldier.

"*As-salaam-alaikum,*" Vivek greeted his new customers warmly and introduced himself. For a split second, he looked closely at Altaf and wondered if they had met before. *The eyes, the pistachio green of the eyes, like an oasis in the snow.* He had seen those eyes before. But no, it couldn't be. The eyes he was thinking of had been closed forever years ago, on a battlefield far away. Shaking off the memory, he resumed conversation.

"Ji, bataiye, what can I show you? Perhaps some lovely jasmine, or musk, or oudh? We distill almost everything ourselves, just upstairs."

"Jannat-e-ward," Altaf said, "the rose."

From under the veil, a whisper floated out, "Taif, rose taif."

Vivek's eyes widened, impressed at the mention of such a rare rose extract. He reached across the shelves behind him and picked up a small, ornate flask. Unbottling it, he held the glass stopper out to Altaf. "From the time of the Ottomans, this has been known as the Arabian rose, growing in the cool suburbs of Taif. Its extract is brought to us directly from there. Harvested in the early-morning hours of March and April, this rose must be picked before the sun rises and the heat of the day penetrates the bud and destroys the fragrance of the legendary flower. It takes about fifteen thousand roses to create a tiny vial of pure taifi essence."

Altaf brought his nose to the glass stopper covered in densely clear liquid, and took a whiff. Wazir Khan, that's what it reminded him of, the sprinkling of rosewater every morning at the mosque. Fresh, sweet, reverent. It was a familiar smell, but not the rose he had fantasized about for the *Alf Layla.* The taif was more powdery that he'd have liked, and hidden within each inhale were tealike hints he hadn't expected. Taking the stopper from Vivek, he held it out to Zainab, who delicately brought it underneath her veil and smelled.

"According to legend," Vivek continued, "over two centuries ago, the rose petals from Taif were carefully collected, tightly sealed, and brought to Mecca on camels' backs, where their infusion was distilled with sandalwood oil, resulting in a floral, woody, soothing fragrance. The very same kind you are smelling right now."

Placing the glass stopper back into the bottle, Vivek gave it a swirl so it was coated with ittar. He then removed it once again and, painting it across Altaf's palms, instructed him how to rub both hands together and deposit the fragrance across his body, over clothes, skin and all. Every scent smelled differently on different skins. And so, the calligrapher complied. But even after being doused in the holy scent, he seemed unconvinced. Finally, he described his need to Vivek, whose fingers began moving across bottles on the shelves, just as quickly as the words escaped Altaf's lips. History, tradition, travel, family, all things that Vivek treasured.

"Roses, roses, let me bring out our roses. Some are pure essences, and others are blends that we have created." He began picking out bottle after bottle, and soon there were clear, yellow, ochre, and light pink hues lined neatly before the Khans. "Although we could also compose something special for the manuscript . . ." the perfumer offered after a moment, thinking out loud, "perhaps adding some geranium essence, locally called lal jari, to the taif. It grows in balmy regions and has similar properties to the rose, so much so that it is often mistaken for the same. But it is less powdery and almost fruity or minty."

Altaf Khan's lips curved up into a half-moon as he held a bottle of pure geranium essence up to his nose. Indeed, it was similar to a rose, but it was also green, lemony, rich, dense, even nostalgic. It compelled him to agree with Vivek on a blend of the two ingredients, and momentarily forget his inquiries about Iqbal or the War.

As the heavenly rose-colored realm began to emerge at the front of the shop, Firdaus let go of her mother's hand and looked around, feeling most out of place. Intrigued by a squeaky sound, she followed it to a low glass cabinet in the back of the ittar shop. Hundreds of small, precious glass bottles inside created a natural fortification between Firdaus and the boy who sat behind it. He was hunched over some empty bottles in the same way that she was often hunched over a book. She found herself smiling as his tongue crept slightly out of his mouth in concentration, in the same way that hers did when she drew. Interest piqued, she placed her small palms on the glass cabinet and peered through.

Half a year into his apprenticeship, Samir was crouched on the ground at the back of the shop, obscured behind a glass cabinet. He drowned each bottle in a bowl of hot water and then, using his fingernails, peeled off the gummy, worn-out labels. Each perfume or ingredient bottle in the shop bore a simple black-and-white label, which was not exactly beautiful, but a functional element for business. Samir had barely got through half the lot when he stopped. Bottle still in hand, he inhaled deeply with closed eyes as a new smell snaked around him. Everything about it was ordinary, yet something stood out so clearly that he was unable to ignore it. He smelled her before he saw her.

Lifting his nose above the curtain of his already perfumed environment, he detected rose and orange peels doused in milk, mixed with multani mud and gram flour. These were the ingredients for ubtan, the ordinary face mask applied by many women. Someone had walked into the shop carrying the remnants of ubtan, but there was something else, something extraordinary adhered to this ordinary smell. It was musky, warm, soft, calming, sweet—yes, it was also sweet. Immediately, he recalled a bottle of the same substance from a faraway island called Haiti, a highly prized ingredient called vanilla, which his uncle pronounced as *vaneel* and his father as *vaneellaa*. Could it be? Samir dropped the bottle in the water and smelled further, eyes still closed. Hints of something vaguely smoky floated into his nostrils. Was it leather, or pepper? No, neither. It was more rudimentary, denser, warmer, ashy like kohl. Allowing this composition to expand his smile and also, it seemed, his heart, he took another deep inhale. Most redolent within this bouquet was the rose. Effortlessly overpowering all else, for a rose could never hide. And just as he brought his nose down from the air, he found a pair of pistachio-colored eyes staring at him through the rows of glass bottles.

It was her, the wearer. It was her.

Samir tried to move but couldn't. In fact, all movement occurred in slow motion, lasting for seconds, minutes, or hours, he could not tell. His brown eyes remained fixed onto her pistachio ones. He was determined not to look away, even though he wanted to stand up, reach across the cabinet, hold her arm and inhale. Smell with his nose, his gut, his heart.

He watched her, and just as unflinching, she watched him. There was such intention in her gaze, and he wondered why she had ventured toward the back of the shop at all. Her smell had drawn him to her, but what had been her pursuit? The two pairs of eyes remained locked. No one noticed this; not a single person disturbed the beginning of whatever this would become. But if from the front of shop, anyone had looked back, they would have found two children, not far in age from each other, clinging to opposite sides of an old glass cabinet full of perfume bottles.

Unwillingly, Samir tore his eyes away from hers. Still crouching on the ground, staring through the wall of glass bottles, he looked at her face. She had skin pale enough to reveal the shadow of veins beneath, and on her chin sat a sole beauty mark, a til, its color as dark as her braided hair. Her face was oddly angular for a child's, and a small glistening diamond was pierced through her left nostril, which brought Samir to her nose. Long, slim, and completely still. It struck him how normally she was breathing, as if the heavily perfumed floral air all around them left her unaffected. Almost instinctively, he took in a deep breath, expecting her to do the same, but she remained motionless. He stared at her nose for a few seconds longer before meeting her gaze once again.

"Firdaus!" Altaf's voice called out from the front of shop, causing her to look away.

"Firdaus," Samir repeated under his breath, savoring the name on his lips.

*Firdaus.* Paradise. Of course, she had to be.

8

Alif

The Khans had left the perfumery with a bottle of taif for Zainab and the promise of a rose-geranium blend for Altaf. In the past, Vivek had fashioned many a bespoke blend of perfumes and oils as wedding presents, anniversary gifts, and even scents to woo a woman. But to create something as animated as a perfume for an object as inanimate as the paper of a manuscript, well, that was an altogether new undertaking, and a challenge he couldn't wait to get started on.

Before exiting the shop, Altaf had happened to glance over at the ordinary black-and-white labels pasted on every perfume bottle. Without a second's hesitation, he offered the perfumer a barter—the design of an original new label for their bottles, inscribed by Altaf and illuminated by Firdaus, in exchange for a vial of the bespoke fragrance for his manuscript. Smiling, Vivek had agreed immediately, embarking on an unusual professional collaboration that would eventually grow into a deep friendship.

All this Samir had witnessed wordlessly from the back of the shop, the air around him still imprinted with the rosy-smoky-sweet ubtan smell. The Khans had left just as gracefully as they had entered, hopping back onto their tanga and disappearing into the crowd, and Samir had stared after Firdaus until he could no longer see the swaying tail of her dark braid. Now, hours later, as he helped his father and uncle clean the shop before closing, he mustered up the courage to ask the question that had lodged itself in his brain.

"Taya ji . . ." he began softly.

"Hmmm," Vivek replied distractedly, barely looking up from the notebook of orders.

Samir paused and swallowed hard. If he closed his eyes and concentrated, he could still smell it, smell her. Firdaus. Firdaus with the soot, Firdaus with the til, Firdaus with the pistachio eyes, Firdaus with the unusual traces of vanilla. He couldn't explain why, out of all the people who came in to the ittar shop every day, it was *her* aroma that had singularly bound itself to him.

"Here in the shop, we make perfumes using flowers, spices, woods . . ." he began.

"Mm-hm."

"Well, is it possible . . . How can I learn to . . ." Samir stumbled through his thoughts. "What I mean is, can we re-create something we have smelled before? Or *someone,* the smell of a person?"

Vivek stopped reading. He turned to look at his nephew square in the face, eyes wide, and rubbed his left hand across his lips and chin. In that moment, Samir felt it difficult to discern whether his uncle was angry or upset, for his expression was one he'd never seen before. Immediately, he regretted uttering even a single word and went back to tidying the space around him.

Vivek, however, remained transfixed. How was it that a child, a mere child of ten years old, could fathom with such depth the intangible nature of their craft? Of course, all perfume was about people, even about a *person*, if the perfumer so desired. And more often than not, they did. People—the inspiration, the admirer, the wearer—were fundamental to the creation of perfume. But to hear this thought float out so casually from his nephew's mouth left him in awe.

He remembered how he had willed his way into perfumery, compelled by a desperate longing like no other. This longing had been the result of homesickness and torment, of misery and fantasy. And only then, eventually, had fragrance appeared before him as his release. It had taken weeks, months, years for him to understand the distillation of flowers and herbs into a single aroma, let alone to imagine a person as inspiration for one.

But here was Samir, so naturally gifted at such a young age that there was no telling how cavernous his understanding of scent could one day prove to be. The incident with the tuberose essence at the river Ravi should have forewarned Vivek about the extent of his nephew's gift, but he had assumed it would be a gradual progression. For this, he was altogether unprepared.

"Come with me." He took Samir's hand and then called out to his brother, who was tallying the day's inventory, "Mohan, we'll be in the atelier if you need us."

"Samir as well?" He looked up from the cluster of bottles, surprised.

"Samir as well," Vivek concurred and led the child out the rear exit of the shop.

In this small atelier connected to the ittar shop, Vivek had constructed his first perfumer's organ in 1921. At first, the organ's four-tiered wooden shelves had held just a solitary vial. Three inches in height, it contained a pale yellow liquid that was the true muse for the perfumery. Ambrette. Having carried it from vilayat, he wrote its local Urdu name, mushk dana, underneath the English label. Then, one by one, he removed the remaining vilayati bottles from the leather case, as well as those he'd procured on his travels, and placed them onto a shelf. It was a cacophony of ingredients, including geranium, ambergris, patchouli, bergamot, ginger, cedarwood, myrrh, black currant, grapefruit, tonka bean, iris, sunflower, costus root, cinnamon, benzoin, sage. Another shelf held local ingredients like bakul, oudh, kastur, genda, chameli, mitti, khuss.

Eventually, several more ingredients were added, and the organ became an altar of liquid and glass, with bottles of assorted heights and shapes with different stoppers, corks, colors of glass, and labels in various languages. To any other perfumer, this method of classification could have seemed chaotic, and over time, the organ would be rearranged in a more customary fashion, in accordance with the respective scent notes—the top, the middle, the base—but at the beginning, Vivek had wished for an atlas of smell devoid of all hierarchy.

A tabletop ran alongside the base of the organ and onto the adjacent wall, which was fitted with a single large window of tinted glass. Through it, deep mustard light streamed in, illuminating the assortment of glass bottles on the four shelves fitted right onto the window frame. Over the years, from perfumers, extractors, bottle-makers, and glass blowers, Vivek had amassed a substantial collection of glass vessels. Each was unique, and had once held a perfume or an ingredient. Even though all were now empty, some still bore traces of their occupants—a lingering rose, a resolute jasmine, a woody juniper. These collectibles ranged from long-necked vessels with metallic stoppers to elegant bottles in the shapes of peacocks, from large, round-bottomed amber bottles with half-torn labels to ones with gilded latticework.

On another wall of the atelier, shelves had been installed for storage. These held apparatus and tools like strips of linen cloth, boxes of empty bottles with golden caps, beakers and decanters and large copper cauldrons. There were scales and measuring devices, mortars and pestles, and various tools to cut raw materials. There were stacks of small sticks called laakri, upon which perfumed-soaked cotton buds were rolled to create smelling strips. On the topmost shelf were placed four kuppis, colossal flask-shaped vessels made with untanned camel leather, capable of holding volumes of liquid.

This atelier had become Vivek's universe, and over the years he'd plunged in headfirst. It was an escape from this world into the past, a place only he could inhabit. Samir knew that admission into his uncle's atelier was not to be taken lightly, and whatever the evening led to, he would emerge forever changed. He walked in nervously, not daring to touch anything, but his eyes and nose explored the room. Hungrily, they swallowed each sight and inhaled every trace of smell that lingered lazily in the air. So entranced was he that he barely noticed his uncle rummaging around. Seated at the table by the organ, he extracted a set of vials from an old leather case—slim, long, like test tubes from a chemistry laboratory. Wide-eyed, Samir approached the table and dragged up a stool.

Each glass vial was shut with a cork, and Vivek carefully wiped the surfaces and examined the labels. Samir leaned in, trying to read the faded Urdu text on each. There was *Lahore,* and *Lahore, Remembered.* There was *Lahore 1916, Lahore 1917, Lahore 1918, Lahore 1919, Lahore 1920,* all staggeringly low in quantity, as if they'd been frequently worn. There was *Reshmiya* and *Anarkali* and *The Disappearance.* Some vials had more abstract labels like *Parwana,* the lover; *Taveez,* the talisman; *Takleef,* the suffering; *Khamoshi,* the silence. But Samir was most intrigued to find names—there was an amber vial reading *Leela,* a brilliant jade green that read *Som Nath,* and a crimson one for *Mohan.* Separate from all others was a half-full test tube that Vivek now held out to Samir.

"*Alif?*" he read the elusive, lean annotation on the label.

"*Alif,*" Vivek repeated, making the first harf of the Urdu alphabet sound more like a complete sentence. "This perfume is called *Alif.* For now, at least. It's unfinished, but I gauge its evolution from time to time. You see, puttar, a perfume is always evolving, whether in rest or on one's skin." Taking a deep breath, he held it out further. "I would like you to be the first to smell it."

Samir took the open vial from his uncle and hovered his nose above it.

*Alif,* though visibly heavy and oily, smelled surprisingly light. It possessed an otherworldly quality, a weightlessness. It was the smell of freshly laundered clothes, of cotton, grass, wood, and lemon leaves. It somehow also evoked the smell of folded skin, of warm sweaty crevasses, of human touch. An old, tender, faraway touch. Unfinished it might have been, but it was still beautiful and rather dreamlike. Samir swayed with delight as his uncle listed some of perfume's ingredients—galbanum, cedarwood, citrus, aniseed, carrot, rose oxide, angelica, and the essential oil of the ambrette seed. A single perfume was a universe in itself, sometimes encompassing over a hundred different notes and smells.

"All perfumes," Vivek broke his nephew's reverie, "*all perfumes* are in some way inspired by people. They become homages, dedications, tributes. In fact, a perfume without memory is a body without soul. One cannot create a perfume for a place, that dialogue is unsustainable. The place can be inspiration, but a perfume is *always* created for people in general, or a person in particular. And our memories, our histories, our desires, our fears, and even our interactions are like any other ingredient—a prized flower, a rare spice, a fine herb—and we must use them just the same."

Vivek chuckled and continued his monologue. "But of course, one has to be just a little bit obsessed to pursue a realm that cannot be seen, that can only be *perceived* through the organs. A perfumer is constantly thinking about the way things smell, what they remind us of, what other smells they would harmoniously blend with. The art of perfumery, thus, is all about association and evocation. It is the union of chemistry and poetry."

Samir nodded cautiously. He did not completely follow, but he refrained from asking any more questions for the moment, for his nose, his gut, and his heart were all attempting to not forget any aspect of the soot-like smell of Firdaus. Some part of him certainly understood what Vivek was explaining, and that part had already surrendered.

The *Alif* vial then, became the first crucial lesson of his apprenticeship—the way in which hints of a person can find their way into liquid. Smelling it once again, Samir asked his uncle what or *who* had inspired him to create it.

"Well, it was . . ." he began, caught off guard by his nephew's directness. "It was a long time ago. Sh-she was . . . Amb—" He paused, pursing his lips, and thought about what he wanted to say. Then, drawing a breath in, he spoke with new composure. "I have been working on this for many years now. But the inspiration came to me from someone I met in vilayat a long time ago when I was, well, I was young and different."

"During the . . . war?" Samir apprehensively said the word he had heard so many times from his elders at home, though he didn't quite understand why or where this war had taken place, and how his uncle had managed to be a part of it; perfume seemed so far removed from any form of physical battle. "Baba said you left for vilayat when he was just a teenager."

A sharp breath lodged itself in Vivek's throat. A long-concealed secret threatened to escape. He looked at his nephew's face, childishly oblivious to the burden the perfumer held inside.

He cleared his throat. "Yes, your baba is right. I was away for many years, having crossed the dark waters, kala paani, to spend my days in a land called France."

"Frraaanss." Samir slowly murmured the word like his uncle, rolling the *r,* elongating the *a,* hissing the *s.* "Is that where you learned to be a perfumer? Was your education like this as well? Can we go there? How far is it? How deep is the kala paani? How much water separates us from Fraans?"

A barrage of questions.

Vivek laughed, choosing only to answer what seemed least complicated.

"*So* much water separates us. More than that of fifty Ravis put together. It was the ocean, vast and wondrous, ungovernable and powerful. You will see it one day, too, Samir, you will see the ocean. Kos and kos of nothing but salty water. A liquid map all the way from Hindustan to France, which is where I first smelled ambrette, mushk dana, the base note of my *Alif* perfume."

"Base note," Samir repeated.

"Yes," Vivek said, looking at his watch. "It's not yet so late. We have time."

In a gesture both unusual and intimate, Vivek held Samir's hands within his own. He smiled at his nephew and wished, fleetingly, that someone had educated him in the elusive realm of smell in the way that he was about to.

But he was also acutely aware of how different the child was from him. They both possessed perfumistic talent, of that there was no doubt, but he knew in his heart of hearts, nose of noses, that Samir's senses were far more nuanced than his own. This child, this monsoon child, was a natural. His nose was intuitive, athletic, robust, hungry, and resilient. It was young. Vivek thought back to the night Samir had been born, of how he had inhaled the untamed storm. And now that it resided within him, it remained a kind of compulsion. His senses were unskilled, devoid of any and all olfactive grammar, and, hence, completely unadulterated.

"Children smell very well, far better than adults," he began. "They amass incredible memories of smells, associating them to things without even realizing. A bit like assigning concrete symbols or images to abstraction."

Samir shifted his weight from one foot to another, hand still sandwiched between his uncle's. He did not understand.

"Do you remember the khuss from when you were a child?"

A cautious nod.

"What did you say it reminded you of?"

"Summertime, when the curtains in the haveli are woven with khuss."

"Exactly." Vivek beamed. "A child is uninhibited in making associations when it comes to smell. They walk into the room and immediately recognize what it smells of. In fact, they are able to smell even before they are born. The infallible strength of our senses is a gift of childhood, but one that recedes with age unless we make a conscious effort to retain it. *You* possess this gift. But you need to learn how to hone it in a way that you are able to wield it, rather than the opposite."

Samir tried to concentrate on his uncle's words rather than Firdaus's disappearing smell.

"As perfumers, we use smell to construct stories. A perfume, then, is more than just a form of opulence or luxury. It has the ability to seduce and allure, to repel and repulse, to persuade and command, to warn and defend. It can evoke long-forgotten memories and enliven those who are no longer alive."

He paused and looked around the workshop, letting Samir's hands drop to his side. He concluded, "A powerful smell is a refuge."

Samir reached over and picked up the unfinished *Alif*. For a few seconds, it lay in his hand before he uncorked it and smelled it again. Otherworldly. He looked up at his uncle, the sole person who could provide Samir with both the answers and skills he desired. He hadn't understood a lot of what his uncle had said, but some things had always been clear.

Nervously now, the boy spoke. "Smells and I, we talk. They pop into my head at strange moments, Taya ji, sometimes just as I am falling asleep, sometimes when I'm doing my math tables at school, sometimes during dinner and even here in the shop. They tell stories, they paint pictures, they ask to meet other smells."

"What do you mean, 'meet other smells'?"

"Well, recently, while cleaning the shelves, I could hear the khuss. I could smell it, of course, but I could also hear it and feel it, as if it had suddenly wrapped itself around me."

Knowing that Samir had never been partial toward vetiver made Vivek doubly intrigued.

"One day, it called out to me. It sounded like a long, mossy tunnel through which an echo had just passed. *Whoooosh.* You know the kinds that exist under the Lahore fort? Baba took me there once. They were endless, and though the air was damp and cool inside, you knew once you stepped out of the tunnel, the hotness of the day would collide into you. It sounds silly, but I . . ." he rambled on, but Vivek was hardly listening anymore. He was witnessing something else altogether.

A remarkable moment of genesis. A composition had been imagined.

When he tuned back in, Samir was still explaining. ". . . so I walked around carrying the green vetiver tunnel in my thoughts for a few days until one afternoon, I was cleaning the bottles in the front window of the shop and I just knew. The smallest one, the light ruby-colored oil, would smell wonderful when mixed with it. You know the one, watery almost, and smells tangy and sweet and fresh?"

"Grapefruit oil?"

Samir shrugged, and Vivek instinctively reached to the top of the organ and brought it down. A top note. Twitching his nose, the child smelled it and smiled. "This is it."

Vivek smiled back, quite aware of the elegant harmony the ingredients produced when mixed. "The future, then, holds promise of a vetiver and grapefruit blend."

"May I watch? May I smell it once it's ready?" Samir asked.

"Puttar, it will be entirely your creation."

Samir jumped out of his seat and embraced his uncle, who lifted him up and sat him on the tabletop. One last thing remained before the evening came to a close.

Picking up the *Alif* vial, he now asked, "The base note for this perfume is the ambrette seed. Do you recall its smell?"

Samir rubbed his hands together and repeated under his breath, "Ambrette." All those months of dusting shelves and bottles had fitted the architecture of the shop into his memory. He nodded at his uncle. "I remember it. Ambrette, or mushk dana, smells like soft flowers and wood and animal skin. Sometimes, Ma calls it lata kasturi when she soaks the seeds to make ayurvedic concoctions."

"That's correct. Can you locate it on the organ?"

Samir tried not to read any of the labels, English or Urdu, relying simply on his olfactory memory. He inhaled and exhaled, deeper into the neck of this bottle and that. His lips moved softly as he whispered the ingredient to himself, again and again like a secret not to be forgotten: "Ambrette, ambrette, ambrette." And each time he said it, Vivek's heart beat faster. *Ambrette, ambrette, ambrette.*

He remembered the sepia-toned photograph of the couple. The woman with doe eyes, the man with a mole on his right cheekbone. Instinctively, his hand reached up to touch his face and there it was—the dark, round mole. He sighed, almost painfully, remembering the smell of freshly washed cotton and sweet jasmine. Vast fields of jasmine bloomed across the terrain of his mind, nothing else to be seen for kilometers. He remembered how the green leaves and white flowers had married the clear blue skies. And as always, there was Ambrette. *Ambrette, ambrette, ambrette.* He remembered the odor of congealed meat, stagnant water, leather, uniform, lead, gas, gunpowder. The taste of blood, the wetness of a trench, the smell of burning flesh. He remembered his fear, he remembered the letters. There were so many letters. Names, villages, dreams, desires, deaths. He remembered endless water and ships like floating islands.

He breathed in sharply and closed his eyes. *Not all things need to be remembered. Some things deserve their place in oblivion.*

In the background, rummaging through the glass labyrinth of the organ, he heard his nephew whisper, "Ambrette, ambrette, ambrette," like the dull rhythm of a heartbeat. And when Vivek opened his eyes again, Samir was holding up a vial of pale yellow liquid.

"Ambrette," the perfumer affirmed.

# 9

## The Barter

"P attoki," Vivek announced one morning in mid-March, "remember the name, puttar." And before Samir could inquire any further, his uncle, smiling wide, continued, "The season of roses is finally upon us. We will travel to Pattoki next week."

Standing at the front of the shop, he tore a piece of paper out from the notebook of orders and drew a rough diagram of the route for his nephew. He placed Lahore at the very top, followed by Kasur on the bottom right and, finally, Pattoki, lower still, on the left. Samir folded the paper and put it in his pocket.

Just then, the calligrapher walked through the door of the shop. Since his first visit, Vivek had spent many evenings composing what he considered befitting of the mythical *Alf Layla,* and he was eager to know what his newest acquaintance felt about it.

"*As-salaam-alaikum, ustad sahib,*" Vivek said. "Welcome."

"*Wa-alaikum-salaam, Vij sahib, Mohan ji,* how are you?" Altaf placed his papers on the counter, removed his cap, and greeted the brothers warmly.

Three stools were brought out for the men, and Samir quietly retreated to the back of the shop, where Savitri was attending to two Sikh sisters visiting from Rawalpindi. They were shopping for their niece's wedding and had set aside several solid perfumes as gifts for the women of the groom's family. They were now looking to fill the box set of six fragrances for the bride herself, traditionally purchased by the father and populated by conventionally seasonal floral smells. In this case, both traditions were put to the test as the bride had been raised by her widowed mother, and the two aunts shopping for her trousseau were interested in anything but ordinary fragrances.

"Something unique, something different, not this regular jasmine-shasmine, gulab-shulab. Something never-to-have-been-worn-or-smelled-before, *kujj changa dikhao na, ji,*" the taller one out of the two—clearly also the older one—requested in her liltingly musical Punjabi. Her nose scanned the shop, braid swaying from left to right. Samir suggested the accords he had come to adore, and his mother offered him the lead.

Small glass vials were carefully brought out from the corners of the shop, for accords were precious potions. Each was a medley of several ingredients or notes, which resulted in a completely new odor. Sometimes, this could be the end product, making it an elementary version of a perfume. Other times, it could be extended and combined with other accords that would eventually make a more expansive, complex perfume. These accords could be animalic, fruity, floral, spicy, green, fresh, and his uncle had named each one thoughtfully.

From their treasury, Samir chose the gem-like *Gauhar,* which combined mandarin, cypriol, and agarwood. *Shafaq,* which meant twilight, was a blend of orange, tuberose, and vanilla. An accord of lilac and citrus was called *Sahil,* which Vivek had composed using the memory of a seashore he'd once stood on. The playful, enchanting *Nargis* combined lemon and rosemary oil. *Parwaaz* was made with basil, mint, and lavender essence. And finally, for the first time since its creation, Samir offered a customer the vetiver and grapefruit accord from his green-tunneled dreams, which he had named *Sapna.* Using the slimmest of glass droppers, he had carefully squeezed out drop after drop of each ingredient, careful not to waste anything. Vivek had observed attentively, reminding his apprentice to make notations on smell memory, and record a list of each ingredient used along with its quantity, for perfumery was an art of exactitude.

Savitri twirled a fresh piece of cotton between her thumb and forefinger, deftly fashioning it into a spindle, careful to keep the cotton completely clean of any residual liquid. She then took a small laakri stick and stabbed the cotton bud with it, which she then proceeded to dip into the light green *Sapna* accord. Gently, she daubed the oily liquid onto the wrists of both sisters, who lifted them to their noses and inhaled.

"*Ab yeh hui na baat,* this is exceptional," the elder sister said with pleasure. "Preeto, *tenu yaad hai,* do you remember the fields behind Pita ji's house, where the long wild grasses grew by the pond? How we used to play hide-and-seek in the unruly khuss patches as children? This smell, this smell has made me feel seven years old again."

Fragrance had the power to deliver one back in time, Samir noted with pleasure. This was his skill; this was his endowment.

Meanwhile, Vivek had gone into the atelier and brought back a maroon felt pouch holding a five-milliliter glass bottle, small enough to be concealed within one's palm. It had a decorative gold top, which Vivek uncapped carefully and, using the thin glass applicator stick, spread a single clear line across Altaf's wrist.

*Opulence,* the calligrapher immediately thought. *Luscious, sparkling opulence.* He recalled the most famous story from the *Alf Layla* collection: A king betrayed by his first wife takes on a succession of wives, slaying each one the very morning after their wedding night, before she, too, can betray him, until one has the wisdom to protect herself by telling a story. A tale that continues night after night, delaying her execution for One Thousand and One Nights, at the end of which her husband emerges a wiser ruler. Taking a long inhale once again, Altaf emerged overwhelmed.

Like the stories in the book, this perfume struck the precise chords of history, legend, mythology, magic, poetry, and delight, and he could immediately imagine lush illuminated borders of green and gold, rose and blue. Taking out a sheet of handmade paper, he offered it to Vivek to test the fragrance on as close to a finished product as possible. A drop was released, and it created a dark, oily circular film over the otherwise glossy surface. The three men smelled it, turning the sheet onto itself, holding it up, fanning it out gently. For a while, they spoke about how the prized ittar was to be added to the pulp during the papermaking process.

And then it was Altaf's turn to reveal his creation. On a sheet with the consistency of butter paper, a wreath of gorgeous foliage surrounded three rows of elegantly handwritten text:

*Ittar Kadā*
*Vij & Sons*
*Estd 1921, Lahore*

To Vivek and Mohan's satisfaction, it was written in both Urdu and English, catering to their diverse clientele. Altaf had even left a blank space underneath, to accommodate the name of the ittar the bottle would hold. The label was to be printed in various sizes, small enough to fit on the smallest vial for purchase and big enough to spread across the large tumblers of base oils. Holding the page up to the light, Mohan marveled at the detail of drawing and the accuracy with which it reflected the Vij family. Warm, grounded, local.

"Ah, it is my daughter, Firdaus, who deserves this praise. She is my apprentice, learning the art of naqqashi," Altaf said with pride. "In fact, she accompanied us on our first visit."

"Of course," Vivek remembered. "Well, this is even more impressive now, because she looked no older than our Samir."

"Samir?" the calligrapher asked, and the prodigy was summoned.

"This is my son," Mohan introduced the boy, "well, *our* son." He smiled and corrected himself as Savitri emerged from the back carrying a tray of everything the Sikh sisters had selected for purchase, the trail of her sari fluttering behind her. She greeted the calligrapher, and then quickly motioned for her husband to join her at the till so they could ring up and pack the order. The sisters followed the couple to the front.

As Mohan excused himself, Vivek held his nephew by the shoulders. "Samir is my apprentice, learning the art of perfumery," he declared proudly.

"Samir"—Altaf bent down so he was the same height as the child— "how old are you?"

"Ustad sahib, I am ten years old."

Samir stared into a pair of eyes identical to hers. Light wisps of honey and gold over a background of pistachio green, darkening into a deep forest color right at the edge of the irises. The vanilla soot-like smell emanated from him as well, and Samir wondered if this was a familial trait. His curiosity heightened.

"Very close in age, indeed. Firdaus turned nine this January."

*Firdaus.* Samir's heart beat faster upon the very sound of her name. He instinctively inhaled the air as if she were standing right before him, but it was his memory that obliged. Firdaus with the soot, Firdaus with the til, Firdaus with the pistachio eyes, Firdaus with the unusual traces of vanilla, Firdaus with the unconcealable rose. The calligrapher stood up tall and looked around the shop at the labels already stuck on every bottle. In studying the childlike Urdu scrawl, he deduced that these labels were Samir's responsibility.

"Vij sahib, I have a proposition. Why not send your nephew to my hujra in Wazir Khan mosque for a few hours each week for lessons in calligraphy? This way, the names of perfumes can be written in an equally beautiful script on the new labels. And in any case, to be versed in the fine art of calligraphy is a marker of sophistication and discipline."

Samir knew well that to speak out of turn before his elders, or, worse, in the presence of a guest or customer, was ill-mannered. But his fingers had begun to tingle and his nose had begun to twitch at the prospect of seeing, *smelling,* Firdaus again, and before he could stop himself, the words slipped out. "Ji, ustad sahib, I would love to!"

Vivek folded his arms across his chest and lifted his eyebrow, amused.

Once a week then, it was decided.

As Altaf gathered his papers, readying himself to leave, Vivek placed a hand on his shoulder. He couldn't explain why, but he felt an unusual kinship with the calligrapher. Though he tried to think of other reasons, the uncanny resemblance to the pistachio eyes from the battlefield wasn't lost on him.

"One moment, ustad sahib . . ." He directed him toward the round wooden table in the center of the shop with six glass bell jars, each with a knot of beige linen cloth doused in the best-selling perfumes. The first four held rose, jasmine, vetiver, and shamama, a popular winter ittar distilled as a mixture of several herbs and spices. The fifth held the first perfume that Vivek had ever composed in France, a fragrance made with geranium from Madagascar, a leathery amber-like resin called labdanum from Spain, and vanilla from Uganda. Overcome with nostalgia upon reviving it so far away from where he had learned the art of perfumery, he named the fragrance *Ibtida,* which meant the beginning.

In the final bell jar lived his newest creation. After careful consideration, Vivek had decided that it was time to introduce his unfinished *Alif* to the world and had, that morning, poured a few drops into a knot of linen cloth and covered it with a glass cloche. Now, several hours later, he lifted this jar and held it out to the calligrapher. Beads of perfumed moisture clung to the glass.

Intrigued, Altaf took a long and gradual breath in. Then he smiled, as if the smell had evoked something familiar and private, and his shoulders gently relaxed. His mind became suddenly overrun with images of Zainab, intimate and amorous—drying wet clothes under the bright golden sun, washing the tomato seeds off her fingers, applying kohl in the morning, braiding the long lengths of Firdaus's hair, humming to herself as she sewed lace onto a kurta, lying next to her husband in the late hours of the night, their ankles entwined. Whatever this fragrance was, it had drenched every inch of Altaf in Zainab. He sighed with pleasure.

"What is this?" he asked the perfumer.

"*Amrit,*" Vivek uttered the name out loud for the first time, "I call this perfume *Amrit.*"

Upon completion, *Alif* had been renamed *Amrit.* Inspired in sound by its muse, ambrette, the word *amrit* meant immortal.

The calligrapher seemed at a loss for words. He simply continued to stare at the knotted linen now exposed to the room, the ittar wafting around, unrestrained. A few seconds later, in a voice unlike his own, thoughts still of his begum, Altaf Khan uttered a single word.

"Dilkash." Alluring.

When the shop closed for the evening, two precious vials of *Amrit* had been poured out—the first for the calligrapher's begum, Zainab, and the second for the mistress of aroma, the woman of the house herself, Savitri.

Later that night after dinner, when everyone had retreated to their rooms, Samir took out the folded route to Pattoki and studied it. Wondering how long it would take to arrive at the season of roses, he ran downstairs to his grandfather's room to find him leaning back on the cane chair by the window, listening to the radio.

"*Baalam aaye, baso morey mann mein, saawan aaya, tum na aaye.*" Eyes closed, Som Nath crooned to a song from Kundan Lal Saigal's iconic 1936 hit film, *Devdas.* Just a few months ago, in December, the Vij family had attended a live performance by Saigal, Zohra Bai Ambalewali, and others at an All-India exhibition held at Minto Park. K. L. Saigal, already a household name, had drawn crowds to the park, and since then, Som Nath had been a loyal fan.

"Dadu?" Samir interrupted the amusing scene.

"Puttar, come in. Listen to Saigal sahib's voice." He raised the volume and sang along, "Come, beloved, and dwell in my heart, the monsoon has arrived, but you are still far. *Wah!*"

"Ji, Dadu, it's beautiful. But tell me . . ." He lowered the volume on the radio and held out the drawing. "Have you ever heard of Pattoki?"

Som Nath nodded knowingly. "Ah, the season of roses is upon us."

Slowly he got up from the chair, walked over to the bookshelf and drew out a heavy volume bound in maroon leather. *Punjab Government Gazette,* read the title, in embossed gold. Som Nath turned the book over to the last page to reveal a large, foldable map of the province of Punjab. Unfolding it out in the bed, he pointed out the place of roses, Pattoki. Samir's index finger traced the road they would likely take to their destination, almost eighty kilometers away, passing peculiar places like Phool Nagar, Flower City, and Rosa Tibba, Dune of the Deep Red, en route.

"For many years, I used to accompany Vivek to oversee the harvest of our roses. Pattoki is a place unlike any other. Imagine, if you can, an entire village transformed into a sea of pink. You will smell it long before you see it. It's the ingredients, Samir, the raw materials of a perfume—flowers, herbs, leaves, spices, and twigs—these are what you must acquaint yourself with. Forge with them an everlasting love affair. Begin with the roses. Over two hundred and fifty species of roses grow in the world and from them, the *Rosa damascena*, the Damascus rose, or, as we call it, damas gulab, the one you will encounter, is the finest. The Queen of Flowers."

It was the first and perhaps the last time that Samir witnessed a passion for anything perfumistic in his aging grandfather. Of fabrics and family, his stories were endless and emotional. But of fragrance, they fell short at mere duty and obligation. He was a forlorn man, his grandfather. And ever since Samir had known him, he'd felt Som Nath to be a hoarder of the years that had long passed. He sometimes wondered at his grandfather's need to dwell in the past. How much solace could be found within things that no longer existed, that could not be seen or touched? Then he'd be reminded of perfume, and how he found pleasure in things that seeped into the skin, lingering in sight only for moments before they, too, turned invisible. And all of a sudden, his grandfather's obsession didn't seem so unjustified.

"When was the last time you went to Pattoki, Dadu?" He returned to the matter at hand.

Som Nath chuckled. "Actually, it was the year you were born, 1927."

He got up again and this time walked toward the wooden wardrobe across the room. For a few minutes, he wrestled with a pile of something heavy at the back—books or ledgers, from the sound of rustling pages—ignoring his grandson's offers to help, waving his hand back to gesture that he could manage. Finally prying out a thick register and carrying it with both hands, he brought it to Samir.

VIJ & SONS, ESTD 1830, LAHORE, the cover read. Samir could make out that this was a ledger from when the family dealt in fabrics. Swatches of silk, satin, lace, brocade, muslin were attached to each page with notes below them. Numbers, measurements, dates, even cities were neatly collated like mementos.

His grandfather's Book of the Past.

"*Woh bhi kya din the,*" he mused, still turning the pages with a deliberate slowness, resting his frail, wrinkled hands across a swatch of fabric every now and then. "Those were the days."

Then he discovered it. Toward the end, between two blank pages, lay a single dehydrated rose. A damas gulab from Pattoki. Samir gasped. Som Nath carefully peeled it off and, for a moment, considered the deep yellow impression it left behind. Having separated the rose from its shadow, he held it out to his grandson. The once vibrant pinkness had faded to a pale blush, some petals now almost completely cream. Light brown veins spread across like filigree, and each edge had dried resolutely into its brittle shape.

"I plucked it from the field during that last visit. And for ten years, it has lived inside these pages," his grandfather, the unexpected flower-presser, remarked. "Go on then, take it. It now belongs to you."

Samir took it delicately—the flower as old as him—and cupped it in his hands, for already, the light breeze from outside threatened to crumble it. Curious, he brought it up to his nose and realized that the rose no longer smelled even remotely of a rose, but entirely of paper. It wafted off an old, musty, slightly acidic, almond-like scent, and, much to Samir's disbelief, bore a trace of vanilla. *Could it be?* The same smell that had emanated from Firdaus and her father resided within this rose. Placing the pressed flower down, he now lifted the book and thrust his nose right into its open spine. He inhaled, and there it was. He deduced that, somehow, a shared element existed in the natural constitutions of handmade paper and vanilla—one that he was determined to explore further.

ℒ

Across the Walled City, in the late hours of the moon-soaked night, the neighborhoods of Delhi Gate receded into stillness. Lights from the houses dimmed, the winter bonfires were put out, and the stray cats curled into furry balls under staircases. In that hour of quiet, the calligrapher presented his gray-eyed begum with a vial of precious perfume. Delighted, she dabbed the ittar onto the pulse points of her body that emitted heat and allowed the fragrance to bloom faster. The perfume kissed her wrists, neck, cleavage, the backs of her knees, as the calligrapher watched in rapture. Eventually, the couple fell asleep, ankles entwined.

But in the same house, in a room overlooking the golden mosque, the young illuminator of manuscripts remained awake. By the light of a single oil lamp, she held a stick of charcoal over a blank sheet of paper. It had been weeks, yet he was still imprinted in her memory. She didn't understand why he had remained there, but every now and then, she found herself wondering if they would meet again. The boy in the ittar shop.

The language of words had never belonged to her; that domain was entirely her father's, and one that she would have to learn as the years progressed. Unlike other children her age, she remained comfortable in silence, relying on ink and paper to render her thoughts. But this boy had made her act out of character, emboldened and resolute in a way that she couldn't understand. She closed her eyes and pictured him. His hands had looked soft, unlike her own, which endured the daily contact with ink and soap; his hair had been neatly combed back, his face was speckled with light beauty marks, and his ears pointed outward, comically large. These

impressions had become difficult to forget, but what had been most striking was the way in which they had held each other's gaze.

Opening her eyes, she concentrated on the blank page, fastening her
grip on the charcoal stick. She began with the eyes, drawing wisps of black
like the veins of a leaf, then the pupils, the eyelashes, and soon, a face began to emerge. Eyes, lips, a jawline, a nose, *the nose.*

# 10

# The Soul of the Rose

It was still dark when Vivek and Samir left for Pattoki in the tanga they'd hired for the day. The Walled City was barely awake as they rode through its narrow alleys. Samir rubbed his tired eyes and suppressed a yawn as his uncle, seemingly wide-awake, directed their horse out onto the main road they would follow until their destination. Only after they'd been on the road for nearly forty-five minutes did the sun rise completely, painting the day golden.

City ultimately gave way to open land—fields of wheat, corn, fruit trees, jasmine—and finally, whispers of the rose emerged. Samir smelled it before he saw it, just as his grandfather had said. He knew it was coming up ahead, Pattoki, where the earth and air were both swathed in rosy blush. An entire village transforming into a sea of pink. From a distance, as they approached the abundant fields, a thin dark man walked toward them, silhouetted by the day's suddenly bright light. He motioned toward a clearing where they could park the tanga.

"That is Bir Singh," Vivek told Samir. "He's spent his whole life in this rose field and has knowledge greater than anyone else here, perhaps even us. He understands every facet of the damas gulab and its habitat, from seed to oil. These fields serve as employment for many members of his family, and in fact, most of Pattoki is engaged with the world of flowers in some way or another."

*Like our family,* Samir thought.

"Vij sahib, namaste. Aaiye, come this way . . ." Bir Singh greeted them with folded hands and led the uncle-nephew duo to the heart of the field. Vivek walked ahead, but Samir followed slowly, enchanted by the sights around him. His grandfather was right, the world had suddenly bloomed into a spectrum of pinks, and he took his time strolling through, luxuriating in the landscape. Short walls of roses surrounded him. The field was cultivated in rows, and each row was peppered with pink. In the plains, the rose bloomed from March to April and had to be picked before sunrise—lest the rays of the sun wither their scent—and distilled the same day.

Men, with heads and bodies covered to protect themselves from the heat, picked the mature flowers. At times, their hands moved with such swiftness through the bush that all Samir could discern were colors and textures in motion. He watched, transfixed, as calloused brown fingers progressed through the bushes, picking open-faced petals and waxy sepals, careful to avoid leaves and thorns, and dropping them into the open sacks tied to their waists and necks. Their movements seemed to be synchronized to a low humming. A picker's song, rhythmic and involuntary, floated throughout the field.

The face of the rose was large, soft, flat, and open, and the pickers grabbed it from the top, often holding more than one rose in both palms before dropping them into the sack. The rouge of the damas gulab was the lightest of light pinks, unlike the darker, more commonly found desi gulab, and caught one's eye as it peeked out playfully from the woven jute. As Samir watched the pickers at work, he was reminded of his uncle at the ittar shop, grabbing vials off of shelves with both hands to present them to customers.

For the next two hours, they walked around the rose field, observing the men at work, studying the soil, and, of course, smelling. Each time Samir inhaled the air around him, he felt intoxicated. He couldn't wait to tell his grandfather all about their day and, as a souvenir, picked a large rose to take back to him. Translucent and lightweight, it looked almost like the flowers constructed with tissue-thin paper.

By mid-morning, the pair was on their way back to Lahore, large bundles of damas gulab weighed and tied carefully in layers of jute sack and cloth, to avoid any penetration of harsh sunlight. The entire cargo was then further covered with a tarp and tied down with rope, in a way that would cause least damage to the flowers. Luggage and passengers aboard, the tanga drove out of the pink-hued village and back to its cacophonic city.

Vivek and Samir arrived back in Anarkali Bazaar to find them waiting outside the ittar shop—Ousmann, Aarif, and Jameel, who operated the distillery above. Samir had spoken to them before, but never as intimately as the afternoon that was about to unfold. They would give him his first lesson in the ancient process of distillation. Pajamas and kurtas rolled up past their knees and elbows, the turbans on their heads tightened, the three men quickly carried the fragrant cargo up the side staircase. And for the first time, Samir was allowed to follow. He walked up slowly, observing how dark the walls were. Like an inverse composition of land and sky, the upper walls had become soot-charred and smoky black, feathering downward to the original light blue paint.

In the open-air distillery, Jameel held a bundle of pale pink in his arms and brought it close to one of the copper pots called a degh, which could hold up to eighty kilograms of rose petals. Several deghs were lined up in a row, placed a few feet above the ground on wood and dung-fire ovens as makeshift furnaces. On the floor of the distillery were several piles of chopped wood. Jameel tipped the sack at the edge of the degh and let Aarif remove the cover and gently nudge the contents in. A river of roses spilled into the open mouth of the vessel.

"*Daalo daalo, poora daalo,* come on, fill it to the top," Ousmann instructed in his husky voice. He was the most experienced of the three; his father had once been Khushboo Lal's chief distiller, and Ousmann had inherited many of his skills. Samir watched as petals fluttered out onto the ground and around the degh until it was full. Jameel and Aarif swept the contents in together, using both hands and feet for balance.

Distillation was a bodily process. It demanded use of the limbs, the mind, and, most importantly, the nose. The three men moved around the distillery in methodical, practiced movements, like dancers. Their muscles flexed each time they lifted the heavy sacks, and beads of sweat trailed down their suntanned arms.

After transferring the flowers, they poured small amounts of cold water over the petals and shut the degh. To ensure that no steam or liquid escaped at all, Aarif brought a heap of clay, wet and coiled up like a three-inch-wide snake, and, mixing it in with fluffs of soft cotton, he uncoiled it onto the edges of the closed pot, like a seal. Dumm, this process was called, and it was repeated for each degh, until no more roses remained. A fire was then lit and the mixture boiled for five to six hours.

Soon a smoky, charred smell began to float up to the sky, alerting the inhabitants of Anarkali that a concoction was brewing. It stung Samir's eyes, but everyone else stood still. Blinking repeatedly, he, too, tried to remain composed. If he wanted to exist in the world of delicate fragrances, then he would have to become accustomed to the tempestuous ways in which they were distilled.

Ousmann wiped his face with a cloth, sweat already having drenched through his vest and shirt. He pointed to the empty jute sacks. "Samir beta, it takes approximately four tonnes of roses to produce one kilogram of pure rose ittar. But time remains essential in all aspects of perfumery, and perhaps all aspects of life. *Time is critical,*" he emphasized, as if drilling the motto into Samir, and then sat on his haunches, motioning the boy to come closer.

"Look." Ousmann's hands moved along the distilling apparatus. "This is the degh-bhapka process." And then, turning around, he called out to Vivek, who was observing from a distance, "*Vij sahib, ennu angrezi vich ki kehnde eh?*"

"Hydro-distillation," came the prompt response.

"Aah, that. Hydro dist . . . lisht . . ." He trailed off vaguely, waving his hands in the air. "Now, look, we put all our ingredients into the degh and light a fire underneath. The hot steam releases the essential oils of whatever is in there, in this case the damas gulab. But the contents could be flowers, leaves, herbs, spices, woods, barks, or even seeds, and sometimes everything together. The vapor of the distilled matter rises, condenses, and flows from the degh, through this attached hollow bamboo pipe called a chonga, into a smaller receiver vessel called a bhapka. This bhapka receiver, as you can see, is placed in a trough of cool water." Ousmann pointed out each element.

Samir made note of the distilling apparatus—two containers, one hot, the other cool, connected through a hollow pipe—exceedingly simple yet remarkably effective in extracting, absolutely, the essence of ingredients.

"And the rope?" He gestured to the jute that tightly covered the bamboo pipes.

"Ah, good, very good." Ousmann was pleased with this observation, "The ropes are made of wild jute and grass and serve as insulators to the pipes. The distiller's job—dighaa, that is what we are called—is a complex one, for he must always remain vigilant. A dighaa must know exactly how long to heat the degh for, because if his attention wavers and it overheats, then the resulting scent will be too smoky and all the ingredients will have been wasted. You see this process is thousands of years old, and over generations, its practice has become like second nature to us. *Yeh bunyadi kala hai,* this is a foundational art."

Ousmann now pointed to the bhapka. "Traditionally, sandalwood oil is mixed into the vapor, which emerges from the bamboo pipes as the core of all ittars. Sandalwood acts as a fixative or carrier oil, a receptacle for aromas that are still in an extremely fragile state. It *fixes* the scent of these flowers and herbs, allows them to last longer."

"Like a canvas?" Samir offered.

"Exactly. It holds all the smells without imposing itself or interfering in any way. Now, when the receiver is filled completely, the dighaa rubs a wet cloth around it for a temporary pause, and then the full receiver is replaced with an empty one to continue the process. The cold water is also changed. This is repeated until the distillation is complete. Sometimes, it's only five days long, and other times, it can last up to a whole month."

"And then the ittar is ready?" Samir asked.

Ousmann laughed. "Not quite, not quite. This liquid is strained and filtered, and then set aside in kuppis for maceration. The mammoth kuppi flasks made of camel leather soak up any excess moisture from the mixture, leaving only the purest oil behind. This last step can last for weeks, months, or even years. In the case of the rose, we can distill the petals into an ittar on a base of sandalwood, or use other methods to extract an even more concentrated essence of the flower. An absolute." He held out his hand and opened all the fingers slowly and magically, like a blooming rose. "That is the soul of the rose, ruh-e-gulab."

Samir exhaled loudly and stared at him, wide-eyed. "How long does it take to learn all this, Ousmann chacha?" he asked, running his hand along the dry mud caked on the cooling trough.

"*Beta ji, yeh sab tajurbe ka kaam hai,* this entire process comes with experience. There are no thermometers to gauge the temperature, no manuals to instruct on the thickness of clay on the deghs, no teacher standing by to tell the difference between a good batch of ittar and a foul one. It all just comes with time and settles in like muscle memory. *Sab waqt ke saath samajh aa jayega,* you will learn it with time. I promise."

He ruffled the child's hair lovingly and then held his face up. "My grandfather taught the art of distillation to my father, who further taught it to me." He paused. "You see, this world of ittar is so fragile and elusive that unless we preserve it and pass it down to the next generation, it will crumble. One day, we might even forget this ancient art. Memorize it, Samir, be its treasurer. Be its keeper, its khazin."

# 11

# The Syntax of Smell

A few days after the distillation of the rose began, Vivek brought Samir to the atelier to trace the history of the enchanting flower and its scent. Since it was too soon for this season's harvest, they sat with last year's rose, making it the first ingredient Samir would learn about in depth. Firdaus's unique rose scent snaked through his memory as he approached the three containers placed on the table. The first was a vial of thin, clear ittar gulab, or rose oil; the second was the concentrated ruh-e-gulab, or rose absolute, thicker and deeper in color; and the third was a long glass beaker with a swan-shaped neck that held gulabjal, or rosewater, obtained as a by-product of the distillation process. Rosewater could be used to wash the face, heal scars, moisten the eyes, or refresh the mind.

"They say that the first Mughal emperor, Babur, was also the first to have brought the damas gulab and perfume culture to Hindustan, going as far back as the sixteenth century," Vivek began. "So besotted he was with gul, the rose, that he named his four daughters as a tender homage to the flower. Gulchihra, the rose-cheeked; Gulrukh, the rose-faced; Gulbadan, the rose-bodied; and Gulrang, the rose-colored. In his diaries, he even immortalized this love through poetry—

*"My heart, like the bud of the red, red rose,*
*Lies fold within fold aflame,*
*Would the breath of even a myriad springs*
*Blow my heart's bud to a rose?"*

Samir picked up the closest vial and inhaled once again.

"Babur's grandson Akbar also had a deep interest in perfumes, scenting his halls with a substance called ambergris, which is a natural product from the intestines of large sea creatures called whales. Here, we call this abeer."

Samir scrunched his nose in disgust.

Laughing, Vivek produced a small piece of stonelike substance from a drawer under the organ. Samir's hunger to devour new smells eclipsed his initial aversion, and he smelled the crumbly, off-white lump. For a few seconds, it seemed completely alien, and then, gradually, it took on shades of smells already familiar. Salty, warm, sweet. *Interesting,* he thought. Vivek told him that the whiter ambergris they smelled now was older and pleasant, whereas the fresher sample, black in color, smelled almost rancid and fecal.

"Oh, puttar, it might not always smell or look as lovely as a rose, but it is just as expensive and far rarer as a raw material! Men go to great lengths to procure it, spending days at sea, and even longer scouring the shores. The very first time I smelled ambergris in vilayat, I was overcome. It was the dark, fresher variety, and emitted a horribly repellent odor. So powerful and commanding that I actually feared it . . ." His voice trailed off to somewhere far away for a few seconds, before he clarified, "I feared to use it for a while."

Samir nodded slowly, nose still suspended over the off-white lump.

"Now," Vivek continued, "*this* is how you know if the ambergris is still good to be used." He heated a slim needle using the fire of a matchstick, and then stuck it into the ambergris. Samir watched as the needle effortlessly entered the stone with a low oozing sound. A lone tendril of smoke snaked up. *Still good,* Vivek indicated, and then, placing it back into the drawer, continued with the lesson.

"Coming back to the gulab. The most famous story of the rose belongs to the reign of Akbar's son, the Emperor Jahangir. According to legend, Asmat bibi, the mother of his Empress Nur Jahan, was making rosewater one day when she discovered an oily film floating on the surface of the hot water. Little by little, she collected it and, rubbing it on her palm, was delighted to discover its strength. That a single drop of the oil was reminiscent of an entire field of blooming roses. The perfume was called *itr-e-Jahangiri* and, in his memoirs in 1614, was described by the emperor as the discovery of his reign, which had the ability to restore the hearts that had been broken and withered."

Then, opening Samir's notebook to an unused page, Vivek drew a triangle and divided it into three parts. He labeled each part—top, middle, base—and began scribbling words inside the sections. The page quickly transformed from a blank sheet to a document busy with names, formulas, and numbers. Once it was complete, he passed the notebook back to Samir, who surveyed the diagram. He recognized some words but mostly understood nothing. He looked up at his teacher, distraught, causing Vivek to laugh.

From his pocket, the perfumer retrieved a tiny key and unlocked the last drawer of his worktable. Samir craned his neck to see, and was confused when he saw only notebooks. Vivek took out a dusty one and began reading under his breath, tracing the pages with his forefinger. Samir tried to concentrate on Vivek's fast-moving lips, but his uncle seemed to be speaking a completely foreign language.

"You must keep all your notebooks, Samir. Every observation and notation is important, for it reflects how you feel about a certain smell at a certain time in your life. Ingredients, formulas, dreams, textures, each and every failed or successful attempt—these things must be noted down. *And throw nothing away.*"

Samir drew his own notebook closer to his chest.

Vivek's journal was a medium-sized blue hardcover. GRASSE, 1916, its label read. A document from over twenty years ago. Flipping through its pages, he arrived at a diagram not too different from the one he has just drawn for Samir. *La pyramide olfactif,* the apprentice mouthed.

"To smell is commonplace; we inhale our environment every day, without question or thought. But just because one *can* smell doesn't mean that one always analyzes those smells. To smell well, *to sniff,* is an art, and the people who practice this art are called noses. I am a nose." Vivek brought his fingers to the bridge of the prized organ. "There are still so many things we don't completely understand about our ability to smell—it is elusive and mysterious. But what is certain is that our nose is an incredible machine, able to both break down as well as construct thousands of different odors into harmony."

Samir nodded, sliding his forefinger down his own nose.

"So, how do we imagine smells that don't yet exist?" he asked, and Samir shrugged. He simplified the question, "How do we make perfumes?"

"The . . . distillery?" Samir pointed to the world above the ceiling.

"Indeed, perfumes are distilled or extracted using the natural elements of fire, water, air, flowers, and herbs. In our part of the world, these are oil-based scents called ittar or itr or attar, as derived from Farsi and Arbi. The oils are viscous and lush, and when rubbed into the skin imbue the body with fragrance. But an ittar is subtle and does not disperse into the air. One can only smell it once close to the body of the wearer, so while the fragrance may be intense and long-lasting, its sillage or trail is intimate and private."

*Sillage,* Samir noted down the term.

"In vilayat, however, perfumes are not made on a base of oil, but rather a solvent called alcohol. Alcohol blends and preserves, and also stabilizes the ingredients of the perfume. The final product is a diluted liquid, sprayed onto the body like mist. As this perfume disperses into the air around the wearer, the sillage becomes tremendously larger than any ittar. It can even be smelled across the room. Vilayati perfumes are also made by blending many ingredients together by hand, as the perfumer desires. Jasmine may be mixed with rose and vetiver, lavender may be mixed with sandalwood, musk, and so on . . ."

"As we blended the grapefruit and vetiver oil to create a new smell?" Samir asked. "We can make recipes of different smells?"

"Quite right," Vivek said, "and it is all about repeated trial and error. Sometimes our ingredients may blend with harmony, and other times they may not. But we don't call this a recipe—that word does not belong to perfumers. What we make is called a composition."

*Composition,* Samir added to his list of new terms.

"We compose our perfumes, and build them in the same way that musicians compose their symphonies, each instrument gradually being introduced. First the harmonium, then the tabla, then the sarangi, then the vocals, and so on. Imagine each ingredient being a separate layer of varying volume, and those many layers together creating a new smell, a blend.

"Customers do not only come to our ittar shop to buy a vial of rose, jasmine, or any other flower or herb. They come to buy our blends, like *Sapna* and *Amrit,* modern renditions of a traditional craft. They come to buy a sensation, a feeling, a transportation, a movement of time, a medium. They come to buy history, memory, dreams, desires, and romance." Vivek's tone was impassioned, and placing a palm on Samir's chest, he continued, "I can only teach you the techniques of perfumery, which in itself are difficult enough. But the real talent in composing original perfumes must come from *within* you."

"But how does one begin?" the young apprentice asked.

"Ah, yes, how does a perfumer begin to compose or even imagine a perfume? How does he understand the structure?" He paused for dramatic effect and then tapped his forefinger on the open page. "By understanding this. The olfactive pyramid. The realm of scent, as we know, is invisible, subjective, and ambiguous. Therefore, understanding its unique language is essential."

Suddenly there was a knock on the door, and Mohan peeked his head in. "Veer ji, Das sahib has come and is asking about the vilayati samples he asked you to procure for his soaps."

"Ah, yes, of course. I'll be right there." Vivek got up and from the shelf, picked up a small package wrapped in brown paper. Das sahib was a new client, perhaps the most popular soap-maker in the bazaar, and he had sought Vivek out to source some foreign oils that could be mixed into his soaps. Leaving his nephew with the open notebooks and a wealth of new information, Vivek promised to be back shortly.

Once alone, Samir sighed with irritation. They had barely begun. There was so much to learn, and yet one had to tend to the everydayness of business. Idly, he leaned over and picked up his uncle's notebook.

"Grasse," he whispered, rolling the *r*'s, hissing the *s*'s.

"Grassee?" he tried again, unsure of what an *e* was doing at the end of the common English word. What was Grasse?

Humming the strange new word under his breath, he turned the pages of the notebook, making sure to keep his finger in as a bookmark. He wanted to read all the secrets of scent, know them all, use them all. Samir could read some English, but these secrets were completely unreadable. Maybe this was the language that his uncle had been mouthing, the language of vilayat, perhaps.

Vivek returned twenty minutes later. Das sahib, having adored the samples on account of no other soap-maker in Lahore having them, had purchased them all.

Over the next few days, Samir learned that perfume could be divided into separate notes, or descriptors of scent. But before one blended different notes, let alone composed a complete perfume, abundant knowledge of ingredients was essential. They were the alphabet of perfumery. Slowly, Samir began familiarizing himself with the different vials on Vivek's organ, classified into their respective notes.

What one perceived upon application of a perfume were the top or head notes. These set the first impressions of a perfume, and comprised ingredients that were light, fresh, sharp, and stimulating, yet had higher volatility and evaporated within minutes. Citrus fruits like bergamot, lemon, neroli, mandarin, and aromatic herbs like sage, rosemary, mint.

The middle or heart note was next, lingering for three to four hours. Florals like rose, jasmine, geranium, frangipani, ylang-ylang, and, of course, Samir's heart of hearts, the tuberose, or rajnigandha. There were green smells too, like grasses, leaves, pine, and tea. There were fruits like raspberry, apricot, mango. There were spices that added to the intensity and ruggedness, like cloves, cinnamon, saffron, pepper. These smells were rounded and mellow, and were also used to mask the initial, seemingly unpleasant nature of the base notes. Together, the middle and base made the body of the perfume.

The base notes lasted for over five hours and sometimes lingered throughout the day. They boosted the perfume, gave it depth and solidity. They were large and heavy woods like cedar, sandalwood, and moss; animalic scents like musk, myrrh, and civet; and lastly, Vivek's own muse, the ambrette seed.

As the pair went through the list, each ingredient was brought down from the organ and smelled. Citrus, herbs, florals, green notes, fruits, spices, woods, and balsam together created the complete atlas of smell.

The young apprentice tried his best to keep up, to not be overwhelmed or seem restless. But every hour or so, he could feel his energy waning, his mind crawling away into his schoolwork, or friends, or even the rose fields of Pattoki. Sometimes, Vivek would catch him fumbling and fidgeting with the bottles, or smelling randomly for his own pleasure rather than for the exercise. He'd reprimand him, but then soften immediately, realizing that despite his astute sense of smell, Samir was only a child, and not everything needed to be learned at once.

⚘

One evening, Samir's nose was so overwhelmed that, using Savitri's trick, he inhaled the crook of his elbow. Vivek smiled, impressed with the tricks of the trade that his young apprentice was amassing. The day's lesson had just ended, and together, they placed the many stray bottles back onto the organ.

Vivek collected his notebooks, put them back into the drawer, and locked it.

"Are the notebooks more precious than the ingredients, Taya ji?" Samir asked, increasingly curious of the secrecy surrounding the bottom drawer.

"Without a doubt," the perfumer replied, slipping the key back into his pocket. "They are irreplaceable." He sat back on the stool, rolling down the sleeves of his shirt, and picked on a loose thread. Samir remained seated, unsure of what was happening now.

"Look, puttar, you may not completely understand these things now, but you will one day. There is much that you need to learn, and much that I know you to be capable of." Vivek smiled at him. "Our sense of smell is unpredictable. Over the years, it will change, it will age, it will become a receptacle of memory and mystery, and begin to contain a sense of . . ." He looked out the window. ". . . of having lived. This is why a record of smell is so important, so that we can remember the way things once were. The way *we* once were."

Samir chewed on his lower lip, trying hard to focus on the words.

"A perfume is not a string of smells one has merely blended together on a whim. A perfume has occasion and history. It has a landscape, a body, and a response. But we may not always feel the same way toward a perfume that we have made and smelled because we are also evolving as noses. Therefore, it becomes important to record our observations at every step in the composition. Our notebooks and journals remain the most important document of our progression as perfumers." He picked the sandalwood and ambrette vials off the organ and said, "An ingredient may easily be distilled or procured again, but the memory, intention, and ambition with which we compose a certain perfume at a certain time in our lives . . . well, that is irreplaceable."

Vivek toyed with the vials in his hands. He was momentarily grateful for the dim yellow light of the workshop, for it concealed the tears that had suddenly lined his eyes. He couldn't let Samir see him this way, but he also couldn't push aside the images that suddenly flooded his mind. If the memory of a perfume was irreplaceable, then so was the memory of the person who had inspired it.

"Samir puttar, always remember that the most poignant compositions will emerge from the things that do not leave us. Like the memories of love and happiness, or periods of deep longing, or"—Vivek's voice retreated into whisper—"moments of unfathomable loss."

# 12

# Carrying an Ancient Art
# into a Modern World

When Firdaus turned five, old enough to hold a qalam and takhti properly, she began to accompany Altaf to the calligraphy studio at Wazir Khan mosque, where she would refer to him as ustad.

Altaf's small studio consisted of ten male students, of varying ages, who arrived at nine in the morning. Everyone sat on the ground and was expected to work silently, showing respect for this sacred art. A typical day began with a lesson in tafsir, Quranic interpretation. Around noon, they would pause for the zuhr prayer and break for lunch, which the ustad took at his home. When he returned, it was with Firdaus. For the remainder of the day, students devoted themselves to mashq, where they copied and practiced masterly verses and inscriptions. Adorning the walls of Wazir Khan were Quranic verses inscribed in the khat-e-nastaliq, khat-e-tughra, and khat-e-thuluth styles of calligraphy, which the students also attempted to reproduce.

Though the majority of Firdaus's education would be in the art of illustration, illumination, and embellishment, she also spent time learning the calligraphic scripts. At the muezzin's call for asr prayer, students would follow their ustad into the mosque compound. But young Firdaus, for whom reading namaz was not yet comuplsary, simply continued her work. The day ended after the maghrib prayer, when again she remained in the confines of the calligraphy studio.

It didn't take long for Firdaus to realize that she was the only girl.

She let a week pass before bringing it up. Then one evening, as Zainab was sitting by the window, scrubbing off the dark ink that had bled into her daughter's nail beds, Altaf appeared at the door. He smiled, for the scene reminded him of his own childhood. But just as he was about to leave, Firdaus called out and asked him why no other girls practiced calligraphy. Zainab, who was already weary of her husband's progressive approach to parenting, said nothing, but the calligrapher came and sat down beside them. Taking Firdaus in his lap, he told her the story of the Princess Zebunissa, eldest daughter of Mughal Emperor Aurangzeb. Showing great intelligence from childhood, she memorized the Quran by age seven, impressing her father with her knowledge of the holy book. She went on to learn Arabic, Persian, Urdu, mathematics, and astronomy; was instructed by female teachers and taught poetry by her great-grandmother.

Holding his daughter's tiny ink-stained hands in his own, Altaf told her that the world of calligraphy could not possibly belong only to men, for Princess Zebunissa herself was a calligrapher skilled in the styles of nastaliq and shikaste. As Firdaus's eyes filled with hope and wonder, he added that Zebunissa begum, her father's undisputed favorite, often even came to court, though always in veil. Carrying his little apprentice to her bed, Altaf promised that one day, he would show her the book of the princess's poetry, collected and published posthumously under her pen name, as *Diwan-i-Makhfi*, or the Book of the Hidden One. With that, he'd blown out the oil lamp on the table.

Later that night, Zainab had reminded Altaf how the tale *actually* ended. Despite Zebunissa being favored by her father, encouraged to learn fine skills and consulted in courtly disputes, it was he who would eventually imprison the princess for her indulgences, in a fort at the edge of the city, for twenty-one years until her death. At this, Altaf had chuckled, commenting that the imprisonment had been due to complicity with her younger brother who'd declared himself the emperor. But to Zainab, this served as nothing short of a cautionary tale.

෴

Years had passed since Firdaus first heard Zebunissa's story, and yet it remained her favorite. Every time she looked around the studio, at the boys bowing over their takhtis or looking up at the inscriptions on the mosque walls, she reminded herself of the princess who had lived the life of a scholar and the father who encouraged her.

Then one evening in the spring of 1938, as she sat in a corner of the studio, head covered and eyes following the nib of her qalam, a new student appeared. The boy from the ittar shop. He arrived with his uncle, the perfumer, who promised to come back to pick him up after maghrib, at least until he learned the route to bicycle there on his own. Samir, the boy's name was Samir, and one by one, he was introduced to the students, including Firdaus, who gave a gentle nod. Her eyes had remained downcast and her fingers had continued to move the qalam, without really paying attention to her work. At the sunset hour, as the azaan was heard for maghrib, everyone apart from Firdaus and Samir dispersed toward the mosque.

For a moment, Altaf stood at the entrance, worried about leaving Firdaus unchaperoned in male company, no matter how young his new student might have been. But across from them was an old calligrapher who offered namaz while standing in his studio, no longer able to sit and pray in the mosque courtyard. When he gestured that he'd watch over the children, a satisfied Altaf joined his students. It was in this way that week after week, for just a few minutes, Firdaus sat alone in Samir's company, though no words were ever spoken.

Sometimes, when her father instructed Samir on how to deftly turn the qalam to start the stroke of a letter, or how often to dip its tip into the pot of ink, Firdaus's pistachio eyes would follow. She would watch his initially clumsy arrangement of alphabets on his takhti, and attempts to display the same decorum and composure that other students had exercised for years. But no matter how much the boy from the ittar shop tried to fit into the world of paper and ink, he would stand out. Occasionally, Firdaus would catch him inhaling the contents of an ink pot or the fibers of paper, and she would smile to herself at the oddity and intimacy of these gestures.

Months passed this way, and one evening, as Samir's head was bowed over his work, brows knitted in concentration, she tried to count the tils on his face. Two beneath the right eye, one on the cheek, a faint one on the bridge of his nose, a darker one by the temple just under the hairline, one below the edge of the left eye, one next to the nose, and one above the right eyebrow—she counted sixteen in total across the contours of his face. And just as Firdaus was committing these beauty spots to memory, Samir looked up, catching her eye.

Even with eyes closed, Samir would have discerned her presence, for her smell had become imprinted in his memory. As he sat in the calligraphy studio, the fragrance of rose with orange peel and creamy milk would waft up to him. The pungent gram flour, the unusual vanilla and smoky substance that somehow felt heightened in the mosque compound, provoked him to steal glances her way every now and then. But it was the smell of her skin, the particular redolence of perfume and sweat, that Samir found most captivating. Often, when he returned to the ittar shop after the lesson, he'd gather the ingredients that reminded him of Firdaus's scent, and inhale them one by one.

Frequently, Samir thought about their wordless conversation at the ittar shop, through the rows of glass bottles, through the locking of their eyes, through her smell and his desire. Though he wished for another such exchange, he'd never actually spoken to a girl his age before. There was a girls' school nearby to his, and Samir would see them skipping rope or playing hopscotch during recess. But what did one say to them? How did one behave? Added to this was the fact that Firdaus never spoke in the studio. Not to him, nor to anyone else. Even when the ustad called upon her, she responded in gesture—a nod of her head, the gentle closing of her eyes—as if her voice was on reserve.

They might have been sitting only a few feet apart, but the distance felt insurmountable. Samir dared not approach Firdaus in front of her father, no matter how liberal the calligrapher seemed. He craved a glance, a gesture, even a glare, another moment like the one they'd once shared. If it had left such an impression on him, then surely it had lingered in her mind, too. He'd almost abandoned the idea until one day, he caught her looking in his direction. Their eyes met, and immediately, she had lowered her gaze, but then she'd looked back, once, and again, and then throughout the evening lesson, and every week after that.

⚖

By the summer of 1939, one year later, Altaf was impressed with Samir's progress in his studio. He seemed to Altaf a changed young man, tranquil and composed, on the cusp of teenage-hood. Unlike other students at the studio, who were proficient in Islamic scripture and several styles of calligraphy, Samir focused only on mastering the everyday nastaliq. Over time, his penmanship had improved considerably, his skill with a qalam finessed, and he'd cultivated respect for the art form.

One day, when it was just the two of them, the calligrapher invited him to help in making a new batch of ink. There were no students that evening, and Firdaus was with her mother at home. The pair walked into the mosque, heads covered, and retrieved one of the large old hemp oil lamps. Bringing it to the studio, Samir observed as Altaf gently scraped the soot off from inside the lamp and collected it in a shallow dish, a pile of soft, silken embers. The soot from the mosque, he was told, was considered divine and imparted a spiritual blessing to the ink. It was then mixed with gum arabic and water, and kept aside.

From a wooden box on the ground, Altaf now extracted small pouches of herbs and spices. Though Samir was not allowed to handle these ingredients, he focused on their smells to identify odd items like gallnuts, henna leaves, and indigo. As Altaf carefully mixed the items into the ink, Samir thought of Ousmann and his uncle, who took pleasure in creating such beauty from the natural elements.

"*Ustad sahib, ijazat ho toh,*" Samir sought permission from his teacher to ask a question.

"Zaroor, Samir, what is it?"

"The formula for your ink reminds me of the formulas for our perfumes in the shop."

"I see the similarity as well." Altaf smiled. "Each calligrapher has knowledge of the natural ingredients that they use to make their ink, but these are specific to every family. My walid sahib, who was also my ustad, perfected this formula and passed it down to me."

After preparing the ink, Altaf covered the mixture and placed it in the corner of the studio. "That will sit for five days, macerating, as the herbs lend their characteristic colors, smells, and qualities to the ink."

"Like ittar, which also remains untouched, sometimes for months," Samir offered.

"Quite right." Altaf wiped his fingers on a wet rag, the ink having bled right into the cuticles. "Tell me, Samir, why are you so besotted by ittar?"

Samir sat down cross-legged and shrugged. "Ustad sahib, I've never thought too much about it. My uncle says that it is something you're born with, the gift of your nose. But my mother claims it's because I am a monsoon child and the smells of the world have settled into me, now inseparable. Monsoon enlivens the world, and that is what fragrance does as well."

Altaf looked at Samir, astonished at the simplistic yet mature thought, and briefly his mind wandered to his own January child. He wondered whether Samir was right; if Firdaus's reserved demeanor was, in fact, a seamless translation of the frigid winter night of her birth.

The following week, teacher and student strained the inky mixture and, using a fine quill, stirred it to the desired consistency. Altaf scrunched up a wad of silk fibers into a ball and placed it inside an inkwell. Upon this silken lump, the black ink was poured, just enough to be absorbed by the fibers, but not drown them. Samir then watched in awe as his ustad dipped a reed in the inkwell and transformed the ebony liquid into the graceful Urdu alphabet.

⚮

Over the year since they had first met, Altaf forged a deep friendship with the Vij brothers, meeting frequently, engaging in conversation and debate on the politics of their days, sending bottles filled with the latest perfumes or even special foods to each other's homes on Eid or Diwali. While Zainab might have been worried by this closeness on account of the Vijs being Hindu, she certainly did not mind the regular supply of new ittar.

When Samir missed his calligraphy lesson two weeks in a row, a worried Altaf inquired why, only to learn that the family was preparing their largest ever shipment of ittars for a single client, and the boy had to help out every day after school. A grand wedding was to take place in the royal house of Bahawalpur, and the guest list comprised royalty, nobility, politicians, and English men and women. Since the Vijs' reputation preceded them in all Punjab, a royal order had been placed for one thousand bottles of perfume, one for each guest. Having gained some skill in the fine art of calligraphy, young Samir was tasked with beautifully labeling each bottle. When Altaf learned of the colossal task, he volunteered himself and Firdaus to help out.

As father and daughter rode through the city, the first monsoon shower of the year broke. Small drops of rain dotted Firdaus's dark green dupatta.

Altaf stretched out his palm, and a pool of raindrops collected. Smiling, he inhaled the earthy, comforting smell. When they walked into the ittar shop, they found it shut to customers. Samir was carrying a crate of small glass bottles when he smelled her at the door. A shy smile broke across his face, and he attempted to place the crate down without breaking all the bottles. Greetings were exchanged between the elders, secret glances between the apprentices, and very quickly, tables were cleared and a production line was set up.

Altaf, Firdaus, and Samir would write labels; Savitri would stick them onto the dainty bottles that had been cleaned and dried over the last week; then Mohan and Vivek would fill each one with perfume from large glass vessels using a metal funnel and, finally, pack them into individual embroidered pouches. The many perfumes to be included in the bride's trousseau had already been poured into more elaborate cut-glass, hand-painted bottles, nestled in velvet-lined silver boxes. The group worked through the day, talking, laughing, passing around bottles of ittar, and breaking to eat puri-cholas and sweet sandesh from the specialty Bengali shop that Samir had run through the rain to buy.

After a while, resting from the tedious exercise of rendering word after word in identical fashion, Altaf stretched his arms to the ceiling and breathed in. Chameli, musk, khuss, rose, sandalwood. He looked over at Firdaus and was surprised to find her smiling as she helped Samir with his labels. Gently dipping his qalam in the ink pot, the novice calligraphy student would write the name of the perfume, softly blow on the label to dry it, and then hold it out to Firdaus for feedback. Altaf had never really seen his daughter interact with anyone her age, and her gestures seemed suddenly open and welcoming, rather than reticent and restrained. There was an uncomplicated joy on her face, the same kind that finishing an illustration or mixing a beautiful shade of ink brought her. Perhaps it was the novelty of an afternoon spent outside the studio, or perhaps it was just the company.

Somehow, in the presence of the Vij family, all formality was cast aside and Altaf felt at ease. Part of him was almost envious of how progressive they seemed, and when he looked at Mohan and Savitri, he momentarily found himself wishing that Zainab had accompanied them. But what pleased him the most was how, like his calligraphy hujra, this ittar-kadā was a place where tradition had been safeguarded and disseminated, and great care had been taken to carry an ancient art into a modern world.

## 13

# The Uncertain Hour

Britain declares war, the headline of the *Tribune* screamed. It was Monday, September 4, 1939. For a moment, Vivek stared at the words, horrified. "GERMANS ROUNDED UP IN BOMBAY AND CALCUTTA. The Prime Minister has broadcasted . . . Great Britain is at war with Germany." With his handkerchief, he wiped his face and neck. *Surely this can't be true*, he thought to himself. *Surely this cannot be happening again.* He looked around to find the world continuing on, uninterrupted. Blinking profusely, he scanned the page.

> *The British Ambassador in Berlin handed the German Government a final note . . . unless we heard from them by 11 o'clock that they are prepared at once to withdraw their troops from Poland, a state of war would exist between us.*

Folding the paper in half, then into quarters and then eighths, he shoved it into the pocket of his pants. Needing to focus his attention elsewhere, he let his thoughts race to the dark perfumed ink he carried. Mohan and Savitri had insisted that he make something special for the ustad, a gift of appreciation for helping their family send off the large order on time, and so Vivek had procured a small amount of ivory black, obtained by charring ivory in a closed vessel. He had ground it to a fine powder, and then a paste with gum arabic water, adding a few drops of the essence of musk and fewer still of ambergris. *Powerful, smoky, earthy, the perfect distraction from war.* It calmed him to think of the loving, laborious process. Pushing the headline from his mind, Vivek caught a tanga to Wazir Khan, where he was meeting the ustad for a cup of chai.

As Vivek stood in the brick corridor outside the ustad's studio, he saw Samir seated with the other students, and watched in wonder as his nephew attempted to participate in a world entirely different from theirs. With a glistening shell, Altaf was burnishing the surface of a paper to perfection so that the water-based calligraphic ink would sit atop it rather than be absorbed within. And though Samir was watching the paper transform from rough to silken, his eyes were constantly darting between the ustad and his daughter. Vivek suppressed a smile, watching from afar, until Altaf saw him standing by the door.

"*Oh, Vij sahib, aaiye na,*" he said, welcoming his friend.

Samir smiled widely at his uncle, holding up the papers he was working on. Over the last year and a half of weekly calligraphy lessons, not only had his nephew's penmanship improved drastically, but spending time at the studio seemed to have transformed him into a more emotive, inspired apprentice as well. Now, looking at the pistachio-eyed illuminator who sat across from him, Vivek understood exactly why. The ustad instructed his students to continue their work, and the two men walked out into the corridor.

"Altaf mian, please wait!" a voice called out just as they were leaving the bazaar, and they turned to find an old man with a slight paunch walking toward them. He had a short white beard and carried a tasbīḥ in his right hand, letting bead after bead slide through his fingers.

"*Ustad sahib, salaam,*" Altaf greeted him.

"I must thank you for the indigo ink you gave me last week, it worked marvelously. Mashallah, the color and consistency were ideal for marbling paper!"

Ordinarily, the calligraphers of the bazaar called one another by name or bhai, brother, or mian, a title of respect. The term *ustad*, teacher, was reserved only for the world outside. But Rizwan Alam was the most experienced Arabic calligrapher in the area, as old as Altaf's father would have been today, had he been alive. Altaf respected him deeply, even though they disagreed on many matters, particularly Firdaus's presence in the studio.

"Shukriya," Altaf replied graciously, and then presented his friend. "This is Vij sahib, whose family owns a prominent perfumery in Anarkali Bazaar."

"*As-salaam-alaikum, ustad sahib,*" Vivek greeted him.

"*Wa-alaikum-salaam,*" Rizwan said, and studied him for a moment. "Now, are you that Hindu perfumer who has been supplying Altaf mian with the rose ittar? And that leathery oudh, and the jasmine he used for the manuscript on Mughal gardens? The day that paper arrived, the entire bazaar was enveloped in the most magical aroma."

Vivek laughed. "Yes, all the ittars come from our shop. It is right next to Beli Ram chemist, and we distill everything on the premises. Please do come by anytime, perhaps we could find something special for your manuscripts as well."

The Arabic calligrapher considered the offer. "Well, your ittar is enchanting, of that there is no doubt. But we don't really venture outside our areas, Vij sahib. I hope you understand that there is an ancient order to the divisions of the guzars around the Walled City. It was nice to meet you. *Khuda hafiz,*" he concluded curtly, and nodded at Altaf.

"What did he mean by '*our* areas'?" Vivek asked quietly as Rizwan walked back to his studio, straightening the cap on his head.

Altaf patted him on the back. "Vij sahib, he's an old man with older thoughts, *purane zamane ke khayal hain.* Don't take it to heart, times are changing." Altaf smiled warmly and then offered to get the chai.

As Vivek sipped on the hot, sweet beverage, he remembered tasting it for the first time in the trenches of war. Till then, the people of Punjab had drunk neither tea nor coffee, relying on the very substantial lassi or haldi doodh. But just a few years ago, the Indian Tea Board had popularized the drink on account of overproduction of the tea leaf. Its employees were made to stand outside people's homes and shops, offering chai along with a bun, free of cost. Now it could be found in every home and little corner shop, with salty and savory snacks as accompaniment.

He and Altaf spoke till the azaan called worshippers to prayer. Rizwan's words were ignored. The perfumed ink was presented. The newspaper was not mentioned, but it was not forgotten either. That same evening, on his way back to Anarkali, an anxious Vivek bought a portable radio, much smaller than the one Som Nath had in his room. Later still, at approximately 8:30 p.m., he listened to the voice of the viceroy, Lord Linlithgow, ring through the frequencies of All India Radio, announcing that His Majesty's Government was, indeed, at war with Nazi Germany, and as a colony of that government, so was India.

&#x0639;

Over the next year, careful to not indulge in even a single conversation about war, Vivek spent most days in isolation at his organ.

From the autumn of 1939 to the spring of 1940, confined to his atelier, the soldier turned perfumer composed a delightfully strong perfume that he named *ab-e-zar*, literally meaning gold reduced to its liquid state, inspired by the luscious color of the ittar. Vivek transported his mind as far from the current war climate as he could—away from all that he knew, from the news, from the army, away even from his war years in vilayat, to a small island touching the southern tip of India.

A perfumer from Ceylon had once traveled to Lahore and, seeking Vivek out, presented him with a bottle of cinnamon essential oil, a prized commodity on the island. As an ingredient, it was sweet and bitter, hot and sumptuous, and left a long and lingering sillage. Composing it into a perfume with ingredients like peach and cumin, jasmine and vetiver, cedarwood and myrrh, *ab-e-zar* became Vivek's refuge through the anxious early months of war.

On some days, walking to or from their home, the Vij family would come across groups of men discussing the international events. These were usually the older veterans of the First World War, sitting on charpais and chatting or smoking long-piped hookahs and hand-rolled beedis. Some would bring out their medals and badges, and show off old wounds like war souvenirs, others would help to round up new recruits, and most would tell tales of horror and death, tales that Vivek himself had struggled to suppress. Like in the previous war, men who hailed from generations of soldiers readily enlisted for battle, but others approached with caution. Some were dissuaded by the stories they'd heard or read in the letters that arrived from battlefields, others were kept away from recruiting parties by their families, and some were even briefly arrested for singing anti-recruitment songs or printing anti-war statements.

The Ahluwalia brothers, who lived a few doors down from Vij Bhawan, were recruited; their father, Ujagar Singh, a veteran, having served in Gallipoli in the First World War, volunteered yet again. Medical practitioners from Savitri's mohalla of Wachowali gali were recruited as doctors and attendants, and a host of able-bodied men of all ages signed up to be noncombatants like tailors and cooks.

Every now and then, the name Hitler could be heard on the streets of Lahore. At school, a classmate of Samir's, whose uncle was fighting in the Mediterranean and brother had become a recruitment officer during wartime, would ominously declare that Hitler's army wanted to take over the world. Mohan made a delivery outside the Walled City, only to learn that German and Italian nationals working at large companies, or even as missionaries and teachers, were now seen with suspicion. But even as global events came to dominate local headlines and conversation, the threat of war on Indian soil felt distant. Against this backdrop, business continued for the Vij family as per usual, apart from the ban on the importing of foreign ingredients like bergamot oil, extracted only in now-Fascist Italy. Often an old customer who remembered how Vivek had left at the onset of the previous war would ask if he was planning on enlisting again, but he managed to deflect the subject each time.

But whenever this happened, Mohan would find on his brother's face a growing unease. While Vivek's time in vilayat remained a subject off-limits, his brother began to observe certain physical traits reappearing. Mundane things that might otherwise have gone unnoticed, had it not been for the all-consuming paranoia with which they were followed. His brother shaved even the slightest stubble off his face, and became abnormally particular about hygiene, sometimes bathing twice a day, even as the weather grew cooler. He dragged a palpable anxiety around the haveli and shop, and began resembling the angular, withdrawn man who had returned home from war. When Savitri noticed, Mohan had no choice but to tell her that the behavior was a repetition from two decades ago, and only with the opening of the perfumery had it relaxed.

Neither Som Nath nor Mohan had ever asked Vivek what had happened on the battlefield. But upon his return to Lahore, he'd shown no interest in spending time with old friends and flatly rejected any mention of matrimony. Back then, the family had simply been grateful that he was alive, unlike so many others who'd perished. And though Mohan often considered whether it was finally time now to ask about his brother's wartime experiences, Vivek's renewed fragility unnerved him.

Meanwhile, as men and women numbering up to two thousand each month began to leave the subcontinent to serve, Vivek thought back to his youth, to the adventures and equality he had once craved, and was struck by how unfamiliar that younger version of himself now seemed. Like a layer of dry, dead skin, he had slowly shed a whole person over the last twenty years, and emerged anew. Sometimes he wondered what else had been scraped off and abandoned in the process.

In the ittar shop, the portable radio played like a background score all day long. But Vivek insisted on listening only to the news bulletin and reports of war. Anxious, agitated, he buried deeper the years that threatened to spill out, vowing not to get caught up in this war. Too much had been lost the first time around. He could afford to lose no more.

14

# The Lahore Resolution

It was rare for Som Nath to receive visitors, but on a spring day in 1940, someone knocked on the entrance off Shahalmi Road, and was seated by Savitri in the front baithak. She had sprinkled the aangan with rosewater just an hour earlier, and escorted her father-in-law through the sweet-smelling courtyard into the formal guest room.

"*Oye, yara!*" Som Nath lifted his arms in delight upon recognizing the visitor, and tall, wiry Basheer Rabbani stood up and embraced his friend. Both men had aged considerably over the years, thick-rimmed spectacles sitting on their noses, walking sticks in hand, hair graying or completely white.

"Basheerey! To what do I owe this pleasure?" Som Nath turned to Savitri. "*Yeh sada bachpan da yaar eh.* His family used to stay just around the corner when we were growing up. But I must be seeing him today after nearly . . . fifteen years!" The excitement had turned the seventy-two-year-old's laughter into a mild coughing fit, and Savitri, pulling her sari over her head in formal company, excused herself to fetch water and tea.

Basheer leaned forward and, placing one arm on Som Nath's shoulder, asked, "Are you keeping well? *Sab khairiyat hai?* I have just come from Anarkali after meeting Vivek and Mohan and your grandson. The business is doing well, I see." From the pocket of his khaadi waistcoat, he took out a vial of khuss he had just purchased from the shop. "This bottle reminds me of our childhood, and the fragrant khuss curtains in this haveli."

Som Nath held both palms up to the heavens. "*Bass sab rabb di deyn hai.* It is with God's kindness that we are surviving."

"Thriving, my friend, you are thriving! Now tell me, have you been getting my letters?"

Som Nath pushed his spectacles up the bridge of his nose. "I received your letters, yes, but I didn't quite understand the last one. What did you mean by 'a separate land for Muslims'? Where will it exist?"

Basheer's family had moved away just after he finished college. The ambitious young man had traveled to England to study law and had set up a flourishing practice in Rawalpindi since his return in the early 1900s. After decades of working as a lawyer, Basheer had joined the All India Muslim League. All the while, he had kept in touch with Som Nath through letters every few months, for nothing could destroy old friendships, not even distance.

"My friend, as long as the British are in Hindustan, differences between Hindus and Muslims will continue to exist. The idea of separation is growing popular within the League, and without the settlement of issues that have come to exist between our communities, there can be no swaraj, no self-rule."

"Basheerey, what are you saying? *Meinu samajh nahi aa raha hai.* Whatever issues there are, *jo vi masle hain,* can be worked out between the leaders, can't they?" Never one to indulge in politics or affairs of state, he studied his old friend's face. "And in any case, Sikandar Hayat Khan is leading the Unionist Party in Punjab. With them in power, surely any separation on the basis of religions cannot be the answer. We have grown up together . . . you and I, both Punjabis . . . how can we just . . . ?" He laughed nervously.

Just then, Savitri came back with a tray of tea and homemade pinnis.

Her glass bangles clinked as she served the gentlemen, and briefly, Som Nath thought back to the festival of basant that he and Basheer had always celebrated together as children. How excitedly they'd run to the rooftop at the crack of dawn with large kites and flown them till they soared high in the sky, higher than all the rooftops in the mohalla, high enough until the sounds of *bo-kataa, bo-kataa, the kite is cut!* resounded.

Historically, was basant Hindu or Muslim? Had the kites been Hindu or Muslim? Had the air been Hindu or Muslim? Could one even divide air, separate it?

Basheer cleared his throat as Savitri left the room. He picked up the cup and saucer and took a sip. "Look, Som Nath, I don't know what will happen in the future, but whatever I know, I want to tell you so you can prepare."

*Prepare?* thought Som Nath. But no words escaped his lips.

"Last month, Jinnah sahib presided over a session of the Muslim League, right here at Minto Park in Lahore. A text was prepared at this session demanding a separate homeland for the Muslims of British India, called Pakistan. We don't know yet what this land will look like, or what it will mean for Hindus or other communities, but I can say with certainty that the day the resolution was drafted and passed will be remembered as a significant day in our history."

Thinking about this later, Som Nath kept coming back to that *our,* for though his old friend hadn't explicitly said as much, he could tell that the word excluded him. In the future that Basheer now envisioned, the lived history of Hindus and Muslims of Hindustan would somehow diverge.

After his old friend left, Som Nath sat for long hours in his room, holding Leela's charred bone within his palms. How he wished she were here. He remembered her scent, how she'd rub the sandalwood stick on the grinding stone each day until a fresh, thick paste would form, velvety, luscious, and deeply earthy; how she'd spread it over her arms, her legs, her face. How she scrubbed it clean never with water but only milk so that her skin glowed golden. How had he existed for so many years without her? How had he endured this solitary life? He looked out of his window, up at the clear spring sky, and imagined it being sliced in half, the unwrinkled air being divided. Oh, Leela would have known what to do, how to feel, what to *prepare* for. Most of all, she would have understood how to calm his racing heart. With his fist still enclosing the bone within it, he closed his eyes and fell into a deep sleep until his sons returned home that evening.

During dinner, Som Nath brought up Basheer's visit. The rest of the family also didn't understand what a separate state would mean. But the air became tense, as if stretched over a surface too small for it. Vivek found it best not to mention what the old calligrapher had said to him all those months ago at Wazir Khan. *Our* areas, and *yours.* The meal ended quietly, for everyone's mind was crowded with questions.

In the master bedroom of the house, camphor burned in the corner to keep mosquitoes away through the night. Savitri changed into her night sari behind a wooden screen, and Mohan lay on the bed, hands interlaced behind his head. She emerged and sat beside him.

"Did you manage to hear anything Basheer mian said to Baba today?" he asked his wife.

She shook her head. "I didn't think it was right to linger. But he stayed for quite a while . . ."

Her husband was silent.

"Where do you think they will create this separate state? Do you think we will have to . . ." Her voice was now a whisper. "Will we have to leave?"

"Savitri, of course not! Lahore is our home. Why would we go anywhere? And most of Shahalmi is Hindu or Sikh, so will we all just be evacuated from here to another city? No. We may not be the religious majority, but we are certainly the economic one. So even if a separate state is created, Lahore *will* remain a part of Hindustan. And how do we know this is not just another ploy by the British to divide us?

"So, listen to me now." He sat up straight and held both his wife's hands within his own. "*Nothing* is going to happen. Hindus, Muslims, Sikhs, Jains, Parsis, Christians, we have all lived together in this city ever since I can remember. Why would it be any different now? Think of the people who come to our shop, do we differentiate between them based on their religion? That would be absurd. Rose oil for the Hindu, marigold for the Muslim, jasmine for the Sikh . . . have we ever thought this way, *socha hai kabhi mazhab ke baare mein?* Whatever this is, it will settle, it will pass. Trust me. Lahore is our home."

He spoke with a conviction that compelled her to nod in agreement.

"Yes, you're right. Of course." She exhaled deeply and grasped her husband's hands tighter. "It's just that, I don't know why, when Baba was telling us what his friend warned him of today, the only thing I could think of was Samir going to Delhi Gate every week, to the mosque all by himself. To that area. And now, I feel so . . . so ashamed. But you are right, Lahore is our home. This is where we belong."

"Savitri, ustad sahib is a good and open-minded person. Nothing will happen to Samir under his care. You know he's always treated him like his own son. But Veer ji and I will speak to him, if it will make you feel better. He may know more about all this . . ."

"Yes, that is a good idea," she agreed and reached over to dim the oil lamp placed on the bedside table.

Kissing her forehead, Mohan turned to his side and curled into sleep.

Savitri waited for at least an hour to make sure her husband was in deep slumber before she stepped out of bed and tiptoed toward the wooden chest near the window. In a thick dupatta, she collected all the valuable jewelry she had amassed over the years and tied it together so that it was in one place. She hoped with all her heart that her husband was right, but it didn't hurt to be prepared, just in case.

Meanwhile, on the upper floor of the house, Vivek leaned on the windowsill, smoking a cigarette—a habit he thought he'd left behind on the battlefield. In the background, the radio played on the lowest volume. He had come to find solace in All India Radio's east-west signature tune, and throughout the day, shifted between AIR and the British Broadcasting Corporation, which had recently begun the news in Hindustani. But occasionally, if he adjusted the antenna just slightly, the frequency could catch a German network. Vivek, who had learned a smattering of French while in Europe, would try to make out any words that sounded even vaguely familiar, but with little luck. He didn't know what news he expected to hear of the troops fighting across the black waters, but he hoped that their lives, caught yet again in a war that did not belong to them, would turn out differently from his own.

From underneath his pillow, he extracted the sepia photograph of the couple and gazed at the woman's face. She was imprinted in his memory this way—doe eyes, a youthful smile, a simple white dress. "May no one endure the losses I had to," he spoke to the lifeless image. "May they be spared the suffering."

He slipped the photograph back under his pillow. Then, with the radio still humming, Vivek fell asleep.


In the room next door, Samir lay awake. For the first time that evening, he realized what it meant for Firdaus and him to be from different religions. But none of his affection for her seemed to have waned, and so he deemed the detail rather insignificant. Two years had passed since their first meeting, and in that time, his curiosity had grown into a tenderness hard to overlook. All those months ago, writing labels together in the ittar shop had shown him a different side to Firdaus. A carefreeness that dulled into reticence at the studio. Sometimes, if he closed his eyes and concentrated, he could remember the curve of her smile and the way her green eyes had shone in the monsoon light.

Since then, they'd begun to exchange greetings in the presence of the ustad and other students. But it was at prayer times, under the irregular supervision of the old calligrapher, that Firdaus began to draw Samir. He hadn't noticed it at first, but every so often she would gesture for him to stay still or hold out his hand in a pose. She never said why she did it; perhaps she didn't need to, for it seemed that she was committing his features to memory as he had her smell. But despite the intimacy of these actions, Samir hadn't summoned the courage to actually tell her how he felt.

The following week, he quietly brought this up with his friend Prithvi. A tall, well-dressed boy with dark brown eyes, Prithvi was popular with the girls from the school down the street, and Samir was certain he would offer some practical advice. He had wiggled his eyebrows up and down and teased Samir, before easing into a tone of seriousness.

Leaning back on the railing where they had parked their bicycles, he said, "Why don't you write her a letter? Like Devdas wrote to Parvati from Calcutta."

"Devdas wrote Paro a letter saying they should only be friends!" Samir exclaimed, recalling the plot of the 1935 film.

"But Samir's letter to Firdaus doesn't have to say that." Prithvi wiggled his eyebrows again.

At the time, Samir brushed off his friend, but the idea stuck. That night, dipping his qalam in a pot of ink, Samir carefully rendered his feelings on a sheet of paper and folded it four times into a discreet square. Slipping it under his pillow, he whispered into the night:

*Tumhari yaad ki kashti iss dil ki darya mein doob gayi hai.*
The paper boat of your memory has drowned in the river of this heart.

﴾

The next day, Samir was surprised to see his father and uncle both accompany him to the mosque. Though his secret note for Firdaus was stowed safely in the pocket of his pants, its presence made him feel more nervous than ever. Usually, he'd have ridden his bicycle, but with both Mohan and

Vivek tagging along, they caught a tanga from Lohari Gate instead. Afraid that they would confiscate the note, he kept his left hand in his pocket throughout the ride.

Upon reaching the studio, Samir greeted his ustad and took his place across the carpet from Firdaus. As always, her eyes remained fixated on the manuscript she was working on, and momentarily Samir felt a stab of disappointment. What had he been expecting, after all? He opened up his qalamdan to take out his pens and poured ink into the dawāt. After allocating work to each student, Altaf accompanied Vivek and Mohan to the bazaar outside. Just as the men walked out, the green eyes glanced up. Firdaus was wearing a deep blue dupatta that day, and her eyes appeared more teal than pistachio. She gestured a *salaam* to Samir and he beamed in return. The folded note remained, and the perfumer wondered how to transport it all the way across the studio to Firdaus without any of the other students getting suspicious.

"Uh . . ." he began, and then paused, not knowing what to say. So many social conventions he had to adhere to, and so many he wished to break. When he spoke again, his tone was unnaturally confident. "Firdaus?"

She looked in his direction, as did everyone else.

"Could you hand me that qalam-e-kafi, please?" He motioned toward the small qalam placed on the ground next to her. The rest of the students returned to their papers and slates, and the gestures of dipping-writing-drying continued as usual. Nervously, Firdaus nodded, picked up the reed, and held it out toward Samir.

He reached across the carpet to take the qalam from Firdaus, and deposited into her hand the folded secret. Color rushed to her cheeks, and quickly, she balled the note within her palm and placed it at the bottom of her pen case. A secret to be devoured only later. Firdaus gave a light nod to say shukriya, and then tried to return to her work. But every now and then, her eyes darted toward the pen case.

‧⸝‧

Over the next seven years, Samir Vij would write Firdaus Khan three hundred and eighty-eight letters, one for every week, whether they saw each other or not. On some days, these letters would be about love and separation, longing and intimacy, and on others, they'd simply run through the most mundane topics—the color of the sky and earth, the smell of flowers, the rustle of trees, the movement of clouds, the sound of his mother's voice, the sadness of his grandfather's stories, the spiciness of chili pickles, the city as he rode through it on his bicycle, the daily slow-moving life. They'd run from pages long to sentences short. These letters would become Firdaus's most prized possessions, and eventually be elevated to the status of heirlooms for all the years to come, when neither she nor Samir remained.

‧⸝‧

Later that night in Vij Bhawan, Vivek, Mohan, and Savitri met in the ground-floor courtyard, after Som Nath and Samir had both fallen asleep. As they huddled around the tulsi plant, the brothers narrated their conversation with the calligrapher, who had assured them that nothing would happen to the Vij family. Whatever this separate state was, whenever it would come about, the city of Lahore would always remain, Altaf had assured them, just as it was now—syncretic, secular, and secure.

# PART TWO

15

---

# Inquilab Zindabad

Sighing loudly, Altaf folded the *Daily Milap* and placed it on the counter of the ittar shop. "So many of our men are fighting in this war. The world must end Hitler's oppression, yes, but how can one expect the soldiers of Hindustan to die for the freedom of Bartania, when it denies us the very same right?"

By the spring of 1941, news of German and Italian occupations continued to hum through the radio frequencies, intermittently broken by song. But just weeks ago, victory of the Indian troops in North Africa had been publicly celebrated with schools and colleges closing, and marching bands parading down the streets of Lahore, cheered on by crowds.

Altaf's fingers smoothened down his short beard. "I wonder what the future will hold for them, for us, for Hindustan."

Vivek scoffed. "Rather than joining efforts against the British, we seem to be at war with one another, just as the British want. They will use this conflict to their advantage, to tear the land apart. Congress is on one side, Muslim League on the other, there is also the Hindu Mahasabha, Akali Dal, Unionist, Communist. Everyone is against each other, and it is all foolishness, all bakwas. We are people of one soil and should be fighting to regain that soil."

"But the rupture between people is beginning to surface, Veer ji," Mohan replied. "Just yesterday the Muslim fruit-wallah by Circular Road refused to sell fruit to the priest of the Hindu temple. To a priest! I could hardly believe it." He now turned to Altaf. "What is the news from Delhi Gate, ustad sahib? What is everyone saying?"

"Well, you are right, Jinnah sahib's call for a separate state is gaining momentum," Altaf admitted. "But like you, I, too, believe that our fight should be against the angrez Raj." The calligrapher's voice took on a faraway tone. "My great-grandfather was a khattat when the first war of independence broke in 1857. He would tell us how the walls of Lahore were razed and freedom fighters shot dead with cannons right here in Anarkali. But till the day he died, he believed that we would, one day, be the masters of our own land."

More quietly, he continued, "My cousin enlisted in the First War, and no one understood why, least of all my great-grandfather. He called it another kind of slavery. I was only eleven, and always thought I'd ask him once he returned, but he never did." He now turned to Vivek. "You, too, fought in the war, Vij sahib. Perhaps you would have known him . . . Iqbal, his name was Iqbal Khan. He was part of the Frontier Force sent to vilayat."

"Iqbal Khan." Vivek's lips released the name into the sweetly perfumed air, and it was returned to him, sharp and bitter. From the first moment the calligrapher had stepped into the shop, Vivek had known that he already knew him. *Those pistachio eyes.*

A scene from spring played out like autumn—khizān, they called it at home, when all the dry leaves fell in shriveled heaps to the ground. But in Vivek's memory, these were not leaves, but limbs. Men writhing in pain, their eyes swollen, their mouths frothing.

*Check all the men to see if any are still alive,* orders came from janral sahib. *Check the Jarmans, too. Do not remove the cloth from over your mouth. Do not breathe the air!*

Vivek had jumped over the parapet of the trench into the now-silent no-man's-land. He approached the bodies, but the field was so peppered with khaki and red that for a moment, he forgot what the actual color of the land was underneath. *How much blood does each body contain?* he thought to himself as he moved from corpse to corpse. *How can the whole ground be covered in blood?* In the darkness, he tried to recognize the faces. Musalmaan, Hindu, Sikh, Gurkha, Punjabi, Pathan, Kashmiri, Dogra, Rajput, nothing mattered in death. Everyone was reduced to a pile of organs.

The stench was unbearable, and Vivek tightened his turban cloth across his mouth and held his breath, trying not to vomit. Many hours had passed since the attack, night had fallen, and yet the strangely poisonous smell of pineapple and pepper still lingered in the air. *Amar Singh, Daya Deen, Majid Khan,* he whispered the names that he had come to learn, *dead, dead, dead,* smelling like remnants of food and tobacco, smoke and blood, excrement and mud. And at the very end of the marshy field was the young Pathan from the Frontier he had met just two weeks ago. The pistachio-eyed man with beautiful penmanship, the calligraphic family in Wazir Khan mosque, and three bullets to his chest, *Iqbal Khan.*

"Vij sahib?" Altaf's voice brought him back to the present, drowning out the battlefield. Met with silence, he asked again, "Iqbal Khan, my uncle's son . . . did you know him?"

Vivek's gaze remained vacant and fixed on the radio in the back of the shop, as it whirred out history through its fuzzy frequencies. He said nothing, but shook his head very slowly from side to side.

&#x2E;

In February 1942, as the commander in chief of British forces in Singapore surrendered to the Japanese, Burma lay vulnerable to invasion, leading the war to India's eastern doorstep. Keen to secure India's cooperation in an effort against the Japanese, the British government sent Sir Stafford

Cripps, a member of the War Cabinet, to discuss its participation during the war and offer dominion status thereafter. But this proposal was swiftly rejected by nationalist leaders of all religions and parties.

On August 8, Mohandas Karamchand Gandhi launched the Quit India Movement at the Bombay session of the All India Congress Committee, demanding immediate independence from British rule. Two days later, the main headline of the *Indian Express* newspaper bellowed, MAHATMA GANDHI, MAULANA AZAD AND NEHRU ARRESTED. And as the entire Congress leadership remained imprisoned, civil disobedience broke out across the country—railway stations and empty trains were burned, post offices looted, and telegraph wires suspended and cut.

Som Nath had sat in the aangan all morning, reading every Urdu and Punjabi newspaper Mohan could get his hands on, and the radio played throughout the day. Fifteen-year-old Samir, who had just passed his matriculation exams, met his friends that evening, and inevitably, the conversation veered toward political events. Schools and colleges were closed, but news spread about the youth of Garhi Shahu parading in the streets and chanting nationalistic slogans. Some of his classmates even had siblings in colleges across the country who had answered Gandhi's clarion call for the British to "Quit India."

"My cousin tells me that a group of students in Allahabad have been shot at by the police for yelling slogans of *Inquilab zindabad, British Raj murdabad!*" Zahir told the group.

"Well, Sunder's brother, who participated in the movement in Benares, has been thrown into the Mirzapur jail and fined a sum of 250 rupees," Prithvi added. Sunder's family were staunch supporters of the Congress Party, and that evening, he was attending a meeting organized by local leadership.

The Quit India Movement was repressed harshly by the government. The leaders of the Muslim League refused to join their Congress counterparts against the British, and in this way remained out of jail, growing in strength. In Delhi Gate, Altaf overheard impassioned conversations about the need for Pakistan. In Anarkali, Vivek and Mohan watched the rift between Hindu, Sikh, and Muslim shopkeepers grow wider and wider. One night after dinner, Savitri narrated how she had passed two young boys in the neighborhood wheeling around a trolley and crying out *Hindu paani, Hindu water.* The fight for freedom was dividing not just land and people, but also the indivisible elements—the air and the water.

Upon hearing this, Som Nath recalled the kites and his old friend Basheer.

Samir's thoughts were of Firdaus.

⚘

A few days later, he was sitting across from her at the calligraphy studio. Maghrib was approaching, and he watched as Firdaus rendered a verse onto a beige sheet of handmade paper. Her wrist flattened the deckled edges of the page, and as she transformed lifeless alphabets into living, breathing beings—the beak of the pot-bellied *jim* sprouted into a swan's face, the length of the *be* resembled the husk of the boats fishermen took out onto the Ravi each morning, a cotton flower grew out of the rounded head of the *mim*—Samir wondered why he had never considered the limber, acrobatic nature of language before.

Watching her work was hypnotic, and he found himself worrying less and less about the politics that strove to bisect their world. But his daydream was soon broken by the ustad's voice. "Samir, *angrezi padh sakte ho,* can you read English?"

When he nodded, Altaf handed him the manuscript of an unusual lughat. It was a *Dictionary of Poetic Urdu Words* he had been commissioned to compile for an English scholar learning Urdu poetry. Altaf had been hesitant to take on the commission from an angrez, but since he did not endorse the division of Hindustan, unlike the rest of the calligraphers in the bazaar, less and less work had been coming his way. The scholar, employed by the Mayo School of Art, had engaged him to make three copies of the lughat, which would then be sent for leather binding. He had already rendered two, but since it was to be written in the basic nastaliq style, he saw no reason why Samir could not produce the third, making use of the skills he'd learned over the years. Altaf instructed the teenager to go through the manuscript while he offered the maghrib prayer.

With his departure, the young perfumer and illuminator sat across from one another, as the old calligrapher watched over them mid-prayer. Samir folded a small piece of paper into a boat and slid it across to Firdaus, who clicked her tongue, pretending to work. But Samir continued to gaze at her, a smile across his face, until she could no longer ignore him. Fixing her dupatta and tucking it behind her ears, she whispered for him to stop, but couldn't help the identical smile that had appeared on her face.

Coolly, Samir withdrew and picked up the lughat. He was only going to pretend to read it, but, flipping through the pages, found himself drawn in. *A, B, C, D, E, F,* the English alphabet was quite different from the Urdu *alif, be, pe, te, se* he had memorized since childhood. Words were written in Urdu and transliterated in English, along with their meanings. *Ada,* elegance. *Be-sabr,* devoid of patience. *Chupke-chupke,* stealthily. *Dil-e-nadan,* innocent heart. *Ehsas,* feeling. This dictionary was written almost entirely in the language of longing and desire. Glancing over at Firdaus, he found her to be consumed in work again. Her bamboo reed made a tense sound as she pressed it down purposefully. Upon completing each verse, she gently blew on the page so the ink dried faster, and then observed it from a distance. Meanwhile, Samir approached the letter *F* and scanned the list of words.

"*Farhat,*" he whispered. Delight.

"*Fida,*" Samir continued down the list, reading out into the room. Awestruck.

Across the room, Firdaus's focus remained uninterrupted.

"*Firaq,*" he read aloud. Separation.

Now the qalam stopped moving.

Samir took a deep breath before the next word.

"*Firdaus,*" he declared, paradise, and looked over at its namesake.

Finally, her pistachio-green eyes focused on him, trying to conceal their pleasure.

"*Ghazal*"—an ode. He recalled his grandfather's humming as he completed the lyrical word.

"*Gulab*"—a rose. The atmosphere of the distillery permeated his nose.

"*Hareer*"—silk. The family's long-forgotten familial trade.

"*Harf*"—a letter of the alphabet. A quick and sharp word.

"*Ilm*"—knowledge. A daily undertaking for the young perfumer.

"*Inkar*"—denial, refusal. A heartbreaking word.

"*Ijazat*"—permission. To cross the invisible frontier drawn through the room.

"*Irada*"—intention. Had this list of words been extracted from his heart?

Just then, much to Samir's surprise, Firdaus put down her atlik and qalam, slowly reached over to her father's things, and picked up the second copy of the lughāt.

"*Ishrat,*" she whispered. Happiness. A nine-year-old girl and a ten-year-old boy in a perfume shop.

Barely able to believe his ears, he stared at her in wonder across the carpeted alcove.

"*Jan,*" she continued down the alphabet to *J*, unusually bold. Life. When Samir still said nothing, Firdaus prompted him yet. "*Jan?*"

Running his fingers through his neatly combed hair, he smiled shyly.

"*Jan-pehchān?*" he asked. Acquaintance.

"*Jasusi?*" came a playful response. Spying.

He laughed and shook his head. How the evening had transformed.

"*Jannat,*" Samir read out the synonym to her name. Heaven.

"*Jhalak,*" she teased. A glimpse.

"*Jurm?*" he inquired. A crime.

"*Junoon*," she completed the *J*'s. Madness, frenzy.

"*Khwaish*," he admitted. A wish.

"*Khamoshi*," she replied softly. Silence.

All too quickly the innocent game had metamorphosed into a conversation of the heart.

"*Khazin*." From the list of *K*'s, Samir had found the word that Ousmann had once proudly bequeathed to him at the distillery. Treasurer, keeper.

For a moment, Firdaus was quiet, as if thinking. She bit her lower lip and then covered almost her entire face with her dupatta, only a single impassioned pistachio-green pupil peeking out.

"*Khazin*," she repeated. "*Khazin-e-firdaus*."

The keeper of paradise.

# 16

# A Hindustan for All Hindustanis

After six years of apprenticeship, in the autumn of 1943, Vivek offered sixteen-year-old Samir a workspace in the atelier. A small tabletop and a drawer with a lock. They would share the organ until Samir created his own atlas of smells. For many months, the pair had been employing their noses to create unfamiliar accords with familiar ingredients. They had smelled musks that reminded them of babies' skin, animals, pears, and beetroot; floral blossoms reminiscent of the ocean; cedarwood betraying traces of pencil shavings and leather; labdanum that evoked the unusual suggestion of waxed wood. They smelled and smelled, their noses hungry, their appetites vast. And while Vivek built many worlds, Samir devoted himself to the creation of a single perfume for his beloved, using his treasured tuberose as the heart note.

Around the same time, the young perfumer escorted his grandfather to Anarkali Bazaar for a special occasion. The owner of Bhalla Shoe Co., Dhani Ram Bhalla, had turned seventy-five and invited his oldest friends for a birthday party. The pair arrived at the shoe store and were greeted by the comically large Peshwari chappal hanging from the front facade. All afternoon, the shop was to be closed so that Bhalla sahib and his guests could celebrate without interruption.

Invited along with his grandfather were the halwais Kundan Lal and Bhagwan Das; Sheikh Inayantullah, who ran a textile store; Narendar Singh, editor of a small Punjabi newspaper; Chunni Ram, the hardware store owner; Dhuni Chand, the cloth merchant; and Mushtaq Alam, who was heir to the most reputed tannery and leather shop of the bazaar. Most men were in their sixties or seventies, and some, like Som Nath, had brought chaperones. Of everyone in the group, the Vijs were closest to Mushtaq Alam and affectionately called him chacha, for Som Nath's father had been instrumental in helping them set up shop in the once predominantly Hindu and Sikh bazaar.

The morning passed in the same way that water glides through old courses. From stories of Prince Salim and his beloved Anarkali, to the leaflets of qissas and poems sold for two pice, to the tales of sahibs and mems trotting around with their bearers holding their bags and opening their doors.

Inayatullah sahib, perhaps the oldest in the group, with his large turban amd long, wiry beard, raised his frail arms in the air to quiet the crowd. His paper-thin voice floated out like a whisper, "*Yaad hai, yaara,* do you remember the days when not a single car could be seen along the lanes of Anarkali? Why, I never thought I'd see a motorcar in my life and now they are everywhere!" He laughed and directed his attention toward Samir. "There were tangas, ekkas, tum-tums, fittans, and even palanquins! If only you could see how magical it used to be. A world of magnificence and gentility, where customers strolled down the road in finery."

Dhuni Chand added, "In those days, we used to live in the Musalmaan mohalla of Bhati Gate, where most women observed purdah. On my way to or from the shop, I remember attaching my bicycle to the back of the tangas that passed me by. If by chance there was a girl sitting on the back seat, and if I caught even a glimpse of her ankle as she climbed aboard, oho, what a great day that would be! You know, puttar, my wife was on one of these tangas, which is how we first saw each other." He chuckled.

"So much has changed," Chunni Ram agreed. "There is progress. Girls are attending college, finding jobs. Why, just the other day, I saw a lady riding a bicycle!" He looked around the group with wide eyes. "But whatever you say, some things will always remain the same . . . like Bhagwan Das's lassi! Oho, sardar ji, that whole peda you blend into the lassi until it's frothy and thick, that is unchanged!"

Everyone burst into laughter.

Catching his breath, Som Nath placed his hand over Samir's arm and said, "Puttar, Anarkali Bazaar has always been the epicenter of culture, society, and politics. Do you know, in 1929, when you were only two years old, Pandit Nehru rode through the streets of this very bazaar on a white horse. We watched him as he crossed in front of our shop, newly elected president of the Congress Party, and was showered with flower petals as he made his way through. Oh, the whole market smelled divine, your father and uncle talked about it for days. But Pandit Nehru got off the horse and came right here, right here into this very store, where Bhalla sahib felicitated him with a garland of currency notes! What a grand sight it was, a day to remember." He looked into the distance, nostalgic.

"But, Dadu, why was Pandit Nehru here in Lahore?"

"To declare our demand for independence, puttar," Narendar Singh spoke with fervor. "Standing on the banks of the river Ravi, he unfurled the flag and addressed the gathering with a plea for complete independence, purna swaraj. Not the independence of Hindus or Sikhs or Muslims or Christians, but for *all* Indians, all of us." He gestured around the room.

"*Lekin oh z'manah hi alag si,*" Mushtaq Alam replied in Punjabi, "that was a different world than the one we live in today. Read the papers, Singh sahib, you print the news yourself. *Khabraan padh ke te mein heraan aan.* I am shocked when I read the paper each day. Look at what is happening around the country. An old friend is in jail in Rawalpindi for anti-British activity, my grandson is joining the youth division of the Muslim League, there are shop owners in this very bazaar who refuse to entertain religions other than their own. This is not *my* Hindustan, the one I was raised in. But is there a possibility of a Hindustan for all Hindustanis anymore? I went to listen to Jinnah sahib speak in Minto Park in 1940, I heard his demands for Pakistan, and I also saw the madness in people's eyes."

Taking off his spectacles, he massaged his eyes. Som Nath placed a hand on his shoulder. The words Mushtaq Alam uttered next would be, perhaps, the most accurate prophecy of the future that Samir would ever hear.

"This war we have embarked on against one another is most dangerous, for it is a war against our own. Neighbor against neighbor, colleague against colleague, brother against brother, Congress Party against Muslim League. I fear the consequences will obliterate *this*." He gestured around the room at his old friends. "If this war continues, then I see no future where each one of us is not the bearer of a deep and irrevocable loss."

After the birthday party, Samir had helped his grandfather board a tanga and, to distract himself, spent the afternoon amidst perfume. But rather than going into the shop, he headed up to the distillery, where Ousmann and the others were distilling the autumn rose. Aarif, sitting on his haunches, cooling the bhapka with a wet cloth, motioned for Samir to come help him. Changing out of his neatly pressed outfit into a pajama and cotton vest like the others, Samir let his mind and body succumb to the mechanical movements. The burning of wood, the heating of deghs, the cooling of bhapka receivers, the uncoiling of snake-like clay, the air, the fire, the petals, the manure, the sweat, the salt, the mud, the earth, the smoke, the sky, the monotonous calm.

Five hours later, as the sun was setting, Samir looked up into the ether, where the gray smoke married the blue-orange yonder, and felt warm tears sting his eyes. He wished that these were smoke tears, just like the first time he'd worked in the distillery, but these were different. These were tears of uncertainty, of fear.

Mushtaq chacha's voice echoed in his ears. *Is there a possibility of a Hindustan for all Hindustanis anymore?* Then perhaps there was also some truth in Basheer mian's warning. But his family had rejected the thought of separate states, as had ustad sahib. Conflicted, the young perfumer looked around the distillery as he breathed in his own heavy, fragrant sweat. Their Lahore, this perfumery, the haveli, his Firdaus. There was so much to lose. *There was so much to lose.*

When he returned home that night, the afternoon's conversation still saturated his mind. The hour was late, the men had already eaten dinner, but Savitri had waited for her son. Sitting in the open courtyard, the pair ate dal and roti with fresh mango achaar and onions.

Doling out a second helping of dal to Samir, Savitri whispered, "Baba mentioned the incident from this afternoon. Your father and taya ji don't agree with Mushtaq chacha."

"Hmm," he replied, biting into a piece of onion.

"Don't worry, puttar, everything will be all right." She tried to console him, but even to her, the attempt seemed futile. They continued to eat in silence. A stray voice called out in the neighborhood. A dog howled in response.

"Ma, I want to tell you something." Samir's heart thumped faster. He looked around the courtyard to make sure no one else was around. Savitri's fingers were sticky with lentils, a piece of coriander stuck to her thumb, but she squeezed her son's hand in encouragement.

That night would be the very first time he would utter the name of his beloved to anyone in his family. From here on, it would be mentioned in Vij Bhawan time and time again until time itself stood still for the old haveli.

# 17

# Yours, Samir

On the tenth day of the year 1944, Firdaus turned fifteen years old, and she spent it at the studio, as she normally would. In the evening, Samir came to Wazir Khan for what would be his last calligraphy lesson, since he would soon be graduating and working at the ittar shop full-time. As soon as they were alone, the perfumer presented to her a birthday note and garland of fresh jasmine flowers. Firdaus spread her dupatta promptly and discreetly over them and tied both into the ends of the scarf.

Upon reaching home, her trembling fingers untied the knot, and the flowers cascaded onto her bed. In full bloom, the jasmine remained white, crisp, and unwilted, despite the day's end. The room was bathed in yellow from the oil lamp, and with an enormous smile on her face, Firdaus pushed aside the flowers and unfolded the note. Lying on her stomach, she read it out.

January 10, 1944

Firdaus, have you ever seen the changing colors of a jasmine flower? When strung into garlands each morning, they are tight buds, bright white and green. Their smell is crisp and floral and green. But as they bloom, their petals become white and pink, softer, open to the world. Their smell is now intoxicatingly sweet and powerful. But with time, a purple color bleeds into the white of each bud, and the green sepals turn dark like the color of jamun fruit. Eventually, if left to the mercy of the environment, the twinkling jasmine turns brown and begins to resemble a paper flower, its crisp sepia petals emitting no smell at all. Some might think that this is the death of the flower, but in fact, it is the state at which the flower lives on for eternity, enduring and unchanging. This is constant. What I give you on your birthday may only be a garland of jasmine, but like it, my affection also shall endure and remain unchanged.

Samir might not have been a poet, but he was certainly well versed in the poetry of the natural world, Firdaus thought as she glanced at the abandoned flowers and continued to read.

Last night, I looked up at the moon and wondered whether you were looking at it too. At a time when Lahoris are being divided to this side or that, I drew comfort from the fact that the same moon illuminated both our nights. That it did not care for Delhi Gate or Shahalmi, a mosque or a temple, it did not read the Quran or the Gita. Surely there will be days of joy beyond these days of division, where there will be a place for us. A place where the jasmine endures. A sky beyond this sky, where the winds, samir, reach up to touch the heavens, firdaus. A place where we converge.

"Tumhara, Samir," it stated. "Yours," the signature read, different from all the others before. She held the letter against her heart and looked out at the sliver of moon in the darkening sky. "There is a world beyond this world, a sky beyond this sky." She then drew her attention back to what had likely been, in Samir's mind, the more important part of this birthday gift. Picking up the jasmine garland, she gingerly brought it to her nose and inhaled every part of the flower. Once, then again, and then a third time. Exasperated, she pushed the garland aside again, and chose to focus on his words that had settled into her heart in a way that no fragrance ever would. Smiling, she folded the note into the palm of her hand.

A knock.

"Firdaus," Altaf called from the other side of the door.

"Uh . . . j-ji, Abba jaan?" She scrambled up and sat cross-legged on the bed, fixing her dupatta over her head, note still in her hand. The jasmine, forgotten, remained where it was.

The door gently opened and in walked the calligrapher, looking for a book that sat on Firdaus's worktable. He picked it up and almost turned to leave, but then sat down next to her. Folding his hands across his chest, he watched his daughter attempt, rather unsuccessfully, to suppress the joy on her face. Bemused, his gaze fell on the jasmine. He was surprised, for Firdaus never would have bought flowers for herself. With his slim fingers, he scooped up the garland and inhaled its sweet smell. Firdaus gasped softly, but watched her father's nose entrap every last trace of scent from the jasmine, as Samir so often did with handmade papers or the ink at the studio. Altaf placed it back on the bed and looked at his precious child.

Unable to help herself, she smiled yet again and, for the first time, felt an affinity with her father that had little to do with the realm of script or prose. The boy in the ittar shop had set her wintery paper heart ablaze.

"*Yeh phool?*"

"They were a birthday present, Abbu," a quiet voice responded.

"And who has given such a present to our daughter?"

Firdaus cleared her throat and weighed her options. For as long as she could remember, her father had fought for her to be raised no differently from how he would have raised a son. Rather than tending to the house, she had been given responsibilities at the hujra; rather than acquainting

herself with salt and spices, she had entered the world of bamboo reeds
and ink. She was the sole heir to everything and, hence, was groomed no
differently.

So easy it would be to get her married off, for she was now older than
her aunt, Nasreen, had been at her wedding. Nasreen, whose name meant
wild rose, had been anything but free and wild. Firdaus knew how differently her father had wished her life to develop, but it was difficult to
disregard how many girls her age had already been wed, mostly to men
considerably older than their brides. Men with the promise of wealth and
fortune, men with the assurance of land and title. But love, the kind that
her parents had, the kind she could imagine sharing with Samir, that love
seemed absent in all these alliances.

In that moment, Firdaus was endlessly grateful to have been raised
as neither submissive nor dependent. It was true that she embodied her
father's calmness and unnatural quiet, but she was also part owner of her
mother's tenacious demeanor, her desires and determination. The zeal
in Zainab flickered in her daughter too, if only rarely. And it was now,
in what would prove to be the most important, intimate interaction she
would ever have with her father, that Firdaus Khan chose to be her mother's
daughter.

"Samir gave them to me," she said finally.

"Samir?"

Firdaus nodded and sat up straighter, and Altaf couldn't help but notice the change in her demeanor. For the very first time, his daughter
reminded him less of the brittle surface of paper and more of the soft
opulence of flowers. Was Samir responsible for this metamorphosis? The
gangly perfumer, the determined calligraphy student, the keeper of scents
and senses, and now, it seemed, the owner of his daughter's affection?
Some things, like matters of the heart, were beyond reason or rationale.

He stood up and leaned against the window frame. The world was
changing, Hindustan was fighting for her freedom, and his daughter de-
served the chance to write her own future. Altaf might have not quite

understood *what* he was acceding to that evening, but he looked over at Firdaus and met her anxious gaze.

"Samir," he concurred with a nod.

At twilight, Altaf walked across the street to the Sunehri Masjid, while Zainab and Firdaus performed the isha namaz at home. The filigree shadows from the windows fell on their faces as the sun set. After, Zainab returned to the kitchen to prepare dinner and was surprised to see Firdaus follow her in. The unmistakable joy on her daughter's face was not lost on her, but she simply attributed it to her birthday. Together they removed the coil of dough and mud that sealed the large biryani degh shut, and laid the dastarkhwan on the ground. When Altaf returned, they sat down to eat. It was three of them—always just the three of them—but the meal of biryani, kebabs, raita, khamiri roti, and zaffran kheer felt as lavish and decadent as a feast at Eid.

Later on, as Altaf was reading a book, Zainab sat at her dressing table. She combed her hair, gathered it to one side, and then began massaging her face and neck with a concoction of rose and sandalwood oil. Turning to her husband, she remarked on how different Firdaus had seemed that evening, noticeably warm and forthcoming, causing Altaf to relay their conversation from earlier on.

"Samir." She said his name slowly and pensively.

Over the years, Zainab had surrendered to the fact that she might never have as much in common with her daughter as her husband did. And though his progressive parenting might have been frowned upon by many, Firdaus had grown into an obedient and respectful, albeit reserved, young woman. But this piece of news was both unexpected and disconcerting.

"Samir is a good boy," she finally managed to say, "and from a good family, but . . ." Her voice trailed into a *tch*.

"But what?" Altaf put down the book he was reading.

Zainab's tone dropped to a whisper. "Khan sahib, they are Hindu. *Please* tell me the thought has crossed your mind. There has never been such an alliance in any of our families, extended relations, or acquaintances."

"So what, my love, they will be the first. It may be unprecedented in our family, but it is not unheard of," Altaf replied. "Tell me, does it matter what religion he is from, or does it matter how happy he makes our daughter?"

Zainab almost could not believe her husband's naïveté. "Samir's religion may not have mattered before, but it does now. Surely you aren't blind to what is happening around us. The city is rife with rumor. This . . ." She inhaled sharply before continuing. "This friendship will only provoke it further. What will everyone in the mohalla or in Wazir Khan say, and what will I tell my brother in Delhi? Khan sahib, just because you are virtuous does not mean you are exempt from the decrees of society."

"Of course, the thought has crossed my mind," Altaf admitted. "But even *if* Jinnah sahib's Pakistan is created, he has said nothing about not allowing people of all faiths to worship as per their traditions. And no one knows yet where this Pakistan will start and begin, or if Lahore will even be a part of it."

Zainab brought her palms up to her cheeks, and her eyes filled with tears.

Altaf walked over to the dressing table and got down on his knees. Cupping both of his wife's hands within his own, he kissed them and looked up at her. "Neither you nor I have ever seen Firdaus as radiant as she was this evening, and it is all because of Samir. Forget for a moment that he is Hindu—"

"I cannot and neither should you," she cut him off. "You should be fighting to achieve Jinnah sahib's Pakistan. Not encouraging our daughter to marry a Hindu boy."

Altaf sighed. One of the things he loved most about his begum was how fearlessly she spoke her mind, unafraid even to disagree with him. But this idea of hacking a land into pieces—a piece for Muslims, and another for Hindus and Sikhs—was inconceivable. "Zainab, *no one* is getting married right now. Firdaus still needs to finish her education, which will take years, and by then, all this madness, all these rumors, will have passed. Mark my words. In the meantime, there is no harm in letting this be as it is."

Removing his hand from her cheek, Zainab wiped her eyes and studied their reflection in the mirror. It was of a couple who lived in two very different realities.

"Ustad sahib," she now addressed him with formality, "I will do as you propose, but I hope you are not promising your daughter something that life will make impossible."

# 18

# Tulsi

Mohan and Samir fitted large glass decanters of sandalwood, henna, jasmine, and frangipani ittar into three wooden crates and tied them together with rope to the back of a bicycle, securing the cargo tightly. Vivek had been in Hyderabad for nearly two weeks now, and in his absence, Samir was taking the monthly delivery to the Koh-i-noor shop in Shahdara that had been selling the ittars distilled by Samir's family for years. When he was younger, Vivek would take him on all his fragrant travels—seeking oudh in Assam, kewra from Orrisa, mitti from Kannauj—but now Samir worked full-time in the shop.

Walking out into the bazaar, he felt the summer heat strike him. His father handed him a vial of vetiver and, pouring out a few drops on his palms, Samir applied the green liquid to his temples, collarbone, the backs of his ears, and the moist nape of his neck. *Nothing like vetiver to cool the body from the oppressive Lahori heat,* Savitri always said.

"Finally, some respite," he said, handing the vial back to Mohan.

"Try to come back as soon as you can, puttar. Your mother is at home today, so it's just you and me at the shop."

"Ji, Baba." Samir promised to be back by lunchtime. He wiggled the bicycle to make sure nothing would fall as he rode through the city, and then, satisfied, climbed on. Through the clamor and chaos of the Walled City he rode, finally emerging at the northern bank of the Ravi nearly forty minutes later. Following the directions his father had given him, Samir passed flower fields, wheat fields, and stretches of green vegetation until he reached the Koh-i-noor ittar shop.

"Namaste, Pran sahib." Samir parked his bicycle and greeted the elderly gentleman who sat at the front, newspaper in his hands, the tail of his turban falling over his shoulders.

"Aha, namaste, Samir beta, where is your uncle today?" The old man smiled a toothless smile.

"Taya ji has traveled to Hyderabad to bring back a shipment of safa marwa and kashish. Perhaps you might place an order for them next time, lovely summer ittars," Samir offered.

"Why not," the old shopkeeper replied. "Many years ago, a perfumer from the nizam's court in Hyderabad came to us with vials of the most heavenly kashish, the composition of which had been in his family shop at Charminar since the late 1800s. The business had survived even the great Musi floods of the city. He told us that during the month of Ramzan, the entire old city is doused in the smell of kashish, overpoweringly floral and mystical." Pran sahib's voice took on the same shade of nostalgia Samir had heard many times from his own grandfather. He began unloading the crates from the bicycle, careful to not break any bottles.

Using the ends of his turban cloth to wipe his face, the old man called out to a teenage boy who helped out at the shop, "Oye, Karanbir, get some sherbet or rosewater for this young man . . . rode on his bicycle all the way from Lahore in this heat, *uff*." He fanned himself with the newspaper.

Fifteen minutes later, refreshed and hydrated, bicycle lighter without its cargo, Samir began his journey back, but stopped to take in the fragrant fields. Shahdara, like Pattoki, was known for its rose crop, and though the variety was not quite as spectacular as the damas gulab, the resulting ittar was fairly pleasing. The next harvest wouldn't be until the autumn, so Samir walked through shrubs intermittently sprouting baby pink buds. At the fringes of the fields were planted small herb gardens, and as he walked by, bicycle in tow, Samir recognized the wild bushes of holy basil. Tall, long-bladed, with hairy stems and dark purplish flowers, it was easily recognizable as tulsi. Since before his birth, it had grown in the courtyard of Vij Bhawan, and day after day, he'd walked by the seemingly ordinary plant. But today, for the first time, removed from the familiar setting of the haveli, weaving its aroma through the nascent roses, it caught his attention. Wild and spicy, warm and wistful, evocative of ritual and tradition. He crushed the leaves between his fingers and chewed them, finding the taste pungent and clove-like, bitter and herbaceous. Smiling to himself, he plucked a few stems, slipped them into his pocket, and within the hour was back in Anarkali.

At the shop, he found Mohan pouring out a long vial of rosewater for the moulvi of the local mosque in Anarkali, a weekly exercise. Samir greeted him and then sat down at the back. From his pocket, he took out the leafy tulsi stems and placed them on the counter. Meanwhile, Mohan rolled down the blinds, closing the shop for lunch, and walked toward his son, steel tiffin box in hand. Vivek's radio played in the back, now more out of habit than anything else.

"Oh! Tulsi." Mohan smiled, holding up a stem. Bringing it to his nose, he inhaled its earthiness with the same delight as his son had. "Did you know that your grandmother used to love this herb? She planted the tulsi that still grows in our courtyard."

Samir watched as he proceeded to open the steel tiffin and lay out bowls of spiced kadi, rice, roti, and onions. Despite being father and son, they rarely did anything just the two of them. So often they were a trio— Vivek, Mohan, and Samir—that in the absence of his uncle, the young perfumer felt a peculiar sense of awkwardness. But if Mohan had felt any, he was better at concealing it, for he continued on passionately about the holy herb.

"It blends well with sandalwood, that's what Ma used to do. Make a fresh paste of sandalwood, crush the tulsi leaves into it, and apply it on her face and arms. Perhaps even add some neem and other grasses."

"Was she a perfumer, too?" Samir asked, suddenly wondering if she was the original bearer of the nose he had inherited from his uncle.

"She was magnificent, puttar. But as far as I know, she didn't have much skill in perfumery per se. She died young of a sudden illness. But when she was alive, she worked alongside your grandfather at a time when women were barely allowed to leave the house. She was educated and fierce and beautiful. Leelawati, that was her name." He paused, a sad smile spread across his face, and then continued, "Each time I smell either sandalwood or tulsi, I am reminded of her."

Never had Samir seen Mohan this nostalgic; he was always so practical and pragmatic. It was strange to learn that even his father had an intimate understanding of smell, something he attributed solely to his uncle. The fact that his father also relied on smell memory was not only confusing, but also made Samir look at Mohan in a completely new light. He pursed his lips together, not quite knowing how to navigate the conversation any further.

"You must . . . miss her," Samir said.

"Yes," Mohan said, "yes, very much."

And then again, there was silence. Neither father nor son spoke, and gradually, sounds from the radio in the background filled the quiet. The news bulletin announced that war had arrived at India's doorstep. The British and Indian soldiers had successfully countered a major attack in Burma by Japan, Britain's enemy in the Far East, but there were reports of the Japanese using all forms of propaganda techniques to lure Indians to their side, of the torture of Sikh soldiers, and of heavy casualties. Mohan was certain it was these many reports of prisoners of war and the details of bloody battlefields that had driven his brother away on this most recent trip to Hyderabad. Annoyed, he reached out to shut the radio, causing his son to turn toward him with purpose.

"Baba, how come you didn't go to war when Taya ji did?"

Mohan raised his eyebrows. Samir had never asked about the war before.

"What I mean is, Baba . . . I know nothing of what happened at the time, and now we find ourselves in another war. When so many of our people are fighting across the world, should we also not be out *there*, rather than in *here*?" The boy gestured to the shop. "What is the point of composing perfumes in the midst of war?"

Calmly, Mohan served out a portion of lunch for each of them, handing a glass of cold water to his son. "Thirty years ago, when your taya ji went to war, he had passion, the very same kind you are voicing now. And though he initially enlisted because he wanted to see the world, he did gradually come to feel that it was his duty to offer himself to the war. Because the world was ablaze, because measuring out lengths of fabric in his father's clothing shop was not quite the same as measuring out lengths of explosives to obliterate the enemy, because what good were silks and satins when there would be no world left to enjoy them in."

Samir nodded vigorously.

"But what you don't know is how that war broke him. What happened to your taya ji in vilayat is something known to him alone. For years, he disappeared, vanished, ceased to exist for us except in memory, to an extent that we were certain he had met his end on the battlefield. Your grandfather wrote letter after letter—about our home, our dwindling business, even about the sudden death of your grandmother—and they all went unanswered . . .

"Finally, when Veer ji returned home, he simply refused to speak. He looked different, he dressed like an angrez, his habits and mannerisms were different. He was afraid of the world around him, cautious of interacting with anyone. The *only* time he reminded me of even a shadow of his former self was, strangely enough, around perfume—an art he had never before shown any interest in."

Mohan walked up to a shelf, picked up a small vial, and placed it between him and his son.

"*Mushk dana, ambrette.* These were the very first words I heard my brother utter after the six long years that be had been away. Puttar, I can't tell you what happened to him in vilayat, I don't know where he learned perfumery, I don't know how and I don't know why. But what I *can* tell you is that perfume was the only thing that made him recognizable to us once he returned to Lahore."

Mohan removed the glass stopper from the bottle and inhaled. The stagnant air around them grew warmer, musky, nutlike.

"Sometimes, when the whole world seems ruined beyond recognition, even the faintest gesture of beauty, like the whiff of a familiar perfume, can bring a sense of solace."

He held out the glass stopper to Samir and watched as his son closed his eyes and inhaled.

"*This* is why what we do is important; rather, it is essential. We have the ability to provide a momentary refuge from the maddening world. Smell is an escape, a shelter, a sanctuary. My son, I am not a perfumer. I am not even a distiller. I don't possess the gift of the nose like my brother or you, to an extent that sometimes I question what value I add to this business. But years of inhabiting this shop have made me realize the potency and persuasiveness of perfume, of its ability to tell stories and evoke emotion."

Placing a loving hand on his son's face, he concluded, "Do not allow the hostile world to erode your gift; do not ever disrespect or belittle the power of your nose. Our sense of smell, regarded by so many as secondary, is one of the most extraordinary ways to preserve intimacy, history, and, of course, memory."

Smiling, he held up the stalks of holy basil as example. "It is this simple. In all the ways I remember my mother, it is her smell that defined my childhood."

Samir, taken aback by the poignancy of his father's words, nodded sincerely.

"Puttar, do you remember that morning at the Ravi, with the vial of tuberose? Do you understand why you cried, why it moved you so?"

The young man shrugged.

"Right from the moment that we are in our mother's womb, our life is defined by smell. The smells that string my life together are evocative of my mother: sandal, tulsi, neem. For Veer ji, it is ambrette. But for you, it could only have been tuberose. Did you never wonder why your uncle presented *that* specific ittar to you?"

Again, Samir looked at his father blankly.

Mohan smiled, almost shyly, his voice now taking on a dreamy quality. "You see, in all the months that your mother was pregnant with you, she tended to the tuberose crop. She worked till the week she was to deliver you, separating flower from stalk, sorting, sifting, even making garlands. In a sea of waxy bright white and crisp green, she sat with a baby in her belly, surrounded always by the heady tuberose flower. It was her companion . . . as it subconsciously became yours."

Goose bumps erupted across Samir's body. In his eyes, tears appeared again, just as they had on the riverbank in 1937. And then, a small smile emerged.

"There is an intimate connection between smell and emotion, for they are processed in the same part of the brain." Mohan placed his palm flat on the top of his head, indicating just where the senses converged. "Veer ji explained that to me, and I understand it, because the sudden presence of a smell is capable of transporting us back to the moment when we first smelled it. Tuberose had *always* been known to you, whether you knew it or not. Always trust your nose, Samir. Allow it to lead you, give you strength and happiness. Wield it to summon everything you love."

The afternoon was no longer painted in any form of awkwardness. In fact, his father's untrained nose appeared to understand the psychological realm of smell far better than Samir's own.

Closing his eyes then, the smile still on his lips, the young perfumer decided to employ his father's advice. He imagined, through the incredible faculty of smell, the place where he found solace. He inhaled deeply, the way lovers did, and, sweeping the warring world away, summoned the smell of his beloved.

# 19

# The Rain Below Our Feet

On Tuesday, May 8, 1945, newspapers across the world reported on the German surrender in Europe, marking the end of the Second World War in the European theater. This meant victory in one theater, as the war was not yet over in the East, where thousands of Allied soldiers, including Indians, continued to fight and thousands more languished as prisoners.

But as Vivek walked to Anarkali that morning, it was with a renewed spring in his step, and for the first time in years, the anxiety that had become his shadow seemed replaced by relief. The front page of the *Times of India* had announced a holiday, with several cities celebrating the victory. Government schools and offices were shut, and on his way, the perfumer passed a group of teenage boys running through the streets with joy.

"*Jeet gaye, hum jeet gaye!*" one screamed while others danced around him. "We won!"

Laughing, Vivek walked closer to them, and asked what they had won. "*Kya jeet gaye, bhai?*"

"*British jung jeet gaye! Hitler haar gaya!*"

Watching the celebration with amusement, a corner shop owner commented, "Oye! They have won the war in vilayat. What are you all dancing here for?"

"Arre, chacha," one of the boys said with a wide grin, "the angrez had promised us. We help win the war, and in return, they will give us freedom. Azaadi!"

Later that day, Vivek and Mohan listened to the news of crowds flocking to the Taj Mahal, and victory parades and marches in New Delhi. At 8:30 p.m., as the brothers were closing the shop, they heard British Prime Minister Winston Churchill's speech relayed through the overseas services of the BBC. His tone was exuberant as he praised the efforts of the Allies, despite the toil and rebuilding that still lay ahead, both at home and abroad. "Advance, Britannia!" he concluded, yet in the same breath, added, "Long live the cause of freedom!"

Mohan scoffed. "Not *our* freedom."

Whether the end of the war meant the beginning of freedom for Hindustan was yet unknown, but the words of the teenage boy from that morning resounded in Vivek's mind.

꒰꩜꒱

It was against this backdrop in June that Vivek suggested a few weeks away from the city. He wished to rid himself of the secondhand burden of war he'd carried around, and sought the one person he knew could rejuvenate him. And so, three months ahead of Samir's eighteenth birthday, Vivek and Mohan, along with the eager teeneager, boarded the morning Frontier Mail. The most luxurious express train, started by the British in 1928, it spanned from Bombay to Peshawar—close to the last frontier of the Raj in India, hence its name—halting in the major cities of Baroda, Delhi, and Lahore. Owning to an old friend of Mohan's in the railways, the trio managed to procure tickets for the intermediate-class compartment.

"Baba, tell me where we are going at least!" Samir piped up halfway through their journey. So far, the brothers had given him barely any information, except that they would be away from home for two weeks. In their absence, Savitri and Som Nath would look after the ittar shop, and Ousmann, the distillation unit.

Mohan laughed, and Vivek leaned over and tapped his nephew's nose. "Puttar, we are going to smell the rain!"

"But it won't rain for weeks, monsoon is still far away," Samir responded.

"Not all rain is found above our heads," Mohan said mysteriously. "There are some kinds that live below our feet, inside the ground. We are going to smell the rain drawn from the earth."

This not only aroused Samir's interest but also excited his nose.

"Samir, always use your nose to smell from the ground up," Vivek added. "Here, we are one with the land, with soil, clay, fields, and even stones. The earth, mitti, dharti, bhoomi, zameen, whatever we may call it, it rouses and inspires us." His words seemed to catch the attention of other travelers in their compartment. The Sikh gentleman across from him nodded his head knowingly, revealing that as a farmer, his allegiance was singularly to his land.

As their train approached Delhi station, Vivek concluded, "Puttar, there may be no escape from this land, no matter how far one travels from it, for your skin is saturated with it."

Samir didn't quite understand, but he was intrigued.

From Delhi, the trio boarded the East Indian Railway, which cut through the United Provinces, allowing them to alight at Lucknow. The day had dimmed to dusk, and under the light of the setting sun, they hired a tanga to drive nearly three hours out to the city of Kannauj, known to be the mecca of perfumery in Hindustan. As they approached the outskirts, Samir's nose rose into the air, sniffing out traces of the mehendi shrubs and jasmine plantations. Vivek was instructing the tanga-wallah with directions to their mysterious location, and Mohan had fallen asleep the moment they'd left Lucknow.

⁓

The next morning, Samir finally met the master he had heard only stories about. Khushboo Lal, whose very name was inspired by his fragrant
profession—*khushboo,* scent—welcomed them at the threshold of his perfumery. Vivek, who had first met him in Anarkali in 1903 when he was
ten years old, and then again in 1920, when he returned from vilayat,
touched the old man's feet with respect and reverence. Decades had passed
since Khushboo Lal left the bustle of Lahore for the genteel Kannauj,
transforming from the robust, adventurous perfumer to a tender perfume
savant. But despite his advancing age, his nose remained employed.

His family had been distilling ittar since before he was born. Beginning
with his grandfather in the mid-1800s, they became the largest and most
important distillers of the woody, smoky, leathery cypriol and velvety sandalwood oils in Hindustan. Now, nearly a century later, Khushboo Lal,
patriarch of the family and business, was assisted by his son and grandson.

"Come, come inside." The old perfumer spoke through his reddened,
paan-filled mouth, hobbling in on his walking stick. "We have just made
some fresh khuss sherbet."

Samir walked into a room smelling of deodar pine and lemongrass.
Samir was led to a low diwan, and Khushboo Lal sat before him, his light
green kurta assuming the shape of his soft, round stomach. The sherbet
was served, and Samir picked up his glass. As Khushboo Lal leaned in to
get a better look at the young man, he continued chewing on the betel leaf
in his mouth, his voice emerging full and muffled.

"You must be Samir. Welcome to our city of perfumes, our *sungandhit
tapobhumi.*"

"*Sugandhit tapobhumi?*"

Khushboo Lal reached for his spittoon and spat out a red squirt of
betel juice. He cleared his throat, prepared to embark on a long-winded
story, and then suddenly chuckled, taking in the young man's western
attire and slicked-back hair, almost a copy of his uncle.

"Do you know, I was seven years old when I accompanied my father to the mountains of Kashmir and smelled the most maddening and intoxicating fragrance of musk, kastur. I knew then that perfume would pave the path of my life. Generations have been able to preserve the craft of traditional ittar here in Kannauj, and no matter how modern you may become, a single whiff is enough to carry you back home. Never forget that. Everything I know, I have learned from my grandfather and father. There is perfume in my blood, just as there is in yours."

He gestured to Vivek, before continuing.

"Sugandh, yes, you understand that word, fragrance. And tapobhumi is a place where one seeks enlightenment and illumination. Kannauj is the land of fragrant enlightenment, drawing in perfumers from the entire world." Khushboo Lal asked Mohan to pass one of the smaller kuppis from the corner, and then, holding it between his hands, he continued, "But *this* is what Kannauj is truly known for today." Uncorking the leather flask, he invited Samir to smell.

"*Agar zameen se koi shayari banti ho, toh wahi mitti ittar ki khushboo hai,* if there were ever a poetic essence to be extracted from the heart of the earth, it would be the smell of mitti ittar."

Khushboo Lal, remarkably active for all his eighty-five years, led them through the lanes of his ancient city out to a taalaab, an old water pit. As they walked through the winding alleys, he told them that though only a few hundred families now continued the laborious work of distillation and extraction, everyone in Kannauj was connected to perfumery in some form or another. Following his nose, Samir noticed how the drains of the city were filled with residue from the many distilleries, causing even the water in them to become fragrant.

When they reached the water pit, they found it dry and excavated. The clay from this pit had once been used to make earthenware cups that would become infused with the rich, mineral taste of the soil. Used and discarded, the piles of these cups would emit such a powerful fragrance that it sent even the animals of the town into frenzy. In the pre-monsoon season, when the aroma of earth was strongest, perfumers employed artisans to make hordes of earthenware cups from the clay from such pits, and these became the source of mitti ittar, the earth's most primitive perfume.

Walking into the distillery unit, Samir felt transported back in time, for Khushboo Lal and his workers retained all the oldest forms of distillation on a scale more substantial than he had ever seen. Samir's eyes burned with the heat, for multiple units were working simultaneously, resembling soot-covered domes.

*If only Ousmann were here,* he thought. Sweet-smelling smoke rose up to the sky, as men equipped with the same skills as Aarif and Jameel extracted essential oils from flowers, herbs, woods, and spices. If perfumers were storytellers, then distillers offered the details. And though the hand that distilled ingredients was rarely seen, each one had his own nuanced method.

In one corner, the mitti ittar was being distilled. In the same manner that the biryani-wallah in Anarkali scooped rice out of his vast pots, the distillers shoveled the clay disks and cups into deghs, the copper distillation units. Then they poured in water and closed the tops, sealing them with fragrant fuller's earth. As the men moved and glided to the rhythm of the elements, Samir found himself itching to be a part of the experience.

Hours later, when all of the aroma had been extracted from the clay, a liquid pool of earth was offered to the Vij men. It would now be poured into leather kuppis and left to macerate, and then bottled, sold, and shipped off to various corners of the country, where, no doubt, perhaps in the frost of winter or the crippling summer heat, a vial of mitti would be uncorked to evoke the sensation of the humid earth.

Two weeks later, when Samir left Kannauj, he was carrying the monsoon in his pocket.

While the trio was away, the Congress leadership, imprisoned in 1942 as a result of the Quit India Movement, was finally released. But in the political arena, their absence had been filled by the Muslim League. Reminders of religious identity had begun to be reinforced such that now any mention of independence was quite naturally followed by talk of Partition.

With the dropping of atomic bombs on the Japanese cities of Hiroshima and Nagasaki in August 1945, the Second World War came to an end at last. Indian soldiers who had been deployed in the Far East made their way back home, armed with stories, souvenirs, and wounds from the battlefields. Only one of the two Ahluwalia brothers, who had lived a few doors down from Vij Bhawan, returned from Burma. Sitting on the stoop outside his home, he showed Samir the blood-soaked cloth he had tied on his younger brother's fatal wound. And as Vivek watched the pair from the window, he felt a familiar sadness take hold of his heart.

# 20

# The Gift

Firdaus scooped her hair to one side and began to braid it, as she did each day. She had scrubbed her hands clean that morning, washed away any remnant of ink or dye that usually stained her fingers and nails. Midway through the braid, she paused. A lithe, plain-looking girl stared back at her. The white cotton shalwar kameez she had chosen for the occasion did little for her pale skin, and she wondered whether the pink dupatta would do any better. She sighed and stopped braiding, letting the hair fall freely down her back and face. *Better, softer.*

Then, reaching for the surmedani that Zainab had once bought her, the bronze pot of kohl she barely ever applied, she unscrewed it and extracted the long suramchi applicator stick. Leaning forward, lips apart, she carefully darkened the waterlines of her eyes. Their usually light pistachio color transformed into a darker green with the soot outline below them. Wiping off any excess, she wondered at how a single gesture had made her look drastically more feminine. Zainab used to line her eyes as a child. Surmageen, she would call her, one whose eyes were stained with kohl.

*Will he like it?* Firdaus wondered. *Will he notice?*

It was the summer of 1946, and she had secured admission in the Islamia College for Girls on Cooper Road, outside the Walled City, studying

Islamic literature. Firdaus would be the first woman in her family to go to college, and to celebrate this occasion, the nineteen-year-old perfumer had gotten permission from her father to take her out, unchaperoned. This, too, was a first. There was a seriousness to this decision, like a prelude to the future.

She tightened her diamond nose pin, put on two silver bangles, and covered her head and shoulders with her pink dupatta. Before she left the house, she slipped a small white envelope into her cloth pouch. She walked the ten minutes from her home to Wazir Khan, smiling widely. Everything about the day seemed like any other, except everything was different. The sun was brighter; the heavy red semal flowers had fallen all across the ground like a sea of crimson; even the chaos of Kashmiri Bazaar seemed a vibrant symphony.

When Firdaus arrived at the mosque, Samir was standing outside. He was dressed in brown pants and a white shirt with suspenders, bicycle in tow, speaking to her father. As she walked toward them, the conversation died down, and her father smiled, patted her cheek, and told Samir to have her back before maghrib.

Aware of the many eyes following them, Samir and Firdaus wordlessly walked across the dusty maidan in front of the mosque and onto the road that led out Delhi Gate. Firdaus played with her dupatta, her surmageen eyes stealing glances until they caught the perfumer's gaze.

"Will you say nothing today?" she teased. "You write so much in your letters."

"Today I have no words," he replied, unable to believe the afternoon belonged to them.

※

Altaf stood at the entrance of the mosque and watched as Firdaus and Samir disappeared. Unable to determine whether he was completely comfortable with this outing, he slowly walked back to his studio, trying to put aside any unease. Rizwan Alam, who had been watching the young couple, stormed up to the calligrapher, catching him unaware.

"Altaf mian, what are you doing?"

"What do you mean, ustad sahib?"

"Your daughter is seventeen now, of marriageable age. No one will marry her if they know she's been wandering across the city with a Hindu boy." *Hindu,* he spat out the word like venom.

Altaf breathed in sharply. "Dekhiye, ustad sahib, you and I have our own opinions on this matter, and it's best if we just let it be."

"*This matter?* This matter is graver than you think, mian. Your father would have agreed with me. If we get independence from the angrez, these kaafirs will not let us Musalmaans have anything."

*Kaafir,* disbeliever. Or in this case, *the other.*

His tone grew more spiteful. "They will finish us, just wait. *Humari salah lo,* take my advice and join the cause for Pakistan. Join the Muslim League. Join *your* people." He gestured to the crowd around the mosque.

The older calligapher's remarks were met with cold silence, as Altaf bowed his head in adaab and returned to his studio. Sitting then among his mute papers and inks, he breathed out a heavy sigh, as if he were finally safe. But what he was afraid to admit, perhaps even to himself, was that dread had slowly begun to grow in his heart like a tumor. Zainab's words echoed into Rizwan's, becoming a single, resounding voice of caution, and Altaf hoped he had made the right decision.

~

Under the stone arch of Delhi Gate, Samir hopped onto his bicycle and held it in place for Firdaus. She held her breath as he helped her up; never had they been so close before, and she wondered if he could hear her heart beating. She sat sideways behind Samir, adjusting her kameez and wiping her clammy hands on its fabric.

"Where are we going?" she asked, tucking her dupatta behind her ears.

He beamed. "You'll see."

As they rode out of the Walled City, a new, modern Lahore welcomed them with her wide, tree-lined streets. The cycle sliced through the hot summer air, and Firdaus's dupatta fell off her head, her hair trailing in the wind. She laughed. For the first time, for the very first time, she felt boundless and weightless, like a bird or a cloud or a stray leaf. Her fingers timidly crawled up from her lap onto Samir's shirt, and held it for safety.

A short while later, they reached Mall Road, which, laid in 1851, connected Anarkali all the way to Mian Mir. Throughout the ride, Firdaus was struck by the sparseness of the new city compared to the congested labyrinthine neighborhood she'd grown up in. They passed tangas, camels, horses, and people walking on the wide pavements of the avenue. They passed angrez mems and sahibs being driven by chauffeurs in their motorcars. They passed the statue of Queen Victoria, a row of car showrooms, striking colonial buildings, and the Regal Cinema, before reaching their destination.

The iconic Standard Restaurant had opened in 1939, catering to both Indian and British patrons. Firdaus waited nervously, fidgeting with her dupatta, as Samir leaned his bicycle against the outside wall. The college she had enrolled in was not far from here, she noted, looking around. Bicycle safely stationed, they walked into the restaurant together and were escorted to a table at the back, removed from the afternoon crowd.

"Full Tea" for a fixed price included as much tea as one could drink, and as many cakes, pastries, sandwiches, and patties as one could eat. Samir smiled each time Firdaus sampled something she had never tasted before—the chocolate cake, a cucumber sandwich, fruit tarts. This world outside the traditions of paper and ink, outside the mosque and studio, felt to Firdaus like a glimpse into the future she might one day share with Samir. Unable to stop smiling, she met his gaze as she picked up her cup to take a sip of milky tea.

In turn, he took out a velvet pouch from his pocket and slid it across the table.

Taking it in her hands, she asked what it was.

"Well, it . . . it's for you," he stumbled excitedly on his words. "A tube-rose perfume I have been working on for several years."

"Years?" she repeated, eyes wide in surprise. Undoing the ties, Firdaus drew out a perfume bottle unlike any she had ever seen before. Its elegant body was entirely covered in gold filigree, and, mesmerized by the delicate flowers, curled leaves, and entwined vines, she allowed her fingertips to trace the engraved surface of the bottle.

Seated across from her, Samir watched, smiling. Several weeks ago, unsure of what critique his uncle might offer, he had first shared the perfume with his mother. All it took was a single inhale for Savitri to realize that this composition, with its sublime floral heart, was meant for a beloved. For Firdaus. Days later, she knocked on his bedroom door bearing an exquisitely handcrafted gold bottle, befitting of the liquid it would hold, older and far more striking than anything they sold at the shop. Samir wondered where his mother would have acquired such an object, but accepted it gladly.

Now, as the seconds passed and Firdaus made no attempt to unscrew the cap, he knit his eyebrows together nervously. "This is my very first perfume . . ." he said, "for you."

Politely, she uncorked it and gingerly sniffed the contents. "Lovely, just lovely," she gushed in the same manner she had heard her mother speak about the Vijs' ittars.

Samir stared at her and then at the bottle.

"You don't like it." His voice was small, hurt. "I can make you something else." Samir now remembered the smell that overpowered her ubtan. "Do you prefer the rose?"

Firdaus did not care for the smell of flowers in the way that others did. She did not like the rose, and the rose had never liked her. But she knew it was a flower that Samir was partial to, so she quietly nodded, and the perfumer smiled, unsuspecting.

Mindful that Samir had expected her to be more excited about the

perfume, she placed her right hand on the table and, despite her apprehensions, slowly crawled it across toward him. If she were braver, she would
have reached out and laid her hand over his arm, but demure out of habit,
she reached just halfway, the napkin holder acting as a natural border between them. Seconds later, Samir reached out and erased any distance between them so that their arms lay next to one another. Firdaus felt his skin
graze hers. No one objected; no one even noticed. The hair on his arm was
thin and soft. *Like the finest, threadlike wisps of linen paper,* she thought to
herself. For a few minutes, neither spoke, their arms still touching, and
she wondered if the body remembered these gestures. Once home, would
she be able to think back to this moment and recall the precise touch of
Samir's skin?

"Why are you looking at me that way?" Firdaus asked shyly.

"I am just"—he searched for the right words—"memorizing you."

For years, behind the veil of silence, had Firdaus not done the same?
The delightful evening of counting the sixteen tils on Samir's face sprang
to her mind.

Suddenly, he got up from his side of the table and sat down beside her.
They were seated at the back of the restaurant, tucked away from everyone's view. Softly, he asked her to roll up the sleeves of her kameez and
hold out her arm. Alarmed, she stared at him, almost frightened.

"Don't you trust me?" he asked in a voice as soft as butter.

She looked around cautiously, and then did as he had requested. He
held the two silver bangles at her wrist. Then, slowly, he rolled up each
fine pleat in the long sleeve of her muslin kameez, all the way past the
elbow. Firdaus held her breath, unable to move. She became acutely aware
of the fact that no item of clothing she ever owned had revealed this much
skin. Again, she looked around nervously and took a deep breath. The
bones on her neck stood out sharply. Their knees were touching, her fingers tingling. Samir gently ran his fingers across her forearm, stopping
right at the inside crevasse of the elbow.

Samir looked around the room. All the waiters were either engaged with customers or in the kitchen. No one was watching; no one was around. He bent down and, holding her outstretched arm in his hand, inhaled the crook of her elbow. *Imagine this plot of skin as an island. Isolated from all smells, a brief interlude, a patch of renewal.* She was his island. The surface of his lips grazed her skin, and she felt his touch reverberate all the way to the tips of her toes. His breath was balmy, sensuous; his touch was disarming.

"This is the only part of one's body that smells entirely of them, no foreign odor lives here," Samir said. He could escape from the whole world within this crook of skin. He could dive, descend, disappear. Her smell could suspend his grasp on time.

"Well, what do I smell like?" Firdaus asked.

He told her to try it, but she declined.

"I want to know what I smell like to *you.*"

Her smell had been imprinted on him since the moment he encountered her nearly a decade ago. Looking into her eyes, Samir said, "It smells like the place I belong to. Firdaus, wherever you are, wherever this smell is, that is my refuge."

"That is my refuge as well," she repeated. "*Wahin meri panah hai.*"

Any fear that had remained in Firdaus's mind was erased by Samir's affection. Around him, she felt brave, encouraged, protected. So, from her bag, she, too, extracted a gift. The white envelope.

"*Aur yeh kya hai?*" Samir asked.

"From me to you. *Humari taraf se, tumhare liye.*"

A few weeks ago, Altaf had taken Zainab and Firdaus to a photo studio near the mosque. For many years now, he had desired to go to Mecca, and finally, having saved enough for the three of them to travel across, he had begun doing the relevant paperwork. At the photo studio, they'd each gotten individual photographs taken for the travel documents, and then a more formal one as a family.

Samir opened the envelope. It was Firdaus, frozen in black and white, wearing a kameez with white embroidery and dupatta over her head, braid trailing down her shoulder and eyes staring into the camera. There she was. Firdaus with the soot, Firdaus with the single beauty mark on her chin, Firdaus with the twinkling diamond nose pin.

Bringing the photograph to his lips, he kissed it and slipped it into his wallet. There she'd remain, Firdaus, always with him.

She said nothing in response, but the simple gesture moved her deeply. *This is the life I desire*, she wished to tell Samir, but couldn't muster the courage. *I wish to be young with you, I wish to grow old with you. I wish for our lives, yours and mine, to mix so seamlessly into one another in a way that your fears and your dreams become my own, and mine become yours.* Under the table, she found his hand and held on to it, tightly. *This quiet love that we have cultivated over many years, I want this love to survive the tides of time.* Unable to say any of this out loud, Firdaus hoped that Samir was versed in hearing the unspoken, that her gaze could convey all this, that he knew how deeply he had penetrated her heart.

Still gazing at one another, they resumed the meal of finger-sized pastries and tea, but an unvoiced concern remained.

"What is this Partition?" Firdaus began, her voice dropping to a whisper. "At the mosques, people talk. They gather and discuss newspaper reports and bulletins on the radio. There are chants of *Pakistan zindabad* sometimes late in the night, from the areas around the mosque. Where will this Pakistan be, and who will decide?"

Samir did not know what to say, mostly because he did not know himself.

"I'm scared, Samir. I'm scared about what will happen to the country and to us. Will Lahore be a part of Hindustan or Pakistan? Will they separate people lane by lane? What about the students in colleges?" After a few seconds of confused silence, she said, "You won't have to leave. Promise me that you won't have to leave."

Now, taking a deep breath, Samir thought of Basheer mian and Mushtaq chacha's prophecy, and how months ago, his friend Sunder's brother, Jagdish, had been released from Mirzapur jail and returned to Lahore to participate in the student movement. He might have been imprisoned for protesting British rule, but was now equally in protest against the creation of Pakistan. At that moment, he chose to disclose none of this to Firdaus.

He sealed his fears about the future deep into his heart and, caressing his beloved's hands with his thumbs, said, "Is it so easy to leave? Our life, our business, our flower fields, they are all here. Just because the land may acquire a new name, that doesn't make it any less ours, does it? Hindustan or Pakistan, Lahore is as much my home as it is yours."

He smiled at her, their fingers now entwined. "All my years have been only for you, and no one can separate us. But if we *are* ever drawn apart, I promise you, Firdaus Khan, that we *will* find a way back to one another."

The glistening, kohl-rimmed pistachio eyes smiled in return.

On the way back from Standard Restaurant, Firdaus chose to sit in the front of the bicycle, Samir's arms embracing her from both sides. She held on to the handlebars and rested her head on his chest. They rode along Mall Road as the sun was still suspended high in the air and found their way to the labyrinthine lanes of Delhi Gate well before maghrib. Under the fiery pink-orange sky, Firdaus directed him to her home right by the golden mosque. Ignoring the gaping passersby, the couple parted ways. Humming to herself, carrying none of the day's summer sluggishness, Firdaus walked into the house and was greeted by her mother fanning herself with a foldable pankhi.

Zainab had spent the afternoon fighting with her husband upon learning that he'd allowed the Hindu boy to take Firdaus out unchaperoned, or at all. Months ago, in January, a program had been organized at Islamia College by the women's subcommittee of the Muslim League, to appeal to female voters during the upcoming provincial election. Jinnah sahib had urged Muslim women to fight for the creation of Pakistan, claiming that no nation could make any progress without the cooperation of its women. Present in the audience was a group of ladies from Dabbi Bazaar, including Zainab, who would cast her vote for the very first time. And though the Muslim League would lose the 1946 election, the passionate speeches by its female members, particularly the principal of the Islamia College, would influence Zainab enough to encourage Firdaus to study under her tutelage. Following this meeting, the idea of Samir had grown even more rancid in Zainab's mind.

"*As-salaam-alaikum, Ammi jaan,*" Firdaus greeted her cheerfully.

Zainab only grunted in response, continuing to fan herself as her daughter sank into the low diwan beside her. In a dreamy tone, she said, "Oh, Ammi, what a lovely afternoon."

"Stop this, Firdaus, you are no longer a child!" Zainab snapped.

The excitement of the day dissolved in a single instant.

Putting down the handheld fan, her mother turned toward her and spoke directly. "Firdaus, listen to me when I tell you that the outcome of this friendship will not be good. I implore you to think with your mind and not your heart, because so far you have only amassed a considerable debt to your abba."

A long and uncomfortable silence prevailed before Firdaus got up and walked to her room, the pink dupatta trailing on the floor behind her. Once inside, she closed the door and leaned with her back against it, tears forming in the corners of her eyes. Then, walking to her worktable by the window, she extracted a wooden box from beneath it. Rows and rows of envelopes sat inside. Love letters of the everyday. Beside them sat the curled jasmine garland from years ago, which had metamorphosed from the waxy white to a crisp mustard brown, as Samir had predicted, smelling no longer of flowers but of the paper it lived with. She ran her hands over these souvenirs of love, and to them added the gold bottle she had just received.

Pushing the box back underneath the table, she lay on her bed, repeating Samir's words like a salve. *All my years have been only for you.* She said them over and over until they drowned out her mother's pragmatism. She tried to recollect every miniscule moment of the afternoon, from the wind in her hair to the feel of Samir's skin against hers. Intoxicated by these thoughts, she fell asleep along with the setting sun.

꙳

Samir walked his bicycle out of Firdaus's lane and into Dabbi Bazaar. Many years ago, as a child, he remembered asking his grandfather where all the perfumers of Lahore lived, and since then, every few years, Som Nath had brought him here to this fragrant lane along the glimmering Sunehri Masjid. Succumbing to the olfactive pleasures, he walked along the shops, sniffing, inhaling, smiling dreamily.

"Oye, Samir?" a voice called out after him. "Is that you?"

Samir turned around to see Rashid, whose family had been old acquaintances of the Vijs' ever since Vivek had opened the ittar shop. Dressed in a maroon and black shalwar kurta, Rashid stepped out of the alcove-like shop toward him.

"*Salaam, Rashid bhai, kaise hain aap?* How are you?" Samir embraced him.

"Everything is all right thanks to Him, *Allah ka shukar hai.* But look at you, how old you have become, looking just like some angrezi babu! Tip-top!" he teased, straightening out the young man's collar. "Are you married yet? Has your family found a nice girl for you?"

Samir looked shyly toward the ground, the photograph of Firdaus sitting safely in his wallet. "There are plans, of course there are plans. But I will marry only in an independent Hindustan, *nayi zindagi ki shuruaat naye Hindustan mein!*"

"Ah, still virtuous. Inshallah, we will be the masters of our own land one day. Free, azaad."

Nodding in agreement, Samir began to leave, but Rashid called him back. "Oh, don't leave so soon. Come in, smell this beautiful ittar that just arrived."

Laying down his bicycle and removing his hat, Samir crawled into the small space and inhaled the familiar aromas. Rashid's family ran the Al-Asghar ittar shop; they were not distillers or perfumers, but instead traded in ittars from across the country.

Rashid brought out a large cut-glass flask and placed it on the low wooden table. "Ittar kadamba . . ." He removed the applicator and held it out for Samir. "Have you ever smelled this before? It is scented with orange flowers that grow in round clusters. The wood from the tree is used to make paper."

Samir brought the applicator to his nose and inhaled. He marveled at the smell, notes of pistachio, sandal, and kewra, with hints of sweetness. He closed his eyes, inhaled again. Within seconds, he was transported to the mithai shops in Anarkali, surrounded by the aroma of traditional sweetmeats like milky barfi and dense ladoo. Smiling, he told Rashid what he thought.

"Exactly! It is from an old ittar shop in Delhi's Dariba Kalan called Gulabsingh Johrimal. Bottles of this usually come to us around Eid, but walid sahib ordered it a few weeks earlier this year." He gestured to the back, where his father sat, tallying up the inventory.

Samir greeted him and then looked around the shop. It had been years since he'd last visited, and yet everything appeared unchanged—identical glass bottles lining the back wall, large globular vessels of rosewater standing on the floor, solid perfumes and pendants displayed to one side, and aromatic wood burning in a bronze incense burner at the back.

How often he used to come here as a child, and how wonderful it felt to be around his own kind—keepers of smells and senses, guardians of perfumes and pleasures. Rashid and his father, much like the Vij family, took great care to preserve the ancient techniques and rituals of perfume. Amidst the politics of separation, this serene, shared craft felt to Samir devoid of all religious disparity. An equalizer like no other, for ittar, liquid and flowing, was borderless. It saw no Muslim or Hindu, no Sikh or Christian. It seeped and dissolved and spilled like water, slipping deftly through the crevasses of all difference.

# 21

# Things Hardly Ever Ruptured
# in Clean Lines

As the summer of 1946 drew to a close, Firdaus started classes at the Islamia College, and was unable to spend much time at her father's studio. Her parents had engaged a daily tanga service to take her to and from Cooper Road, which was a brisk ride outside the Walled City. Each morning began with an assembly speech, where the principal prepared the girls for their national duties in the fight for Pakistan. Every so often, she would invite members from the women's subcommittee of the League to deliver equally emotional lectures, which would rouse both students and professors. Firdaus began to make friends, though many would spend their time campaigning for the League by selling badges or distributing propaganda material. And no matter how struck she was by their appearance in public, shedding the conventions of purdah and interacting with the masses, it unsettled her that every conversation was centered around Pakistan, which remained vague in geography yet increasingly concrete in concept. While the topic of discussion among many remained this potential partition line, Firdaus and Samir rarely broached the subject. In fact, leaving the Walled City each day allowed Firdaus to leave her mother's bitter words behind, for after her classes and before the tanga-wallah arrived, she would find Samir standing outside the college gate, leaning on his bicycle, waiting for her.

Just weeks later in August, Altaf was unlocking his studio door after the asr prayer when he heard a crowd gathering outside the Wazir Khan mosque complex. Confused, he walked toward the main steps to find dozens of men, most with their prayer caps still on, some with large photographs of Jinnah sahib, noisily talking among themselves.

"Bhai sahib," he stopped a passerby going to join the group, "what is happening? What's the commotion about?"

"Ustad sahib, there is news from Calcutta. Come, join us!"

Altaf walked down slowly and stood at the foot of the staircase, watching in horror as the group became larger and larger, louder and louder, men raising their fists in the air with fervor and zeal. "*Pakistan ka matlab kya? La ilaha Il-lilah!* What is the meaning of Pakistan? There is no God but Allah!" they screamed. Their slogans tore through the otherwise tranquil air, "*Maarenge, mar jayenge, lekin Pakistan banayenge!* We will kill, we will die, but we will create Pakistan!"

The Calcutta chapter of the League had appealed for a complete strike of Muslim workers across the city. Processions, prayers, and rallies would culminate in a mass mobilization, putting pressure on the British government for the cause of Pakistan, now that the war had been over for a year. August 16, 1946, was thus termed Direct Action Day. Muslim citizens—a majority in Bengal—swayed by speech and vehemence, interpreting the vagueness of "direct action" as immediate extermination, proceeded over several days to commit heinous acts of violence in order to secure the imagined Muslim state.

As a result, nearly 1700 kilometers away from Lahore, Calcutta lay ravaged. Thousands of men with sticks and brickbats in their hands, and the same fire in their eyes as Altaf saw that afternoon, had roamed through the city committing murder and arson. The Hindu sectors were set on fire, shops were vandalized and gutted, homes and business were looted.

As dawn broke on the morning of August 17, the city on the banks of the river Hooghly was littered with corpses and blanketed with the noxious odor of death. With this defining act of violence, the ancient system of shared identity had been effectively and officially obliterated. No longer was it merely a question of allegiance to the Congress or the League, of Hindustan or Pakistan, or even the mere ideology of a separate state. No, the question had been stripped—with knives and cleavers and sticks and brickbats—to its ugliest, most rudimentary, skeletal form of difference.

Hindu or Muslim, *us* or *them.*

❧

In March of the following year, Zainab Khan sat by the window, surveying the fabric in her lap. A single, sharp tear ran through the otherwise intact tapestry. Placing the two halves as close to one another as possible, she tried to align the tear to sew it back together.

"*Uff yeh ladki na,*" she muttered to herself. Earlier that week, Firdaus had gotten the shawl caught in a door and, yanking it forcefully, she'd torn it right through the middle. Zainab tucked her dupatta behind her ears and adjusted herself to face the light. The parrot green shawl had been a present from Altaf to Firdaus two months ago on her birthday. Hand-spun and intricately embroidered all over in pink Kashmiri sozni work, the garment had cost him a small fortune, but it was her eighteenth birthday, after all. Still, the girl had carelessly split the precious present down the middle, and naturally, it was now Zainab's job to mend it. Sighing, she wished Firdaus would withdraw herself from the world of manuscripts or her college coursework long enough to learn a bit of housework. It was all well and good when she was a child, but with her teenage years nearing a close, other responsibilities would soon emerge, for which Firdaus was completely unprepared.

Shaking her head angrily, she threaded her needle with a green silk thread and began mending the tear, slowly and carefully. A running stitch emerged like a river. Strands of ragged fabric stuck out in places like slim tributaries, and she attempted to smoothen them down with her flattened thumb, with little luck. Things hardly ever ruptured in clean lines. She was halfway through when her attention was diverted by the sudden commotion outside. Quickly adjusting her dupatta, she looked out the window.

Hundreds of flags with the crescent-moon-and-star emblem of the Muslim League were fluttering in the spring breeze. A large mob of men, women, and youth had collected in a procession outside the Sunehri Masjid, while many others watched from the sidelines. Banners, portraits of League leaders, sticks, and fists were thrust in the air against the rapid chants of "*Pakistan zindabad!*" and "*Jinnah sahib zindabad!*"

Coerced by violence across the northern belt of Hindustan and the postwar bankruptcy of their treasury, the British government had announced its intention of a transfer of power to Indians by the very next year, 1948. Since the announcement, however, the violence and demonstrations had only worsened, arriving at the threshold of Lahore. Shops and businesses had remained sporadically closed, and marches had become a common occurrence. With the League gaining such aggressive momentum, even the Unionist premier of Punjab, Khizar Hayat Tiwana, staunchly against Partition, had resigned just the previous evening. The crowd gathered today, on its way to Mall Road, was presumably celebrating this resignation.

Zainab watched as the shop owners of Dabbi Bazaar rolled down their shutters one by one. Women in the overlooking multistory houses pressed their faces against closed windows, peeked through the slats, and ran up to the rooftops to get a better view. "*Leke rahenge Pakistan!* We will take Pakistan!" the crowds chanted, gaining momentum in both numbers and volume.

And then it happened. The green, white, and sunshine yellow suddenly gave way to blood red. So far, she'd only overheard rumors from hawkers in the bazaar and from women around the mosque, but that day Zainab saw with her own eyes the beginning of the battle for Lahore.

A group of men emerged from the sidelines, their faces covered, sticks and kirpaans in their hands. *"Jo mangega Pakistan, usse milega qabristan!* Whoever demands Pakistan will be shown the graveyard!" they bellowed. In response, the League crowd grew louder, more deafening. Insults and abuses of "kaafir, non-believer" and *Khizr dalla hai,* down with Khizr, the pimp!" flew across the dusty road. And then, suddenly, a man from the smaller group drew a knife and struck a body from the opposing party. Zainab, watching the confrontation from her window, gasped and retreated.

She slumped under the windowsill, still holding on to the torn shawl. Her eyes were wide open, her breath was racing, and slowly, she laid the shawl out on the floor before her.

Two halves. This was the future of Hindustan, Zainab realized. There had been women in that crowd, there had been children; it could have been her husband, it could have been her daughter. Murder and arson had now become visitors in broad daylight. For better or worse, everyone's fate was now bound to the fate of the land. From her place on the floor, she heard police rush to the scene. The crowd disappeared toward Delhi Gate, and the lifeless body remained in a pool of its own blood. That day, Zainab vowed that no matter what her husband said, no matter how liberally they had raised their daughter, Firdaus was no longer to see the Hindu boy.

Things hardly ever ruptured in clean lines.

⚘

Across the old city in Anarkali Bazaar, the dense smell of sandalwood had settled over the ittar shop. The extravagant wood was being distilled for the last many days, and Samir felt the heat from the degh collect in beads of sweat across his body. Now whenever he smelled sandalwood, the grandmother he had never known would appear before him, aromatic and magnificent. And during the quieter moments of the day, the concept of a tulsi-sandalwood perfume had begun to take shape in his mind. Full of earth and green, history and tenderness.

He was lighting fire to the dung cakes when he heard a crowd gathering below. Wiping his face with a cloth, he walked to the front of the open-air distillery and looked down. Ousmann came and peered over his shoulder. A crowd of turbaned men—Hindus and Sikhs—could be seen making their way through the bazaar toward the entrance of old Anarkali.

Just then the servant boy from Bhalla Shoes ran up, clearly having done the rounds of many other shops beforehand. "Tara Singh . . . Master Tara Singh!" he gasped breathlessly, "Kapurthala House. He is giving a speech on the grounds." He paused momentarily, crouching on the ground, trying to catch his breath, and then ran back down to notify the other shopkeepers. Samir and Ousmann looked at one another, the creamy sandalwood aroma closing in between them, and made their way downstairs. Aarif and Jameel were instructed to continue the distillation. In the shop, Vivek and Mohan were preparing to leave.

"Puttar, stay and watch the shop," Mohan instructed him, in a tone firm and parental.

"But I want to come!" Samir insisted, angrily. Over the past few months, so many of his friends had become active members of organizations and parties fighting against Partition, and he did not want to be left behind. "If this is about a united Hindustan, then I want to be there. I want to fight."

Vivek placed a hand on his shoulder. "Which is exactly why you will stay here. There will be no more battles fought by this family. Ousmann, aap aaiye, come with us."

Indignant but silent, Samir remained in the shop. Ousmann trailed hesitantly behind his employers, patting down his beard, removing the topi from his head, anxious of what the speech might reveal.

Aarif and Jameel packed up and left for the day, afraid to get caught up in any commotion. Only Samir stayed in the shop, an army of bottles surrounding him, the alchemist of displeasure. He was certain that his friends had gone to listen to the speech, particularly Sunder and his brother, Jagdish, who had been rallying student support against Partition. Samir wanted to be out there with them, rather than stuck inside. Two hours later, the Vij brothers returned to a shop emptied of any customers. They frantically hurried Samir out of the shop and caught a tanga back to Shahalmi. Once inside, Vivek secured Vij Bhawan, locking every door and window, and the family collected in Som Nath's room to discuss how the day had unfolded.

"The premier, Khizr Tiwana, has resigned," Mohan informed his family. "At first, the League was rejoicing, but the procession turned violent near Sunehri Masjid."

Samir's heart sank. "What kind of violence?" he asked, fearful for Firdaus.

"Someone from the procession was knifed in broad daylight, the police rushed to the spot, but that was just the beginning. This morning, Master Tara Singh, the Sikh leader, spoke against Pakistan to an angry crowd at the Assembly in Garhi Shahu. Then, along with the Congress leaders, he repeated the same sentiments in Anarkali. In fact, he vowed to finish the Muslim League. Ousmann had accompanied us, but we lost him quickly. After the speech was over, I believe the crowd attacked innocent Muslim shopkeepers in Bansawala Bazaar, just outside Shahalmi, beating them with sticks and poles."

Mohan let the information settle heavily among them. "Baba," he now addressed his father, "the days are going from bad to worse. *Sachi baat batavaa'n.* There is rioting across Punjab. Hindus and Sikhs on one side, Muslims on the other. It is madness. I have never seen anything like this before."

Som Nath studied his family's worried faces one by one. "But Partition is not a permanent solution. It *cannot* be implemented and it *will not* uphold."

"Even then," Savitri whispered, "even then, Baba, please consider that

for now, we may not be safe in Lahore. There is family in Amritsar, barely
an hour away. We can go there."

"When your world begins to fail you, the last thing you should do is
also fail yourself. In times like these, we must stand by what is right," Som
Nath began gently. "*Puttar, Savitri, ab saadi gall sun,* listen to me now. If
need be, I will offer myself to this madness outside, I will be sacrificed,
but I am not going to abandon this house. *Kurbaan ho javanga, lekin iss
ghar nu nahi choroonga!*"

Then his voice grew simultaneously stern and melancholic. "I was born
here and my wife was married into this house, she died here, and so will I.
You all can go anywhere, *tussi jana chande ho toh jao,* but I will stay here."

Silence.

As the sinking fear continued to grow in Samir's heart, he abruptly got
up and began walking toward the door. Was she all right? He had to know.
Had her family been hurt?

Four pairs of eyes followed him.

"The . . . the sandalwood . . ." he stuttered, trying to make up an excuse to go outside. "We need to remove the sandalwood from the deghs or
the entire batch will ruin."

"Forget the sandalwood," Vivek said. "No one leaves this house tonight."

⚜

Alarmed at the rate with which the violence was unfolding, the government had imposed a strict curfew from 8 p.m. to 7 a.m., leaving the streets
eerily desolate all night. The once crowded Mall Road was barely populated, resembling a dusty, rural road rather than the imposing boulevard
it was. The shops in Anarkali remained closed, the batch of sandalwood
ittar had likely decayed, and residents of the Walled City were confined to
their homes in fear.

When Mohan slipped out to try to contact relatives in Amritsar, he found the phone lines at the post office to be dead; Savitri visited her kin in Wachowali to learn that they were migrating to the mountains of Shimla for the next few months; Vivek heard the neighbors claim that the water supply had been poisoned, and rumors of kerosene being poured into the drains, ready to alight at any time, flew through the mohalla. A dismal stillness had descended upon old Lahore, fractured every now and then by violence. Then, amidst the mayhem, a new viceroy was sworn in: Lord Louis Mountbatten, brought to transfer the power from British to Indian hands.

During this curfew, Samir, like many others, felt suffocated and cut off from the world outside. In the long hours of the day, he often sat by the window, hoping for some news from his friends, or ritualistically writing Firdaus the weekly letter.

And in the next room, Vivek spent his idle hours unable to confront the world outside. From his cupboard one day, he drew out a small bundle of linen cloth. Unwrapping it carefully in his lap, he retrieved a bamboo reed and ran his thumb along the once ink-darkened qatt, the nib. Iqbal Khan's brilliant pistachio eyes flashed before him, his face covered with mud and blood. Sounds of gunfire rained in the background, a faint greenish gas still descended, the smell of pepper and pineapples filled the air around him.

For over three decades now, Vivek had held on to a secret friendship and an even more secret death. The bamboo qalam that should have been rightfully bequeathed to another sat in his guilty hands. He wrapped the reed back in the cloth and returned it to the cupboard, burying it as far as it would go. It had taken him so long to overcome the memories of war, and now another kind of war was at their doorstep. In what seemed like another lifetime, he and many others who had traveled across the black waters had wished one day to be free from British rule. But they had never considered what the price of this freedom would be.

Those who were now considered *other* had until recently been part of oneself. As if a single body had been bisected into two ravenous halves, feeding upon one another. Incidents of violence had begun to appear as frequent dots of red on the labyrinthine map of the city—tiny flowers blooming into bouquets of blood. A battlefield. A quest to claim territory, where no one would emerge victorious. *Red, crimson, vermillion, carmine, maroon, rust, brown.* In March of 1947, the festival of Holi was played with blood rather than the usual powdered color, staining indelibly the memories and histories of those who survived to remember it.

# 22

# To Pause on the Plateau of Some Uncertain Hope

By April, the city still lay under curfew, but the violence had ebbed, and this brief calm lulled Lahoris into a false sense of normalcy. After breakfast, Altaf would leave for his studio, but following an attack with tear gas and lathis on a procession of female students from Firdaus's college rallying in support of the Muslim League, she was no longer allowed to venture out. Instead, Zainab took this time to domesticate her daughter.

Samir would bicycle past her house on days the curfew was lifted, delivering weeks' worth of letters to his beloved. He'd wait under Firdaus's window till she appeared, and in the basket that her mother had tied with a length of rope to the railing of the verandah to bring up vegetables, Samir would place the letters. Firdaus would never speak of the secret delivery to anyone, for her mother had forbade her to see Samir. Apart from this irregular exercise, the lovers had been successfully kept apart.

One morning mid-month, Altaf walked through the sparsely populated Kashmiri Bazaar to Wazir Khan mosque. Hardly any of the calligraphers opened their studios any longer, lessons having terminated completely.

Even the khanas for religious scholars located inside the courtyard of the mosque lay empty. But even if there was little work, Altaf chose to come to his studio. Some days, the confinement, coupled with Zainab's insistence that her husband join the processions and meetings of the League, was simply too much to bear. On days like those, his heart went out to Firdaus, who wordlessly and obediently indulged her mother.

As he walked up the steps of the mosque that day, a distantly familiar smell greeted him, so powerful that it completely absorbed the months of massacre. Gulabjal—the caretaker had sprinkled rosewater. What had once been a daily routine had now become rationed and reserved only for the Friday prayer. Standing at the mosque entrance, Altaf wondered how his friend the perfumer was doing. Every now and then, an urge would tug at his heart to cross the city to Anarkali. But some things had been rendered impossible, for while the external world was warring for land, a smaller, more intimate battle was being fought within the confines of the Khan residence. Eventually, Altaf's ingrained secularism had lost to Zainab's inflexibility, abruptly severing so many sincere ties.

The day passed unusually quietly, and after asr, the calligrapher locked the studio and walked down the stairs of the mosque. Hardly a soul lingered in the open maidan, but from a distance, Altaf noticed a lump-like mass by the marble fountain. Drawing in a breath, he surveyed the area and then walked across toward it. But before he reached the lump, a trail of sticky red confronted the calligrapher. Panicked, he followed it to the source to find a mangled body, blood spewing from an open wound in the back, a kirpaan still lodged in. A long stick lay abandoned close by. Flies hovered hungrily.

Turning the body over, he gasped; it was Rizwan. Unable to balance himself, Altaf fell back on the ground. The world around him turned suddenly gray, splattered with blood like an ugly sheet of marbled paper. Gathering his things haphazardly, he ran all the way home. The very next day, the Khan family packed their bags and left for Nasreen's home in the suburb of Badami Bagh.

⋏

In May, Ousmann knocked on the door of Vij Bhawan. His eyes were anxious, the usual black crochet kufi was not on his head, and he had tamed his unruly beard—precautions to enter the predominantly non-Muslim neighborhood of Shahalmi. Vivek, Mohan, and Som Nath sat with him in the baithak. Samir lingered by the door. Savitri had no choice but to serve a dark, murky black tea. There was a shortage of rations and no milk to be found anywhere. Amidst the violence, those who worked at the gau shala were afraid to come back to work. Embarrassed at the meager offering, she set the tray down and darted out.

Som Nath sighed. "There isn't much we can serve you with the tea, puttar. Please excuse us."

"You shouldn't have bothered even with this," Ousmann said, taking a bitter sip. Then, extracting a large guchcha of keys from his pocket, he placed them on the diwan.

"Vij sahib," he addressed Vivek now, "I have come to tell you that I can no longer work at the distillery. I thought the violence would die down eventually, but near Mochi Gate, things are spiraling out of control. My cousin Yasser, who works for Beli Ram chemist, was threatened in broad daylight. I've seen the violence with my own eyes, and cannot risk the safety of my family by"—he hesitated for a moment before continuing—"working for Hindus any longer."

He pushed the keys to the distillery and perfumery toward the brothers. "Please forgive me if you can. It should never have come to this. Aarif and Jameel will also no longer be working."

"Ousmann, people don't change, only governments do," Vivek said. "*Yeh sab siyasati chaal hai.* You have been with us from the beginning . . . We will protect you if anything happens. You have our word."

Ousmann smiled sadly. "That may be so, Vij sahib, but we always protect our own first."

"And are you not our own? Lahore has never belonged to any one religion," Som Nath appealed. "*Sikh te Hindu te Musalmaan,* living together. We are Punjabi, this is our shared culture, and no politics can fracture that. *Tussi apne aap nu humse alag thodi na kar sakte ah,* you cannot sever yourself from us."

"In the army, there was no difference between us. The Muslim soldiers were as much my brothers as a Hindus or Sikh," Vivek added. "We spent months in the trenches together, fighting against a common enemy, for a shared cause. It must be the same now, don't you think? There is no me or you, Ousmann, there is only *us.* Together. Please consider returning to work when all this is finished."

The chief distiller looked down at his feet. "With all due respect, sahib, I think you should leave the city until this violence subsides."

"But Ousmann chacha—" Samir began before the distiller cut him off, shaking his head sadly.

Som Nath took in a sharp breath. He thought of Basheer and the kites. He thought of all the oldies of Anarkali, sitting together despite their different religions. He thought of Lahore—the city of his birth, the city by a river, the city of Sikh maharajas, the city of Mughals, the city of the ancient Hindu Rajputs. He thought of Mushtaq Alam's prophecy, inching closer to fulfillment with every passing day.

Surveying the locked windows, the fortified doors, the morbid air, he spoke. "Till now, all communities of Lahore have shared everything. So, this violence, this suffering, this sorrow, even the memory of these days shall be shared. Whether we leave the city or not, Ousmann puttar, we will all be equal inheritors of its loss."

ᴔ

May 20, 1947
    Firdaus, this curfew has become a death sentence, and we
are amputated from the outside world. Sometimes, there is no

water. Sometimes, we cannot fire up the chulha. Sometimes, the air is so heavy with rumor that it feels stagnant. Even the natural world can no longer lift our spirits. The amaltas have wilted and the neem pods have browned in the sun. Last week when the curfew lifted, I rode past your home to find it locked. My heart sank as I rode to the mosque to find the studio locked as well. Then the moulvi told me that ustad sahib had taken his family away until things settled.

These long and unbearable days of curfew have deprived us of the extraordinary aromas at the shop. Jasmine, sandalwood, and rose have been replaced with the mundane smells of smoke, kerosene, mealy rotis, and half-cooked dal. My father once said that our craft provides people with comfort and calm, relief and respite. That at times when the world is unrecognizable, even a whiff of familiar perfume can bring us back to the place where all is safe. I'm beginning to think what he said no longer applies. The ittar shop is closed, there are random stabbings across the city, and Gurkha troops have begun patrolling the streets. There was a fire by the mosque just days ago, burning areas of Wazir Khan Chowk, Akbari Mandi, and kucha Wanwattan. I was relieved that you were far away.

Lahore feels at a standstill, like we have paused on the plateau of some uncertain hope. Even you seem so unreachable that on most nights, I yearn to be one of your pressed twigs, the curl of your dried leaves, the surface of your polishing stone, so that I may remain forever confined in the palm of your hand, warmed by your skin. As the keeper of paradise, khazin-e-firdaus, I am waiting here for you.

Yours, Samir

✿

By late May, worried that Muslims were determined to burn Hindus and Sikhs out of Lahore, the Vij family began to collect valuables that would be safer under lock and key at the shop in Anarkali than at home, should their non-Muslim neighborhood be the target of arson. Mohan and Som Nath gathered money and the deeds for their home, shop, and Pattoki flower fields; Savitri added the dupatta full of jewels, Samir his notebook of formulas. Most of Vivek's treasures—the journals from vilayat, the brown leather case, the vials of perfume—were already in the atelier. But to the pile, he added an old tin box with Iqbal Khan's bamboo reed and the sepia photograph of the couple, too precious to lose. Then, after much thought, he put in another antique from the war—a sharp, hand-carved knife in a wooden sheath—and shut the box. Assembling all these items in a hard leather suitcase with brass clasps and corners, they now waited as the city went silent.

Then, on the first day of June, the curfew was lifted. Shielding their eyes from the sunlight, the Vij men headed apprehensively to Anarkali Bazaar, accompanied by the small suitcase of riches. Savitri and Som Nath watched from the windows in fear. Citizens of Lahore, who had not ventured out for months, trickled out to buy vegetables or open their shops and offices. And by Sunehri Masjid, the Khan family, who had returned from Badami Bagh just the day before, settled down for whatever meager breakfast Zainab had managed to whip up from the rationed groceries.

But on the eve of June 3, 1947, the Vij family and several shop owners of Anarkali listened to the voice of the Viceroy Mountbatten on All India Radio confirm that in mere weeks, undivided Hindustan as they knew it would disappear. Independence would be granted in August 1947, and Partition would be its price. Though the exact border was left to a Boundary Commission, a division of the land into India and Pakistan was now certain, and the provinces of Punjab and Bengal would be split between both. After Mountbatten, Nehru spoke from the Congress, Jinnah from the Muslim League, and Baldev Singh representing the Sikhs, all in support of the decision to partition.

The announcement pacified almost all parts of the country, except Punjab. Here, communal war hovered with the sinister darkness of monsoon clouds. Since it was difficult to tell Punjabis apart, many Hindus had begun to wear a tilak on their forehead and Muslims the Jinnah cap. Newspapers advised Christians and Anglo-Indians to wear a cross as a mark of their identity. In marketplaces and alleyways, one could hear whispers of "*Lahore kidhar jayega?*" as people discussed what side of the border Lahore would fall on, and whether to remain or flee. The Vij family had no intention of migrating elsewhere; they simply assumed that the violence would pass and they would continue to live in Lahore, regardless of which nation it became a part of. But Samir, who had not seen Firdaus for months, feared a future he did not know how to plan for. Casual stabbings and arson resumed in many parts of the city, non-Muslims began to put up barricades or hide up on their roofs with bricks and stones for protection, and yet again, a night curfew was enforced.

Meanwhile, Sunder and Jagdish had gathered a sizable group of Hindu and Sikh youth vowing to fight for the city of Lahore, often joining the cause at the expense of their studies. Many had seen the recent fire set by Muslims in Papar Mandi, and how the police, overwhelmingly Muslim, had not allowed Hindus to leave the Walled City, as there was curfew. Losing confidence in authority, they decided to take matters into their own hands, claiming they wouldn't allow even a sliver of Punjab to be sliced away. After three Muslim boys threw a bomb into the Lachman Das Hospital outside Shahalmi in mid-June, causing over forty casualties, the group's blood boiled further. A meeting to draw a plan of action was called, and the news made its way to Samir through Prithvi.

"This is the fight for Lahore," Prithvi had said to him with zeal in his eyes. "Our home, the land of our birth. We cannot let Hindustan be partitioned or Lahore be divided. If nothing else, think about Firdaus and your future together. And for her sake, join us."

# 23

# The World Ablaze

The meeting was to take place past midnight outside the Walled City. Hours earlier, Samir, who longed to see, to *smell* Firdaus once again, sat by the window and wrote his weekly letter. He would cycle round the next day to see if the Khans had returned. The conversation with Prithvi had rattled him enough to envision a future that would not be disturbed by a partition line.

June 21, 1947

   Firdaus, it is difficult to remember a time before you. Without you, my life seems only half lived and I don't know how to grow older in any other way but beside you. August will bring a new dawn, both for the land and for us. I dream to be married to you in the Lahore of an independent nation, and whether that nation is called India or Pakistan is of little concern to me. This land will still be our land, this history will still be one which we have forged. You and I will remain the same, on this side or that.

                                                        Yours, Samir

He folded the letter twice, kissed it, and tucked it safely into his wallet. Then, lying back on his bed, he waited till just a little after midnight, when he heard the soft tap of a pebble on his window. Looking down, he saw Prithvi waiting for him, bicycle in tow. Stillness had descended upon Vij Bhawan, the moon had ascended in the sky, and barefoot, shoes in hand, Samir snuck out the side entrance on kucha Reshmiya and rode off with his friend.

⚘

That same evening, Zainab handed her husband a letter, requesting that he read it. It had arrived from Delhi just that morning. She sat beside him, carefully peeling the skin off an apple and slicing it into quarters. Clearing his throat, Altaf read the contents out loud. In the run-up to Partition, Zainab's brother, Muhammad, had decided to migrate to Lahore and was writing to let his sister know that the family—his wife, Nadira, and their son, Fahad, and twin daughters, Saira and Sitara—would arrive by July.

Zainab's eyes twinkled as she listened to her bhai jaan's words. "Oh, it has been years since we saw the whole family, how wonderful that they will be here now. And Khan sahib, I was thinking . . . Fahad works with bhai jaan in the carpet business. He is twenty-two now, just a few years older than Firdaus. Don't you think they'd make a lovely couple?"

Immediately, Altaf eyes darted toward the open door of Firdaus's room. He gestured to his wife to lower her voice. Zainab swatted his hands away and made a mental note to respond to her brother the very next day. Altaf sighed, caught in the middle of a silent war between his wife and his daughter.

Later, as Zainab was washing the dishes, Altaf knocked on Firdaus's door. From a distance it seemed as though she was lost in a book, but the moment she looked up, it was evident that she had heard everything. Her eyes were bloodshot. She looked at him—her advocate, her soldier—with confusion and helplessness, but he refused to meet her gaze, focusing out the window at Sunehri Masjid. Rizwan's brutal death remained fresh in his memory, and daily reports of Muslim victims in *Dawn* newspaper filled him with fear.

"Abbu," she whispered. "Samir . . ."

"I think it's time you forget him, Firdaus. This war is bigger than you or him." Altaf crossed his arms over his chest. "Not all love stories are meant to end in happiness."

Firdaus stared at him, unable to understand how history had intervened so ruthlessly in her life, suspended and dismantled all possibility of hope. She had been so careful to keep the intimacy of her world safe, guarded, sacred. How, then, had the chaos outside swept over her father and changed his beliefs? With labored breath, she opened her mouth to speak, but no words came out. She looked around her room, at the crisp mustard garland of dried jasmine now hanging on the wall, at the large box of love letters under the desk, at her father, at the floor, at the moon outside, boundless and untethered. She felt anger, but knew no medium to express it.

"Abbu, please," she begged as tears filled her eyes.

Altaf clenched his jaw.

"But Fahad . . . bhai?" Defeat filled her voice. "We are cousins."

"Firdaus, don't be naive. You are well aware that such alliances are common." Then, with a sharp breath, he offered the final betrayal, words escaping his lips like unfamiliar poison. So much for the years of education and independence, so much for her father's principles—it had all been but to demand this ultimate sacrifice. That day, Firdaus realized that she had lost.

"After all that we have done for you, this is the least you can do."

⚘

Samir and Prithvi slowly and discreetly pedaled through the old city, sneaking past the sentries who patrolled during curfew, and onto the wide avenues of new Lahore. By the time they had crossed Government College, its big clock had struck one o'clock. Prithvi headed down the deserted Mall Road and Samir followed, beads of sweat trickling down his face. They approached a small nondescript park off the main road, where twenty or so young men had gathered, illuminated by moonlight. Most were students in khaadi and kurta-pajamas; many of the Hindus wore Gandhi topis, and the Sikhs wore turbans. The perfumer hung toward the back, still holding on to his bicycle, as Prithvi walked up ahead.

Sunder stood at the front of the group next to an older man in a white kurta-pajama, who seemed like the leader. Samir assumed it was his brother, Jagdish. Tall, lean, with a slim mustache, he bore a scar on his cheek. After nearly a half hour, he got up on a park bench to address the crowd with the ease of a trained orator.

"Doston, friends, all of you present here are true sons of Lahore. Generations of your families have made this land their home and dreamed of its freedom. Azaadi! And now that freedom is within our grasp. But we did not endure centuries of British Raj only to bow down to Muslim rule!" The crowd broke into applause. "The Muslim League wants to cut up Mother India to create their Pakistan. Carve Bengal and Punjab in half. It wants to take Lahore. That is unacceptable! We do not accept the Partition of India! We do not accept the division of Punjab! We will not forgo Lahore!"

The crowd raised their fists in the air. "Lahore does not belong to them! We will not give up Lahore!"

"We will not give up Lahore!" Jagdish repeated passionately. "It is the hour when the youth must take back what is ours. By force or violence, if we need to. If they can burn down our houses and shops, if they can throw a bomb into our hospitals, then so can we!"

If Samir had naively assumed that this was a nonviolent meeting, he was proven wrong. This was nothing short of extremism. He could never have imagined his classmates, Prithvi, Sunder, boys he'd known since the age of five or six, would take up any kind of arms.

His thoughts were broken by Jagdish's ominous words. "On Direct Action Day, they mercilessly slaughtered our Hindu brothers in Calcutta. In March, they attacked and abused our women in Rawalpindi. Now they are determined to drive us out of Lahore. Shame on the Congress for accepting the Partition plan. We do not accept Partition! We will not give up Lahore! We will not give up Lahore!"

As the crowd repeated the chant, Samir found his breath caught in his throat. Jagdish's ideology might have begun with the demand for independence from British rule, but with time, it had morphed into the rejection of Partition in order to keep a unified India, and had now turned vengeful and violent against the perceived other.

Samir's eyes were wide with horror as they scanned the scene, and his thoughts were only of Firdaus. What was happening to their world?

⚘

Back at Vij Bhawan, the family attempted to sleep. Ordinarily in the summertime, they would carry their cots to the respite of the open roof, but with the ongoing violence, that was no longer an option. Meanwhile, at the entrance of Shahalmi Gate, when all the oil lamps and dim bulbs had been dimmed, a group of local thugs devised a plan. Two large drums of flammable solution were snuck past the sentries at the gate of the Hindu and Sikh stronghold, and splashed across wooden facades of homes and shops, on cycles, vehicles, and anything else that lay out on the road. Locally made bombs were placed at various locations and the open drains were filled with kerosene.

Then, as the clock struck one o'clock—when Savitri was tossing in her bed, thinking of her family in Shimla, and Mohan, stretched on his stomach, was dreaming of the day where Lahore resumed its syncretic glory, and Som Nath, curled in fetal position, was remembering his brown-eyed Leela, and Vivek, face illuminated by the moonlight, was embroiled in memories of war and love, jasmine and crushed lemon leaves—a match was struck.

Within seconds, lane after lane of the congested, mazelike Shahalmi was ablaze. Fire unleashed itself on the wooden houses, swallowing everything. The lampless alleys glowed orange. Smells of spices, oils, tires, cloth filled the air. And somehow still, over the roar of fire, screams and cries could be heard of people asphyxiated by the smoke, burning within the confines of their homes. Some ran up to the rooftops, others escaped from windows covered in soot and fire, but most perished. From a distance, the perpetrators watched as Shahalmi, the fortress of Hindus and Sikhs, disappeared into ash.

⨎

Samir didn't remember how it started, but all of a sudden, panic seized the crowd. One moment, Jagdish was claiming he would draw every Muslim out of Lahore, and the next moment, someone was shouting about a fire swallowing Shahalmi Gate. Samir looked toward the old city in the distance and saw flames touching the sky. Alarmed, he jumped on his bicycle and began to pedal back as fast as his legs would take him, down the Mall and to the mouth of the old city, where an overwhelming, sizzling smell greeted him, ashen particles fluttering in the air.

The fire had been burning for over an hour, and still it raged on, swallowing as many structures as it could. It lingered in curls of orange and flickers of blue all along the mohalla. The houses tucked deep inside the lanes had managed to remain standing, but the structures along the main Shahalmi Bazaar Road, which had been doused repeatedly with the flammable solution, had caught fire and collapsed. This continued all the way down to Papar Mandi. Some of these houses, nearly a century old, made of frail bricks and wood, were destroyed beyond recognition.

When Samir finally reached the place where Shahalmi Gate had once stood, he found a crowd of people staring into the smoldering alleys inside. A fire brigade and two military fire engines had arrived on the scene, but they seemed to have no water supply.

"Oye, puttar, don't go inside!" a man screamed as Samir rode in.

"The fire is still burning, mundeya, come back!" yelled another.

"It's the Vij boy! *O' khoteya,* Samir, don't be stupid, you will die in there," a shopkeeper from Anarkali called out. He tried to grab onto the bicycle, but Samir continued to pedal down the road. After a few minutes, he abandoned the bicycle and ran as fast as his feet would carry him, shirt coming undone from his trousers, suspender falling off one shoulder. In the distance, he heard a gunshot go off, but he continued on. The street was charred; even the gutters had exploded, fashioning small craters in the ground. He coughed as he tore through a screen of thick smoke.

Upon reaching the corner where his home had once stood, he stopped in his tracks. Standing motionless, he looked at the burning structure, unable to believe his eyes. The floors and walls had collapsed into piles of blackened wood, some still on fire. There was no trace of the prayer room, the jasmine flowers, the holy tulsi. Amidst the rubble, he tried to make sense of the floor plan. Where were the rooms, the beds, the gauzy mosquito nets, the hand-carved jharokha windows, the staircase? Where was the kitchen? Everything smelled of smoke, all traces of henna, sandalwood, rosewater, chai, and spicy red chilies, all that had been synonymous with home, had been expunged. He looked around, dazed, and stepped on a piece of glass. Half a bangle. Green, dusty. He bent down to pick it up. His family, where was his family? He prayed they had fled, but then the smell of charred flesh floated into his nostrils and he went numb.

Samir got on all fours, his face now black with ash, his fingers tearing through the debris, trying to drag away the large pieces of stone. The heat was unbearable, and parts of the structure were still burning. For what seemed like hours, he scoured the blackened stone, but in vain. No one could have survived this brutal an inferno. He heard a bomb go off somewhere a few streets away, and it jolted him out of his daze.

He collected whatever he saw of whatever remained—his mother's broken bangle, an incinerated book probably belonging to his grandfather, an ornate corner of a balcony railing—and made a small, charred pile of belongings. Slumped against half a broken wall, Samir closed his eyes, sewed them tightly shut, ready to awake from the world of death. Minutes later, he opened them to find the world unchanged. Everything had perished, but somehow, he had remained. It felt as though he had swallowed the world and the weight of it had multiplied inside his body. His arms felt immobile, his feet like cement, his mouth was parched, and his face was filthy. But on the inside, Samir felt no rage or madness. There was disorder, and confusion, and many, many questions. *What happened?* he demanded from the slow-moving smoke, in a voice no louder than a whisper. *What happened here? How did it happen? Who did this?* His heart beat faster now. *Why wasn't I here?* He cursed Prithvi and the meeting on Mall Road, Partition and politics, Nehru and Jinnah and Gandhi and Mountbatten. *If only I'd been here,* he told himself repeatedly, *I could have saved them, I could have got them out.*

In the distance, he heard the shuffling of people and trucks. He closed his eyes again and, for a brief moment, thought back to a summer night years ago, when the family had taken their beds up to the rooftop. Nestled under the moonlight, twirling a fragrant white flower between his fingers, Samir had listened to his grandfather's tales. Now, cradling the charred book like a treasure, he asked, "Dadu, do you remember what you had said then? You told me that no matter what happened to the world outside, this haveli was our refuge. This was home. Do you remember, Dadu? Now tell me, where shall I go?"

Samir sat motionless for hours. Night gave way to dawn, and morning brought parties of police officers, military personnel, and the local magistrate to survey the damage. None had noticed the living, breathing person lying in the rubble. It was only when a crowd of manic voices punctured the air, chants of *"Allah hu Akbar"* followed by *"Pakistan zindabad,"* that Samir opened his eyes.

For a moment, he considered sacrificing himself to the Leaguers. How could he go on when he would never again see his mother paint henna upon her hands, his father button his khaadi waistcoats over his kurta, his grandfather unearth pressed roses from the pages of old ledgers? And his uncle, the greatest teacher of all—how could Samir continue on when he could never again sit in his uncle's shadow, learn by his side, watch him enliven the invisible, magical world of perfume? Why should he survive? Guilt filled his heart until something else jolted him to his feet.

He had to find her.

# 24

# Like a Body Abandoning
# Its Shadow

Samir ran down Shahalmi Bazaar Road, past Rang Mahal and to-ward Kashmiri Bazaar. *She* would be the reason to survive. The dark beauty spot, the pistachio eyes, the smell of roses and ink. He arrived at Sunehri Masjid and turned toward her home. *She will know,* he reassured himself. *She will know what happened.*

He knocked as loudly as he could on the front door, something he had never done before. Bringing his hands to his face, he wiped the dust away and found blood trickling along his forehead. Using the cuff of his shirt, he rubbed it off and waited. The door opened and Altaf stepped forward, dressed head to toe in black.

"Ustad sahib." Samir embraced him, relieved to see a familiar face. "Our home, ustad sahib, the mohalla, a fire. A large fire," he gasped through his words. "Everything is finished, everyone is, everyone is . . . dead." His tears rolled into his mouth as he tried to catch his breath.

Altaf peeled his student away from his body. "*Khuda kisi aur ko aise dinn kabhi na dikhae,* may god never bestow days like these upon anyone else." He meant it, for his heart had shattered upon hearing the news, and yet he could not meet Samir's gaze.

"Firdaus?" Samir asked, looking behind him at the dark staircase that led up to the house. "Firdaus? *Woh theek hai,* is she okay?" He craned his neck to look up at the window.

"Everyone is all right," Altaf said, and then grimly continued, "but you cannot see her."

The perfumer looked at his old master, uncomprehending.

"You are a Hindu, Samir beta," he said firmly, "and we are Muslim."

Beta, he called him. *Son.* A word now lacking all definition.

"Look at what is happening around us. This is no longer your land, and there is nothing for you here. You must leave Lahore."

His tone was no longer of the man who had taught him and Firdaus to render beautiful and complex scripts, or the teacher who indulged Samir's love for the smells of paper and leather. That day, Altaf Khan was a Muslim, and Samir Vij was a Hindu, and the threshold of the Khan house became a border he could not cross.

Panicking, Samir looked up at the window again. A cloth curtain had been drawn over it. Closing his eyes, face up to the sky, he relied on his most treasured organ. Inhaling vigorously to a point that his ribs caved in, shaping his belly in a deep concave, he smelled past the oudh on Altaf's kurta, past the ash-speckled surface of the window. Samir channeled his reliable gut to smell past Zainab's half-cooked eggs, tea leaves, and pods of fragrant green elaichi, past the smoke collected in the air pockets, and toward his beloved. He fought the barricade of all other smells in search of roses and oranges, milk and ink. She was around; he could smell it.

"Firdaus!" he called out in desperation.

"Firdaus!" he repeated, louder now, and still, she did not emerge. But he had smelled her out from behind the curtain. She was there, somewhere, a mere veil of cotton separating them. The neighboring women had come out to their windows, watching the scene from underneath their purdahs, and the hawkers outside Sunehri Masjid now directed their attention toward the calligrapher's home.

"Firdaus," Samir said her name again, softer.

"Firdaus?" Softer still, his voice overcome with love and melancholy.

"Firdaus . . ." The keeper of paradise had nothing more to lose, and falling to his knees, he whispered for the last time, "Firdaus."

For a few moments, no one moved. Altaf longed to reach out and pick Samir up, Zainab stood by her daughter's door, and Firdaus stepped up to the window. As the curtain parted and she emerged, Samir's nose reached the air before his closed eyes did, sensing his beloved. But the brightness of her pistachio eyes was diminished, and for the first time, Samir smelled something new on her.

Tears. Salty, briny trails mixed with saliva and something else pungent, running from her eyes into the folds of her dupatta. And despite all the distance between them, the terror around them, and her father's bitter words, Samir shut out the world and concentrated only on the smell of Firdaus. The one from the ittar shop, the one he had memorized over the years. As if encountering it for the very first time, as if possessing it for the very last time. Firdaus with the roses, with the gram flour, with the unusual traces of vanilla and smoky soot. This was his Firdaus. And when he finally looked up, there she was, lovelier than ever, the dark til on her chin inviting him to drown in its depths.

Firdaus thought twice before saying what she eventually did, but her mother's ominous words encircled her mind like a summer dust storm. *So far you have only amassed a considerable debt to your abba,* she had forewarned. Was it true, Firdaus now wondered, her fragile world at the brink of collapse. Was it so terrible to love as one wished to? She had been the ideal daughter—obedient, reserved, dignified, hardworking. The only mistake she'd made was to fall in love with a boy who happened to be Hindu.

*How can you leave him,* she fought herself. *After everything that he has lost, how can you, too, leave him?* With the ends of her maroon dupatta, she wiped the tears flowing uncontrollably down her face and thought back to the days of her childhood. Her father had battled his wife so that their daughter could grow up an educated, self-sufficient woman. A true heir. But little had Firdaus realized that this was both a gift and a sacrifice, for she now understood what she had bartered the moment she picked up that first qalam. Her freedom.

In her life, henceforth, there would be abundant knowledge and history, books and poetry, but there would exist no freedom and not a trace of love. So, in a voice she barely recognized as her own, she said, "Chale jao, Samir, you must leave. Abba jaan is right."

Unable to comprehend or believe anything that had happened, Samir remained still. A few minutes later, he picked himself up and turned to leave. As Altaf began shutting the wooden door, his heart heavier than ever, Samir called out and handed him the very last letter to Firdaus.

Then, as if from the heavens above, a dupatta, maroon cotton, lathered in Firdaus's smell and tears, fell upon his head. *It's not what you want,* the gesture said, *but it's all I can give.* He turned around and saw her—his paradise, his decade of love—helpless, swimming in tears, collarbones jutting out, hair out of place and head alarmingly naked without the dupatta.

Samir said nothing, but his eyes betrayed everything. Silently, he begged Firdaus to be courageous, to be defiant of her family's wishes and grant herself a lifetime of happiness. But he was asking for the unaskable. Some things were impossible. That day, two hearts broke, like the fragments of a newly divided land.

Yet some part, some vital part of him, would remain with the woman he loved, without her even knowing that she was in possession of it. Then maybe one day, a long time from now, this part of him would gently unfurl over her skin like ittar, drift into her memory and settle there like it belonged.

The mid-morning sun followed Samir as he dragged himself to the ittar shop, hoping for it to have survived intact. A ghostly cloud of gray and black still rose from Shahalmi. Carelessly, the perfumer walked down the middle of a deserted Anarkali Bazaar. Drained of life and unafraid of death, he fumbled with his keys and unlocked the door.

A familiar combination of smells greeted him. Roses, jasmine, vanilla, cloves, vetiver, lavender, neem. But everything was different, everything was a memory, everything had become a faint reflection of some other moment. He recalled how his father had hung up the black-and-white photograph from the first day Samir joined the shop in 1937, and walking up to the cash counter, he took it off the wall. Blowing a sheet of dust off of it, he rubbed the happy faces with his thumb. Who would have known that in ten years' time, all happiness would cease to exist.

He tucked the photograph underneath his arm and stepped farther in. He remembered his mother by the bell jars in the center of the shop, lifting each one every day and refreshing the linen cloths with perfume. Walking through the unlit shop, he lovingly touched all the items that his family had once made. There was so much beauty in this fragrant world that his uncle had dreamed to life. Who would populate this world now? At the tap outside the atelier, he washed all the filth, blood, and debris off his body. Cupping his hands under the running water, he quenched his thirst. And for the first time that day, when he inhaled the world around him, somehow it smelled of nature alone. He breathed in the dry earth, smelling dusty beets and unglazed earthenware cups.

Samir unlocked the atelier, and a myriad of smells assaulted him. For months, the altar of delights had remained untouched, each bottle secure in its place, each tool left exactly where it had been. The only new item was the suitcase containing the Vij family's treasures. Using a heap of linen cloth as a pillow, Samir stretched out on the floor and fell into a deep sleep.

When he awoke, a thousand shards of colored light rained down on him, reflected from the empty glass bottles lined along the window. He was drenched in sweat and his head was pounding. Surprisingly calm for a man who had lost everything, Samir gathered his bearings, reminding himself that nothing of the day before had been a dream. All promises of the future had been fractured; all life had become unrecognizable.

He reached into his pocket, retrieved his wallet, and extracted a black-and-white passport-sized photograph. Its corners had been creased, but the face of the illuminator still retained its splendor. He traced his finger-nail across her dupatta, along the embroidered neckline of her kurta, over the dark til on her chin. Staring at Firdaus's face, Samir toyed with the idea of destroying the photograph. As tears stung his eyes, he shoved it back into the wallet. Perhaps they were both cowards in their own way.

There was nothing left for him in Lahore. Family, home, land, and love had all been seized. Ritualistically, he took each ingredient bottle from the organ and smelled it, inhaling deeply, as if for the very last time. Some he would take, and the rest he would abandon. He found Vivek's traveling apothecary, with compartments to hold perfume bottles, and be-gan to stack his most beloved, one by one. He packed every perfume that his uncle had composed in vilayat, his masterpiece *Amrit,* all the accords they had made together, and the tuberose ittar for Firdaus.

Opening the leather suitcase his family had packed just last month, Samir carefully added the framed photograph from 1937, along with the broken items he had collected from Vij Bhawan. Then, breaking open his uncle's sacred drawer, he extracted, hesitantly and reverently, his note-books from vilayat, and placed them in, along with his uncle's case of handheld tools and his own perfume journals.

Samir picked up Firdaus's dupatta and smelled it. His weakness con-quering reason, he folded it into the suitcase as well. Looking around the deserted shop, he now felt alone, completely and utterly alone. Mo-mentarily, he thought of the crook of his elbow, and how his mother had offered it to him as an island tucked away from the world of smell. He could have never imagined that one day, he would become an island him-self, stranger to a city he called home. A desolate sense of incompleteness settled over him as he walked out of the shop for the very last time, and into the unfittingly vibrant sunshine.

# PART THREE

# 25

# Are You There, Can You Hear Me?

Samir bhai." Ehsan gently shook him out of sleep. "Uthiye, wake up."

The perfumer awoke to find the teenager holding a glass of water in his hands. He handed it to him, along with a handkerchief. Beads of perspiration trailed down Samir's face and neck.

*The fire, the debris, the heat*—he had been dreaming again.

Samir pulled his body into a seated position. "Shukriya, Ehsan."

He wiped his face and gulped down the cold water. Morning had broken and Lahore was nowhere in sight. A month had passed since he'd been in Delhi, and still his days were colored by flames. All this time, he'd felt as though his nose was deceiving him, and despite being the bearer of so many losses, it was this that truly devastated Samir. Unable to depend on his nose, he wondered whether moments of great sadness and abandon could betray our senses. Nothing smelled the same anymore, except Firdaus's dupatta. But he was certain that by now he'd memorized the fragrance to such an extent that it needn't have been present for him to feel its presence.

Before leaving Lahore in June—after the fire, after the separation, after everything had been lost—Samir had sought out the one person he still trusted. He had collected his meager belongings from the perfumery and walked through a deserted Anarkali to Mushtaq chacha's home. *Delhi,* the old man had suggested, *go to Delhi, my son.* Many decades ago, Som Nath's father had helped his, and now, with Samir at his doorstep, Mushtaq Alam paid off his debt in full. So, suitcase in one hand, and the address of Mushtaq chacha's cousin in the other, the perfumer had boarded a train to Delhi.

Despite the Partition line not having been announced, Delhi was already teeming with refugees. Ehsan, Mushtaq chacha's nephew, had received Samir at the station, and as they rode home on a tanga, Samir was struck by old Delhi's likeness to Lahore. Similar mosques dotted the landscape, the labrythine streets reminiscent of the ones he'd left behind. Lahore was somehow embedded within Delhi, and it was this very fact that would eventually unravel Samir.

For a while, he kept to himself, just as his uncle had when he returned from the war. Ehsan's family would inquire about what had happened, or what the situation in Lahore was like, but Samir could say nothing. Yet in his mind, he would replay the night over and over. What if he hadn't snuck out, what if there hadn't been a fire, what if there were no riots, what if there was no talk of Partition, what if, what if, what if. Eventually, to distract himself, he began to make himself useful around the house or pick up odd jobs around Chitli Qabar. The vials of perfume lay unopened in his suitcase. They would remain that way for as long as he could help it, for perfume was a language into a past he was not ready to relive or revive.

And yet, much against his wishes, each morning he would wake up thinking about Firdaus, and each night, looking up at the sky, he would invite her into his dreams. *Are you there?* he once whispered to the moon after Ehsan's family had gone to sleep. *Can you hear me?* But no answer came, and Samir eventually fell asleep with Firdaus's maroon dupatta swathed across him. Hints of roses, oranges, vanilla, and soot were all subsumed under the newest addition to the odor of love—salty tears.

※

Meanwhile, across the northern plains of Hindustan, the calligrapher stood on the mountain of rubble that had once been Vij Bhawan. All the buildings around it had been destroyed, their insides ruthlessly exposed, wooden skeletons standing bare. Crumbled walls and ceilings had been cleared, along with the corpses excavated from under the debris. On the morning after the fire, Altaf had watched the dark, dense cloud suspended above the non-Muslim locality in horror as he walked to the mosque for fajr, and Firdaus had awoken to bits of black soot plastered against her window, carried there by the hot summer air. It had been a few weeks since, but still the air felt singed.

Having located the house, Altaf had entered its ruined premises and imagined what a grand haveli it had once been. Inevitably, he thought of Samir and wondered where the boy, alone and orphaned, could have gone. As guilt arose, he held his hands ceremoniously out to the heavens and asked for forgiveness.

"*Ho sakey,*" he spoke to the open sky, "*toh maaf kar dena, dost.* I wish that I had found the courage to help you, to hide you, to change the course of this fate. Nothing I will ever do or say will right what has been wronged, but wherever you are now, I beg you, desperately, to forgive me, my friend." He took a deep breath in and looked around one last time before walking out of Vij Bhawan and to the ittar shop in Anarkali Bazaar.

There was no logical explanation for why Altaf's feet carried him to the places once inhabited by the Vij family. He had, after all, driven away its last surviving member. But in the abandoned shop, he allowed the perfumed air to embrace him, hoping to expunge the weight he carried, with little luck. Altaf moved like a ghost through the rows of deserted glass bottles, guilt and regret gathering with every step.

Every now and then he'd pick up a vial, jasmine, shamama, marigold, carrot oil, lavender, rose—their first encounter—the unmissable rose. He'd hold each vial up to the light and read the labels that he and Firdaus had made together a decade ago. He shuddered as sweat trickled down the back of his black kurta, and picking up the item that his friend had once been desperately fixated on, the calligrapher walked out of the ittar shop with the portable radio under his arm.

Once home, Altaf walked up to the roof to find Firdaus squeezing water out of the freshly washed lace table mats and hanging them up to dry. Still not allowed to go back to college, she had become a bird in a cage, a prisoner in her own home. Obediently, she carried out task after task, for later that evening, Zainab's brother, Muhammad, would be arriving from Delhi with his family, including Fahad, Firdaus's betrothed.

Altaf walked up to the clothes string and placed the radio on the ground. It made a dull metallic sound against the cement.

"I went to Shahalmi," he announced, but Firdaus continued monotonously squeezing, airing and draping the lace.

"Everything is finished," he added, watching her silhouette move behind the wall of lace. She had not spoken to him since the day after the fire. Still, Altaf persisted. "*Sab khatam,* Firdaus, there's nothing left," he said, and then, in a voice barely audible, "I don't know why I thought I would find Samir in the shop in Anarkali, but there is no one there either. It is only full of ghosts."

Through the delicate lace eyelets in the mats, he caught a glimpse of her, green eyes downcast, face impervious. Not once did she look up, not once did her fingers stop moving, not even at the mention of the perfumer.

"Firdaus!" Zainab called out from downstairs. "Come help with the gosht, please. You must learn how to cook it. And we must lay the extra beds for tonight before bhai jaan arrives!"

"Ji, Ammi, I'm coming," she called out, and then, picking up the empty metal bucket, she held it against her body, adjusted her dupatta, and, without so much as a single word to her father, walked away.

# 26

# Freedom, and Partition

When the month of August finally arrived, rumor and riot began to engulf Delhi, as they once had Lahore. Newspapers had been publishing projections of where the final border might fall, deliberating over how much of Hindustan would be carved out to become Pakistan. Afraid of being on the wrong side of the border, Muslim families began exiting Delhi, heading either to the train station or to Purana Qila refugee camp, where they were assured they'd be safer than in their neighborhoods. The homes they left behind were soon occupied by the Hindu and Sikh migrants, and the businesses they abandoned were adopted by those looking to start fresh.

Ehsan's family, however, like millions of other Muslims, had decided to remain in Delhi, their loyalty bound to the land their ancestors had been born on and buried in. As they exchanged passionate words of patriotism and allegiance to their homeland, watan, Samir's displaced heart would find its way back to Som Nath.

At the stroke of midnight on August 15, 1947, as Samir listened to Pandit Nehru deliver his first prime ministerial speech on the radio, independent India awoke to life and freedom. Incidentally, it was also the Islamic holy month of fasting, and within Ehsan's household, August 15 was celebrated not only as independence, but also as the Prophet's Night of Destiny. Fleetingly, Samir's thoughts turned toward Altaf and the festival of Eid, just a few days away. Each year, generous portions of seviyan, kheer, biryani, and sweet almond sherbet would be sent across, as tradition, from the Khan house to the perfumery. But so many things had now been driven to dissolution.

Over the following days, the newspapers were crowded with declarations of independence and sovereignty, stories of migration and outlines of the new border. On one such evening, Samir sat at a chai shop in Chitli Qabar, listening to the radio. Several men had gathered round, all paying close attention to the broadcast, wondering what side of the border their ancestral villages would fall in.

"Gurdaspur, India . . . Lahore, Pakistan . . . Amritsar, India . . . Nankana, Pakistan . . . Calcutta, India . . . Chittagong, Pakistan," the voice on the radio crackled out, followed by an eruption of whispers all around. The landmass of undivided British India was now an India sandwiched between two Pakistans. Muslim-majority areas had been given to India, Buddhist hill tracts fell in Pakistan, the birthplace of the first Sikh guru lay separated from worshippers in a now-Muslim-majority land. Parts of Punjab in the west and Bengal in the east, where there had long been a marriage of religions, remained shrouded in misinformation and rumor. *To stay or to flee.* Even refugees who had arrived in Delhi came bearing little information. They had braved destruction, arson, murder, rape, and riots, had walked for miles and boarded trains toward a new life, but few understood the new order.

Through the chatter, the Muslim owner of the tea stall called out to Samir, whose steaming earthenware cup sat undrunk in his hands. "You have come from there, na?" he asked, offering the young man a flaky fan pastry. "What is happening? This news-shews, gormint-shormint, Jinnah, Gandhi, Nehru, I don't understand. Why is the country being divided?"

What was the answer to this question? Samir said nothing.

"Will we all have to leave?" the chai-wallah asked. His family had lived in Chitli Qabar for generations, his ancestors were buried in Delhi, his great-grandfather had witnessed the twilight of Mughal rule, his father had started this tea stall.

But Samir had no answer. He had become like the wind, idly carried around by life. Similar to his uncle, who had continued to listen to the broadcasts of the Second World War day after day, obsessive and dazed, Samir, too, stared ahead and listened to the frequency, uttering not a word of reason or comfort.

A transfer of population, which had never been officially discussed or announced, occurred virtually overnight. Driven by force, coercion, fear, and, at times, even by choice, Hindus and Sikhs fled to India, and Muslims to Pakistan. Around Chitli Qabar, refugees lay wounded and hungry, some cradling the dead, others mourning them. They arrived in caravans with or without family, with or without luggage, some having left children behind, some having watched them die before their eyes. No matter how many stories of horror and sadness Samir overheard, the sentiment remained the same—*Why did this happen? How did this happen? How could we have done this to one another?*

Punjab and Bengal were divided. Families, too, were divided. Happinesses and losses were divided. As Mushtaq chacha had prophesied, it seemed that only sadness was gained. The subcontinent, transformed, in a single night, into two self-governing dominions, with Delhi on one side as Indian, and Lahore on the other as Pakistani.

The British government hastily departed and bequeathed the people of the subcontinent with azaadi, freedom. At night, as Samir ran his hands over the framed black-and-white photograph of the Vij men at the perfumery, he pondered the meaning of this freedom. A word that was once Som Nath's dream and now Samir's reality had become devoid of all meaning. An empty sound. There was no freedom to be found in his heart, or in his voice, or in the stories of refugees around him.

‚ƒ

Kilometers away in Pakistan, on the first day of its independence, Firdaus awoke at dawn to the sound of the azaan. No one had been allowed to leave the house for days, and lorries drove around, announcing that the city remained under curfew. She had heard of the locked havelis of Hindus and Sikh families who had fled in fear and haste, leaving everything intact within, with innocent hopes that one day they'd be able to return home. On many such abandoned, half-incinerated buildings, posters reading *This building is now a property of Pakistan* had been pasted, and Indian currency overstamped with the words *Government of Pakistan* was now in circulation. The word *Pakistan* was still gaining meaning and filling into its partitioned shape.

Quietly, Firdaus crept out of bed, careful not to wake Saira and Sitara, her twin cousins and soon-to-be sisters-in-law from Delhi, who were staying in her room. As the sun rose, she looked out her window and wondered about the sky beyond the visible sky—past the delicate pinkness, wisps of sunlight yellow and powder blue—where Samir had promised her that there'd always be a place for them. That sky seemed paler, withered, farther away than ever now.

Firdaus understood that some things were far beyond her will and control. Life would now be dictated by the politics of nation and community. Her land and his land would now be different. Her history and the one he would forge would now lie on separate sides of an unnatural, man-made border.

She would be on this side, and he would be on that.

‚ƒ

In late 1947, Mushtaq Alam wrote to his family in Delhi, asking if the now twenty-year-old Samir had resumed work at a perfumery. But for the last several months, the young man had deliberately distanced himself from the world of fragrance, instead picking up all kinds of work from selling coal at the train station to selling fountain pens in Chandni Chowk market, earning a meager living. Encouraged by his uncle's letter, Ehsan took the perfumer to visit the Gulabsingh Johrimal shop that had distilled and supplied the evocative ittar kadamba to Rashid Al-Asghar in Dabbi Bazaar. Samir followed him through the lanes of Dariba Kalan, until a strong stench overpowered his nose. Instead of roses, sandalwood, and frangipani, Samir smelled waste and the odor of unwashed, ragged bodies. He left immediately, leaving a confused Ehsan behind.

After months of misery, Samir wished desperately to shed off the oldest layers of his skin. He needed to divest himself of Lahore, to discard childhood, to peel off love, to remove all the known landscapes. And to do so, he would need to get as far away as possible from everything familiar. He considered finding Savitri's relations who had settled in Shimla, or Som Nath's side of the family in Amritsar. But in his heart, he knew he could only begin life again in a place that knew nothing about him or his world.

In the early weeks of 1948, he traveled by train to Bombay and found himself amidst the herds of people who had migrated there from various parts of Sindh. They crowded the docks, homeless and helpless, echoing the young perfumer's own predicament. Once again, Mushtaq Alam came to his rescue, helping to find accommodation with an old friend while Samir waited for travel documents and a berth on the next available ship westward out of India. The vessel would get him across the black waters to Britain, and from there, he'd find passage to France—the only other place, apart from Lahore, that his uncle had talked about with fondness.

It was in Bombay that he heard news of Gandhi's assassination, and watched the last British troop ship carrying the First Battalion of the

Somerset Light Infantry back home through the Gateway of India. Then, weeks later, ticket in hand, Samir stood at the Bombay docks, waiting to board the brand-new RMS *Caledonia V,* vowing never to set foot again on the land that had taken everything from him except the breath in his lungs.

And just as Samir was making this unbreakable vow, Firdaus was being married to Fahad.

# 27

# Meeting the Ocean

For as long as he could recall, Samir had spent his childhood listening to stories of the ocean. Never having seen it, his imagination transported him only as far as Lahore's river Ravi. *Ah, but it is more than fifty Ravis put together,* his uncle had once said, arms outstretched as far as they would reach, trying to demonstrate its boundlessness. Vivek had promised his nephew that one day he would meet the ocean. Perhaps this was how it was always supposed to be, that the ocean—dark, mysterious, immeasurable, carrying men and their dreams across to foreign lands—was to be Samir's passageway to the depths of the past, and into the truth.

From the ship's railing, Samir looked down at all the families waving goodbye to the passengers, and felt a sudden tightness in his chest. But folding it into his stride, he proceeded toward his assigned cabin on the RMS *Caledonia V.* It would be a three-week journey from Bombay to Liverpool, stopping at Karachi, Aden, Port Said, and Gibraltar.

Samir had been assigned a shared cabin with two single berths, and found his cabinmate already unpacking his belongings. He looked to be in his mid-fifties, of average height and slim build, skin dark with a few

pockmarks on his cheeks, and graying hair. He was well-dressed in tailored pants with a tie and jacket, and the ease with which he settled in
made Samir believe he had traversed many an ocean before. Introducing
himself as Mr. Syed Ali and referring to Samir only as Mr. Vij, he said
nothing about what he did or his purpose of travel, but turned to his
newspaper, as Samir found his bearings. The cabin had just enough space
to move around and included a porthole, washbasin, chest of drawers,
mirror, wall-mounted fan, and flask of drinking water.

After all passengers had boarded and the baggage was stowed away,
the ship backed out of the dock and locked into the calm waters of the
Arabian Sea. Instinctively, Samir held on to the side of the bed, causing his
cabinmate to inquire whether it was his first voyage overseas. Soon after,
he asked whether Samir would like to join him on deck, and the young
perfumer gladly accepted. The pair walked up onto the wooden promenade, where several other passengers, a mix of Indian and British, had also
emerged from their cabins to explore the ship.

As Mr. Ali sat down at the verandah café and read his papers, reading
glasses perched on his nose, tendrils of smoke snaking up from his cigarette, Samir stood by the open railing. He was particularly struck by how
the massive ship cruised along the water as if weightless. Taking a deep
inhale of the salty ocean air, he watched as the landmass of India become
smaller and smaller, until it disappeared.

On the second night, Samir lay in his berth, unable to fall asleep. When
the ship left Bombay, the water had been calm, but as it approached Karachi, the ocean suddenly rumbled. Like always, his nose smelled out the
storm before it arrived, but rather than delight, this time his body was
filled only with fear. Quite unlike the one that graced his birthday each
year, this tempest smelled salty and brackish, metallic and mineral. As
the ship crashed into a wave, Samir sat up with a start. He looked over to
find Syed Ali fast asleep, breath rising and falling. Holding on to the side
of the cabin, Samir undid the clasps of his suitcase, retrieved the maroon

dupatta, brought it to his face, and inhaled. So sweet was the smell of roses that emerged, so seamless was the marriage of Firdaus's salty tears to the salt in the air, that Samir couldn't help but feel comforted by all his familiar ghosts.

Through the next day, the waters remained volatile and Samir experienced terrible seasickness. Mr. Ali had arisen early for breakfast and upon his return found Samir curled over in his bed, face pale. They hadn't exchanged many words, but the older man now came over with a small brass box.

"I always carry this with me." He handed over an imli pod. "It will help to ease the nausea."

Samir sat up with a groan and broke the hard tamarind shell open to reveal the soft, pulpy inside. Out of habit, he smelled the tart fruit and then placed in his mouth, sinking into the nostalgically tangy taste. If he closed his eyes now, he was certain he'd be able to see the halwai Bhagwan Das seated on a low stool in Anarkali Bazaar, overseeing a large cauldron of bubbling oil. Behind him, an assembly line of boys would be filling a mixture of mashed potatoes, spices, and vegetables into doughy envelopes of fresh samosas, ready to slip into the oil and fry until deliciously golden and flaky. The air would be saturated with the aroma of pickles, onions and peas, cumin seeds, green chilies, and mouthwateringly tangy imli chutney. Home, he realized, would remain the hardest thing to unlearn.

"Are you by yourself?" Mr. Ali asked, breaking Samir's daydream.

His question was simple, but it was followed by a silence filled only by the sound of crashing waves.

"I am alone," Samir said finally.

The gentleman's eyebrows rose. "And where is your family?"

"They are . . . no more," he admitted. "I have no family, no home, and I have now left my land behind." Then, in a voice that betrayed his loss, he repeated, "I am alone."

Mr. Ali's brown eyes looked into Samir's. He didn't inquire further, but seemed to have understood the presence of a deep and profound pain.

"To be by oneself is the hardest condition, Samir," he said. "It can make us feel small and isolated, particularly when it is not of our choosing. Bichhinno, we say in Bengali. And you have chosen water to be the carrier of your disconnectedness. It is a way to remain untethered from the rest of the world."

The tightness in Samir's heart returned, but he wasn't sure if it was seasickness or sadness.

"With time, even history recedes into memory. You will see, we forget everything."

*When?* Samir wanted to ask. *When will I forget everything?*

Mr. Ali continued, "I was very young when I was forced into work to provide for my family. Arduous work, the kind no child should ever have to do. It took me far away from home, away from Sylhet, to live on many oceans and lands, and encounter many misfortunes. As a boy, I used to have nightmares, but as the years have passed, there are no more nightmares to dream, no more history to haunt me." He got up, brass box of tamarind pods still in his hand, and repeated, "Remember, in time we forget everything."

Every day after breakfast, while Mr. Ali spent his hours in the library or writing room, Samir would walk circuits of the entire ship, settling down on the sun deck. With nothing to keep him occupied, he would look out at the ocean view and think about the journey ahead. But inevitably, by midday, the chairs beside him would be occupied by a group of older Indian ladies, dressed impeccably in saris and shawls, knitting nonstop. Some groups played cards, others deck tennis or shuffleboard, and there was Scottish dancing in the afternoons. Dinner was served in two installments—an informal one at 6 p.m., and a more formal meal where passengers were expected to be appropriately dressed at 8 p.m. The young man more often than not chose the informal dinner, which had abundant choice of European or Indian food. Afterward, he would return to the deck, this time to take in the boundlessness of the starry night sky. As the days passed, just as Mr. Ali had prophesied, Samir's thoughts of Partition began to be consumed by the sea.

⚶

Two weeks into their journey, the *Caledonia* entered the Suez Canal, and a sandy landscape appeared on both sides, with the occasional palm tree. The ship anchored at Port Said, and a small crowd of bumboats approached the ship, selling a range of souvenirs at bargained prices that would be thrown up to the rails. An Egyptian magician called Gully Gully Man came on board to entertain the children with tricks like blowing out fire from his mouth and making objects disappear, all to cries of "Gully, gully, gully!" Samir and Mr. Ali, who were observing the scene from one end of the promenade deck, now turned to face the beautiful blue waters of the Nile. Wiping the sweat off his forehead, Samir patted down the short beard he'd grown out in the last few months. He wondered if Firdaus would recognize him this way.

Suddenly, the wind swept a sheet of dust toward the ship, causing Samir to rub his eyes vigorously. The salty air had made them scratchy, and now the sand stung even more. There were two other times his eyes had felt this sting—once on his first day at the distillery when Ousmann had lit the rose-filled deghs, and then again the day Vij Bhawan had burned down. Closing his eyes tight, he began to rub them harder, to remove the sand but also to abrade his memory.

To his surprise, Mr. Ali chuckled and pulled Samir's hands away from his face. He held up his palms as if to say, *Wait,* and then, from the inside pocket of his coat, took out a tiny, cylindrical object just a few inches in height, with a glass dropper.

It was a perfume bottle.

"Wh-what is this?" Samir stammered.

"Oh, it is only rosewater, gulabjal, but it will calm the itching in your eyes. Yet another thing I have learned not to travel without."

Samir gingerly reached for the bottle. He studied it from all sides, holding it up to the light, tapping on the glass with his fingernails, and then placing it on the railing between them, as his uncle had once done many years ago with the tuberose bottle at the river Ravi. Then, Samir opened the bottle, releasing the sweet aroma of rosewater.

All at once, his senses were overwhelmed. He thought of emperor Babur's four daughters, each named after the tender rose, Nur Jahan's rosy bath oil, the blushing fields of Pattoki, Ousmann and his pink-tinted distillations, the many roses showered on Pandit Nehru as he rode through Anarkali Bazaar in 1929, the pressed rose as old as Samir, the fragrant courtyard of Wazir Khan mosque, Altaf and the *Alf Layla* manuscript, and Firdaus—*Firdaus, Firdaus, Firdaus*—always smelling of the rose, for the rose could never hide.

Opening his eyes wide, Samir squirted in two drops of the heavenly rosewater. Immediately, his pupils felt refreshed.

"You are a strange young man." Mr. Ali looked at him curiously, and then, turning back to the horizon, narrated his own tale of family and perfume. "When I left home for the very first time, my walida gave me a vial of rosewater. She grew up in Calcutta, near a large flower market where roses were found in abundance. But after she married and came to Sylhet, no roses grew around our house. In memory of the flower, she named my younger sister Roza." He chuckled sadly. "And then, when I was to leave, she begged an old toothless hakim to bring her a vial of rosewater, and gave it to me. She claimed that pure rosewater could cure anything . . . seasickness, rashes, cuts, and fevers. Even a broken heart."

Samir turned to look at Mr. Ali, who continued to look out ahead. Then, touching his face where the rosewater had trailed down from his eyes like tears, Samir said, ". . . everything except a broken heart. Rosewater can cure everything but that."


Later that afternoon, while Mr. Ali was touring the pyramids of Egypt with a group of passengers, Samir returned to the cabin. Placing his uncle's leather case on the bed, he gazed at it for a while before trailing his fingers along the hard leather corners and the cold metal clasps. Grateful to be alone, he opened the case.

Within seconds, the ittar shop filled the cabin. Wisps of fragrant air formed the foundational columns, wooden shelves, stone walls, and glass windows. Trails of perfume adhered to the carpeted floors and bed linen. Was that ambergris? And how did traces of lavender crawl into the suitcase? He did not remember packing it. He smelled jasmine, carrot essence, cedarwood, and ambrette musk, opening the bottles with both hunger and sadness. Then, closing his eyes, he surrendered to the delight of his old craft, for this was not an indulgence he would allow himself often. If thoughts of the ittar shop flooded his memory, then the fire was not far behind. There remained just too much pain in perfumery.

⚜

"Look." Mr. Ali pointed to where the different waters married each other. They had reached the narrow Strait of Gibraltar, where the sea met the ocean under an orange-pink sunset. The shallow Mediterranean basin held saltier water than the Atlantic, and as these two waters passed through the narrow strait, they caused the ship to roll over merging, undulating pulses.

Samir held on to the railing as the waves rocked the ship. "Can you determine a border over water?" When Mr. Ali said nothing, he continued, "*Are* there any borders over water? When every outline is swallowed by waves and tides, how is a border marked, and how do we know when we've crossed it? A rising sun illuminates both sides of the land equally, a wave rolls from one body of water to another, a bird flies over many lands without . . ." His sentence trailed off. "Only humans must conform to borders. Even in freedom, they are never really free."

"Where are you from, Samir?"

There were only days left until their arrival in Liverpool, and no real personal details had been exchanged between the cabinmates.

"From nowhere," Samir spat out, and, immediately regretting it, said, "Lahore . . . I am from Lahore."

"Land of legends and historic kingdoms."

". . . and of Partition."

"Ah," Mr. Ali said, as if he finally understood what Samir had been circling around. "Partition has awarded Sylhet to East Pakistan, where my mother is, while her family continues to live in Calcutta, across the new border. The same people, the same blood, separated to either side."

Samir bit his lower lip. "And you? Where do you live?"

"I have decided to remain untethered," Mr. Ali said. "This is why I love the water. Here, you don't *need* to determine where something ends and something else begins. Water is borderless."

That evening, convinced that Mr. Syed Ali was a man with resources and contacts across the world, Samir revealed that he wished to travel further on to France but didn't know how. Asking no questions, his cabinmate produced a well-creased document from his briefcase. It was folded several times over, but when Samir unfolded it, the entire world looked up at him. Cities had been marked out in black ink, some annotated with dates, others connected to each other by the routes of trains and ships; notes were scribbled in various corners, and at the very top was a tally of years. This precious document was Mr. Ali's life, from his very first voyage to the one he was currently on. With his fingers, Samir traced the world, touching city after city after city.

"Paris," Mr. Ali said, placing his fingertip on the French capital. It had been labeled with the year *1916* and then again *1943,* revealing that he'd been there during both world wars. "I have a friend, Patel, who will help you get settled."

In the many months that had passed since the perfumer left Lahore, this was the closest Samir felt to a kinship, to what he had lost. Carefully folding the map back into its creases, he returned it to its owner. Mr. Ali looked at the document for a few seconds, and then, with a deep sigh, relinquished the possession.

"Keep it as a way to remember," he said.

At the port of Liverpool, the perfumer and the mysterious gentleman parted ways, never to encounter one another again. Sitting on a bench beside his suitcase and traveling apothecary, Samir Vij brought his forefinger to his nose and ran it along the bridge. Then he brought his hands to his nose and smelled them deeply, making sure to inhale in the crevasses between fingers. The warm, earthlike aroma he had embarked with from Hindustan had been replaced completely with an aquatic, mineral odor. Grainy, fishy, salty, moldy.

Was there any purpose in reminiscing about something which could never be retrieved? All his memories—those he had lived, those he had inherited—seemed to now possess the flatness of a failed perfume. For the longest time, Samir had felt the death of his family and separation from Firdaus as the beginning of his solitary life. But sitting on a lonely dock in a lonely city far away from anything familiar, Samir understood that *now* he was truly alone.

# 28

# A Land for Our People

Firdaus lay awake as her husband slept peacefully. They'd been married for three weeks, but she remained reserved, even when they were alone.

After the fire, things had progressed quickly—her wedding fixed, her trousseau assembled, her future decided, and all mention of the perfumer forbidden. Zainab and Nadira had together spent weeks hand-stitching Firdaus's bridal outfit, a pink silk kurta and gharara, with chaandi work across the dupatta. From her own bridal trousseau, Zainab bequeathed to her daughter a jewelry set that had once belonged to her mother, handmade in gold, with ruby and firoza stones. As refugees continued to migrate across the new border, the nikah was a quiet affair in the spring of 1948, in the presence of family with an imam to legalize the ceremony. Following that, Firdaus moved into the home that Fahad's parents had rented in Bhati Gate.

It was made clear from the very beginning that Zainab's brother and now Firdaus's father-in-law, Muhammad, was uncomfortable with women of the family going out to work or study, so nineteen-year-old Firdaus dropped out of college. She had not accompanied her father to the studio since the Shahalmi fire, and barely conversed with him at all, apart from formal greetings. In her absence, Altaf had no choice but to hire an assistant from his group of students, which made him think of Samir. Not that he needed a reason, for the young man and his family remained on the calligrapher's mind, a constant source of guilt and remorse.

Now, Firdaus turned toward Fahad and watched his breath rise and fall in the darkness. He was a tall and lean man who slept on his back, with one hand by his stomach and the other behind his head. He had no beauty marks on his face and kept a short, neatly trimmed beard. His nose was sharp like his mother's, his eyes light honey brown like his father's. She remembered him from their childhood, flying kites on the rooftop of his home in Delhi, or buying jalebis for his sisters and Firdaus.

Biting her lip, she turned away from him and, when the moon was at its brightest, crawled out of bed and onto the stone floor. After a few seconds of contemplation, she removed the gold wedding band from her finger and gently placed it on the floor beside her. Then, using both hands, she extracted a heavy box out from the trunks that held her trousseau, and wiped the dust off from its surface with her dupatta. Bringing both palms to her cheeks, she stared at the unopened box, and then up at Fahad, who was completely unaware of her history. Then, in a single, soundless motion, she opened it.

Dried leaves, a garland of brittle jasmine, a bottle of ittar, and rows and rows of letters stared up at her. Three hundred and eighty-eight letters, each one individually folded and addressed to *Firdaus Khan* in simple, unornamented Urdu. She longed to reach out and touch Samir's handwriting, imprint herself with his words, but her guilt would not permit it. She had no idea where he had gone, whether he was even alive. And yet here he was, shrunk to the size of a cardboard box, into the crisp mustard petal of an old jasmine garland, into the liquid of a perfume, into the rectangle of a folded love letter.

Tears welled up in her eyes as she realized that her whole world was constructed of paper. Delicate, fragile, beautiful. But this was the quintessential thing about paper—a single flame and the entire world was reduced to ashes.

⚜

"*Allah ka shukar hai* we left Delhi before the riots," Firdaus's father-in-law, Muhammad, said to Altaf, holding his palms up to the heavens. It was Firdaus's first visit to her parents' house as a married woman, and the men were sitting in the baithak, while the women prepared dinner in the kitchen. "So many Muslim families are still stranded in refugee camps, waiting for a train, a bus, *any* form of transport across to Pakistan."

"But many Muslims have chosen to remain in Hindustan, haven't they?" Altaf inquired. "Far more in number than have come to Pakistan."

Muhammad tsked in response. "But how will that work, bhai jaan? In the long run, will they be safe, will be they be cared for, will they not be made targets in a nation with a Hindu majority? Pakistan was created for Muslims, it is *our* nation, where *our* people can practice their traditions, customs, and religion with freedom. Take Lahore, for example, there used to be Hindus and Sikhs on every corner, in every shop, in every government office. Where are they now? They have fled to Hindustan because they know it is a land that will take care of them, a land that is theirs. Just like Pakistan is ours."

Firdaus overheard this from the kitchen and looked out. Her father said nothing in response, making no mention of the riots that had caused their neighbors to flee, of the fires that had violently smoked them out, but she watched as his face tightened. If decorum allowed, she would have interrupted her father-in-law to say that Lahore without its Hindus and Sikhs felt like a body missing vital organs. But she remained in the kitchen, a silent new bride, head covered with her dupatta and ears adorned with annoyingly large gold earrings. She looked down at her hands, once painted with henna and now fading, and noticed the way her wedding band sat on her finger. No longer could she recognize her hands; no longer could she recognize herself.

Then, a new voice emerged from the baithak. "We are fortunate to have found refuge in Pakistan, Abba jaan. But aren't the Muslims of India only of a different faith than Hindus or Sikhs, not of a different upbringing or soil? Were we not all once Indians?"

Firdaus peeked out to see her husband enter the discussion. Upon hearing his words, she felt the skin across her arms tighten, and her heart begin to pound.

"Did Bakshi chacha not keep the keys to our house, promising to safeguard it? Did he not transport us to the train station under the cover of darkness? Was he not the same man whose wife packed parathas and achaar for the journey?" There was a sentimentality in Fahad's voice that could not be found in his father, but had once resided in his father-in-law.

"Of course, beta, without Bakshi sahib's help, we might never have made it across safely," Muhammad agreed. "I am lucky to have known him since our college days. He was a good friend, but he is a Sikh, after all, and in desperate times, we all look out for our own first. See, even Gandhi, Nehru, Patel were not able to keep us safe. Muslims were unable to survive inside their own homes—brutally murdered, wounded, taking shelter in refugee camps. Outside of Delhi, there were mass burials, whole families massacred together as they attempted to flee the city, I have heard the news, I knew men who are no longer alive. Beta, you are young, take my word—we may be born from the same soil, but there *is* a difference. There always has been."

There was a taut moment of silence before Fahad finally said, "Forgive me, Abbu, I have left too many friends and too many memories behind."

Firdaus watched as Muhammad reached out to pat his son's cheek in a way that seemed to be equal parts love and condescension. In the kitchen, her mother and mother-in-law were stirring deghs of richly seasoned meat and fluffing the pilaf. Turning her attention to the raita, Firdaus gently stirred the yogurt and folded in dried mint, coriander, and salt, sprinkling the pomegranate seeds unconsciously into illumination patterns. When she finished, she felt the smallest ray of hope.

⚘

The next day, Altaf rose before dawn to offer fajr and then, quite unlike himself, returned to bed rather than beginning his day. Zainab had barely stirred, neither when he left nor when he returned. Curled on his side, the calligrapher thought back to the previous night, when his daughter had come home for the first time with her new family. Unsurprisingly, the warmth that Samir had so tenderly cultivated over the span of a decade had frozen over within mere months. Instead, Firdaus now carried an air of traditional formality, as if she were entering not her own childhood home but that of a complete stranger.

He recalled how Nadira had taken a bit of kohl from the corner of her eye and, with it, made a black dot on the side of Firdaus's face. Nazar battu, an intentional blemish to ward off the evil eye from all perfection. "*Mashallah*," she'd complimented her new daughter-in-law, as Firdaus's eyes remained downcast.

With her departure from the Khan household, Altaf felt crushed under the weight of his actions. When the alliance with Fahad was decided, Firdaus had mutely agreed. During the assembling of her trousseau, she had picked nothing, relying entirely on Zainab's choice. Before the nikah, she had stood rigidly, allowing Saira and Sitara to drape the pink and silver embroidered dupatta across her head. She hadn't laughed or smiled or betrayed even a trace of emotion, but the family had mistaken this as merely the apprehensions of a new bride. Firdaus had spoken just once throughout the entire wedding ceremony—*Qubool hai,* she'd responded to the imam's question. *I accept.*

Trying to shake Firdaus's sustained silence out of his mind, Altaf turned to face his wife. He caressed her cheek, more out of habit than desire.

"*Salaam, Khan sahib,*" she whispered, still half asleep.

"*Salaam . . .*" he replied, distractedly.

"What's the matter, *kya hua?*" she asked.

For a few minutes, he said nothing. Zainab cradled his hand within hers, and opened her eyes. "*Bataiye,* tell me, what's wrong?"

"Firdaus," he began. "Did she seem . . . different to you last evening?"

Zainab tched. "Khan sahib, *aap bhi na,* how silly of you to worry over this! Firdaus is a married woman now. She has the responsibility of a husband and in-laws. And it's all still so new. Naturally, she will adhere to a certain decorum while around them."

Altaf nodded, but extracted his hand from her grasp. He wondered whether she was actually convinced of the words she was saying, whether the memory of the past few months never rose to the surface of her mind. Ever since the morning of the fire, a single question had been gnawing at Altaf's insides. Had he always known that the world would never allow Samir and Firdaus to be together? If so, he had never acted on this knowledge. He let their alliance continue, even gave his approval, and, in turn, acquired his daughter's trust. Trust that he should have found a way to uphold.

Often, he would return to the tale of Princess Zebunissa, and the ending that Zainab had always narrated to him—how it was no enemy or conqueror but her own father, Emperor Aurangzeb, who imprisoned her till death. Despite his deep love, he banished her to a life of captivity. Had Altaf not consigned Firdaus to a similar fate?

Throughout dinner, she had caught his eye but once, with a look he could not recognize. She was no longer his January child. Not the collector of leaves and love notes, nor the connoisseur of poetry and history. No, this was an altogether different person, mature and withdrawn, a woman of anger and regret, heartbreak and sorrow.

"Begum," he now called out to Zainab. She mumbled a low response, so he turned toward her and whispered, "Samir . . ."

Immediately, her gray eyes flew open. "So *that* is what this is all about. Well, what about Samir? He's gone, hasn't he? They've all gone to their Hindustan. Trying to take Lahore, too . . . imagine that." She scoffed. "Muhammad bhai was right, we should be glad to have Pakistan."

"Are you listening to yourself? *Kya keh rahi hain aap,* what are you saying?"

Altaf used to love that his wife never hid behind her words. But after witnessing the violence of Partition, Zainab wore her opinions like armor. Opinions that Altaf clearly differed on.

"I am not saying anything wrong, Khan sahib! All I'm saying is that this is no longer Hindustan." She sat upright and covered her head with her dupatta, enunciating her next words with great intention. "*Apna alag mulk,* our separate country. *Apna hissa, apni zameen, apna mazhab, apne log.* Our share, our land, our religion, our people. *Our people.*"

"Who is *ours?* Was Vij sahib not *ours?* Was Samir not *ours?* Was a decade of friendship not enough to make them *ours?* Look what happened to them. Look at what became of this city—the riots, the arson, the looting, the devastation. Look at what this Partition has done!" Altaf's voice was hoarse. He knew that there would be no resolution to this discussion, it was futile from the very beginning, but he needed to, at the very least, say the words out loud.

Zainab didn't respond. Standing up from the bed, she began to fold the blankets. "*Khwaab hi dekhte rahe aap,* you just keep dreaming, Khan sahib. Your idea of the world doesn't exist in *this* world."

Altaf sighed deeply. Though she might have been right, he preferred the idea of his world to the reality of this world. "Begum, I don't know where he is . . . Samir, I don't know where he is."

Letting the ends of the blanket fall to the ground, she shook her head. She pitied her husband, his idealism, his goodness. Even after he had made the right decision for Firdaus's future, he could not stand behind it.

Many years ago, when Zainab had first urged her husband to separate Firdaus and Samir, he had not only ignored her pleas but also belittled them. She wanted to remind him of this, to spit out that he could have prevented his daughter's heartbreak, but she couldn't inflict any more suffering on an already suffering man. In a gesture more intimate than the couple had engaged in in a long time, she climbed back on top of the bed and held her weeping husband in her arms.

"What happened to the Vijs was unthinkable. I wish it never to happen to anyone. But you couldn't have prevented it, and we couldn't have married Firdaus to Samir. You have always been an idealist, but even you know that, Khan sahib."

She tried to assure him that in time, Firdaus would find her happiness with Fahad, but Altaf knew this might never truly be. Though he allowed Zainab to comfort him and wipe his tears, he realized that they would never understand each other's point of view. An ideological tear had emerged between them, never to be sewn or repaired. Their own partition.

# 29

# To Leave a Beloved Behind

When Samir arrived at Gare du Nord, he was met by Patel, who seemed only a few years older than Mr. Ali but carried none of his mystique or refinement. A stout Gujarati man, he had traveled to Paris in the early years of the twentieth century to work for the Indian merchants and traders who dealt in luxury goods like jewelry and silks and had settled in the 9th arrondissement. By the 1930s, this population had all but left Paris, though Patel stayed on and eventually settled a stone's throw away from Gare du Nord, in an area known as La Chapelle or, more popularly, Little India, where he now owned a grocery shop.

"During the war, Paris saw curfews and food ration cards. Only potatoes and leeks in the market. Till this year, there was rationing of bread, and there remains shortage of oil, sugar, coffee, and rice," Patel told Samir as they walked through the streets. "But in 1940, millions of Parisians fled to escape the advancing German army. It was Paris's great exodus."

It was difficult to not be reminded of his own exodus, but Samir said nothing of it, and asked instead, "You didn't think to leave and go home?"

"Oh, dear boy." Patel laughed. "There was nowhere else *to* go. I have lived longer in Paris than I had in India. Now this is home." He tipped his hat to the city. "I remained here as sandbags barricaded the streets, I could hear the sounds of artillery fire in the distance, and when the city was finally occupied, German soldiers sipped espressos in our cafés, riding our métro. Paris was deserted of its residents, completely silent. But now the people have returned, along with new immigrants; there are Bretons in Saint-Denis, Algerians, Italians, Spaniards. Not many Indians anymore, but every now and then, a few find their way to La Chapelle." He turned and looked Samir up and down, taking in his now clean-shaven face, neatly combed hair, and tailored clothes. "Not like you, though."

As they walked through the streets, Samir looked up at the tall buildings, some damaged and weathered, others covered in places with soot, but all with identical windows and wooden shutters. These streets were unlike any that he'd seen growing up; they were cobbled, labeled, and had pavements with ornate lampposts on every corner. Fleetingly, he wondered whether his uncle had ever been here.

After a swift half-hour walk from the station, they arrived at an old building on rue Chaptal, where Patel had managed to secure a small studio apartment for the young man. The building, at least a century old, had a stone courtyard and a facade that had seen better days. But the elderly proprietress, Madame Blanchet, took to Samir immediately, recalling with fondness the gallant Indian soldiers who had arrived in France during the First World War. Samir was tempted to say that his uncle had been one such soldier, but stopped himself, for there wasn't much to tell about a history he knew nothing of.

His second-floor apartment, uninhabited since the war, had once belonged to a jazz musician. It was a comfortable space for a single person, with wooden floors and a kitchenette. There was a fireplace that hadn't been used for years, and the floral wallpaper was peeling in so many places that the discolored wall was visible beneath. A long corridor separated the toilet and bathroom from the living space. The apartment offered a single bed, table, chair, and wardrobe, all covered with a thick sheet of dust. But what appealed to Samir the most were the windows and the lush golden sunlight that would sweep through the apartment most of the day.

Once alone, he sat on the bed and opened his traveling apothecary. With both hands, Samir took out each vial, uncorking and smelling its contents. The bergamot oil and grapefruit accord reminded him of a day of discovery at the ittar shop; the rose evoked a conversation with his grandfather; the vetiver reminded him of the ayurvedic remedies concocted by his mother; the sandalwood belonged to his father and the ambrette seed to his uncle. Each vial was a solace, and for a while, Samir indulged in the familial habit of smelling and adorning, surrendering to fragrance as he'd been trained to do.

He cradled home, in the same way that he hoped it would cradle him in exile. For it would have to be *within* his heart, deep within the pumping, beating, fist-sized organ, that a new Lahore would need to somehow sprout. Using his handkerchief, he cleaned each glass vial and placed them back. Perfume was his past, not his future, he resolutely reminded himself as he stored the case on the top shelf of his wardrobe.

Samir now turned his attention toward the larger suitcase, inside which was the remainder of his life. He unpacked only his clothes and left all the remnants of Lahore inside. Firdaus's maroon dupatta, Som Nath's dried rose, Savitri's broken glass bangle, none were granted an audience, for they carried the weight of his guilt. The sole item the perfumer chose to display by his bedside was the photograph of Vivek, Mohan, and a ten-year-old Samir, taken in front of the ittar shop on the first day of his apprenticeship.

⚜

In Paris, Samir became a creature of habit, loyal to routine. Patel had helped secure him a job at a hospital as a porter, with the assurance that when he learned French, he would find better work. Each day, Samir walked to the Claude Bernard Hospital, where his duties included moving patients between wards and departments, lifting them from their beds for baths or tests, and transporting medical equipment, linen, blood, and other samples throughout the hospital. The medicinal odors and bodily stench in the building couldn't have been further from a perfumery. It was exhausting, labor-intensive work, but kept his mind occupied, so the sadness of the past hardly had a chance to filter in. After his shift, he would take pleasure in the quiet walk home, and on weekends, strolled all the way down to the river Seine and back, trying to acclimatize to his new habitat.

When 1949 opened, he had been in the city for six months. One evening, as he was climbing up the stairs to his apartment, Madame Blanchet stopped him to show an old edition of *L'Illustration* that she'd kept from 1931. The yellowing newspaper had an image of Gandhi at Gare de Lyon on the cover, on his way to the Second Round Table Conference in London. With pride, she recalled how she'd caught a glimpse of the Mahatma on the eve of his speech at the Magic City Dance Hall on the Left Bank. As she was speaking, it began to snow—Samir's first snowfall ever—and he stepped outside, arms childishly outstretched, and mouth open to the sky, swallowing the magical snowflakes. For the first time since he'd left Lahore, he felt youthful and unburdened, as snow fell like cotton on his shoulders and melted into his hair. Madame Blanchet, who by now had begun to care for the young man like her own son, remained at the threshold, laughing at the scene.

Later that evening, soft snow continued to fall, but nothing disturbed the stillness, apart from the mechanical ticking of the clock on Samir's bedside. He lay awake staring at the ceiling, Firdaus's dupatta in his hands. Maybe her aroma still vaguely clung to the weave, or maybe he simply imagined it, but the deeper he inhaled, the further back his memory took him. *The studio, the charcoal drawings during maghrib, Standard Restaurant, her laughter, her skin, the beauty spot on her chin, her pistachio eyes, the curtained window in June, the smell of fire, the glow of the golden mosque, the descending of the dupatta.* He took out her photograph from his wallet and stared into her eyes. They looked back, blank, mute. While all of Lahore lay banished in his suitcase, he had not the courage to part with this.

He turned his attention to the clock. *Tick, tick, tick.*

As it struck midnight, a new day was born. January 10.

"*Saalgirah mubarak, Firdaus,*" Samir whispered, wishing his beloved a happy birthday.

⚘

Ordinarily, there would have been a letter.

Written on lined paper, it would have expressed the deepest desires of a besotted heart. It would have included something more special than the regular weekly notes, like a sher or a ghazal—this was a birthday letter, after all. It would have been folded in half, tucked into an envelope, and slipped discreetly into her hand, or deposited into the basket under her window, to be drawn up and read. Most importantly, in careful Urdu alphabets, the envelope would have borne her name. From Samir's heart to his lips to the page, *Firdaus Khan.*

But a year and a half had passed, and not a single letter had arrived. Today, on her twentieth birthday, Firdaus opened the box of old letters and stared at their crisp corners, arranged in neat rows. Unread since his disappearance. Tucked beside them was the gold filigree bottle of ittar, which she removed and placed on the ground. Paying no attention to its glimmer, she shuffled through the letters, lingering over one from spring 1947.

Then in a hurried motion, she opened the envelope.

"Firdaus, I wish to be as profound as a poet or ornate like a painter"—she remembered this letter, remembered it well—"but I am only a perfumer, and my medium is invisible. It disappears into the air within seconds, disperses onto the skin like balm. And yet, to arrive at the creation of perfume, one requires the inspiration of something, someone permanent. Do you rememb—"

"Begum?" a voice called out before knocking on the closed door.

She shoved the letter back into its envelope and slid the box under the bed just as Fahad walked into the room. Finding her seated on the cold floor in birthday finery, her husband laughed and sat down beside her. She pulled her shawl tighter around her body and covered her naked head.

"What are you doing?" His eyes then landed on the ornate gold object. "What is this?"

Firdaus inhaled sharply.

"*Aapko yeh pasand hai?*" Fahad was surprised, for his wife never wore perfume. "Do you like ittar?"

"It–it's very old . . ." Firdaus began nervously, reaching out to take it from his hand. But before she could, he uncorked it, dispersing the tuberose aroma across the entire room.

Fahad closed his eyes and smiled. He looked so serene, just like Samir used to when he inhaled something of insurmountable beauty. Her husband swayed gently, just like Samir used to. Bringing the bottle up to his nose, he inhaled again, a deep and cavernous breath, just like Samir used to. Firdaus stared, paralyzed by the similarities, her pistachio eyes following Fahad's every move.

She continued to stare, but felt her body soften, its posture no longer defensive and uptight. The grasp over her shawl loosened, and the thick fabric fell down softly around her shoulders. "What does it smell like?"

Smiling at his wife, Fahad offered, quite unlike his reserved self, to apply some to her skin. She declined, but asked again, "What does it smell like *to you?*"

She listened to Fahad describe the floral aroma in words more similar to Samir than she could have ever imagined. And later, when Fahad deposited two drops of the amber liquid on his fingers and rubbed it gently into the skin of her wrists, she did not hesitate. And when he reached out to graze the bones of her neck, she did not retreat. And when he removed the thick shawl from her small body, she did not reject his advances. That night, Firdaus gave herself to the likeness of Samir that she glimpsed in her husband, which led to the conception of their first and only child.

Aayat, she would name their daughter nine months later; *aayat,* meaning a miracle.

# 30

# A Family of Three

Five years after his arrival in Paris, Samir was now well settled. He had enough to live and eat comfortably, pay his rent, and appreciate the stillness of his days. But sometimes, when dreams of fire crawled into his sleep and memories of home wove themselves tightly over his heart, he'd make his way to La Chapelle. Patel would cook a pot of moong dal and small round chapatis, Samir would inhale the familiar aromas of turmeric and cumin, and it would feel as close as home could be.

Apart from these rare episodes, Samir continued on day after day, determined to untether himself from the past, without any real aim or hope for the future. Until, one day, he met a woman.

Léa Clement was born in Marseilles in the unbearably hot months of 1928. During the war, she had been training at the nursing school of the French Red Cross when she was sent to serve in the field hospitals at Normandy. She remembered aircrafts flying overhead and the sound of bombs and artillery fire in the distance. But what haunted her the most were the young wounded soldiers, sometimes not much older than herself, who often cried themselves to sleep. It was there one day, at the very tail end of the war, that she came across the mangled body of her own beloved,

Michel. A young man she had known since childhood, who had enlisted as a private at the outbreak of the war with the promise of marriage upon his return.

Michel's death had shattered her, and following the war, she had returned to Marseilles to complete her studies. But unable to remain in the place that they had once shared, she moved to the largest city she could think of, a place where her sadness would dissolve into the deafening noises of the crowd. *Paris.* Léa Clement found work as a nurse at the Claude Bernard Hospital, and in 1953 met Samir Vij in the patient ward.

This time, there was no locking of eyes through clear glass vials; there was no intoxicating smell of rosewater and sandalwood, vanilla and soot, but something far more intense, pungent, and familiar. Earlier that morning, Léa had found an old photograph of her deceased soldier tucked away in her purse and, upon discovering it, she had cried. What Samir smelled on her then was no heavenly odor, but the furthest thing from it. It was the smell he had now come to associate with love. Samir had smelled her tears.

It was not maddening love that brought them together, but the shared experience of having lost a beloved. In those early months, Samir and Léa conversed in the language of sadness. They each took comfort in the fact that the other always understood that there had been *someone else* before, someone irreplaceable, whose love had gone unfulfilled. Rather than deep affection, it was deep loss that brought them together.

Finally pulling out his old suitcase, which for years had been relegated to the back of the wardrobe, Samir had looked through the treasures inside. Unknotting a thick bundle, he found a part of his mother's trousseau that she had wrapped away during the riots. A few gold bangles, a set of meenakari bracelets, a string of pearls, and two rings passed down to her from his grandmother.

With an heirloom ring of gold and emerald, he offered Léa himself and his history. In doing so, she would become the first person to whom Samir would reveal his cavernous losses and vulnerabilities, his guilt and

remorse. Already armed with the knowledge of the lover he had left behind, she now listened to the story of the uncle who had arrived in France
as a soldier during the Great War, and somehow left as a perfumer. She
imagined a clothing shop that had transformed into a perfume shop and
then to a shop no more. She cried when he described the state of Vij Bhawan, the destruction, the smoke, and all who had perished within. She
held the photograph from 1937 to her heart and listened to stories about
family members she would never meet.

Léa accepted his proposal with the dream of a future they could share,
and gave birth to a baby girl, Sophie, within the first year of marriage.

⚘

Fahad sat on one side of the boat with seven-year-old Aayat, and Firdaus
sat on the other. The hull must have been painted bright white at one
point, but its surface was now scratched enough to reveal the dusty wood
beneath. The boatman sat facing them at the very front, rowing across
the river Ravi. The morning was lovely and bright, with a slight chill in
the air. Aayat leaned back into her father's chest, and timidly dipped her
hands into the water, watching in awe as it rippled out.

They were rowing toward a pavilion built on an island in the center of
the ancient river. Listening to the rhythmic movement of the wooden oars
slipping in and out of the water, Firdaus looked pensively to the far edge
of the river, where the papermakers of Lahore used to produce handmade
sheets and dry them flat under the sun. They, too, had a similar rhythm to
their movement, a muscle memory which had been ingrained over generations. Sometimes, Altaf would bring Firdaus to the banks, and she would
watch in rapture as mushy pulp was transformed into beautiful silken
sheets by way of bamboo molds and screens. She was thinking about the
last time she'd laid her hands on a sheet of handmade paper when Aayat
flicked a bit of water at her.

"Ammi!" she squealed, and both father and daughter burst into laughter, causing Firdaus to giggle as well. She was wiping her face dry when Fahad caught her eye and smiled in a way that made the color rush to her cheeks.

When they got back home that afternoon, Aayat fell asleep almost immediately, and Fahad settled on the bed with the newspaper as Firdaus folded the pile of clean laundry. She'd barely made her way through a few kurtas when Fahad turned to look at her over the paper.

"You used to love to draw as a child," he remarked, bringing his hand up to his chin.

"You remember that?"

"I remember you."

Unable to meet his gaze, Firdaus smiled into the half-folded dupatta in her hands.

"Do you still draw?" he asked.

"I . . ." she began, unable to forget that her last subject had been Samir. ". . . not for a while."

"Well . . . maybe you could draw me," he suggested, folding the paper and sitting upright.

"Now?" Firdaus's heart raced, and she looked over at Aayat, deep in slumber. Fahad shrugged playfully, as if to say, *Why not?* She sat with her hands still over the pile of clothes for a few seconds, contemplating what to do. Then, walking over to the metal trunk by the window, she slowly took out the tools of her trade. Sitting on the chair beside the bed, she rested her paper over a rough pad called the atlik and picked up a piece of charcoal. She was partly surprised to find her fingers grasping the ashy stick with the same intention they were trained to, for she had never held charcoal as a married woman.

Firdaus became acutely aware of her every gesture, the posture in which she sat, how her dupatta collected around her shoulders, and the deliberateness with which she now studied her subject. The distance between them seemed to have evaporated completely as she allowed her gaze to linger on the sharpness of his jaw or the small cut that ran through his right eyebrow, on the dimples that appeared when he smiled or the shape of his ears. As she rendered his features on the page, allowing muscle memory to guide her, Firdaus couldn't deny that her husband was a handsome man, nor could she ignore the tenderness of his demeanor.

But there remained a tightness in her throat, and she couldn't help but feel as though she were performing. Thoughts of the maghrib hour flooded her mind. The past and the present played out simultaneously, where Firdaus was both a teenager and a married woman, and her subjects were both Samir and Fahad. Drawing a sharp breath, Firdaus closed her eyes and reminded herself that she could not retrieve what had already been lost. When she opened her eyes again, she was in the present, and her husband was looking at her with concern.

"This is a very good likeness," he said when she finally showed him the rough sketch. "You should start drawing again." Then, after a few seconds, he suggested, "Or perhaps begin working on manuscripts with Abba jaan again. You may no longer be able to go to the studio at Wazir Khan, but the work can always be brought ho—"

"No," she cut him off, "I don't work on manuscripts anymore."

Fahad bit his lip. "As a child, I recall you being your father's shadow . . ."

Firdaus looked away as tears pricked her eyes. It was true that she no longer spent time with her father, but she hadn't thought her husband would notice the rift. She turned to look at him now, her face soft and open.

"It is an old wound, between my father and me. A deep and painful wound."

He nodded, but said nothing, and then reached out and held her charcoal-covered hand.

Fahad never brought up the subject again, nor did he find out what had happened all those years ago, on the day the fire had engulfed Shahalmi. But from that moment on, Firdaus felt the memory of the perfumer recede ever so slightly.

⚘

Following Sophie's birth, Samir and Léa moved into a larger apartment in the same building. They continued to work at the hospital; Samir was promoted to a desk job with better pay, allowing Léa to spend more time at home with their newborn. Madame Blanchet eagerly took over the role of grandmother, indulging Sophie with fairy tales she could not yet understand in the language she would adopt as her mother tongue.

Then, for the first time in a long time, something that Samir could only describe as normalcy prevailed. He seldom indulged in the realm of perfume, and the memory of Firdaus was slowly swallowed by the passing days. She would still arrive unexpectedly—in a dream, in the petal of a rose, when he walked by the old bookbinder's shop that smelled of paper and ink—but she was no longer ever-present. As the months passed, Lahore, too, began to exist only in memory, paving the way for other things to be consciously forgotten. English and French replaced Urdu and Punjabi, which were banished from his tongue, not to be shared with Léa or endowed to Sophie. The maroon dupatta was no longer granted the luxury of touch or smell, though Firdaus's photograph did still remain in Samir's wallet.

These were years that Paris saw an influx of immigrants. Now and again, people would mistake Samir for an Iranian, Algerian, or Moroccan, but this hardly bothered him. He could be from anywhere and nowhere as long as it expunged the specificities of his past, sweeping him into the wave of general migration. He never intentionally brought up his family, for he could not yet find a way to reconcile himself to their deaths, and seemed to believe that if he didn't make any mention of them at all, then their memories would gradually fade and eventually disappear.

Sometimes on weekends, he and Léa would wheel Sophie's stroller down streets and into little gardens, where they would eat lunch under the sun. Samir would observe this little girl who called him Papa in crisp and feathery French, rather than the rounded, sonorous Baba he had grown up with. She had inherited his olive skin, but that was the extent of their physical similarities. Their noses were different; hers was smaller, shorter, and certainly not as astute. She had vivid hazel eyes and brown hair like Léa, and in all senses of the word would be considered typically French. She was so removed from Hindustan, but that was no fault of hers. Samir never wanted Sophie to feel encumbered by the memory of a place she would not understand and likely would never encounter. Perhaps it was unfair to make that decision on behalf of his daughter, but the past was too complicated and tangled, and certainly no place for a child to go wandering in.

⚭

A week after Sophie turned three, Samir was walking past a new Iranian café near the hospital when a familiar smell wafted up to his nostrils. In the past ten years, many smells had reminded him of Lahore, but none had managed to assail his senses this way. Unable to restrain himself, he trailed the smell to a plant resting on the café windowsill. It had a hairy stem, with highly aromatic green leaves that were slightly toothed at the edges, and rows of tiny brown-purple flowers. Samir's heart beat quicker, tears lined his eyes, and within moments, he was transported from the Paris of his adulthood to the Lahore of his childhood, for this had been the epicenter of Vij Bahwan: tulsi. The herb his grandmother had reverentially sown in the courtyard and his mother had lovingly raised till her death. Rayhan, the café owner called it, and Samir left that day with a stomachful of its tea, and a pocketful of its seeds.

Léa had a longer shift at the hospital, so once home, he cleaned, dried, and laid the seeds out on one corner of the table. Even from afar, they smelled intensely fresh, herbaceous and medicinal. In Vij Bhawan, tulsi seeds had been the most familiar and mundane thing—boiled in water for tea, chewed raw for digestion, soaked in milk until they became gelatinous, brewed as a tincture, dried, powdered, made into a paste—and yet here, in Paris, they seemed as alien as the language he had locked within himself.

Wrestling with his memories, Samir closed his eyes and allowed the scent to cocoon him. Savitri's laughter rang in his ears so loudly that she felt almost within his grasp. Som Nath's little temple bell chimed in the background. Samir envisioned Mohan breaking off the stems of the tulsi plant and carrying them into the prayer room. Outside the kitchen, Vivek lit the incense sticks and watched their ghostly smoke rise up in a dance. And Samir, young Samir, hardly understanding the world beyond the courtyard, ran around the holy plant, as golden sunshine encircled the entire Vij family. He dropped his nose to the table and inhaled the seeds. *Again, and again, and again.* He might have been unprepared, but the fragrance of the past had arrived.

When Léa reached home that night, Samir proudly presented the small pile of fragrant seeds. Their dinner was replete—for the very first time since Samir had proposed—with stories of Vij Bhawan, and Léa had witnessed a side to her husband that she never imagined she would. *Samir the child, the Lahori, the nostalgist.*

Léa understood why he had vowed never to return to his homeland. It pained her to think of all that he had lost, but it pained her more to see how he punished himself for it, how guilt had become a companion to loss. There were parts of her husband that no one, including himself, could access. It worried her that he practiced such a resolute forgetting, year after year after year, particularly when Sophie was born. She watched him become a person with no past, whose life began only when he set foot on French soil, and on some days, she felt as though he had erased his own shadow for fear of being engulfed by it.

Naturally then, it baffled her to see her husband surrender to a mere sprig of holy basil.

# 31

# The Discovery

A few months after the incident with the tulsi leaves, as Samir was feeding Sophie a spoonful of her breakfast, Léa overheard him narrating to her how, as a child, he'd once cut down a sky full of kites during basant. Standing some feet away in the kitchen, she had nonchalantly continued to prepare her lunch, but found herself smiling.

As the weeks passed, more stories emerged, slowly, hesitantly, innocently tucked between the most mundane of daily activities. As she listened, Léa began to observe where her husband paused, what made him happy and when history became unbearable. Cities she had never heard of before started to enter their vocabulary. Though a full spectrum of Urdu or Punjabi was never offered, the few words and phrases Samir repeated assumed concrete shape. Léa gathered that *dhoop* was sunshine, and *mitti* was earth, and she would sprinkle them in their conversations. She memorized the words *Shahalmi* and *Pattoki*, knew of Vivek and Mohan and Savitri and Som Nath and Leela, and from the owner at the Iranian café even learned to brew tulsi tea. The realm of perfume might still have remained untouched and undivulged, but for a while, an equilibrium between past and present appeared.

One evening, as winter could be felt stealing the length of autumn days, Samir embarked on one of his longer walks. Hands nestled inside his pockets, he left home and walked just short of an hour to the banks of the river Seine, strolling leisurely to where the bouquinistes—with their rows of wooden boxes painted in a uniform wagon green—began.

According to legend, in the sixteenth century, peddlers used to wander along the banks of the river, selling books and pamphlets. In the seventeenth century, their numbers increased, and ultimately, in the nineteenth century, they were granted official rights to establish their businesses. Over time, their wares, once displayed on the railings of the quays, found homes in the iconic green boxes on the banks of the Seine. Today, they stretched from Quai du Louvre to Pont Marie on the Right Bank, and from Quai Voltaire to Quai de la Tournelle on the Left, essentially forming a bookshelf of three kilometers, selling secondhand books, antiquarian objects, maps, magazines, stamps, and even rare newspapers. Samir seldom stopped at their stalls, but today he walked along the quay as if browsing through a bazaar.

"*Bonjour, monsieur,*" a middle-aged bookseller greeted Samir as he strolled by. "*Je peux vous aider?*" He gestured to the stall, asking if he could help.

"*Non, non, merci.*" Samir made it clear that he was just browsing.

He peered at the selection of books, mostly in French, all displayed in neat rows, with their spines up and titles clearly visible. His fingers trailed the paperbacks and then moved onto the piles of maps. There were postcards of Gare d'Orsay, lovely etchings of Gare de l'Est and street scenes from 1900, showing the cathedral Notre-Dame and Pont Saint-Michel, or the Arc de Triomphe and Champs-Élysées, surrounded by horse-drawn carriages, women in voluminous skirts and men with top hats. Samir now turned his attention to the rack of newspapers hanging at the bottom of the stall. Yellowing, faded, even torn in places, they were dated as far back as nearly a century ago. Bending down, he brought his nose to the newsprint to find the familiarly musty, vanilla-like aroma, and browsed through them until he chanced upon a familiar image.

On the cover of the July 16, 1916, edition, no. 138, of the newspaper *Le Miroir* was a photograph of four men—three British officers and one Hindustani with a trailing turban, preparing for an offensive during the First World War. The turbaned man, "lieutenant-général hindou Sir Pertab Singh," was obviously important enough to be featured on the front page of a French newspaper. Curiosity piqued, Samir began searching the stall for other editions, hoping to learn something about his uncle's history. He didn't know anything about the war, except that his family had always referred to it as *jung* in a tone grave and onimious. He found an edition from July 29, 1917, which showed the English king, George V, visiting his troops on the Western Front, but not much else.

Samir asked the bespectacled bookseller if he had any more newspapers from the time. He didn't think so, but rummaged through the boxes in the back and emerged with something equally as old. "Do you speak English?" he asked.

"Uh, oui, yes, I do," Samir affirmed.

"Voilà, then I have this. *The War Illustrated,* a British magazine, also from wartime." The bookseller presented the thick magazine to Samir, a compilation of several issues printed over the course of the war.

Samir thanked him and placed the heavy bound volume on the wooden surface. With a thud, he opened it to the back and then made his way to the front, idly flipping through photographs of European soldiers until familiar features from a lifetime ago caught his attention. Rows of men with dark skin marching in the streets, setting up camps, working guns and other arms, posing with French children, and squatting around a fire. He looked around the bouquiniste to find the bookseller tending to another customer, a young woman studying a scrapbook of stamps, and an old man tapping the keys of a typewriter as if it were a piano.

HERE AND THERE WITH OUR GALLANT INDIANS IN FRANCE, a headline read on May 8, 1915. It showed three Indians sepoys washing their laundry in a village fountain, turbans on their heads, puttees wrapped tightly around their legs. Grainy photographs of lonely turbaned sentries, a sepoy quenching his thirst from a water fountain, and a pair of Indian cooks were arranged on the page with captions. There was an image of a sepoy holding a French baby, both of them laughing joyously. Samir caressed the sepoy's face.

He then flipped to the very front of the book, to when the first divisions of sepoys had arrived in France. The headline from October 10, 1914, read, INDIAN CONTINGENT REACHES THE SEAT OF WAR, accompanied by several images. Placing his forefinger on the first caption, Samir read it out softly: "Lithe, keen, and fit, these Indian troops, who are seen here in the transport that carried them to Marseilles, disembarked eager for the smell of powder and were not long before they were bearing their part in the hard fighting in Northern France." Above the text was a photograph of sepoys standing on the deck of a ship, clutching the rails. At first glance, they looked indistinguishable, but on closer inspection, Samir found that their turbans were all tied differently; some bore large insignia and badges, and others sported full beards. These were *his* people. And then someone caught his eye.

Samir stared at the photograph. A thousand thoughts were suspended in his brain, but he couldn't grasp at a single coherent thread. Abruptly, he slammed the thick volume shut, paid for it, and carried it back home, barely paying attention to the road.

Léa had been standing by the tulsi plant they were growing in the kitchen, smelling its leaves as she rocked Sophie in her arms. But upon seeing her husband, she immediately put the child down to rest in the crib and went to him. Samir was mumbling to himself, protectively clutching a large leather-bound book against his chest. She pried it from his grasp, and the only words he managed to utter were "Page 173." Flipping through the book, she arrived at a photograph of Indian sepoys. With a trembling finger, Samir pointed to a man in the center of the image, his head titled to the right in order to be fully seen by the camera. There, captured in grainy film, was his uncle, Vivek Nath Vij, having embarked on the adventure of a lifetime.

In their bedroom, Léa compared the image in the book to the 1937 photograph, and though there were physical differences, it was very much the same person. Behind her, Samir was rustling inside the wardrobe, and took out, for the first time in front of his wife, the leather apothecary case. Within seconds, the apartment was filled with a bouquet of sublime smells, and Léa found it difficult not to succumb to their splendor. Many times, she had wondered how her husband could bury this part of himself. Perhaps only the deepest pain could eradicate the deepest love.

She watched as he began removing vials of perfume one by one, searching every inch of the case. "What are you looking for, mon amour?" she asked.

"I–I don't know. Something, *anything*," he said helplessly, before discovering a compartment at the bottom that held a stack of journals. Placing his palm over them, he hesitated for a minute, remembering how precious they were to his uncle and how secretive he had remained about them.

"He kept these under lock and key, you know," he told Léa, "always claiming that they were irreplaceable, more important than any perfume."

Samir brought the journals up to his nose, and inhaled their surface, deeply and desperately. In the pile was a small brown journal different from all the others. It was barely a few inches in height and width, and its cover was embossed with the words VIJ & SONS, ESTD 1830, LAHORE. The very same words were printed on the ledger that Som Nath's dried rose had lived in. Samir picked it up, assuming that this was where it all began, but he found the first few pages to be filled only with measurements and purchase orders. Of course, this was a document from the original family business.

But as he leafed through the journal, he froze. "Vilayat, 1914," an otherwise empty page read. Samir stared at his uncle's Urdu script, rendered pale by years and weather.

"Vilayat," he repeated, feeling the warmth of a familiar language on his lips.

"What does that mean?" Léa asked.

"The foreign land," Samir replied, and began reading out loud, translating for Léa.

August 26, 1914

We have been sailing for two days now, and Hindustan has long been left behind. I have not a fear of water, but last night, I felt as though I would not survive to tell the tale. Large waves crashed against our ship, some taller in height than Vij Bhawan. Men swayed as if intoxicated, unable to remain steady. Thunder and rain struck the wooden decks, strong winds swept us up, and we held our breaths in fear until the ship fell back down again. What will a man who is so afraid of the ocean do on a battlefield, I wonder. No one in my family has ever ventured farther than Punjab, let alone across a liquid body so grand. I am the first. Of so many things, I am the first.

Samir shut the notebook and held it against his body. This was no ledger of textile orders, nor was it a record of perfumistic secrets. This was a private journal of an even more private man, on his way to war. For a moment, Samir was overcome with guilt for having glimpsed into a past he had no business entering. And then reality hit him. There was no one left to tell him about these expeditions: no grandfather, no parents, and certainly no uncle to give voice to the long-silenced years that eventually led the family to perfumery. And yet here in his hands lay the truth, ready to be unraveled. He looked at Léa and she looked at him, but neither knew what to say. After a few minutes, Samir took a deep breath and opened the journal again. He sat on one edge of the bed, and she sat on the other, and between them emerged the story of Vivek Nath Vij.

# 32

# With the Indians in France

In August 1914, twenty-year-old Vivek bid farewell to his family in Lahore and caught a train to Karachi, from where he and other sepoys were to board a ship westward, where they would fight in a war alongside British soldiers. Many of Vivek's comrades who had served in battles before shared tales of their gallantry. But none knew anything about the expedition ahead, why this war had begun, and who was fighting in it. Vivek had left Vij Bhawan armed with his family's prayers and the journal Samir now held in his hands. In Karachi, he waited four days before the ships were ready, and then the ports came alive with sepoys and officers of various regiments, and additional servicemen like cooks, mule drivers, porters, doctors, stretcher bearers, even tailors and water carriers. For many of these men, hailing from villages and hamlets enclosed by dry fields and mountain passes, the boundless blue water was a sight to behold. In summer khaki they had strolled along the harbor with the carefree disposition of men not at the onset of battle but on the cusp of adventure.

"He was never like this, my uncle." Samir looked up from the page at Léa. He was struck by the incredible detail Vivek had committed to writing. "For as long as I knew him, nothing was so easily divulged, things needed to be pried out. Words were scarce, and memories even more so. Yet here he is, chronicling every breath."

"Did he never tell you these stories?" she asked, surprised.

Samir sighed. "He never told me, nor anyone else in the family. All I knew was that he had been to war, but as a child, I used to wonder what perfumers did in battle. And these . . . I always assumed these were journals full of formulas. He was so particular about keeping a record of every composition."

"Well, what else does he write?"

Samir returned to the pages. "That he is one of two educated men in his regiment, and when news of his literacy reaches the British officers, he is appointed official scribe, with extra allowance for the post."

Léa crawled closer to Samir, peering at the pages she could not understand.

Through the night, the couple escaped into Vivek's journal. The SS *Teesta* carried three brigades of the Lahore Division westward from Karachi, stopping at Aden and Suez, where the Sirhind Brigade was left to guard the canal. The Lahore and Jullundur Brigades were then herded back onto the ship, but no one knew how much farther their destination was, or even which country constituted "vilayat." Samir was impressed with how faithfully his uncle chronicled the hours. His language became a discourse of wind and sea, stories of fellow sepoys and of starlight casting its net across the sky. He wrote about how one of the machine-gun mules had succumbed to the heat, and about daily drills, parades, and exercises. Some men played cards, others read holy texts, and Vivek became better acquainted with his regiment, which included companies of Sikhs, Dogras, Punjabi Muslims, and Pathans.

On September 11, he wrote his first letter for Lance-Naik Balwant Singh, who hailed from the mighty Rajputana region and addressed Vivek as kaatib, the formal word for scribe. Having grown up in a sandy desert, he was eager to describe in his letter to his parents the small fish he had seen leaping and flying above the water's surface.

On September 16, as the sepoys disembarked briefly in Egypt, Vivek turned twenty-one years old.

On September 26, they had been afloat for twenty-seven days. "Twenty-seven dawns and dusks, twenty-seven sunrises and sunsets, and twenty-seven twilights. The men have lost count, but I persist. Each day is a shadow of the next, yet each day holds the promise of something unaccustomed." Samir looked over at Léa, who had fallen asleep.

Sleep evaded him, and so he returned to the journal, carefully inspecting it. It was pocket-sized and fragile, subjected to oceans and battlefields. At times, his finger traced a word, a phrase, a scribble, a note that he could imagine his uncle making, and he would smile sadly. His hungry nose smelled the pages—muddy, salty, fetid, metallic, unfamiliar. His nails grazed the old binding, as if wanting to slip into history. Part of him was grateful for this discovery. Yet the more he read, the smaller he felt for never having asked about the past.

September 26, 1914

In the morning hours, we stood on the deck and caught first sight of the majestic vilayat.

As he read these words aloud to Léa the next morning, Samir wondered whether Vivek could have known that this foreign land would alter not just his own life, but also the lives of generations of his family. With his index finger, Samir traced a tiny drawing of ships lined up at the port of Marseilles.

We disembarked to disorder on the port. Men, animals, cargo, and rations were being off-loaded into carts and lorries. Welcomed by soldiers and seamen in baggy red trousers and blue coats, we assembled into our companies, inadequately clothed for the cool weather. The Baluchi soldiers were the first to march out into the streets, and we followed suit with rifles resting upon our left shoulder, held upright toward the sky.

"Mar-say," Samir read out from the page, tracing an invisible word from right to left, connecting the alphabets like a poem—*mim* to *alif* to *re* to *sin* to *baree ye. Mar-say.* The strangeness of reading a mother tongue so far away from the motherland was not lost on him.

As Léa poured coffee and milk into two cups, she said, "My father was a teenager at the time, present in the crowd waiting to greet the Indians. It is a story that all of us who grow up in Marseilles are told—a landmark event. My grandmother would often recall how valiant they looked as they marched down the wide avenues to the beat of drums and pipes."

Placing the journal facedown, Samir smiled at his wife. "What else did she tell you?"

"Oh, the scene was apparently delirious. The crowds went wild, they clapped and screamed, *Vivent les Hindous!* and *Vivent les Indiens!*—waving flags and dropping embroidered handkerchiefs on the cobbled streets." She laughed. "She told me that children swung from their necks and women pinned roses on their lapels. The French people were grateful the Indians had arrived in their time of need."

At work, Samir spent every spare second thinking about his uncle's first impressions of France and comparing them to his own. On his way back from the hospital, he purchased a map, and later unrolled it out on the kitchen table with the intention of tracking his uncle's movement as the war progressed.

The next day, he read Vivek's descriptions of the different companies of soldiers, based on their unique uniforms. The 15th Sikhs bore an iron ring on their turbans and shoulder clasps. The Gurkhas carried the fish-shaped kukri knives. Vivek's khaki turban had a dark blue cloth on the left side with a fringe. The Brahmins and Jats wore tall turbans, the lancers sported a long tail, the Pathans placed a kullah between theirs, and only the Gurkhas and Garhwalis wore no turbans. It was evident that despite the rejection of his father's profession, the habits of a cloth merchant's son were ingrained.

He had also noted that the Indian camp at Parc Borély was separate from the British one. Within it, there were sections for bathing and cooking, and an enclosure for horses, mules, goats, and sheep. There was a kitchen for Hindus and Sikhs and another for Muslims, clearly demarcated. The locals, whom Vivek referred to as Francisi, watched on as the evening meals were prepared by campfire and the smells of chapati and dal wafted through the air, mixing with meats, spices, cigarettes, and hookah coals.

September 27, 1914

The air is cold and dry, and unable to sleep, I write by the light of an oil lamp. Sucha Singh, who has left his new bride, Gul, in the village of Moga, is strumming on his tumbi a few tents away. The wind carries his voice across the open park as he croons a Punjabi song about forlorn lovers. His lament warms my heart and I find myself praying that he may return to Gul, unaffected by this war.

September 28, 1914

When we meet the Francisi people, they shake our hands or invite us into cafés. They are fair-skinned like the sahibs, but the men sport long twirling mustaches, which makes them distinct. None have witnessed people with our coloring. Some women, upon seeing the Sikhs, offered to shave their long beards, thinking they had been on the ship for far too long on the voyage across.

From the kitchen, hands covered in tomato and fennel, Léa said that her grandmother always mentioned how handsome the soldiers were, and how women offered them everything from fruits to flowers, and some-times even asked for their uniform buttons as mementos. Unable to tell if she was teasing him, Samir chuckled, but he reflected that if his uncle had never traveled to France, then Samir never would have found his way here either. Holding on to that thought, he walked to the crib and sat down beside Sophie. Then, reading as much to her as to his wife, he continued.

> We do not understand the Francisis, or they us, but we try to communicate. In shops, we point to a souvenir to know the price. At the post office, the stamps are labeled. So far, we are ad-justing well without a common tongue. This evening, the Faith-ful were called to prayer, and I sat in the far corner watching a Sikh sipahi from Lahore, a teenager no older than Mohan, offer a cup of milk to a cat, as Francisi children looked on, enthralled. There is something tender and rare about this meeting of East and West, unbound or dictated by any sarkar, except the com-passion we share as children of the same earth.

Inspired by all this talk of her hometown, Léa had used her grand-mother's recipe to make bouillabaisse soup for dinner. The spicy fish stew was a delicacy from Marseilles, having originated as a poor sailor's meal made with vegetables and leftover fish scraps likely too bony to sell. The couple had invited Madame Blanchet, who arrived carrying a freshly baked lemon yogurt cake for dessert. All through dinner, dipping crusty bread into the soup, Samir inhaled the familiar aromas of saffron and gar-lic, and smiled to himself. Then, after Sophie was asleep, the couple curled into bed, and Samir took out the journal and the map.

During their final days in Marseilles, a Russian artist had come to speak with and sketch the Indian soldiers at their camp. For most, this was a new experience, and the men were curious to see a white lady among them, unencumbered by color or creed. They gathered from surrounding tents to get their caricature drawn by her, posing and modeling freely. She sketched the Afridi subedar with his elegant nose, and the muscular jemadar of the 59th Sikhs as his khaki kurta fluttered in the breeze. She drew men huddled in groups around campfires, and preparing the midday meal. She even drew the the large water barrels of drinking water, and the herd of goats by the kitchen.

> At the end of the day, the Russi sahiba's book was full of drawings and signatures. Next to my portrait, I signed my name and regiment, and men who did not know how to sign left impressions of their thumbs. I wonder what interest these names and faces will bear in the years to come—the Singhs, Khans, Bahadurs of the East.

> October 4, 1914
>     Three days ago, we boarded a train from Marsay and have now halted in the town of Orleeyaans on the banks of river Lowaar. The weather is getting colder and the trees are changing color. Sipahi Ram Chand dictated a note to his father in Ferozepore, describing the beauty of France, with the greenest of pastures and the bluest of skies. "How can war ever be waged on a country so fine?" he asked. Of everything we have seen here, I think the same question is present in all our minds.

Vivek had written at length about the new rifles they'd been kitted with once in France, and the new friendships he'd forged these last few weeks, taking an immediate liking to the musically inclined Sucha Singh. He also devoted pages to his janral sahib, an Englishman born in Baraut, United Provinces, who had, to date, served in fourteen different campaigns and expeditions across Hindustan and took pride in commanding the multicultural Indian Expeditionary Force which held within its ranks more religious, regional, linguistic, and ethnic differences than any other army on the planet. As British and Indian troops began to assemble in the camp, Vivek had hoped that this was how the East would conquer the West—through camaraderie, loyalty, honor, and brotherhood. That perhaps, through their efforts in this war, the perceptions of color might slowly fade away from their lives at home.

And despite the excitement of being in vilayat, no matter how worldly or untethered Vivek aspired to be, there was no escaping the sudden flicker of Hindustan. For embedded in the lines of his palms and the depths of his heart, there remained the silhouette of home, quietly mirroring Samir's own predicament.

October 14, 1914

I have written many letters today. Sipahi Daya Deen thanked his mother in Peshawar for the Quran she sent him. He held the holy book against his heart, and by the time we had finished the note, a sadness had settled into me as well. We have been away from Hindustan for two months now.

October 16, 1914

The subedars are calling this the Jarman di larai. We do not know who these Jarmans are or why they have begun this war, but we have received orders to move northward tomorrow. The destination is unknown. This morning I have sent home a bundle of newspapers, collected over the past two months, by packet post. In this country, the news is very up-to-date and pictures of the war appear nearly the very next day after anything happens.

October 18, 1914

We were collected in red buses and driven across to the country of Belljum, where the battle is being fought. I am writing this from a lookout stoop in a village the men are calling Whitesheet, whose residents had fled from their homes. No one knows what will happen tomorrow. The evening has been filled with muffled sounds of gunfire in the distance. The war is no longer far away.

"'The war is no longer far away,'" Samir slowly repeated.

## 33

## In the Trenches

Since the discovery of the journals, Léa had listened with fascination to how the Indian soldiers had acclimatized to new landscapes. But it was when Samir's uncle described battle for the first time, detail after detail of all the eye could see and all the heart could feel, that something began to shift deep inside her. Images of war she thought she had buried, sounds she hoped she'd never hear again, the smells and textures, the terror, trepidation, unease, and loss, all began to reveal themselves again, prompted by Vivek's visceral words.

"October 27, 1914. Wipers." Samir held the journal in one hand and, with the other, marked Ypres on the map before he began translating.

My regiment charged across a rain-soaked field, under a darkening sky, and after a short bombardment, attacked the Jarman trench. I remember blood, and bombs. And the sound, I cannot forget the sound. Shell after shell, burying men, blowing up others. A whole body exploding within mere seconds. There are no words in any language to describe it. Here, I have seen a dead man for the first time. Subedar Mansoor Khan was slain by a

bomb before my eyes. So close he was that my uniform bears
the remains of his blood and body, along with mud, trench water, and my own vomit.

Samir paused and then concluded the entry, "'This was not what I had
imagined.'"

"Well, what had he imagined?" Léa asked plaintively from across the
room where she was knitting a woolen hat for Sophie. "This is war. Why
did he enlist?"

"I think he is wondering the very same thing . . ."

Continuing down the page, Samir noted how his uncle had returned
to the billets and written about his soiled uniform in great detail, recording every tear and stain, as if taking an inventory of battle. His leather
boots had emitted a foul, moist odor. The woolen puttees wrapped tightly
from his ankles to his knees had left his legs numb and swollen. The wet
turban and saffa underneath were soaked to his skull. He lightened himself of the leather waist-belt, ammunition cross-belt, water bottle, haversack, rifle, bayonet, and peeled off his trousers and kurta, splattered with
the remains of the subedar.

> There are thousands of thoughts in my head, yet none have the
> clarity of reason. A low beating of bombs mirrors my heartbeat.
> In the trenches, our actions are beyond control, we are fearful
> and desperate and suddenly aware that any moment could be
> our last. The ground vibrates as if it may erupt at any moment,
> clouds of dust enclose us, and the world is drowned by our bul-
> lets. All those who have survived this battle are afraid.

Vivek's regiment became the first Indians to enter the trenches of the
First World War in the Belgian farmlands at Ypres. These initial entries
betrayed a fear that managed to reverberate across the decades and onto
the page Samir held in his hands. They were written in haste, leaving

messy, inky fingerprints, and placing his own fingers upon them, Samir pressed himself into the traces of his uncle, like a palimpsest.

Léa watched as Samir buried his face in the journal, taking in whatever smells of war and misery had endured, as if inheriting his uncle's very memories. She noticed that as much as he was using the journal as a way to trace his family's unknown history, he had also begun to use it as a means of belated conversation with his uncle. The brutality of battle had led him to interrupt, interpret, comment, and question, and there was something unbearably sad and tender about witnessing this relationship unfold.

&

From Ypres, Vivek was sent to Messines, which Samir faithfully recorded on the map.

> November 5, 1914
>
> The fighting in Wipers left many dead. Trenches were bombed through the nights, with noise loud enough to drive a person to deafness. Bodies were scattered everywhere, whole or in parts. There was no cremation, so all were simply buried together. Unholy, some men called this. Sant Ram is dead. Munshi and Waryam Singh are dead. Sher Khan, Mahant Ram, Sardar Ali, Jung Bahadur, all dead. The wounded soldiers have been sent to the hospital, but many men are missing, rendered invisible by the bullets and smoke in no-man's-land . . . Khan Bahadur, Jagdir Singh, Jaffar Ali, all have vanished. In this age, there has never been such a war before, and there may never be one again. If I leave this land unharmed, then I shall look upon it as a new life.

Léa closed her eyes tightly and exhaled. Snow might have been falling in Paris, where she sat with her husband in a corridor of the hospital on their break, but it was stifling summertime in the Normandy of her mind. Vivek never saw such a war again, but Léa had witnessed it mere decades later, when stretcher after stretcher of wounded soldiers had been brought in before her eyes from the front line, in conditions no different from what the journal described. Field hospitals had to be located close, so close that sometimes they bore the brunt of incoming fire. Soldiers were brought in without arms or legs, with burns or in shock, and Léa remembered doing whatever she could to give them hope. Changing bandages, giving shots, administering oxygen, even declaring the dead; sometimes there were not enough beds so patients were laid out on the ground; sometimes the bloodstained operating theater looked no less than a battlefield. But almost always, the soldiers who survived their wounds considered it a second chance at life.

She had heard that sentence so many times that to hear Samir repeat it now, so far removed from the site of war, unnerved her. Léa was trying her best not to descend into darkness, but Vivek's graphic account was not helping. She stared down the sterile corridor, trying to erase the images from her mind as Samir's narration carried on.

That evening, after she had finished her shift, she sat in the nurse's lounge contemplating what she was about to do. Léa was so certain she had laid her ghosts to rest, and yet now, for the first time in years, the seams of her heart had come undone. Perhaps against her better judgment then, she retrieved a creased photograph from a compartment in her purse. Carefully, her fingers caressed the sepia-toned face she'd fallen in love with at first sight, the coiffed dark hair she had run her fingers through as a teenager, the lips she had kissed by the port, the eyes she had gazed into before he left for battle. All this talk of war had resurrected her dead.

Two weeks had passed since they'd started reading the journals together, it had become their routine, but that night, Samir felt a tautness between him and his wife. Vivek's words left no room for lightness or romance or respite. There was only imminent tragedy, recalled through the secret records of a dead man. But if Samir had any chance of knowing what had happened to his uncle, then he would have to continue reading till the end.

The unexpected intensity of battle had left many men desperately searching for a way out and back home. This led to an outbreak of self-inflicted wounds, but none felt to Samir as grave or terrifying as the letter sipahi Muhammad Deen from the United Provinces addressed to his brother about a rare plant he desired.

November 7, 1914

The smoke of the bhelwa plant, used to fumigate a part of the body, results in inflammation of that particular part. It can also be mashed up and smeared on the skin, or ground to a fine powder and lathered across one's loins. The result of correctly using it will last for three days, and by then, the sipahi would already be transported to the hospital. Assuring me that the doctors would believe the condition as genuine, Muhammad Deen rambled on about how to make one's eyes sore with the ground seeds of the rand plant, or apply the wax from one's ear into the eyes with blunt needles, or provoke a fever or injure one's foot with a knife and then insert a piece of copper in the wound. Horrified, I quickly sealed his letter and thrust it toward him with shaking hands, though it is my opinion that the censor sahibs will withhold it.

Shuddering, as his uncle might have, Samir turned to Léa. "This, this sounds inhuman."

"War makes men do things they never imagined they would have to."

The details of battle are both repetitive and gruesome, and I wish not to burden anyone, so I write only when necessary. Yet as an escape from this frightening world, home remains constantly on my mind. Its light is golden and its sky is full of evening clouds. I see the rain, I feel the sand, I breathe in the morning air. I see the Ravi, the wheat fields, the kites and the pigeons. Each night, Lahore unfurls before my eyes.

Samir awoke in the middle of the night to find himself brokenhearted by borrowed dreams, and haunted by a land he might never see again. It had been a long time since the loss of Lahore had gnawed at his heart, and reaching under his pillow, he held the journal until he fell back asleep.

Nestled beside him, Léa remained awake as the darkness of night gave way to the brightness of dawn, for each time she closed her eyes, she saw Michel's face. The day he left for war, a halo of sunshine on his hair, the promise of their future on his beautiful lips. And then again, on the day he was brought into the hospital tent, when all life had left his body. Unable to move, unable to speak, Léa had watched in horror as the doctors declared her betrothed dead long before he'd been brought in. His face was undisfigured but covered in mud, as if it had been trampled on; his body was badly wounded, with bullets in both his legs and shrapnel through his arm. But it was the eyes that wouldn't leave her now, wouldn't let her sleep or forget, Michel's pale blue eyes, hollow and lifeless.

The next morning, she decided that she needed to stop listening to the journals. Perhaps, then, it was sheer coincidence that while she tried to find an excuse that would help her retain both sanity and marriage, she was transferred to the intensive care unit, requiring her to spend more time at the hospital, a promotion she readily accepted.

⁊

It would take Samir a few days to get used to being alone with Vivek's words. Often, he would read something that would prompt him to look around the room for his wife, only to remember that this was now a solitary journey. As a result, the journal became his constant companion—he would read at his desk, while he walked to work, as he put Sophie to bed or waited for Léa to return.

He read as his uncle attempted to learn the Francisi language, a list of words—*bonjour, merci, oui, non, soldat*—their translations and pronunciations rendered carefully in Urdu. He read as the regiment marched to Essars, where word reached the camp about two sepoys from the 15th Sikhs who had each been sentenced to thirty lashes in public for being asleep on their sentry posts in the trenches. He read as they were sent out to inspect a ruined hospital in the town of Festubert, close to the front line. Then, as he turned the page, a pressed fern revealed itself, and Samir discovered perhaps the first ever deliberate smell memory that his uncle would evoke during the war.

> We passed through a dense passage of dark green, and I thought it extraordinary that some herbage had withstood the wrath of man. I broke a stem off the very tall tree and found it to be covered in flat, needlelike leaves. Taking off my gloves, I crushed them with my hands and brought them to my nose. Inhaling, I discovered a sublime form in this otherwise lifeless terrain. I couldn't tell whether my senses were deceiving me, but the needles smelled like fresh lemons. It seemed like I had quite accidentally raised the curtain of winter and discovered a window to another world. My first thoughts were of Khushboo Lal and how through the years of my childhood, we traveled the world by way of the many perfumes in his collection. Now here I am, with the world at my doorstep, wishing only to find my way back home.

Samir picked up the dried leaf, first surveying it and then, out of compulsion, smelling it. Fir, a middle note. With a sigh, he set the leaf and journal down on his lap. Though the loss of his family settled deeper with every page he read, his uncle continued to be his most influential teacher. He remembered how, when Samir was a teenager, Vivek had concocted an eccentric composition of woody fir and sour green mango, to which Mohan had suggested adding a hint of jasmine buds for sweetness. The trio had laughed at their experiment, but the resulting ittar, mixed with beeswax, had been an intensely fresh solid perfume for the summertime, loved and purchased by a British sahib. And now, with no one to ask, Samir wondered whether the war could have, in fact, been the inspiration.

The weather became colder, the battles intensified, and Vivek's entries became sparser and stranger. Sometimes he would write about the fat rats and wet sandbags in the trenches; other times he'd fixate on the gorgeous tendrils of smoke emitted from a hookah in the Indian camp. Notes on nursing wounds would be followed by a page on the foul taste of stale bread. A scene of a cavalryman brushing his horse, the redness of a tobacco-chewing sepoy's teeth, a low-hanging cloud, the isolation of sentry duty, the taste of vilayati milk. Within these entries were moments so lucid that Samir could furnish an entire landscape of war, as if the world had been engraved onto his very brain. But there were other things that remained mere whispers, mentioned as fleetingly as a ray of passing sunlight.

Vivek also continued to write for his fellow sepoys, admitting that many, including him, were still unclear on the reasons for this war. Their correspondences home passed through the British censors, and were sometimes withheld, leading many men to omit things they could not openly write about. But in addressing letters and postcards to places that he had never seen or even heard of before, Vivek realized the scale of their service. The Hindustani sepoy was spread like grains of sand across the world, from East Africa to Mespotamia and across France and Belgium on the Western Front, where throughout winter, Vivek spent weeks in and out of poorly constructed trenches, braving the weather and constant enemy shelling. His words no longer bore excitement or even fear, but were imbued instead with desperation and defeat.

November 27, 1914

Engaged in a significant attack to recover enemy-occupied trenches. After the attack, we climbed back in our trench and cleared the dead. In the three months that we have been in vilayat, these are the first Jarmans I have seen from up close. As we emerged victorious, they lay lifeless, in heaps of blood and dirt, their bodies contorted and their eyes lightless. Some of the sipahis went around collecting the coats of the dead, their weapons and other stray items. But not me, for I have already surpassed the threshold of my barbarity.

December 5, 1914

The weather is cold and the wind is high. War continues, day and night. No matter how much I write in this journal, it falls short of the reality. This land, which we once considered a paradise, now seems worse than any hell. We are not allowed to light a candle or match, let alone a fire to warm ourselves. There are many who will not survive the night.

December 18, 1914

We have given up our lives for a mere eleven rupees a month. No man will return to Hindustan in one piece. If not a physical wound, then an emotional wound we are all sure to carry. For days now, regiments have been engaged nonstop in battle with the Jarmans. There are many casualties, and many of our men have been taken prisoner. Sucha is wounded in the leg and has been sent to the hospital. At my own survival, I am astonished. My cowardice compels me to conceal myself when faced with the enemy, in a way that none of my other comrades do. I do not belong on this battlefield, and wish to disappear. Perhaps Baba was right, for this is no place for the son of a cloth merchant.

With all that Vivek had survived so far, he began to think that only one of two things were now possible. Either death had somehow taken pity on him, or the Lord Yama was mocking his cowardice, refusing to claim such a man. "Maybe I am made for a prolonged suffering," he wrote, leading Samir back to the memory of the Shahalmi fire.

As the year drew to a close, Vivek's regiment was relieved by British troops. The sepoys also witnessed snowfall, described by Vivek with rare delight. For the first time since their arrival on foreign soil, they had felt ageless, playing in the snow with the abandon of men who had never known war. And yet, by the very next day, the temperature had dropped, confining men to their billets and turning the snow to ice.

Then, on Christmas Day in 1914, seventeen-year-old Princess Mary sent each soldier at the front a present—a brass box filled with sugar, fruits, candy, nuts, and other treats. Along with food, there was a pair of warm socks, cigarettes, and writing material. On top of the box was engraved the princess's profile, along with the names of countries that were British allies during the war. Reading this, Samir looked out the window, where Christmas had arrived in Paris as well. Léa and Sophie were in Madame Blanchet's apartment downstairs, helping to prepare the evening's feast, leaving him alone with his uncle.

Turning to the very last entry of the year, he read about the visit of a British photographer. There had been a fall in the level of fighting, which was, apparently, the perfect time for a visitor to tour the trench. He carried a slim portable camera and, standing at the parapet, captured images of the devastated landscape. He snapped away at the Hindustani sepoys' makeshift kitchens, their routines and customs in the filthy war tunnels, and shot several jolly portraits.

> We smiled for photographs, while carrying on with our daily duties. Young Kullu Singh posed with the Jarman helmet he found in no-man's-land. Ashraf Khan showed off his hand-carved

pocketknife made from a thick piece of discarded wire. We were photographed with our rifles pointing up to the stillness of the sky, holding shovels, lifting wet sandbags, drinking tea and tying our turbans. No doubt this is how they will remember us, wearing our hearts upon our uniforms in service to the sarkar. This is how they will remember us, footnotes of battle, in the nethers of damp tunnels. But if we remain alive beyond the war, how will *we* remember this land? What stories will we tell?

# 34

# We Were Here Too

The new year arrived simultaneously for uncle and nephew, separated by forty-four years. Vivek began a new journal issued by the army, its spine covered in red cloth. Inside, a blue-and-white sticker read, TO THE FORCES OF HIS IMPERIAL MAJESTY, NOW IN THE BATTLE-FIELD IN EUROPE, printed at the Model Press in Anarkali, Lahore. Much like the soldiers, the notebook had been sent far away from home, only to find its way to Vivek, who now craved home.

In the dinginess of cold billets, in an effort to enliven their spirits, the Hindustanis observed the festival of Lohri, which marked the end of winter in Punjab. As a part of the soldiers' fund, pinnis made with flour, cooked in ghee, and spiced with nuts and cardamom were distributed throughout the entire Indian camp. There was no customary bonfire or telling of folktales or singing of songs. But home remained on Vivek's mind as he returned to the trenches soon after.

The most important lesson I have learned in this war is that a family does not always share blood. It does not always share religion either. Following an evening of shell fire, sipahi Teja Singh dictated a letter to the family of the slain sipahi Akbar Khan.

They had grown up together in Attock. Addressing his friend's mother as if she were his very own, Teja asked her not to shed tears, for not only had Akbar gained martyrdom and found a place in heaven, but one son of hers still remained.

A lump grew in Samir's throat. What kind of half-life would now prevail in the shadow of Partition? Such letters would likely no longer be written; no longer would a Sikh sipahi adopt a Muslim mother. A Hindu neighborhood would be burned by Muslims with little mercy, a Muslim distiller would be threatened by Hindu thugs in broad daylight, a decade-long love would be buried. With sadness, he closed Vivek's journal for the night.

In February, the enemy shelled the Allied front line, and close to dusk, large guns were fired for hours. Many were wounded, many more were killed, and Vivek just barely escaped death. A havildar from the reserves saved him from a large piece of shrapnel, but by the end of battle, he was found buried under the rubble.

February 16, 1915

In the hospital tent, smoke floated in freely, the air was heavy with the stench of unburied dead, and firing continued in the distance. On the cot next to mine was the lifeless body of young sipahi Bhatta Singh, shot down in no-man's-land while attempting to save another. I often wrote his letters home, and read out those that arrived from his father in Sialkot. The last one asked how many times he had been in the battlefield of Laam, and should he die serving the sarkar here, then he would become as glorious as the sun. He would attain paradise. He was advised to have no fear of death, for the honor of his family, village, and caste would be upheld in this way. Life and death were in the hands of the omnipotent one, after all. But looking at Bhatta Singh's corpse, I saw no honor or paradise, no glory as bright as the sun. All I saw was a boy who would never again walk on his soil.

After being incapacitated for four days, Vivek returned to the trenches. A few weeks later, the sepoys prepared to march out again. "Another town, another camp, another defense line, another trench, another battle awaits"—his words were dry and stale. The fighting continued, the ground thawed, snow melted into slush. The break of day brought bursts of shell fire on both sides, and in the unusual stillness of night, the enemy could be heard working on their defenses. There was no end to destruction, and no news of their return home. "The work of days and months will become the work of years," he noted.

Soon, Vivek's company was ordered to relieve the Gurkha regiment in Neuve Chapelle, where the badly damaged trenches needed reconstruction. As they worked, Vivek chronicled every detail, and in this way, Samir finally understood what a trench was.

It started with the artillery line, where the largest field guns and ammunition were located. The communication trenches came next, tunnels used to move between the front and rear, or transport injured soldiers to the field hospitals. The support trenches were made next in case the enemy captured the front line. These also contained first aid and makeshift kitchens. Underground bunkers were created to store food and artillery, doubling up as command stations erected with telephone lines.

The front lines of the trench were tunnels dug to a depth of eight to twelve feet underground, and six feet in width. On most days, the ground of these trenches was filled with heavy water from rain or mud from shell fire, and to prevent them from becoming waterlogged, the men built narrow channels that allowed the water to drain out at regular intervals. Parapets were constructed on the front line to climb up and look out at the enemy. Dugouts or small hollows were built into the sides of trenches, where men could rest, if they had the chance. Sepoys were supposed to spend one week at the front, and one week at the rear trenches or a rest camp. But in the last month alone, many had remained confined to the barrage of shelling at the front, almost always until it resulted either in victory or in death.

Beyond the front line lay no-man's-land, fortified with barbed wire on both sides. This area of barren earth—mushy and boggish, undulating with mounds of mud and dirt, littered with artillery guns, scraps of uniform, bullet casings, stray weapons, grenade shells, and piles of mutilated corpses, and stretching between the two sides of trench lines from 50 to 250 yards—was the land both sides were fighting to gain control over.

Vivek had drawn a map, and Samir turned the small notebook on its head, on its side, and traced each line of the labyrinthine design.

As the year crawled on in Paris, Samir dislocated from the present and committed himself to the journals. He read pages again and again, over weeks and months, until he could narrate passages from memory. Often, he'd refer to the route he had traced on the map, make lists and timelines, and he had begun venturing into bookstores to find anything on the front lines his uncle had written about. When he wasn't reading the journals, he was thinking about them, unable to keep up at work, which led to his termination from the hospital. If he wasn't so consumed by the record of war, he might have been embarrassed or remorseful, but he simply took it in his stride.

Léa, however, watched with great agitation as her husband descended into obsession. He would stand by the window, rocking Sophie to sleep with songs and stories of air raids and frozen battlefields, trenches and encampments. Léa would watch as the child followed the sound of her father's voice with wonder, and if she didn't know any better, she could have believed that he was telling her stories of dragons and knights, fairy tales from faraway kingdoms. Even on days when they went out for a walk or a picnic, Samir was distracted, and she felt him growing anxious without the familiar shape of a journal in his hand.

Feeling in part to blame, she wished she hadn't receded so abruptly. There were times when Samir had tried to share anecdotes, but Léa had feigned a headache or busied herself in Sophie's routine. And though a distance now grew between them, she took consolation in the fact that it was temporary. That one day, the journals would end, and on that day, her husband would have to exhume himself from the past and return to the life they had built together in the present. Léa held on to this hope.

After a week or so of unemployment, Madame Blanchet introduced Samir to an artist who had recently moved to the building, and was looking to hire part-time help for his upcoming vernissage. The pay was meager, and the work involved stretching, building, and transporting canvases, but it was better than nothing and allowed Samir freedom with his time.

One day, after he and Sophie returned from doing the vegetable shopping, they sat on the bed as she played with her dolls and he settled into the journal. Even by mid-April 1915, Vivek's mornings opened in a blanket of fog. By day, he worked on the trenches, and by night, he nursed his misery. No longer was there any warmth to be derived from the outside world. All heat, all hope, had to emerge now from within. He began crawling into himself, into the years of his childhood when he had taken for granted all the moments he now desperately wished for. The present had never been enough until it became the past.

Without any reasonable explanation, Vivek then chose smell to extricate himself from the battlefield. As he wrote less of the world outside and more of the senses inside, Samir began to trace the emergence of a strong yet untrained nose. He rendered phantasmagoric memories of sweet khuss curtains, spicy mango pickles, and luxurious sandalwood paste. And the deeper Samir descended into the prism of this distressed memory, the more he understood the origin of his uncle's nose. Words that had meant little to him as a boy sitting in the atelier suddenly gained new meaning.

It had been longing, homesickness, and misery that drove Vivek to perfumery and fantasy.

In Neuve Chapelle, sepoy Sucha Singh, having spent the last four months in Brighton Hospital with a broken leg, returned to the front. While in hospital, he had received many letters from his village and a package from his new bride that included, among other things, a stick of sandalwood. Relieved to see Vivek still alive after months of battle, Sucha now broke the stick in half and offered it to his friend.

"My heart is the day and the night is fixed on home"—Samir read the final lines on the page, and before he could change his mind, he got up, climbed on a footstool, and brought down Vivek's traveling apothecary. Sophie stopped playing and stared at the vintage leather case with fascination. Ghostly traces of perfume had already begun to escape, and as Samir unclasped the case, the room came alive with powerful fragrances.

Finding the vial of sandalwood, he uncorked it and inhaled deeply. Within moments, he was suspended in the heat rising from the deghs in the distillery. He was afraid that years of deliberate disuse would have rendered his nose incompetent, and yet he returned with ease to the language of his childhood. An affliction was what his uncle had once called perfume, and rightly so, for Samir could not help but surrender to its power.

Holding out the vial to his daughter now, he watched as she leaned toward it, and then turned her attention back to her dolls. She was nearly four years old, an age at which young Samir was smelling everything he could get his hands on. Realizing that Sophie might not possess the gift of smell, his heart crumpled, but he was also glad to not have passed the affliction on further.

Taking another deep inhale, he closed the sandalwood vial and, with the apothecary still beside him, returned to the journal.

Due to the depleting numbers of their company, reserves from the Frontier Force had arrived, and it was then that Vivek was introduced to

Iqbal Khan, a sepoy from the Frontier Province. As Samir read the passage now, he found the words already too familiar.

> Iqbal hails from a long line of calligraphers who worked on the Quranic inscriptions of Wazir Khan mosque, and now run a studio in the bazaar. For the first time since I arrived in vilayat, I feel I have met someone not unlike myself. A man raised on the finer things in life, whether they are scrolls of poetry or reams of silk, is inherently disconnected from the psyche of battle. Like me, he, too, is the first in his family to enlist in the army, wishing to see a world beyond Hindustan, and this fact has brought me great comfort. Noticing this journal in my hand, he smiled, and from the leather cross-belt of his uniform, which usually holds our ammunition, retrieved a small bottle of ink and a bamboo reed. So long it had been since I'd seen such a thing of beauty. Bringing the dawāt up to my nose, I smelled the ink with pleasure, and felt as if home were suddenly within grasp. Taking the journal from my hands, he rendered in it an inscription in the finest hand.

"*Subah ro-ro ke shaam hoti hai, shab tadap kar tamaam hoti hai,* I weep morning into evening, all night I tremble in restlessness." Samir read the ghazal, rendered in a manner so elegant and ornate as he'd only seen Firdaus or her father do.

"Zafar"—Iqbal had even noted the poet below, and Samir remembered how Altaf would often recite his ghazals and qitaats. Bahadur Shah Zafar, the last badshah of the Mughal Empire in Hindustan, banished from his beloved hometown of Delhi by British forces following the revolt of 1857, doomed to spend the remainder of his frail, elderly life in exile in Rangoon. Though this ghazal had been composed in lament of Delhi, it spoke not only to Vivek and Iqbal's plight on the battlefield, but also to Samir's self-imposed exile.

Could it be true that, separated by decades and waters, his uncle had already befriended a part of Firdaus's family? The coincidence was too unsettling, and Samir felt exhausted that the journals contained more secrets than he was prepared to inherit.

That night, he held Léa in his arms as she slept, but found himself thinking of Firdaus. Prompted by his uncle's words, he imagined a history older than their years. No matter how much he'd deny it, there was comfort, a depth to the memory of Firdaus, which the reality of Léa had yet been unable to attain. He wondered if Firdaus ever thought of him. Staring at the dark ceiling, he thought of her soot-colored beauty mark, wishing he could see it one last time. Then, with a deep exhale, he returned to his marriage, locking away futile desires.

# 35

# Breakable, Mortal Bodies

ivek's journal continued to spiral from memories of home to reports of war until the spring of 1915. In the months of April and May, a multiracial force including British and French regiments, with their respective colonial troops from India, Algeria, and Morocco, would fight the series of battles known as Second Ypres. To Samir, the war now seemed unmistakably mechanical. But this time Vivek would leave other clues for Samir.

As he turned the page, the young man was astonished to find a torn scrap of khaki tucked inside. It looked like cloth from a uniform or turban, ragged at the edges, as if it had been violently ripped from its parent garment. Lifting it cautiously with his thumb and forefinger, Samir brought it to his nose. After so many years, it betrayed no trace of battle, for the smells of the trench had evaporated, leaving behind a strangely medicinal dead-leaf odor.

The Lahore Division had been summoned to the trenches on the Franco-Belgian border to repair a breach in their line. They then engaged in a counterattack on the enemy in broad daylight. Companies of Allied soldiers had jumped across the parapet and advanced over rolling farmland toward the Germans, but most were killed or wounded immediately.

Guns had been fired, and violent shells had sent men and their artillery flying back several feet in the air. The sky thundered with the sounds of battle. The Hindustani trench was empty, empty apart from Vivek.

Everyone else had advanced into the field and I had remained. I climbed up the ladder but my feet would not cross the parapet. I was unable to move, like I'd forgotten how to walk. And then suddenly, the weight of a body flung to our side threw me back into the trench. A blackened, mud-covered face. The man was dead, but his eyes were still open, and fresh blood gushed out of his wounds. Men were being flung tens of feet into the air. Empty shells were collecting in the same way one stores heaps of grain, and the stench of blood was overwhelming. I felt sick and vomited across the trench, and then, unable to advance into battle, crawled into a dugout hole. It was the only way I was going to survive.

In one hand, Samir held the journal, and in the other, he grasped the piece of khaki. Vivek had hid in the burrow as bodies began to collect, piling one atop another. He breathed the stagnant air, inhaling his own fear, watching men he'd spent months with die before his eyes. Bodies, malleable enough to bear holes. Bodies, split into fragments of organs and mass. Breakable, mortal bodies.

As horrible screams tore the air, Vivek shrank further into the dugout. Samir read these intimate confessions, ashamed of his uncle's actions yet still sympathetic. Vivek had looked out from the dugout to see British officers, dumbfounded, immediately placing their thick uniform sleeves over their mouths.

A yellow-green curtain hung in the air. It took a while before I understood what this was. We had heard that just days ago, the Jarmans used dhuaan, poison gas, against Francisis, and we had cast it aside as rumor. But now hordes of still-alive infantry begun crawling back to the trenches on all fours, gasping for air. I may never forget the sandpaper-like sounds of their breathlessness.

Samir's face was inches away from the journal. Vivek's handwriting was becoming harder to decipher, the Urdu accents dancing around the words. He felt suspended, like he was reading a story, like this could have been one of the myths or legends of war narrated by his ustad sahib during his childhood. Samir had to consciously remind himself that this was not fiction, for he was entering the darkest depths of his uncle's memory.

I sewed my lips together, shut my eyes, and prayed for the nightmare to end. Prayed and prayed, I thought of Mohan and Ma and Baba, and all the goodness of the world, and Lahore before this war, and the creamy sandalwood. But when I opened my eyes, I was still in the dugout, still holding my breath, still not wanting to give in to death by drowning in poison. The effect of the pineapple-and-pepper-smelling gas caused the eyes and nose to water, throat to close, and mouth to froth in agony. An unforgettable image.

Samir shut his eyes, hoping that when he opened them, the words would have miraculously altered, and his uncle would have fought the Second Battle of Ypres rather than crawling into cowardice. When he opened them and read on, Vivek had emerged. Enemy shelling had subsided, but even in the darkness, the air felt so thick that he could have reached out to touch every particle of gas suspended within it. And over his mouth—tied tightly to prevent himself from inhaling the poisonous air—was his turban cloth, soiled with thick blood, mud, debris, and the foul residue of his own vomit.

Samir was now painfully aware of what the khaki bookmark had meant. He brought it to his nose once again, half expecting it to smell like vomit or blood this time round. Still, it betrayed no foul odor. He read the pages once more, slowly going over each detail. When he was finished, he stared into the darkness, motionless, mouth half open, recalling all the times in his past that his uncle had recoiled from loud noises and commotion—the celebratory crackers on Diwali, the joyous screams on Baisakhi, the dances around the fire at Lohri, wedding parties and processions that led through Anarkali, and even the protests during the months of Partition. Vivek never indulged in any of these, preferring to stay inside, windows closed, in silence. The truth was that the sounds of war had settled into him like a second skin, and if one hadn't known the origin of this fear, one never would have even noticed its manifestations. Samir had never noticed them. But now, as he read this journal, so many things had begun to make sense.

In March 1947, when Master Tara Singh had made his speech in Anarkali against the Muslim League, and Samir had insisted that he wanted to fight against Partition, Vivek had looked at him with an anger in his eyes. *There will be no more battles fought by this family*, he had said that day, and how Samir wished he had listened.

Deciding that he'd read enough for the night, he shut the notebook, stretched out on the sofa where he was sitting, and fell asleep. For hours, Samir tossed and turned, writhing in his sleep as the men had writhed on the battlefield, intoxicated with poison. In his dreams, he was huddled with his uncle in the dugout hole, both of them cowards. He woke up suddenly, beads of sweat dripping down his face, his clammy fingers searching for the journal. He needed to know what happened next, and read into whatever hours remained till daybreak.

From the mouth of darkness, Vivek had crawled out. What propelled him out, he had written, was not the stench of battle, but the simple fear of being caught. The fear that someone, somewhere, would know that he had been hiding in the dugout while his comrades had advanced into battle and to their deaths. He had climbed over the parapet and onto the battlefield, which was littered with the many limbs of dead and wounded men. Arms, legs, foaming mouths, all having inhaled their way to death. Not a trace of any earth was to be seen, for everything was painted red with blood. An Afridi jemadar, who had held the line until nightfall, was now single-handedly removing the bodies of dead and wounded soldiers. He called out to Vivek to check the land for any sign of life.

Across the killing field, Vivek shook men lost to unshakable sleep. No empty space remained on the ground, so he had no choice but to walk over the corpses of men. He heard Sucha gasping for air under the body of another, and carried him back to the trench. A single body lay closer to enemy lines, and Vivek crawled to it, lifting the face up in his lap. With pistachio eyes wide open, and a face caked in mud, it was the lifeless form of Iqbal Khan, bearing three bullets in his chest.

Samir gasped into the silent room. *Pistachio eyes.*

> I shook his body vigorously, but he was long gone, and so I closed his eyes and prayed for his soul to reach heaven. I don't know what came over me then, but I opened his cross-belt to find the hand-carved bamboo qalam. Pocketing it as a way to remember, I lifted Iqbal in my arms and carried him back to the trench.

Horrified, Samir stopped reading. In the darkness of the apartment, he walked to the wardrobe, careful not to wake his family, and carried out Vivek's case, where he had found the journals. He searched for anything small and pen-like, a discreet piece of someone else's history hiding in plain sight. When he found nothing, he opened his uncle's perfumery toolbox and found a slim object wrapped in linen. Unwrapping it, he exhaled heavily, for there sat the qalam, its nib partly darkened with ink. Samir held it as his ustad sahib had once taught him. It was in this way that Firdaus had been connected to Samir since before either of them had even been born. If their meeting wasn't destiny, then he didn't know what was. He wished he could mend the threads that had once bound the two families together. But the people whose stories these were to tell had now passed into the other world.

When Léa awoke the next morning, she found Samir sleeping on the sofa. Beside him on the ground was a slim metal toolbox, and in his hands was the journal he'd fallen asleep reading. Passing him, she took a sharp breath in and walked to the kitchen, only to find the remaining journals strewn across the table. There was a small pile of books, the map with notations, and many, many lists. She glanced at her sleeping husband, then sat down and began shuffling through his papers to discover that Samir not only had transcribed a detailed itinerary of his uncle in the war, but also had begun to keep a record of the living and dead in his regiment. Next to a few were dates; next to others were villages—whatever he had found in the journals. Pushing everything to one side of the table, she stood up and walked to the stove.

Measuring out a cup of milk for Sophie, she heated it in a saucepan and poured it into a feeding bottle. Then she paused, eyes narrow, fire still burning on the stove. Grabbing one of the journals from the table, she ran her fingers over the aged handwriting she could not read. Biting her lower lip then, Léa brought it to the stove until it was inches away from the flame. She considered how easy it would be to erase the past, reduce it to nothing but a pile of ash in mere seconds. These journals had stolen too much of her marriage, and here was her opportunity to reclaim it.

Just then, Sophie let out a cry from the room and Léa felt her breath catch in her throat. With trembling hands, she shut the stove and placed the journal back on the table. Tears filled her eyes, because even if she had destroyed them, she knew in her heart that it would change nothing at all.

Vivek might have survived after the Second Battle of Ypres, but he did not know how much longer he would remain alive or whether he'd even return home. In subsequent entries, Samir noted that he had stopped writing letters for any of the soldiers. He could carry no more burdens and placate no more fears; the only weight he was willing to bear was his own. The new soldiers from the reserve forces didn't know Vivek to be the company scribe, allowing him to slip somewhat into invisibility. In fact, after this battle, he began to retreat into himself, only thinking of ways to escape and how the world would commemorate the valor of men who had survived the limits of human endurance.

May 16, 1915
     The stories of our sipahis will disappear into history, buried like the many bodies in this unknown land. But history must remember that we were here too. We were here too.

Thereafter, Vivek's entries dwindled. If he wrote at all, it was predictably enough about being herded on and off the battlefield. But usually weeks would pass, causing Samir to grow frantic to know what had transpired in the meantime. Gradually, it dawned on him what the family must have felt having no communication from the front. If, decades later and a generation removed, Samir could be shaken by the lack of news, then certainly so would his grandparents have been. Far away, across foreign lands and waters, they must have waited for letters that were never going to come. He soon realized that Vivek's efforts to not provide any news of his whereabouts or health were, in fact, quite deliberate. It was cruel, but shame and guilt would come to define his uncle's experiences in the war.

Through June, the bombing continued, but casualties were few. Vivek's regiment remained inside allotted houses on Loretto Road, where a company of French soldiers joined them. The Hindustanis had begun to speak in the foreign tongue, and words that were once no more than sounds had transformed into comprehensible language. *Keskersay,* a sipahi would ask Vivek during mealtime, pointing to the food, and he would respond with *la-soup-o-pwa,* spooning the sickly pea broth. When orders were given, the Indian Corps was asked, *compray?,* did they understand? Milk became *doolay,* and water *doolow*. In this way, the sepoys formed friendships with their comrades across the world, and Vivek befriended a private named Paul.

> From his wallet, he took out a black-and-white photograph of a small cottage, behind which were fields of flowers. I looked at it closely, and such a heaven I found in that little image as I hadn't even in dreams. I wished to fall into the fields, be blanketed by petals, leaves, fragrance. To erase all other memory, especially of war. "Oo?" I pointed to the house, and raising his nose to the air as if inhaling a beautiful perfume, he said, "Grass. Cey Grass." Tonight, after a long time, my heart has felt light. Everything has changed, for I have found an escape. I must find a way to reach this Grass.

Samir looked up from the notebook. *Grass.* Where had he heard that word? Where had he seen it? Closing his eyes, he brought his palm to his chin and rubbed it. He remembered being ten years old, and sitting with his uncle in the atelier as a pile of secret journals were extracted from a locked drawer and placed before him. The very same journals he was now in possession of. Samir had not been allowed to touch the pages, but it was where he had seen the word. Unfolding his map, he searched across the country until he found it.

"Grasse," he whispered, rolling the *r* and hissing the *s*, just as he had in 1937.

At the close of the month, a disillusioned Vivek had made up his mind. He had seen too much, endured too much, lost too much. He could make his peace with the dampness of uniforms and boots, the outbreak of lice and disease, the hardship of drills and marches, the lugging of trench mortar and guns, the trembling of earth and sky, the toil of crawling in trenches and the isolation of sentry duty. Even the desperate cold could become a thing of no account. But what petrified him still was that a man could be alive in one moment and dead the very next.

> In all my time in these trenches, I have not come across a single sahib who has risked his life to save one of us, and yet we have offered our bodies in their service. We have bound ourselves to a flag that may soon become our shroud. Every day, I hear talk of death. Young boys, old men, who would ordinarily be tending to the fields, rearing cattle, sewing shoes, cutting trees, talk about death as if it were the weather. Every day, counting the dead. Every day, smelling the dead. Every day, picking up the fragments of uniform, hair, badges, shells. Every day, the mangled bodies, the opened eyes, the clenched teeth, the stains of blood. The everydayness of death is fast erasing the possibility of any life existing beyond this war.

And so, the allure of Grasse grew stronger. A town dedicated entirely to perfume, Paul had claimed, where the shadow of war had not yet fallen. It was the furthest smellscape Vivek could imagine from a trench, and thus, it became his resolve. Finally, in July, a seed of escape germinated.

> There is no more space in the hospitals in the north of France. Now all convalescent troops will travel by train to the Hindustani camps and hospitals in the south in Marsay.

The next few pages were haphazard. So far, Vivek had retained a sense of sequence; now he was unraveling. But he left clues, indications of where he was headed and how. First, he recalled the various methods of harm soldiers had inflicted upon themselves or detailed in letters over the last year—how to fake an inflammation, or redden one's eyes, or cause fevers and pneumonia. There was one method that had proven most effective, a measure that, when followed correctly, almost always drove the injured soldier far away from the battlefield and into a hospital in the free land of France. Plotting his escape, Vivek wrote,

> Smear a paste of red berries called rattis across a cotton thread and pass it through the folds of skin on one's neck with a sewing needle. A particularly frightening malady, wherein the glands of the neck and collarbones will become inflamed, tender, and appear to be infectious.

And that was it, the final entry.

Confused, Samir turned the next few pages to find them all empty. That was where Vivek had chosen to stop writing. Henceforth, the notebook was completely silent. Samir figured that his uncle had found a way to administer the berry needle, and had traveled south from the front to Marseilles. But so many more questions flooded his mind that in search of answers, he inverted the entire notebook and shook it vigorously. To his great relief, several folded pieces of paper fluttered out. Out also fell the fir leaf, the scrap of khaki, and a stray cigarette card. One by one, Samir unfolded the pages and read them. Letters from home, each was a letter from home.

Tears stung his eyes as he read his father's childish script. There were several letters from his grandfather written in all shades of emotion, and a single note from his grandmother, from late July 1915. He held it up, balancing it on the tips of both hands, and inhaled its musty, woody, cardboard-like smell, almost expecting to find Leela's signature sandalwood scent embedded within the page. Samir figured that his uncle must have fled right after he received this, for there were no letters dated after.

Then he dove into the pile of journals. If Vivek had somehow made his way to the perfumed town, as Samir imagined he would have, then the journal he was searching for would be the very same one his uncle had used to teach him the olfactive pyramid as a child—a medium-sized blue hardcover, a little worn and tattered. And there it was, exactly how he remembered it. Samir Vij drew a sharp breath in and opened the journal to its title page to find the words he knew would be there.

*Grasse, 1916.*

# 36

## Grasse

April 15, 1916

It began with a hundred-petaled flower. Centifolia, growing in the garden of a cream-colored cottage with a maroon tiled roof, on the outskirts of a town nestled between the mountains and the sea. Here, in Grasse, with the salty air and alpine breeze, Rose sahiba cultivated a flower so beautiful with a fragrance so intense that a single whiff was rumored to melt all the cares of the world. Standing in her fields, I can affirm that it is an experience of pure intoxication, for if there were a heaven on earth, it would be here.

Samir read and then reread the first entry of the new journal, terribly confused, for it seemed to have been written by a completely different person than the Vivek he had come to know. There was no dark hue of battle overshadowing the words, no bullets penetrating the page, and no smellscape of death. In fact, the tone was unrecognizably effortless. But too much seemed amiss—from autumn 1915 to spring 1916, there were simply no entries, as if for those few months, Vivek had camouflaged himself into the silence of the French terrain and emerged here, in Grasse, seemingly renewed. Samir wanted to call out to Léa in the next room so they could talk through this drastic change, but he stopped himself. The journals, it had been made clear, were his burden to bear.

In the past few months, he'd amassed secrets and mysteries beyond expectation. So much of his life had already happened before he was born that reading through the years had made him age without aging. But he had realized that history was never just about the events that had once transpired. It was also about who narrated the events and who heard them; who wielded time, fashioned the years, lived, or resisted them; and who ultimately was bequeathed the archive.

It appeared that Vivek had arrived in Grasse bearing little more than his twenty-two years and a desire for tranquility. But somehow, in the time that the former sepoy had spent there, he had sown the seed of smell that would later be borne by his nephew. If there were answers to be found, they were in these pages from the perfume capital.

Through the early entries of 1916, Samir gathered that Vivek worked as a flower-picker on the farms of the family deRose. Alongside this, he also learned the history of Grasse, which his uncle had very meticulously chronicled, beginning from a time when the town was best known for leather. Tannery workshops filled the streets, as did the foul odor accompanying the trade. Legend stated that a maharani of France was fond of leather gloves, yet their smell repelled her, and so she sought a tanner named Galimard—"Gallymaah"—to scent the leather. Soon, farmers began to grow flowers on their fields for this purpose. Roses, beautiful pink roses, cultivated to ward off the naturally forceful smell of animal hide. Over the years, the trade of leather receded, yet the rose continued to grow, and so to use up the valuable flowers, a new trade was born. Perfume—parfum. In 1747, Jean de Galimard set up the first perfumery of the region.

Vivek found remarkable connections between the life he sought to shed and the one he wished to adopt. He noted that in 1830, around the same time that his family was setting up their clothing enterprise in Lahore, Madame deRose was setting up her eponymous perfumery. Having recently been widowed, she had tended to her garden as a means to pass her days. A single rose grew into a bush of roses, which eventually became a garden and then a field. By the time Parfum deRose opened, the barren land her cottage had once stood on was now flanked on either side by fragrant rose fields. It was from these fields that her name was derived: Madame deRose, or Rose sahiba, as she was to Vivek. Spending time with other flower-pickers, he learned that she had had one son, Antoine, who died in early adulthood, and one grandson, Édouard, whom she had raised. After her passing, he came to be known as Monsieur deRose, or Rose sahib, and though he had many children, it was his eldest, Gaspard, who had inherited the family nose.

One of the most valued smells in Grasse was the otto of the rose. Samir repeated this word, *otto*, with curiosity, and as he read further, a smile appeared on his lips.

> I did not understand the word when I first heard it, *otto*, but the pickers use it often. Upon listening closely, I realized that the word *otto* is another word for our *attar* or *ittar*, derived from the Farsi *itir*, by way of the Arbi *itr*.

From dawn to dusk, Vivek devoted his days to the fragrant fields, cultivating an intimate relationship with the land. He disclosed no fear or apprehension, letting slip not a single word of regret for having left military service the way he had. It appeared that he had progressed straight from sepoy to flower-picker, erasing the role of deserter completely.

"Since it is the season of Rose de Mai, our days are quite busy," he wrote. For eight to twelve hours, the pickers collected up to six kilograms of roses per hour, after which the baskets were transported to the distillery in town. In the evening, they collected at the edges of the fields to receive the day's wages. Many of the women pickers belonged to the Roma clan

and were called La Fleur, The Flower, which Vivek commented on being
a rather befitting name.

Everyone knew of him, the foreign picker, the traveler from the orient—
Grasse was small and news traveled fast. But Vivek never wrote of making
any friends in the fields, or mentioned anyone by name, apart from his
landlady, Madame Pauline. He had taken up a small room near the deRose
distillery, sparsely furnished with a bed, table, and cupboard. The mistress
of the house, a flower-picker in her day, not only provided all the meals
but also had helped Vivek in securing his job. Years of picking, season
after season, had allowed the vocabulary of scent to settle into her as she
attempted to teach the young man the nuances of their profession.

May 17, 1916

Madame Pauline says that perfume is a language, *le parfa
ett uhn longaage.* Without flowers, Grasse would not be Grasse.
I no longer map the year through fabrics or the news. I see no
monsoon and no snow. I follow only the seasons of flowers.

"*Khushboo ek zubaan hai,*" Samir repeated, reminding himself of this
fact. He read through these carefree entries, but wondered about the prag-
matics of beginning again—money, uniform, his rifle and other arms,
his self-inflicted wound, his limited grasp over language, what story his
uncle might have spun in order to receive the hospitality of the people of
Grasse, and how he must have stood out within the populace, brown in
a sea of white. But these details were not divulged. In fact, so far, almost
nothing in this new journal betrayed the fact that Vivek had once been a
soldier at all.

Having lived the past year in the most catastrophic of battlefields,
where the surface of land was the first thing to rupture, Vivek did admit
to finding it extraordinary that in Grasse, it was soil that was most sacred.
But with each page, Samir could feel the skin of war being peeled back,

little by little, to reveal the desire that lay beneath. Of all the organs in the human body, Vivek was learning to rely on his nose.

May 20, 1916

The perfume of not a single bud is wasted here. In the distance, out in the open country, rows and rows of lavender grow like a lush carpet of purple. Electric in their smell, they are a sight to behold. Travelers are often told to simply follow the lavender fields to reach Grasse, so iconic they are in appearance. If you take a sprig, rub it between your fingers, and inhale, the smell is intense and razor-edged. It smells like kapur, camphor, or the first splash of cold water on one's face in the morning!

For the first time in his life, Vivek allowed his senses to dictate his wanderings, something he'd refused to do while on the battlefield. He admitted to the pleasure of getting lost in the web of little streets, often discovering an arch or doorway leading into a prism of delightful smells.

While Vivek was attempting to fold himself into a life far from war, however, the newspapers of the region continued to publish its stories. His grasp over the language bettered with the help of Madame Pauline, and gradually he began to pick up snippets of conversations around town, from families whose husbands and sons had enlisted in the war. Listening to their fears, he confessed to wondering how his family was doing without any news of him. "I know I must write, but I do not have the words . . ."

Though Grasse remained physically unaffected in many ways, Madame Pauline would often read out the news from cities like Paris, where the Grand Palais was converted into a military hospital, laws were extended to the rates of eggs, wheat, milk, and other necessities, and as more and more men were recruited to the army, the women took their places in all kinds of jobs, including transport and factory work. Samir imagined Vivek listening to these headlines over the breakfast table or a dinner of rationed bread, sitting nervously with a cup of tea and overwhelming guilt, because by midyear, his fears flickered openly.

In Grasse, no sounds of battle can be heard, no odor of death lingers. Perfume has built a defensive wall to protect the town, and yet I continue to look over my shoulder, fearful that I may be found out. My heart jumps even when Madame Pauline accidentally drops a metal colander on the ground. I know what happens to soldiers who desert . . . I remember the rumors— the naik serving five years imprisonment, the Sikh sipahis who were publicly lashed. I cannot be found out, and I cannot get caught. But each day, I am afraid that the newspaper will print a report on the authorities looking for a Hindustani sipahi who has deserted the war. Each morning, I wake with the fear that Madame Pauline will discover my uniform and haversack— things I should burn, clues I should destroy, an entire year I should erase. The only truth of the matter is that it is necessary for a man to save his life by any means possible. One must protect the body one inhabits, and this is all that I have done.

By July—when a major battle in the region of Somme was underway— Vivek had become a palimpsest of fear. Fear of the black water, fear of the trenches, fear of death, fear of desertion, and now the fear of being discovered.

He even wrote about Paul, the soldier from Grasse who had first introduced him to the perfumistic town. Looking up at each house he passed, he tried to remember the exact details of the cottage in the black-and-white photograph. Vivek imagined Paul returning home from the war, exhausted, maybe even injured, chancing upon him on a cobblestone lane or flower field, and his secret spilling out. But during Vivek's time in Grasse, no soldier returned, for the war was still very much ongoing.

Eventually, though, he told Madame Pauline to stop reading out the news completely.

"I wish not to imagine it, the war," he pleaded.

And then, instead of writing about fear, he consciously strove to write about pleasure. Through the latter half of 1916, he created distance between himself and the war, attempting to erase it first from his vocabulary, then from his mind, and lastly from his memories. A slow and painful attempt, but an attempt nonetheless. Whenever asked about his origins, he simply stated that he was a nomad.

During the war, writing had become Vivek's release, but now, he wrote only when something happened. Unconnected days of discovery and delight that Samir tried to string together in order to follow a life being lived. Vivek's desertion from the battlefield, thus, was proving not just to be his greatest act of cowardice, but also his very first act of self-preservation. Realizing this, Samir was suddenly struck by the thought that he and his uncle were more similar now than ever. Both men had fled situations beyond their endurance and understanding, without ever considering the ramifications of their flight. Had anyone ever come looking for Vivek? he wondered. Had Firdaus ever come looking for him? Now he would never know.

Feeling small under the weight of a half-finished story, Samir reflected on whether cowardice, too, was a trait that could be passed down. If apart from his nose, he had also inherited his uncle's faint and fearful heart.

# 37

# La Tendresse

On the morning of August 10, 1916, Vivek awoke with the memory of war. But as day bloomed in the jasmine field and he began picking to the usual rhythm, the thoughts subsided. By noon, he was arrested by the smell of lemons and freshness, a starchy, thick waft. Instantly, he was reminded of clothes being beaten and washed on the banks of the Ravi, frothy soap lathering across the rocks by the shore. He looked around the field, desperate to find the origin of the smell, and felt it pass him by. It belonged to a figure with short dark hair tied under a beige scarf, carrying a basket of flowers.

Yet again, the shade of Vivek's writing had transformed, and for a moment, Samir felt he was reading about the first time he had encountered Firdaus. Intrigued, he read on. Day after day, Vivek inhaled the comfortingly fresh aroma and wondered who the woman was. Having never seen her before, he gathered that she was a new picker, and would watch as she moved quietly through the crop, making sure not to bruise a single petal. Vivek knew not her name nor where she had come from. "All I know is that, in her presence, I feel somehow renewed. She is the woman I am going to marry."

Samir chuckled as he read the bold declaration, for he knew this exact feeling; he *understood*. He, too, had once been transfixed by the scent of another, and he, too, had surrendered to it willingly. Whether it was Firdaus's rose in the ittar shop, or Léa's tears in the hospital ward, he knew what it felt like to be consumed by odor in a way that was out of one's control. At the thought of Léa, Samir bit his lip and set the journal down.

Sometimes he felt like he was living with a stranger, for there were clear moments when neither knew how to be in the other's presence any longer. If there was intimacy, it was practiced; if there was joy, it was out of conjugal duty. For a while, he'd wondered how responsibilities at work could have made Léa so distant and began worrying that there was something else awry.

But he would never realize what his uncle's memories had done to his wife, because she would never tell him. She would never allow the words to escape her lips, to acknowledge the depth of feeling that still surfaced for an impossible love, nor the fact that her husband had become a prisoner to his past. In very different ways, their marriage had come to be overshadowed by memories of both their dead, and now the tightrope they straddled had begun to thin to a point that any provocation might have torn it.

With a sigh, Samir returned to the journal, only to discover that while two hearts were diverging in the present, a convergence was underway in the past.

August 28, 1916

The oils from the flowers rose up with the heat, creating a blanket of sweetness around us, and by mid-morning, we met in the center of the field, baskets full of waxy jasmine. Like the other women, she wears a long dress with full sleeves, an apron tied to her front, a scarf around her short hair. Basket attached to her waist, she reached up and wiped the sweat off of her forehead. An oval face with light brown eyes and a sharp nose. She smiled at me, uttering just a single word, rendering me transfixed. "Bonjour."

To Samir's knowledge, his uncle had never married or loved, nor had he ever been intimately acquainted with any woman in Lahore. Was she the reason why? Samir imagined his uncle stringing his infatuation into garlands of jasmine from the fields, as he once had for Firdaus in Lahore. These entries about a new love should have brought Samir closer to Léa, but in fact, they lured him into the deep folds of memory. That day, for the first time since he arrived in Paris, he dug out Firdaus's dupatta.

⚘

On September 16, what would have been Vivek's twenty-third birthday, he went to work with the singular intention of learning his beloved's name. Half a season had passed, and he had barely found the courage to speak around her. On that day, he went in prepared, having rehearsed a patchwork of French well beyond his novice level. Since she was new to the fields, he was going to tell her about how revered the jasmine flower was where he came from. This was no idle conversation; he wished to offer her a part of himself, a real memory. But the closer he got, the more her aroma distracted him and the less he remembered what he wanted to say. She had looked at him in confusion as he fumbled through a mixture of English and badly constructed French, eventually abandoning the attempt and returning to his work in embarrassed silence. But at dusk, after depositing her final basket, she walked up to Vivek at the edge of the flower field.

*Excusez-moi?* she had called out, and Vivek had turned around, surprised. *Toutes mes excuses, mon anglais n'est pas bon.* She'd barely understood him that morning, and yet some otherworldly force had drawn her to him.

She locked her eyes squarely onto mine, and spoke in the way
that longtime lovers do—without words. Ambrette. Her name

is Ambrette, after the musky, sweet ingredient, for perfume runs in the blood and on the tongues of everyone in Grasse. I try and try to say her name as she does in Francisi, but my tongue just does not contort that way. So instead, I call her by another name, a word that is mine, *Amrit,* which means the immortal.

Samir closed the journal and leaned back, unsure of how to feel. For the second time since he found these journals, Samir felt like an intruder. As if he were reading a story he wasn't allowed to, about a person he didn't know at all.

*Ambrette was not just an ingredient; it was a person. She was a real person.* Samir learned that Ambrette was the daughter of the local laveur, a profession that lent her the signature smell of freshly laundered clothes and lemons. As she and Vivek began to spend their days together, the year passed. They strolled the narrow lanes, hand in hand, talking, dreaming, and smelling all that Grasse had to offer. Ever since the desertion, Vivek wanted to write home, but never had. He never could. As his relationship with Ambrette progressed, he wrote about wanting to tell his mother. Arriving at this mention of Leela, Samir winced, for his father had once revealed a truth that his uncle hadn't known at the time—that halfway through the war, their mother had died. Som Nath had written to Vivek, but having deserted when he did, he'd never received the letter, and so wholly unaware, he dreamed of an introduction that could never happen.

Nearing the end of the jasmine harvest, Vivek walked to the fields well before dawn. In the darkness, he lay under a tree beside the carpet of white flowers, listening to the birds stir from their sleep, finding it incredible that such beautiful forms of life should be allowed to exist alongside the war. Taking out Sucha Singh's sandalwood stick from his pocket, he cradled it in his hand. The smell reminded him desperately of home. It was then that he heard a sound behind him, and turned around to find none other than Rose sahib, standing there, his nose inching toward the earthy sandalwood.

Through this interaction, Samir learned that the sandalwood tree did not grow in France, so naturally, the perfumer was surprised to see it in the hands of the young man. Careful not to mention the war, Vivek spoke of his mother, her love for sandalwood, and the reverence that it inspired in his household. Intrigued at the lengths of the world this flower-picker had traversed, the perfumer offered a memory in return. When he was a boy, his grandmother Madame deRose had kept by her bedside a stick of sandalwood procured off a traveler from the Far East. So enamored she was by the exotic wood that each day would begin and end with its aroma.

Vivek had watched as his employer rubbed the sandalwood into the palm of his hand, warm, buttery, ochre-brown, causing the sweet jasmine air around them to grow creamy and thick. The pair spoke until the other pickers began trickling in, and when they parted, Vivek had been promoted to the status of distiller.

Each day, the deRose distillery received baskets and baskets of tuberoses, and three men, including Vivek, would work the machinery for distillation. He described laying all the flowers out like a carpet of pearls, then weighing them, and finally beginning to distill their essence.

October 30, 1916

There are two methods of distillation. For the flowers that continue to produce fragrance long after they are picked, like jasmine, mimosa, and tuberose—too delicate to steam—the method of cold enfleurage (*an-flah-raj*) is practiced. A large framed plate of glass called a chassis (*shasee*) is smeared with a thick layer of animal fat and allowed to set. Then the flowers are carefully placed onto the fat and their scent diffuses into it over the course of twelve to fourteen hours, until the oil is completely odiferous.

Women are most skilled in this method, and they sit among the fresh flora, carefully handpicking and depositing. Their fingers move in choreographed gestures to and from the pile to the frame, placing, pressing, preserving. It is time-consuming work, but perfumery is an art of serious discipline. The second and oldest method to extract the oil of flowers like roses, violets, or orange blossoms is hot enfleurage. The flowers are immersed into large vessels with animal fat, and heated. For hours, we must stir this mixture, strain it, and replace with fresh materials, until the fat itself is saturated with fragrance. Then we filter the matter through layers of fine fabric.

His uncle had always stressed the different ways the East and West distilled perfumes, but Samir had never seen anything other than the degh-bhapka technique that Ousmann taught him. He now realized what a treasure these journals were, and suddenly understood why Vivek had remained so protective about them.

November 10, 1916

Hand in hand, Ambrette and I walk home in the evenings, and I cannot help but wonder if such a friendship would ever be allowed in Hindustan. But here, far away, I have attained freedom in life and in actions. My escape has become my privilege. The people of this land are free from rumor and gossip, caste and religion. Men and women choose whomsoever they wish to befriend or even marry. In the army, I knew sipahis who kept relations with women in the towns we encamped in, and men who married those women as well. There were those who wove tales in the letters they wrote home, so fearful they were of their actions, as if those at home would consider them unholy. But when I see Ambrette, I know that no such relation can ever be unholy. I see not her color, nor her religion, and least of all that she is Francisi. I see only that my heart greatly desires her.

Week after week, Vivek was growing into a skilled distiller. One afternoon, Rose sahib visited the distillery and motioned for Vivek to follow him to the basement, which appeared no less than a laboratory, with rows and rows of bottles containing clear and colored liquids.

This was to be his new abode, as he began working as an apprentice directly under Édouard deRose. It was a rather unusual arrangement, for a non–family member had never trained under the master perfumer, least of all someone so nomadic. But Vivek was different, and Rose sahib was quick to realize that. Having advanced promptly from the fields to the distillery to the atelier, Vivek now spent his days surrounded by bottles and vials, books and notes on the practice of perfumery. He noticed that several of Madame deRose's original formulas, some dating as far back as the mid-1800s, continued to be composed and celebrated by the family. And soon, he was introduced to the man who would be his companion on this educational stint, Gaspard deRose, Rose sahib's oldest son. Close in age, the two young men became friends, and at times collaborators in their experiments in the atelier.

Sometimes when he watched Rose sahib and Gaspard in the atelier, Vivek thought back to working with Som Nath in the clothing shop, and though his hands now held vials and droppers, they still remembered the feel of linen and silk. They instinctively understood how long a gaz of fabric was, had memorized the lengths of turban cloth.

"The body does not forget the movements it has been born with, and muscle memory remains stronger than any form of forgetting," he wrote. Upon reading this, Samir looked down at his hands. Did he still remember how to properly handle a kuppi, how to lather mud along the sides of a degh, how to tell when the sandalwood was distilled to perfection? If he understood his uncle's words correctly, would his own body still retain the gestures of a perfumer?

Vivek's entries now became less personal to make room for sensorial observations. Lists of essences and raw materials emerged; formulas, notes, and smellscapes were constructed. Rose sahib offered his two disciples the aromatic lore of the wide world, and faithfully, twenty-four-year-old Vivek transcribed it into his journals.

December 22, 1917

Smell is the emperor of all senses. In lands far away, where earth and body converge harmoniously, it is regarded as no less important than the language one speaks—essential, intimate, and often even elevated. Smell is voluptuous, it has volume, it blooms. And since it is invisible, a product of desire and imagination, it is also limitless.

*Indeed, it is,* Samir thought to himself as he flipped through the remaining pages of the journal to find only notes on ingredients and their measurements. He felt heavy, like his body was made of stone and his mind of sponge. But he rummaged through the journals until he found one labeled *1918.* And when he opened it, there she was.

For a while, Samir stared at the sepia photograph of Ambrette standing next to his uncle. She had beautifully large eyes, the kind his mother would have called mrignayani, and was dressed in a floor-length, full-sleeved white dress. In her hair were two white roses. She wore no jewelry apart from a ring on her left hand. Samir brought the photograph up to his face for a closer look. *A wedding band?* Immediately, his eyes focused on his uncle, who was dressed like the pakka sahib he remembered. A white shirt, dark trousers, and a jacket. On his lapel was pinned a single white rose. He hugged her from behind, his right hand nestled at her waist. And on his clean-shaven face, Vivek wore a smile that Samir had never seen before. Serene, buoyant, radiant almost. A smile that hid no secrets beneath its crease. He turned the photograph over.

*Ambrette & Vivek Vij, 13 Avril 1918. Grasse, France.*

# 38

# The Confession

On the evening of March 30, 1918, Vivek led Ambrette to the edge of the flower fields, with the intention of telling her the truth about his life.

Hindustan. She repeated it slowly and carefully. *Hindoostaan.* She silenced the *h,* sharpened the *d,* tightened the *t,* and in typical French manner barely pronounced the *n* at the end, but even so, the word she uttered was *mine.* I belonged to it. Hindustan. It took me home, whatever home had metamorphosed into.

For her, Vivek evoked the ochre of Lahore shehr, the brown of the dust, the brick walls of his home, the carved wood of the window frames, the sounds of hawkers and children in the lanes, the smell of the chilies, the samosas, the grass, the sky, the earth, the rain. He described all the smells he could remember. He could tell that she was surprised and curious and confused and amused at his sudden wistfulness, his sudden need to share. Vivek recorded her smile to be like the curl of a rose petal as she posed a question. It was a single word, but sufficient to conjure an entirely intimate yet distant world. *Famille.*

So I tell her about Ma and the sandalwood and Baba and the clothing shop and Mohan. So many stories about Mohan. I describe his teenage face, his hopes, his kindness. In this way, I reveal my deep yearning for home, for *ma famille*, speaking with my hands, body, heart, and memory. Ambrette nods like she understands. But how could she? She was born in Grasse, and has never once stepped outside this land. She has never yearned for a different sky, or dreamed in a language left behind. She has not worn her home on her back, concealed it, protected it, even suffocated it. She has only ever *lived* it. So how could she understand?

If he wanted any form of future with Ambrette, then she would have to know everything, for in love, there was no room for deceit. And so, in an effort almost identical to how Samir had unraveled himself before Léa, Vivek exhumed the past for Ambrette, emptying himself of it all.

Lahore, Karachi, Aden, Suez, Marseilles, Orléans, Wytschaete, Ypres, Messines, Essars, Festubert, Neuve Chapelle, Grasse, I recalled every land traversed. I told her about the black waters, and the friends I fought alongside, about the Russi sahiba, pistachio-eyed Iqbal and his bamboo reed in my possession, about the uniforms, rifles, bayonets, airplanes, and bombs. I told her about being buried under the rubble. I left nothing out, not the bodies nor the mass burials, the smell of charred skin or the ghostly vacant towns. The sounds, all the sounds of war. I told her about the voices and languages, the lonely nights, the filthy trenches, the smell of death, the lice, the rats, the gas. The poison gas. I emptied myself of it all.

Samir tried to imagine what Ambrette must have felt, what kind of man her beloved must have seemed to her in that moment. Did she think

him a coward, or a liar, or the kind who felt too guilty to write home, or
the kind who fled, deserted, absconded, escaped without a trace? But the
floodgates of Vivek's memory had been opened; it was a deluge without a
dam. Samir's face tightened as he read on.

> I would have died. Had I not escaped, I would have died. I
> described threading the toxin of berries through the skin on
> my neck. I described the pain, as if I'd been set on fire. But as
> expected, my neck became enraged and I was transported from
> the front to the Indian hospital in Marseilles. After my wounds
> had been tended to, I escaped and ran as fast as my feet would
> carry me. Hour after hour, until I arrived in the lap of my ref-
> uge. The flower fields of Grasse.

After one year of being confined to tunnels, trenches, and billets, Vivek
had walked free and unrestricted. He had stretched his body and breathed
the fresh and unsoiled air. Ending his confession with the kindness of
Madame Pauline, the knowledge of Rose sahib, and the love of Ambrette,
he revealed the stark contrast of civilian life. How in battle, one lost touch
with all kinds of intimacies; that outside of war, even the gentlest of gestures reverberated. When he finished his tale, he felt wrung out.

> Before leaving, she said only a single word. *Demain.* And so, I
> wait.

Samir turned the page to tomorrow to read that when Vivek arrived at
the distillery, Ambrette was already sorting through the wild mimosa. A
smell of sweet almonds and honey, cucumber and violet, emanated from
piles of the feathery flower. In Grasse, the mimosa was soft, fuzzy, and
a sun yellow; in Hindustan, it was pink. Vivek had stood by the door,
watching her fingers picking each flower and depositing it carefully on the
layer of fat. She had repeated the movement until the frame was full, and

only then did she look up to find him standing there. Their eyes met, and Vivek found her expression hard to read. Everyone else continued working, while she rose and walked in his direction. Samir imagined the petals of the feathery mimosa fluttering in the air.

> She held out a single yellow bloom, as an offering. And then asked, *c'est tout,* is that all, is there more you need to tell me? Shaking my head, I replied, *c'est tout,* that is all, I am emptied. She held my hand, as if nothing had changed.

Two weeks later, they were married. And separated by decades and death, Samir Vij had inherited an aunt he never knew.

As the hundred-petaled rose bloomed across Grasse once again, the newly married couple fell into a rhythm. Every morning began with boiling a pot of water for tea. Vivek laid out two cups side by side; then breakfast and chores and they left the house, walking toward the distillery. Some days he was required to oversee the distillation, and others he spent in the atelier. In the evening, the couple walked home together, hand in hand. If war was death, and perfume was life, then Vivek, suspended between both, anchored himself to Ambrette.

In the summertime, Ambrette had asked Vivek the unaskable, *When will you write?*

Home, she meant, when would he write home? How would he tell his family? When would he tell his family? *Soon,* he had promised her, *soon.* She had inquired whether he was afraid of what they would say, for he had married a Christian woman, in secret, out of their knowledge. But holding her hand, this extraordinary wife of his, he had assured her that there was no fear, nothing that could diminish what he felt for her.

Thereafter, Vivek attempted to compose Lahore—pages and pages of formulas and ingredients. It appeared that since Vivek could not muster the courage to compose a letter, he began by composing a sensation. He wove together his lived years, the histories of his ancestors, the story of his departure and his yearning. He attempted to build a fragrance around the flower—the same flower that Ambrette had presented him with, the same flower that was considered both traditionally Hindustani and French. A flower serving as a bridge became the inspiration for a perfume called *Lahore*.

Yet again, Samir found himself returning to the leather case in the wardrobe. Rummaging around the oldest-looking vials, he found a set of test tubes, each labeled with the word *Lahore*. As he uncorked bottle after bottle, the aromas cascaded like invisible vines all around him. For many minutes, he remained motionless, breathing very gently. Then his back straightened, his eyes closed, and he took a deep and hungry inhale, detecting mimosa, honey, iris flower, sandalwood, cashmere wood, and something that smelled like an insect note. Then, evoking his own long-unused olfactive imagination, he pictured the delicacy of the mimosa flower and mentally added a note of bergamot, a hint of jasmine, and anise. *Spices evolved,* he remembered his uncle always saying, *they took up volume.* With a pencil, in the margins of Vivek's compositions of *Lahore* from decades ago, he noted his own additions.

Smell was so personal, its memory so powerful, its intonation so precise, and yet the element of surprise was a quintessential component of the art.

In the autumn of 1918, Vivek wrote almost exclusively about his education, filling pages with formulas and measurements, tables and alterations, diagrams and tests. Only twice during this interval did he write personal entries. But so cryptic were they that Samir could have easily missed them among the technical idioms, had he not been following the dates.

"Four years have passed, and the SS *Teesta* now resembles an image from a dream," he had written on August 25, 1918, recording the anniversary of his departure from Hindustan.

And then, mere weeks later, on September 16, 1918, Vivek wrote, "Twenty-five today." Another birthday had passed.

In early November, Gaspard traveled to Paris, leaving Vivek alone with Rose sahib in the atelier. A few days after that, the newspapers announced that the war had come to an end, the act of surrender signed, causing Vivek to finally feel safe. Such an alliance had been built between him and his teacher that Vivek had often wanted to explain how it was the trenches that led him to perfumery, but he could not. Too much would have had to be accounted for; too much would have had to be disclosed. It had been difficult enough to confess to Ambrette, but in admitting the past to Rose sahib, Vivek would have risked his position at the atelier. He would remain no mere traveler, but become a recognized deserter of war. The more time the pair spent alone, though, the more these thoughts magnified in his mind.

And though he would protect himself from all the tangible traces of war, Vivek would never truly anticipate what intangible, invisible assailants like smell could do, or when they might appear. This became clear when, one day, Rose sahib offered the young man two small, waxy, stonelike lumps, one black and one white, both varieties of an ingredient called ambergris. When Samir read this, he recognized it immediately. Abeer, Vivek had called it in Urdu; the abeer incense that burned in Emperor Akbar's Mughal court.

November 24, 1918

Of the two varieties, the white is smooth and pleasant. This is the aged ambergris, and its smell is earthy and mossy, like the sedate dampness of a dark forest. As it floats in the water, it ages, fading into a smoky, cigar-like fragrance. This is the variety that perfumers look for. But fresh ambergris, black, soft, lumpy, is strongly unpleasant. To many, it smells of rotting wood, but to me, it smelled of rotting corpses. The moment I inhaled its odor, I found myself paralyzed; every movement felt a burden.

Rose sahib continued to speak, but the muscles on my face tightened, and before my eyes appeared the lifeless faces from the battlefield. Excusing myself suddenly, I placed the ambergris on the table and left the atelier. I ran all the way home, and with a pounding heart I poured my memories out into Ambrette. She listened as I lightened myself, and now, as she prepares the evening meal, I write these words.

Samir pictured his uncle sitting at a writing desk, the room illuminated with the light of oil lamps, pouring himself into the pages of his journal. Closing his eyes, Samir imagined the smell of food wafting into the room, of Ambrette's lemons and starch. He wondered whether Ambrette knew the extent of what Vivek wrote; he wondered whether she ever asked, or whether she'd read it. He imagined her, this faraway aunt of his, returning to his uncle's side from time to time, food left unattended on the stove, apron around her waist, her hands massaging the gentle folds of skin at the back of his neck, her fingers in his hair, willing him into tranquility, whispering words of affection and the secondhand memories of home that she had inherited from her complicated husband.

By the end of the year, Vivek's entries had become so peppered with mentions of Lahore that Samir was certain he was on the verge of writing home. He composed accords called *Reshmiya* and *Anarkali, Age 10* and *Age 17,* and as Samir looked at the formulas for these, he found at the heart of each oils and pomades quintessential to the most sacred Hindustani ittars: cypriol, lotus, frangipani, agarwood, saffron, sandalwood. Vivek was wading through Rose sahib's cabinets, searching for the formula that would lead him home.

And then, when one year had passed since they'd been married, something wonderful compelled Vivek to decide that home could no longer remain a place of the past: Ambrette was expecting their first child.

## 39

### The Slow Wilt

As Samir read through Vivek's journal from the year 1919, he took out the ittar his uncle had composed using his wife's namesake as the heart note, *Amrit*. Enclosing it within his palm, Samir shut his eyes and recalled the day he first smelled it. The same day he had first met Firdaus. The same day he had been granted access into the sacred atelier behind the ittar shop. The same day he had asked his uncle about the intersection of smell and skin, perfume and person.

Now, just like then, Samir uncorked the vial and inhaled. Freshly laundered clothes, starch, cotton, grass, florals, woods, and lemons, altogether. It was the smell of summer in Grasse. The smell of folded skin, of warm crevasses, of human touch. Having come to know Ambrette through these journals, Samir realized that this was the smell of enchantment and bliss.

Ten-year-old Samir had asked after the perfume's muse, to which a stuttering Vivek had confessed inspiration from *someone* he'd met in vilayat. Samir had never questioned this someone—he had had no reason to—and yet now he realized that his uncle had distilled love into liquid. *Amrit* turned out to be the Vijs' best-selling ittar, hundreds of people had donned the heavenly concoction, and yet only a single man had known the perfume's truth.

Carefully placing the cork back on the bottle, he returned to the page as questions began to flood his mind. He was certain that Vivek had returned to Lahore alone, but what had happened to Ambrette and the child? Why had the marriage fallen apart? Could it be that, at this moment, there was a cousin he had never known?

*

By June, a bump had emerged. Vivek could see it even across Ambrette's apron, the little round shape as she sat among the flowers and chassis. The Roma women rubbed her belly and Madame Pauline fed her delicious sweets. Her cheeks had become flushed and round, and in her hair were strings of jasmine flowers. Vivek now wanted for nothing but a simple existence, where his family would one day be reunited.

> August 7, 1919
>
> In the mornings before the sun rises, we lie side by side, Ambrette and me, skin to skin. My fingers graze the insides of her arms, causing her body to smile. I rest my ears upon her swollen belly and hear the heartbeat from within. The colors of our skins, our eyes light and dark, the shape of our fingernails, the bones of our ankles, the bridges of our noses, the points of our ears, my smell of sweat and sandalwood and hers of lemons and grass will all conjoin into a single, perfect person. A baby girl whom we will name Anouk, after Ambrette's grandmother. And when she is old enough, when she is strong enough, we will go to Lahore.

At times, Samir still felt a sense of invasion, particularly with these entries of intimacy that took him back to the days of his first love. Rubbing his fingers across his lips, he tried to ignore the growing guilt in his heart as he thought about Firdaus. Nothing, not even marriage, it seemed, could erase how he missed her skin, her smell, her presence, her *everything*.

For the first time since he left Lahore, he felt overwhelming regret for not having fought harder for his beloved. For not having fought at all, in fact. She had told him to leave, and without question, he had walked away. He wanted to undo all the threads and retie them in a way that he and Firdaus would never be parted.

Carrying this dual feeling of love and guilt, he read the remaining pages, drifting through flowers, fragrances, plans of Lahore, and language lessons between the couple. He picked up their photograph again and wished he and Firdaus could have taken something similar in their years together. Memory was invisible, and even the most memorable of experiences eventually faded. And so, he wished for physical proof, to reaffirm that a world belonging only to them had once existed.

Meanwhile, in Vivek's world, two were becoming three, and perfume remained the only constant. In the course of these months, he composed minor accords that he called *Parwana*, the lover, and *Taveez*, the talisman. The formulas of these were written in manners different from before, for together with ingredients and their measurements, the perfumer had jotted down verses of poetry. So close he felt to these compositions, so personal and intimate they were—drawn from the world that he and Ambrette were constructing together—that there essentially remained no other form but the poetic to communicate their emotion.

Gingerly, Samir stroked the words with his forefinger, he lifted the notebook and smelled the pages, as if within the woven fibers was stored the scent of love. He continued on until he reached December. And quite abruptly, the entries ended.

December 10, 1919

She has died, they have both died. And now, nothing remains

Breathing heavily, Samir tore through the remainder of the journal to find it empty, save a few notations at the very back. Tears had collected in the corners of his eyes, and wiping them away, he tried to make sense of the cryptic words and dates.

Grasse 01.01.1920
Cannes 03.01.1920
St. Tropez 07.01.1920

Many others, too, were listed, but he couldn't understand why. Overcome with grief, he let the journal fall from his hands and the tears fall from his eyes.

Years ago, years before he was born, the aunt he never knew and the cousin he never had had died, and with them, part of his uncle, too, had perished. And *no one* had known; not a single person had known. How far could one suppress memory? How could his uncle have kept this to himself, silently living day after day with such tremendous loss? Samir understood how the story of Vivek's desertion from war might have brought shame upon the family, but to have to suffer *this* in self-imposed silence and seclusion was another form of torture altogether.

Samir felt insignificant when faced with how his uncle's life had unfolded. Both men had been separated from their beloveds at young ages, but Firdaus had quite knowingly made that decision, and Ambrette had simply been snatched away.

Samir unfolded the map that Syed Ali had bequeathed to him, and plotted the cryptic list of dates and locations. If he understood this to be Vivek's journey home, then the route seemed to be an aimless and haphazard one. Following the dates, Samir traced his uncle's footsteps, leaving Grasse on the first day of 1920, just weeks after Ambrette's passing, and returning to Lahore sometime in the late summer. By these indications, he had traveled for over six months, with no details or clues as to what he'd done for survival, employment, or passage. There was no information on his position at Rose sahib's atelier, or whether or not he had ever intended to return. But the most alarming aspect was that all sense of smell was completely absent. During his journey back across land and water, there was not a single mention of what anything smelled like.

Samir recalled how after he fled from Lahore, loss had seized his nose; how for the entire duration of his time in Delhi, he had been unable to *trust* his nose. Composition had become impossible, but to smell and feel pleasure—the simplest function of his anatomy—was unbearable. As a child, he had learned that humans inhaled over twenty thousand times a day, and yet at that moment, all his inhales had become vacant. In fact, he had felt as though he couldn't breathe anymore, as if pockets of stale breath had been lodged in his throat. Suffering had perforated his senses in the most alarming way, and he wondered whether his uncle could have felt the same.

Separated by decades, Samir Vij shadowed his uncle's journey home, using a pencil to lay down a path, creating more and more distance between Vivek and the mecca of perfumery.

Grasse 01.01.1920
Cannes 03.01.1920
St. Tropez 07.01.1920
Hyères 10.01.1920
Arles 15.01.1920

Vivek had traveled along the coast, through small towns and hamlets, sometimes quickly passing through, other times lingering, but carefully avoiding destinations that the sepoys or army had once inhabited.

Nîmes 16.01.1920
Montpellier 17.01.1920

Paris 20.02.1920
London 01.04.1920
Liverpool 10.06.1920
Bombay 02.08.1920
Lahore 20.08.1920

*Lahore,* Samir said first in his mind, then out loud, "Lahore." The familiar word felt foreign when released into the Parisian air. It returned to him as empty as an echo.

# PART FOUR

# 40

# From the Paris of the East

When Samir arrived in Grasse in 1959, the season of roses
was upon them. The legendary hundred-petaled Rose de
Mai blossomed all around. He had traveled by train from
Paris, suitcase in one hand, Vivek's leather apothecary case in the other,
leaving his wife and daughter behind, promising to return in a few weeks.
It was in this land of perfume that he would finally unearth a complete
past. Walking through the undulating, hilly terrain, Samir paused as he
caught first sight of an ocean of pink in the distance and remembered
Vivek's words.

> In Grasse, if I put my touch to the ground, I can detect the salt
> of the earth, bestowed upon it by the surrounding water body.
> No doubt it adds something unique to the flowers, a salty mar-
> itime splendor, for the rose I have smelled here exists nowhere
> else with such intensity.

Letting his suitcase and burdens fall to the ground, Samir touched his
nose to the soil and inhaled. A deep and complete inhale, an inhale to
claim the elements.

⁂

"*D'où? D'où venez-vous?*" the ninety-year-old, wheelchair-bound French-man asked, looking up from the desk piled high with perfume and paper. The floor was covered with a rich, maroon carpet; the tables were scat-tered with folios tied with string and droppers leaned inside half-empty vials. The wall was filled with shelves of leather-bound books, and the record of a violin concerto played in the background. The aging perfumer pushed his gold-rimmed spectacles higher up his nose to get a better look at the visitor without an appointment.

Samir looked down at his feet nervously. He had wandered through the quaint town, apprehensively seeking directions until he was pointed to the palatial Villa deRose, perched atop a hill on the outskirts. Once there, he was led into a library-cum-study, and now, upon entering, his nose was undergoing an assault he could not ignore. There was a curtain of sweet sticky honey smells emanating from open bottles on the table, smoke from the loban burning in the corner, and something else soft, mildly peppery and green, snaking around the room. Samir tried to focus.

"Excuse me . . ." he began.

Édouard deRose wheeled himself out from behind the desk, speaking now in English, heavily lathered with a French accent. "Young man, from where have you come?"

"L-Lahore, Rose sahib," Samir replied.

"Ah! From the Paris of the East! Lahore, with its ittars of sandalwood and agarwood, vetiver and cypriol." The old man's face softened. "Many years ago, a young perfumer worked here, he was also from . . ." He let his sentence linger, unfinished, brought his fingers up to his chin, and began counting the years. "And . . . Rose sahib," he said slowly. "Oui, that is what he called me, too."

Rose sahib now studied the young man's face for a few seconds. Then he looked him straight in the eye, and Samir could tell that he, too, was lost for words.

*It can't be,* the old man thought to himself. *It just cannot be.*

And picking up on this unspoken dialogue, Samir gave a gentle nod. *But it is. It is.*

"*Êtes-vous, uh, pardon,* are you, by any chance, the son of Vivek Vij?"

"His nephew," Samir replied softly. "He was my uncle."

Édouard deRose sat motionless for a moment, and then, suddenly, his face broke into a wide smile and he invited the young man in for an embrace. Questions erupted—*How is your uncle, what is he doing, what is he composing, has he accompanied you, does he speak of us, does he remember his time here?* Rose sahib called for his son Gaspard, who was equally as delighted to receive Samir. But with their every question, Samir's loss seemed to grow more pronounced.

"He *was* my uncle," Samir finally repeated. And then, opening his suitcase, he retrieved the dusty black-and-white framed photograph from 1937.

Morning passed into afternoon, and afternoon spilled into evening as Samir spoke. He began with everything Vivek had not begun with, for the beginning was essential to the end. The enlistment, the voyage, the trenches, the war, the desertion, and then Grasse. Drawing a breath, he paused, allowing the deRoses to absorb Vivek's history.

"He was gifted," Rose sahib's raspy voice broke the silence. "Of that, there was no doubt. The moment I met him in the jasmine field, I knew that his was a nose to remember, but to learn that the war bestowed Vivek with that nose." He sighed deeply. "We are not all born with the gift of smell, and, well, he betrayed nothing of his experiences in the battlefield, not once. He seemed . . . nomadic, as though he had arrived in search of something, and in Grasse, that something had been found. I always wondered where he derived his imagery from, for all his compositions carried an element of escape."

"One could often find him just lying in the fields," Gaspard added. His English was just as precise as his father's, but with an accent less

French and more ambiguous. A few years older than Vivek would have been, the sixty-nine-year-old perfumer had a handsome face with light blue eyes, a hawk nose, and tousled gray hair. He was now *the* nose of Parfum deRose, the third-generation inheritor of an institution. "Vivek craved simple pleasures—waxy petals, green leaves, damp soil, clear sky, the silence of dawn."

*I know this,* Samir wanted to say. *I have read it.* But he was not yet willing to reveal the journals in his possession. There were some secrets that would remain between his uncle and him.

"After he left in 1920, there was no news of him," Rose sahib recalled. "I waited for a letter, a postcard, any information. But none ever came. He was with us only for four years, and in the nearly forty years that have passed since, not a day has gone by when he hasn't crossed my mind." He then tapped his forefinger on his nose, similar in shape to his son's. "Are you also a perfumer?"

After a moment, Samir nodded. "I was told that I was born with the monsoon in my nose."

As Samir detailed the twenty-seven years from when Vivek had left Grasse to the Shahalmi fire, father and son had quietly listened. Cups of coffee were brewed and drunk; bread, vegetables, and fruits were nibbled on; tears were wept, and the dam to the bygone years was forever opened.

"Only I survived," Samir admitted, "and I don't know if I will ever forgive myself for it."

Gently, Rose sahib reached out for the young man's hand. But Samir looked on beyond the two men at the book-lined wall, and asked, "Can you tell me about Ambrette?"

Since his uncle had written nothing, save a single sentence, about her death and his hasty departure from Grasse, Samir now relied on the deRoses to fill in the gaps. But at the mere mention of her name, both men looked visibly unsettled.

"Life was not fair to Vivek," Gaspard began, his fingertips massaging his temples. Then he got up from his chair and looked out the window at the twilight hour. "Ambrette, what shall I tell you about Ambrette? For a while, it seemed that no two people could have been happier. They had nothing in common, not even language, and yet they fit together, seamlessly."

He relayed the details that Samir already knew, about how a dalliance was born in the jasmine fields, how it knit two hearts into one, and then how suddenly it was shattered. Gaspard had been with Vivek, waiting outside the house as Madame Pauline and the midwife had aided with the delivery inside. The couple had even picked a name.

"Anouk, like Ambrette's grandmother; Anouk, which meant grace."

It was Gaspard who had first received the news of death, it was he who had broken it to Vivek, and it was he who had consoled the devastated widower in the weeks that followed.

"It was in the small, almost unnoticeably mundane things that his heartbreak echoed. Like how their day began . . ." Gaspard cleared his throat. "Two cups. Every morning while she was alive, he would pour out two cups of tea. After she died, he continued this for days, weeks, I think. Two cups—one used, with tea residue at the bottom, and the other unused, untouched, inverted. Like one half of a whole. Her clothes were still hanging in the closet when he left Grasse, her chassis remained unused by anyone else at the distillery . . ."

He then took a deep breath and repeated, "Life was not kind to my friend."

"What happened to him after she died?" Samir asked.

"It was painful, he fell completely apart." Édouard spoke now. "After Ambrette, Vivek had no control over anything. Not how he felt, not what he did, not even how to smell."

Samir's eyebrows shot up.

"Oh, yes, he could not smell. Suddenly, his nose was vacant, gone, *c'était fini.* All beauty had escaped into sadness, and all he smelled was filth. He spoke repeatedly about smelling corpses and blood, wet metal and marsh, pineapples and pepper."

The battlefield, Samir realized. His uncle had unraveled into the battlefield.

"In the atelier," Gaspard added, having spent every day with Vivek, "the peach note smelled like rotting greens to him; he would mistake a sweet caramel note for the fecal-smelling black ambergris. And taste . . . well, with the absence of smell, all food also lost its appeal."

Rose sahib offered an explanation. "But he was heartbroken, you see. He was like turbulent waters, and his experiences were propelling him to compose, for there were so many emotions he wished to bottle and hold on to. In the days immediately following Ambrette's death, smell was something he desperately wanted to control, but just couldn't. He wanted to compose something about her, for her, something that possessed her memory, but it was too soon. The sadness was too dense, and his nose was saturated with it."

"Is this . . . normal?" Samir asked.

"Mais oui, but of course. It is quite normal, and usually a temporary condition, lasting until we cease to feel suffocated by our grief. Le nez, the nose, is a unique organ, and being a nose is even more so. We wish to hold on to the smell of a beloved's skin—the sweat, the air, everything that has been absorbed into it. We want to re-create and bottle what we love, particularly if we have lost it. But this process of creation needs time, distance, and recollection. How we remember the smell of another is changeable by our experiences, alterable by time and weather and light, and the maturation of our own senses. It is a forever kind of yearning that few have been able to capture, where each attempt becomes a refuge."

Recalling all the vials composed as homages to Lahore, Samir nodded. He wondered whether Rose sahib was speaking from experience, if he had lost a lover, a wife, a father, a mother, a grandmother; if he had attempted to bottle them.

"Samir, ce la mémoire . . . this memory is a rather distressing endeavor."

For the second time that day, the young man reached into his suitcase and began shuffling through the contents. The rustling of papers, the shifting of clothes, and the rattling of perfume bottles filled the otherwise silent room.

"He did it eventually," Samir said. "In Lahore, nearly twenty years after her passing, he composed something beautiful and powerful, inspired by her."

He placed Vivek's vial on the table before them. Ambrette as an elixir, immortal, *Amrit*.

# 41

# The Perfumed Land

Holding Sophie's hand, Léa walked down the stairs from their apartment to Madame Blanchet's, where she dropped her daughter off and headed to the hospital. Buttoning up her cardigan, she held on to her nurse's cap as she walked against the wind. It had been a few days since Samir had left for Grasse, and if she was being honest, it had been a relief not to fall asleep or wake up to his figure hunched over a pocket-sized journal. Over the last few months, all he'd paid attention to were words from a time he could not change.

The final unraveling had happened last week, when she was at the hospital and he was supposed to pick up Sophie from Madame Blanchet's after his shift at the artist's studio. But he was so engrossed in the pages of the journal that not only had he forgotten to pick up their daughter, he had not gone in to work at all. Léa would have been more furious had she not returned that night to find her husband weeping on the apartment floor, a pile of journals strewn around, and open bottles of perfume enveloping him in a cloud of sorrow. Stitching her anger into silence, she had cradled him in her arms like a child as he finally revealed what had happened to his uncle. From the battlefields to the flower fields, from a secret desertion to a secret marriage, the content of the journals had left her husband in a state of delirium.

Their marriage was fragile. It had felt so devoid of love for the past several months that when Samir revealed his wish to go to Grasse to search for answers, Léa thought that some distance might actually rejuvenate their relationship. They had never once been apart, and she wanted to give him a chance to miss her and their life together so he could carve a path back to it.

Two or three weeks, he had said when she dropped him off at the train station. Kissing her forehead, Samir had promised to return with closure.

⚶

Each morning during his stay at Villa deRose, Samir stood on the balcony of his room and stared out at the gentle green hills, citrus trees planted by the hundreds, and hectares of flowers blanketed by sunshine. Nestled within this Eden was the village of Grasse, a cluster of tiled, sloped roofs built over pink and yellow homes, distilleries, and factories of fragrance.

Samir had never inhabited a home this grand, and his meager belongings took up very little room. The only thing he had been particular about was hanging the framed photograph from 1937 on the wall in front of his bed. Sitting in front of it, he thought about the very first time he had opened the vials of perfume in his Paris apartment, the sublime assault of aromas and his insistence to repress them. But he knew now that he would always be nurtured by smell. And though he had come to recognize the malady that accompanied his occupation, the benefits of its artistry outweighed everything else.

Perfume had once been his mother's island, his father's livelihood, his grandfather's nostalgia. But most importantly, it was his only connection to his uncle, and an homage to the nose he had bequeathed him with.

⚶

Every day began with Samir and the aging patriarch eating breakfast together, for it was in this way that Vivek would be returned to his Rose sahib. Samir would talk about Léa and Sophie, and his cautious yet inevitable return to perfumery, and in return, the aging perfumer would narrate stories from his youth. Then, for the remaining hours of the day, Samir would follow the journals through town in an attempt to discover exactly what his uncle had discovered decades ago. Samir also used his nose to navigate, but unlike Vivek, it was not fear that followed him around but secondhand memory. Though the harvest in Grasse might have varied year to year, the streets and its stones had remained the same. The air was unchanged, the sky was the same shade of azure, and fragrance had proved its strength by surviving two world wars.

He went to see Madame deRose's ancient cottage, strolled the lengths of Place du Petit Puy to arrive at the town's majestic twelfth-century cathedral, walked the garden that a famed Russian writer had once frequented, and even found the wooden door where Vivek and Ambrette were photographed after their wedding.

One day, while passing by the cathedral, he came across a strange monument—a tall, arched form with a rounded roof and four pillars. The beige stone structure was enclosed within a metal gate on all sides, and opening it, Samir walked up the three steps to survey it up close. His face tightened as he realized that it was a memorial to the two world wars, *monuments aux morts.* Walking around, he passed the pillars engraved with *1939* and *1945,* to arrive at *1914* and *1918.*

The First World War, the Great War, the Long War, Laam, Jarman di larai.

On each pillar were engraved names of the French soldiers who died serving in battle. "Amart, Anes, Allary, Allegre, Amic, André . . ." Samir scanned the list, whispering each name. He was searching for nothing and no one in particular, yet the act brought him comfort.

Weeks passed into a month, then another and then another, until Samir had been in Grasse for half a year. He began working first in the fields and then in the distillery, as Vivek once had. Every week without fail, he wrote to Léa and Sophie, and had made trips back to Paris, but insisted that he needed more time with the deRoses. He could sense Léa's growing anxiety, but would try to explain how each conversation revealed something new about Vivek and Ambrette's life, and he could not leave without collecting every detail.

Often, he would open the journals to the wedding photograph and stare at the faces long enough to imagine them speaking to him. Sometimes, he would peruse the pages speaking of an everlasting love and bearing such optimism that it became easy for Samir to forget how life had eventually unfolded.

November 14, 1916

Sometimes, when Ambrette helps with my Francisi, it feels like I am back in the billets, learning from the Francisi sipahis. The words from the battlefield were of sustenance and survival, the coarse language of everydayness. But Ambrette's words are of love and lightness, the language of pleasure. To these, I surrender. "Waazo," she tells me as it flutters by, a bird. "Ter," she gestures to the moist earth. "Po," her fingers run across her skin. "Kurr," she places her hand over her heart. I cannot pronounce this last word, but I offer her my own in return. One I have carried on my tongue across the oceans of the world. A word reserved for her. I take her hand and along with mine, place them both upon my heart. "Dil," I tell her, "dil."

Reading this, Samir's thoughts meandered to Léa, who had helped him to learn French, as Ambrette had Vivek. He remembered the early days of their courtship, how she would slowly correct his pronunciation—running her fingerips across his nose to emphasize the nasal *n,* focusing on the shape of his lips, using beat and pulse to teach him the rhythm of each syllable in a phrase, how both her voice and intention changed when she switched from French to English. He remembered her laughter when he failed, and her joy when he succeeded.

And in thinking back to these moments, he also recalled the memories that he had buried with great difficulty then, just as he was trying to now. But the realm of language belonged so profoundly to Firdaus that Samir couldn't help but give in. Immersed once again in perfume, the days of his childhood and, by extension, his childhood love had begun to find an effortless passage back to him. The power of smell resurrected their intensity, and any guilt that arose alongside was weaker than the desire Samir surrendered to.

He imagined Firdaus, sprouting flowers and birds from the lean stems and fat bases of Urdu letters, as her pistachio eyes followed the qalam on the page. Firdaus, dipping delicate squirrel brushes into inkwells. Firdaus, mouthing Arabic poetry along with her abba. Firdaus, crushing lapis for the dyes. Firdaus in a sea green dupatta holding Samir's first letter. With closed eyes, he wondered if there was a way to bottle these moments of daily life. Why had his uncle not taught him that? He would have distilled Firdaus's drifting laughter from the bicycle ride over to Standard Restaurant, seized the evening sky on the first day she spoke to him in the studio, taken captive the color of her eyes; he would have composed with the warmth of her breath, the feel of her skin, the movement of her hands, the fall of her hair, even the sound of her voice.

Opening his eyes, he slammed the journal shut. With his heart still pounding in his throat, he shook off the past, and he penned a letter to Léa, filling the envelope with sprigs of fresh flowers, and posted it out the very next day.

When Samir returned from town that morning, Édouard deRose was waiting for him at the breakfast table. He was no longer able to walk or smell well, age having defeated his body and its senses, but he was still a gifted storyteller, and would spin the tales of history like Som Nath once used to.

Two wars had swallowed the world, but through both, Grasse had survived. Men had enlisted; they had lived and died on the far fields of battle. But no blood had been spilled on southern soil, which had made Grasse the perfect escape for men like Vivek. In the years following the First World War, it became a cultural center, home to artists, writers, and musicians from around the world. Even perfume thrived, for American soldiers who had been stationed in France during the war took bottles of French fragrance back with them, driving renewed international trade. The export of the centifolia rose flourished. During the Second World War, Grasse became a more official refugee camp, as people from across the occupied areas of France were evacuated into the tiny town. Through Rose sahib's raspy voice, a story of tragedy and triumph unfolded, not quite so different from the one Samir had abandoned on the other side of the world.

Over eggs and croissants, Samir asked Rose sahib the same question he had once asked his father, and the answer he received was miraculously similar.

"What are perfumers to do when our world, our freedom is under attack? How do we play our parts in war; how do we fight?" From all the stories that Rose sahib had relayed, the Second World War had imperiled not just land and power, but the essence of humanity. It had stripped millions of identity, exterminated those who were considered *other,* and resembled, in misery and misfortune, the days of Hindustan's Partition.

"Ah." He peered at Samir through his gold-rimmed spectacles. "Oui, there were those who fought in the battlefields, bien sûr, men like your uncle. With arms and weapons, some had no choice but to enlist, some volunteered." His fist rose slightly in the air. "And then there were those of us who fought another kind of war, a resistance war. We were the soldiers of beauty and art. Throughout the war, when bullets and blood covered the land, when battles consumed every mind and heart, *we were the transporters.*

We bottled memory, painted paradise, wrote on all that was being forgotten, transcribed the world we were witnessing . . . a world that may later have required the clarity of retrospect. You see, we were the bridge to the lost civilization. It might seem an insignificant undertaking, when compared to fighting in a battlefield, but it was also essential. *This* is what art did, what music did, what perfume did, it elevated human life during crisis. *We* were the transporters, we took people *somewhere else.*" Rose sahib's hands now moved across the table in a wave, like a ship carrying folk from somewhere to somewhere else. His voice was barely louder than a whisper, as if he were imparting to Samir a secret of great worth.

"The transporters . . ." Samir repeated after him.

"*Oui, exactement.*"

# 42

# The Second Apprenticeship

When Sophie turned five, Léa brought her to visit Samir for the first time. She had started school, and whenever anyone asked her where her family was from, sensing the foreignness of her surname, her answer would simply be "Grasse." One year of postal envelopes filled with fragrant petals and leaves had eclipsed any memory of the years her father had spent in Paris.

As for Léa, she would need to get used to this new version of her husband, not at a desk, not lifting patients or moving beds or constructing painter's canvases, but indulging in the ancient art of perfumery. She found him transformed, almost unfamiliar. There was a delicacy and finesse to his movements that she was witnessing for the first time.

She noticed his effortlessness as he took them on a tour of the flower fields and the riviera, greeting pickers and distillers, townspeople and shopkeepers. His eyes seemed to sparkle; the smile she remembered from when they first met had now returned; even his physique had improved from working in the fields. She noticed the tenderness with which his hands grasped a stalk of tuberose or wove a string of jasmine in Sophie's hair. He was attentive and romantic, intimate and present. For the first time in a long time, Léa found herself drawn to her husband, and wondered whether it was distance that had rekindled her feelings, or the stability he had achieved here, or simply the fact that he was returned to his most natural state of being.

But no matter how charming his work as a perfumer seemed, it had rendered their marriage into a task. She hated that he chose to live here, in Grasse, so far away from her and Sophie. She hated making excuses when Madame Blanchet asked when he was returning. She hated that his state of mind rendered him incapable of the commitment he had made to her. She hated that he no longer made love the way he once used to. She hated the distant feeling of his skin, even when it was pressed against hers, and how the expression in his eyes was always far away, looking toward some other day, some other memory, perhaps even some other person. But what she hated the most was that he seemed to have left her behind.

All through the visit, Léa wrestled with this sense of abandonment. Then one evening, as the couple sat with their daughter in the garden, she brought up the future.

"*Tu reviens quand?*"

Distractedly, Samir looked up from the painting he was making with Sophie. "*Quoi, mon chérie?*" and so she asked again.

"*Tu reviens quand à Paris? Ou on va vivre à Grasse ensemble?* When will we be together again?"

"Soon." He smiled, turning his attention back to the piece of art. "Very soon."

And that was it; her husband never brought up the subject on his own, as if this arrangement was completely normal. A week later, when Léa got back on the train to Paris, child in tow, she felt more confused and lonelier than before.

"It takes ten years to master the art of smell recognition," Gaspard deRose stressed. "An average person may be able to remember a few hundred odors, but a perfumer, *a nose,* knows and recognizes thousands!"

One week after Léa and Sophie had left Grasse, Samir began the second apprenticeship of his life, this time under Gaspard deRose. Since he had first worked as picker and distiller, this new role would complete his perfumistic education and lay the foundation for his future in France. On that particular morning, the pair occupied the darkened basement laboratory, where Vivek had also worked. Lined up on the shelves were hundreds of brown bottles in every size, arranged in alphabetical order, holding ingredients from around the world. This was the collection Samir would have to memorize.

Gaspard led him into the adjoining room, which contained a small perfumer's organ, almost identical in shape and form to the one Samir had grown up with. He approached it in the same reverential way as one did an altar, carefully letting his fingertips glide across the bottles. On a table, a unique initiation had been set up, modern and more clinical-looking than any that Vivek had undertaken. Samir approached the table apprehensively. Ten vials were laid out, with blotting cloths and droppers. Each smelling exercise was to be separated by a pause of several minutes, after which ten new vials would be brought out and the exercise repeated. Gaspard was testing his new apprentice's knowledge, for not everyone could hold the monsoon in their nose, after all.

Vial after vial, Samir smelled and identified, some easily, if they were natural elements that he'd been exposed to in Lahore—rose, orange flower, vetiver, musk, civet. These sat at the very tip of his nose. But with the advent of science in modern perfumery, synthetic compounds had been produced to supplement the limited extraction of natural substances, and to those, Samir paid the most attention. Complicated chemical names gave no indication of the corresponding smells, so all identification began and ended in the nose. Deconstructing the synthetics was difficult, a combination of concentration and association, pausing all other senses to rely only on smell.

Gaspard dropped a spot of colorless liquid upon a piece of linen, and held it up for Samir. A pleasant odor emanated—sweet, sticky, nostalgic, melancholic, familiar. Even beloved.

"Vanilla." Samir swallowed his Firdaus-shaped sadness, trying to ignore the montage of papers and inks that had appeared before his closed eyes. ". . . along with something bitter?"

Gaspard was impressed. "This is coumarin, discovered in 1868."

Linalool resembled rosewood, coriander, and lavender.

Jasmone was a pale yellow liquid with hints of woody, floral, heavenly jasmine.

Calone gave the impression of a seashore.

There were synthetic molecules that smelled of boiled rice and comfort; those to be used only in trace amounts like saffron and algae; those that smelled like a dirty scalp, or like petrol and earth; and those that offered an incredible range from soapy and waxy to lemony and floral, all in a single molecule.

With each vial they studied, Gaspard paid close attention to Samir's vocabulary. He watched the younger man as he inhaled and contemplated, associating odor with memory, his nose meandering from wheat fields to monsoon rains, from the moist earth to a dawn sky. He also knew well that his student was neither a native English speaker nor a Frenchman, and yet in perfumery, the specificity of one's olfactive grammar was essential. Language was the hallmark of connoisseurship and sophistication. While describing how a particular odor was perceived, Gaspard encouraged Samir to combine his sense of smell with his sense of touch. Thus, a smell could be hard or soft, velvety or prickly, sweet or tepid, spicy or stiff. It could smell like wilted roses in the nighttime, or the first drops of morning dew.

Perfumers invented the object of their creativity, gave it shape and body, volume and tenacity. And though most of Samir's education in

Lahore had been in the classic deRose way, in this method of exacti-tude, the teachings of Gaspard deRose differed from those of Vivek Nath Vij.

⸎

The next time Léa visited, Samir brought her to the atelier. Walking over to his desk, she found it littered with notebooks of formulas, used and unused smell strips, and several ingredient bottles. Watching him move through the perfumed space with deftness, she imagined how he must have craved it all these years. She had realized what her husband feared the most was the loss of his memories, but wanted to show him that there was space enough for memory and reality to coexist. He gestured to a composition he was working on, and she brought the vial to her nose. The wistful scent of tuberose snaked in, reminding her immediately of silks, satins, and heavily perfumed chambers. She imagined the warm breath of a beloved, inches away from one's skin. Closing her eyes, she inhaled it again.

"There is tuberose, bergamot, cedarwood, vanilla, indole, peach, lav-ender, and amber . . ." Samir listed. "A few months ago, I added some cacao to the formula, making it sensuous and slightly spicy, but also fuller and thicker in texture."

Léa smiled, almost unable to associate the words he was saying to the person she had known him to be. In some ways, she felt like she was meet-ing her husband for the very first time.

"*Noor,*" she now read out the label on the vial. "What is the story of this perfume?" She assumed it also began in Grasse. The smell was warm, sultry, sticky, sweet, just as she remembered the deRoses' tuberose fields to have been.

Samir leaned on the countertop. Tuberose was a notoriously complex flower, he told her, involving the micromanipulation of ingredients. *Noor* had taken him years to make, and had been the product of intense inspi-ration.

"Well, it was actually the very first perfume I composed in Lahore, in the 1940s," he admitted.

Léa watched as her husband was visibly drawn back into the past. His face became softer, almost joyous, as if he were in possession of a secret. She realized then that this perfume meant more to her husband than he was letting on.

A novel thought struck her, and though she tried to push it out of her mind, it escaped nevertheless from her lips. "*C'était pour* elle, *non?*" she asked, her tone solemn. "You composed this perfume for *her?*"

That night, after tucking Sophie into the cot by their bed, Samir held Léa as they slept, or pretended to sleep, for each was immersed in their own thoughts. Her face was nested into his chest, her soft brown hair scattered across his arm, and her feet touched his. The evening in the atelier replayed in his mind, where the name Firdaus had been uttered for the second time since they'd met. Samir wondered why he hadn't rebuffed Léa's accusation, why he'd acknowledged Firdaus as the muse for *Noor*. As his thoughts drifted back to the afternoon at Standard Restaurant a decade and a half ago, he marveled at how memory could have such a hold on him, while the skin and smell of someone in the present could not. He wondered if, like his uncle, he, too, was meant to love only once. Then, with dread, he leaned into his wife and inhaled the smell of her body, only to affirm that he did not recognize it at all.

Meanwhile, all the joy that Léa had felt upon seeing her husband again had fizzled into sadness. She felt foolish for assuming it was the realm of perfumery and family history that had consumed her husband, keeping him in Grasse, for it appeared that the lure of first love's memory was just as powerful. A memory that was evidently accessed and nurtured through fragrance. Léa felt betrayed, suddenly unseen and unloved; she couldn't stop thinking about the depth of intimacy that had emanated from the vial, and how now, she'd never be certain whether Samir was thinking of his future with her, or of his past with the woman he had left behind.

꙳

Barely six months later, in 1961, Rose sahib passed away at the age of ninety-three, leaving the perfumery and estate to Gaspard, and added responsibilities to Samir. Around the same time, Léa left Paris and moved back in with her parents in Marseilles, finding work at the local hospital. With there now being no definitive date to her husband's return, Léa decided that she could no longer raise Sophie on her own, that the child should grow up with her grandparents. Samir had taken the train from Grasse to help them settle in, but accompanying him had been a set of Vivek's early journals from the war, which he used to retrace his uncle's movements in Marseilles, taking Sophie on daily excursions through parks and cobbled marketplaces, ports and war memorials. With trepidation, Léa watched as her husband withdrew deeper and deeper into a past that she would soon have no place in.

꙳

In Grasse, as the weather cooled, Seville oranges were picked to distill the traditional vin d'orange, the smell of pine permeated the hills, and Samir began working on his first composition in France. For months, he had gazed at the photo of his uncle and aunt, imagined her veil of fresh lemon, pictured their rendezvous in the jasmine fields, and had dreamed up a composition for Vivek and Ambrette.

When he presented his work in progress to Gaspard, the perfumer had leisurely picked up the vial. "A heart of jasmine with . . . lavender, musk, amber, and . . ."

"Sage," Samir added, naming the sacred Roman herb, "and sage."

"Mm." Gaspard's nose now drew out the peppery freshness. Though the composition was already interesting, there was more to build on, still. Perhaps the addition of a green note or a trace of velvety civet, he thought to himself.

Then, placing the glass bottle on the table, he observed Samir's setup of vials and droppers, formulas and notes. Like an examiner, he walked around the younger perfumer, picking up bottles, *hmm*ing and clicking his tongue, and breathing in the sweetly suspended cloud. Arriving at a formula sheet for the jasmine Samir had used, he realized that no flower had been distilled to provide the floral heart note, but an entirely jasmine-less jasmine had been especially composed. Samir had undergone multiple attempts in his endeavor to create something original and exceptional, modifying, comparing, starting again and again over the course of many months.

So much of perfume was about failure, that Gaspard was most interested in the unsuccessful attempts. They showed persistence, ambition. Reading through, he found them noted as "too animalic and fleshy" or "lost character quickly" or "orange-like" or "too dense" or "far too transparent," until the final jasmine smelled as close as possible to the variety that Samir remembered from his childhood. Gaspard examined the formula under his breath, genuinely intrigued by the olfactive connections Samir had made with natural and synthetic smells: "A note that smells of bananas, to give volume; a note that smells of papier-mâché; a note that smells of lemon and dust; a note that smells of a transparent rosy-lime; a note that smells of geranium; a note that smells of ink; a note that smells of naphthalene; the essential oil of ylang-ylang."

Several attempts in blending these ingredients together had created the perfect jasmine, upon which Samir had anchored his entire perfume. The composition was alive, it vibrated, and though incomplete, it was intimate and personal. The young man was talented; his mastery had been inherited through blood and augmented through experience. But there was something quite unique within his methodology and vision, something that Vivek, too, had once been an expert at bottling—the attempt to possess a home no longer within grasp.

Gaspard smiled. "It smells like gardens of India, *les jardins de l'Inde*."

Samir held the phrase in his heart, along with the Hindustan he had carried across the oceans.

꙳

In 1964, three years after he began the jasmine composition, Samir offered to Gaspard a completed perfume. To the images he collected from Grasse and Vivek's journals, he added his own memories of the jasmine trail in southern Hindustan. He remembered how the pickers collected the twinkling white flowers in their flowing saris at 3 a.m. He dreamed of his mother quietly making garlands and stringing them into her hair. He longed for the Punjabi city of gardens sprawling alongside a river in springtime. He pictured a field where lovers met and crushed green leaves between their fingers and swallowed the glorious sunshine.

*Arzoo,* he named this fragrance.

After smelling this homage to Vivek and Ambrette, Gaspard asked Samir something quite unexpected: "Would you like to visit her?" And then, in response to the young man's bewilderment, he clarified, "Her grave. Would you like to visit it?"

Gaspard led him down through the winding lanes of boutiques and cafés, to the main square of Grasse at Place aux Aires, and farther down the provincial stone steps to a cluster of homes. Tall buildings, painted in bright colors with wooden shutters and metal balconies, were erected on either side of streets that curved in a leisurely manner, creating the shadow tunnels that Gaspard and Samir now moved through. Men and women carrying baskets of flowers, fruits and vegetables greeted the famed perfumer with "Bonjour, Monsieur deRose." As his mentor walked purposefully across the cobblestone, Samir trailed behind.

He didn't know what to expect. He had never even witnessed a cremation; the burning of Shahalmi was, in fact, the closest he'd ever been to any kind of death. Growing up, he used to visit the mazaars of saints and the graves of emperors in Lahore with Som Nath; he had even been to the mausoleum of the famed dancing girl Anarkali after whom the bazaar was named. Within the walls of Wazir Khan courtyard itself, predating the construction of the mosque, was the tomb of a thirteenth-century Sufi saint, Miran Badshah. With ornate arches and pillars, hand-painted with florals, it was a structure Samir used to love walking around as a child, particularly when the courtyard was empty. But he had never visited a graveyard before, let alone the grave of someone who was once family.

Walking up a staircase of long, narrow, moss-covered steps, Gaspard stopped in front of a building and pointed to the upper floor. It was ochre yellow, with deep green shutters. It didn't have much of a view, for the street it stood on was so narrow that the balcony looked out only at the building in front. But Gaspard needed to say nothing more: this was their home, the apartment that Vivek and Ambrette had lived in until December 1919. This was where they had loved and dreamed and forged morning rituals and shared nightly whispers. This was also where she had died, and where a part of him had died with her.

*This was the place.*

Samir looked up at the balcony, where a clothesline hung and a faint song drifted out of the window. For a second, Samir had the desperate urge to run up to the apartment, knock on the door, and—regardless of who lived there now—sink into the walls, throw himself onto the floors, inhale the air that his family had once inhaled. But the dead would still be dead, and so he stood motionless, staring up at the wet laundry as it fluttered in the breeze.

"Okay, *on y va*," Gaspard said after a few minutes, and began walking down the steps.

Samir followed, and for the next half hour, the pair walked downhill through the town until they arrived at the gate of a cemetery. The older perfumer led the younger one through rows of neat graves, some grand and monumental, others modest and intimate, all erected in the same dull gray stone. Moss had begun to grow on some, and others had been weathered by time and discolored by rain. Everything was cloaked in shadow. Samir walked carefully, mindful not to step on any plot, gazing at the large stone crosses and decorative epitaphs. In comparison, Ambrette's grave was not large, it was not monumental, it bore no flowers or ornate carvings, but the moment Samir laid his eyes on it, he recognized it to be unique.

Unable to believe the sight before him, he looked over at Gaspard, who was smiling sadly. "Well, what shall I say? He did not want to wait for an official gravestone . . ." He shrugged. "And this is better, anyway, *n'est-ce pas?*"

Samir nodded, slowly at first and then with purpose, and before he could stop himself, he burst out into laughter. It was a laughter laced with sadness, for after several seconds, tears began pouring down Samir's face. He walked over to the grave and fell down on his knees. Then, with a hesitant hand, he reached out to touch it.

There were no embellishments, no epitaph, not even the cause of her death or the nature of her life. The gravestone had not been engraved, but rather *inscribed* by Vivek in Urdu. His long, slim index finger had dug into a block of wet cement and carved his late wife's name, testament to the fact that she would never be separated from his touch, even in death.

*Ambrette Vij,* the stone simply read from right to left, *7th July 1897– 10th December 1919.*

She was only twenty-two when she died, Samir saw. And since he did not believe in prayer or hymn, he performed the act which to him felt most sacred. Taking the vial of *Amrit* ittar out of his pocket, he sprinkled a few drops onto the grave. The smell of cotton and grass, woods and lemons floated up. Week after week, Samir would perform this ritual without fail. Sometimes he'd read parts of Vivek's journal out to the grave; other times he would speak to her about the days unfolding. After a while, he became just as particular about this weekly visit as he had once been about writing Firdaus her weekly letter.

⚜

Meanwhile, across the world, India and Pakistan engaged in their first battle since Partition, over the disputed territories that had remained along their border. A war, beginning in August 1965, continued for seventeen days with thousands of casualties on both sides, until a United Nations–mandated ceasefire was finally declared. During this time, Radio Pakistan stopped its broadcasts of Hindi film songs, replacing them with patriotic poetry and songs in the voices of Noor Jehan and Mehdi Hassan, dedicated to soldiers who had offered their lives for the land.

Day after day, Fahad sat in front of the radio, listening as reports from the battlefield made their way to the airwaves. The western border had become an impassable terrain, communication and trade were banned, and families who had once been drawn to opposite sides in 1947 were now severed completely from one another. At first, sitting by her husband's side, Firdaus had assumed that he was listening for Pakistani victory. But one evening, she found him weeping during a broadcast, and discovered the reason for his obsession to be decades older.

"When I left Delhi, I never believed it would be permanent. For long years, I hoped that Partition simply meant a separation and not a divorce," Fahad confessed.

Upon hearing this, her heart filled with sadness, and turning to face her husband, she wiped his tears with her fingers. But taking her hands in his, he shook his head slowly. "You have never had to leave Lahore, you will not understand. But with this war, *home* finally feels out of my reach. Now I don't know whether I will ever see Delhi again."

With a sigh, he dropped her hand and went into the bedroom. But as the static from the radio continued in the background, unable to help herself, Firdaus wondered whether somewhere across the border, her perfumer might be thinking the same thing.

## 43

## Firaq

Since his arrival in Grasse, Samir had nurtured the tulsi plant he had brought with him from Paris, until one day, Gaspard led him to a pale, golden-colored vial on the organ, labeled *basilic sacré*. Gaspard explained that, centuries ago, a Roman naturalist, Pliny, had reported on the medicinal qualities of the herb. In the Far East, it had been used as cough medicine; in America, to ease headaches; and in the continent of Africa, it was used to expel worms. Tulsi, sacred since the Vedic age in India, believed to promote longevity of life, became the first step Samir would quietly take to reclaim his homeland.

It had begun innocently, by breaking a stem off the plant and holding it up to the light. The color was formidable—the kind of green reserved for rain showers. He had crushed a few leaves between his fingers and popped them into his mouth. The strong aroma had mixed with saliva to create a warm, astringent taste. Samir had chewed slowly, purposefully, until he was immersed, until he had swum the waters backward from Liverpool, reboarded the train from Bombay to Delhi, back to Lahore, and found himself at the heart of Vij Bhawan's courtyard, standing in front of the tulsi plant. He had chewed until the sharpness of the herb gave way to the clove-like taste, and only then did he swallow. For a few minutes he had remained still, bare stem in his hands, and then began imagining a formula.

For years, a perfume of holy basil had resided in his nose, and now, taking full advantage of the ocean of memory, he commenced. He laid out smelling strips, glass droppers, measuring instruments, and then he proceeded toward the organ. The vial of tulsi, steam-distilled from its leaves, was retrieved, along with cinnamon essence. The pair shared a chemical component called eugenol, giving them both a sweet, spicy aroma, and making them harmonious. Samir also selected vetiver to enhance the herb, and sandalwood to imbue it with warmth. Thus began his composition.

Into clear vials were dropped varying quantities of ingredients, resulting in a cluster of yellow-green hues. Samir blended, smelled, and made notations. Woods lasted longer, the citrus family diffused rapidly, musks adhered to the skin for days. Like Vivek, Samir, too, wanted his fragrances to hold within them a passage of time. He wished to compose larger, more voluminously, a structure bigger than he had before. He wanted to fit an entire world within a single vial. But the most important thing drowned within the liquid—along with flowers, herbs, woods, memories, and history—would be time itself.

꜀

A few years had passed, and a fuller composition had begun to take shape when Samir settled into the atelier one morning. He dove into his old journals, those he had kept as a teenager in Lahore, to re-create the images with which he wished to suffuse the perfume. He read his first impressions of the tulsi plant, along with whatever memories he'd been able to gather about his grandmother Leela, for whom the plant was sacred. As a middle-aged man, Samir receded deeper into a past that predated his own birth, to draw out a smell that would define his family. Like his uncle with the ambrette seed, he became quite defenseless to the powerful aroma of holy basil.

A few hours later, Léa knocked on the door of the atelier. By now, roughly half their marriage had been spent living in different cities with diverging priorities. Over the last several years, they had exchanged letters, postcards, phone calls, and visited one another when they could, but it had become clear that while Léa's concern was the future of her family, Samir's remained suspended in the past. Bitterness grew in her heart as obsession took hold of his.

When she walked in the room, she found him in a daydream. His eyes were closed and around him hung a fragrant cloud of fresh green. She laid a hand on his shoulder, and when he opened his eyes, Léa noticed a strange look on his face. It was the same look she had seen when the first tulsi leaf had sprouted all those years ago in their apartment in Paris. A look that betrayed a trip to the past, a look of lament and reminiscence. Her gaze fell on the bare stem on the desk, she smelled the chewed leaves on his breath, and she knew that a portal had been opened.

That day, Léa finally understood why her husband had been so adamant on erasing his history at the beginning of their marriage, for she had witnessed just how it devoured him. Samir had so swiftly and impulsively moved from shutting out the past to completely immersing himself within it that he'd failed to maintain any balance with the present. She thought back to the afternoon he had proposed to her, the promises he had made, and looked down at the dainty heirloom emerald that sat on her finger.

The journals might have long since ended, but Samir's obsession had only grown, and it amazed her how something invisible and ungraspable could ever be so powerful. Now, inspired by an herb, Samir had decided to descend the ladder of memory even further. On multiple occasions, Léa wished that the holy basil had never come to him, and that things could return to the normal, albeit uninspired, way they had once been.

"At some point, if they are unreachable landscapes, should we not just let them dissolve?" Léa asked Samir a few days later, at breakfast, as they sat by a window overlooking the flower fields. For her to begin a conversation in English meant that it was serious, that she needed all of her husband's attention, unimpaired by language.

He watched as she broke apart a croissant, neatly painted a layer of jam over the flaky inside, and took a bite. He thought about what she had said and also the way she had said it. There was a directness in her voice that he had never been on the receiving end of.

*Dissolve,* she had said. If only it were that easy, if only he could let the past dissolve. It wasn't as if he hadn't tried. But upon encountering the holy basil all those years ago, Samir's boundary wall had come crumbling down.

"Mon amour?" she called out to him.

"*Ce n'est pas facile pour moi* . . . it isn't easy." Samir looked into her hazel eyes. "You know better than anyone how much I had wanted to let this all go, but now, it seems impossible to. There is . . . there is too much to take care of before it slips away."

Then, suddenly, in a manner quite unlike him, Samir asked her, "Are you tired of me?"

Léa remained calm. It had been several years since the holy basil first entered their life, and if she really thought about it, it seemed an exceptionally ridiculous thing to have disrupted their relationship. She had tried, but she had failed, and now her husband's submission to the past just exasperated her.

"Yes," she admitted, "because I no longer know you. All I know is your absence."

The moment those words left her mouth, Samir knew that a fracture had occurred. A fracture that he had caused. Looking out the window, he weighed the life he had vowed to live when he left Lahore against the life he was living presently. He thought about his grandfather and the grandmother he never knew; he thought about his uncle and the secret aunt who died in childbirth; he thought about his parents. He thought about how each of these people had cared for the past, however big or small the past might have been. It took courage to continue to remember, to hold on to the heaviness. To honor it.

In that moment, he could not think beyond his own obsession. Later in life, he would regret this deeply, but in that moment, the past seemed so much more important to guard than the present. So, he callously attributed Léa's perspective to a fundamental difference between them, between East and West, between the people of two different worlds. That perhaps relationships were ultimately bound by culture, no matter how intimate they became. That there were some things Léa might never understand, for even if Samir didn't return home, he would still feel his association with Lahore as unfinished.

"One day, I am afraid I might forget everything I once was," he began, but she cut him off.

"But what about who you are now? What about our marriage, and . . . and Sophie? She is just a child . . . Do you expect her to grow up without you?" There was anger in Léa's voice, but she had asked this question so tenderly that Samir couldn't tell whether it was an accusation or a plea. Collecting her courage, she continued, "Mon chéri, sometimes it is essential to forget the days we have lived and left behind. They cannot be returned to us . . ."

When she reached out across the table to hold her husband's hand, there were tears in her eyes. Samir watched them trickle down her face, and momentarily, he was overcome with visions of the first time he encountered Léa, and the last time he encountered Firdaus.

"Let me help lessen the load of your memory, *s'il te plait*," she offered.

With his hand still in Léa's, he replied, "But without memory, there is nothing. Without memory, we are nothing."

When Samir awoke the next morning, the room was empty of Léa's belongings. Part of him had anticipated this, and he remained in bed for a while, contemplating her departure. Perhaps he had made a mistake, he thought, as his mind drifted to Sophie. But then his gaze fell on the journals by his bedside, the stalks of tulsi nestled between the pages of formulas and memory, and deduced that what he was preserving was his daughter's history, too, and Léa just hadn't understood that. Then he walked to the desk by the window, where a single envelope was propped up, ironically, against a vial of perfume. As the sunshine streamed in, he read the letter that asked for a divorce.

"I can no longer look in from the outside," Léa had written.

⚶

Samir spent the remainder of the day in the atelier.

Upon entering, he walked right toward the bell jar on the worktable. Late last night, he had deposited a few drops of what he considered a finished perfume in some linen cloth, and covered it. All night, the fragrance diffused into the enclosed space. Now, as Samir lifted the bell jar, a rich greenness radiated out into the room.

Samir had recalled all the greens that had once filled his childhood days, and he had poured their memories into this perfume: freshly washed tulsi, the rain shower of neem pods in the courtyard, the moss on the stepwell in Shahalmi, the green stones near the river Ravi, the khuss curtains, the greenest of unripe mangoes, the greens of henna in his ustad sahib's inks, the jade dyes of illuminated manuscripts, the yellow-green tile mosaic of the Wazir Khan mosque, Firdaus and her pistachio eyes.

Samir had hoped to create a perfume that filled the unfillable spaces between life and death, between him and his Lahori family. But the years of its composition had facilitated other unfillable spaces, vast physical and emotional distances which he had not anticipated.

Situated at the threshold of many separations, shaped by the form of many absences, he named the perfume *Firaq*.

# 44

# The Hyposmic

In Lahore, under the light of the afternoon sun, Firdaus ran her fingers over each leaf from her collection, the same way she used to as a child. The texture was brittle and dry, and the leaves made a cracking sound against her fingers. But once held up to the light, the veins running through them illuminated instantly, like the alleys of her old city, or the tributaries of a river. Each leaf had a story to tell, which made this childhood collection a treasure unlike any other. The red chinar from Kashmir, the forest green ziziphus leaf from Persia, the heart-shaped maple from Baku, this was how she had once traveled the world.

"Ammi," a voice called out from behind her. Aayat, now nineteen, came and put a hand on her mother's shoulder. "Nanu is calling you."

The year was 1968, exactly twenty years since Firdaus had been married, twenty years since she had spoken to her father. And now, here she was in her childhood home, hours after her mother's funeral. Last night, Zainab Khan, only in her late fifties, had died suddenly of a heart attack. Altaf had been in the next room, cleaning the day's ink off his qalams. When he finally came to sit with his wife on the bed, he realized that she had passed away, her departure uncharacteristically quiet. The once-spirited gray eyes were still open, yet all the light had dimmed from them. Trembling, Altaf had touched her face, her lips, the hands he had loved so much in his youth. Tears had fallen from his eyes, but his heart felt lighter than it had in years.

Upon receiving the news, Firdaus had felt nothing, for the relationship had been severed decades ago. Obediently, however, she had arrived in the middle of the night with Aayat to help her father prepare for the funeral in the morning. Through the night, men and women from the neighborhood and family had gathered to give their condolences; women had beaten their chests and wept. Firdaus's father-in-law and Zainab's brother, Muhammad, along with Altaf and Fahad, made arrangements for the funeral prayers and burial.

It was the responsibility of women in the immediate family to wash and shroud the body, which Firdaus began quietly and without fuss. Her mother was unnaturally cold now and her muscles had stiffened within a matter of hours. Firdaus bathed the body with warm water, as her mother-in-law, Nadira, consoled a weeping Aayat. Once the skin was cleaned and wiped, five pieces of simple white cloth were used to shroud Zainab's body. Firdaus mechanically covered the shoulders, the feet, the soft skin of the arms, and tried to ignore her mother's voice in her ear. Hours later, in the morning, the body was taken for prayer and burial, but Firdaus and the other women had remained at home, preparing to recieve the mourners.

Now, as she carefully placed each leaf back into its resting place, she heard her father walk up behind her. So many years later, she still could have picked out his footsteps in a crowd. She turned around, and two pairs of identical pistachio eyes stared at one another. Firdaus remembered the last time they'd been alone together in this room, the day of the fire and of Samir's banishment.

"*As-salaam-alaikum, Abba,*" she addressed him formally, fixing her dupatta over her head.

"I was waiting for you . . . I sent Aayat in here, too." He looked disheveled and tired, and his black kurta had been buttoned up wrong.

She gestured to the leaves to show him that she was occupied, and in turn, he opened his wrist to reveal a fistful of dark maroon roses that had fallen off Zainab's shroud. Something to remember her mother by. But Firdaus merely stared at the flowers, remaining completely still.

"Firdaus jaan . . ." Altaf's expression was suddenly one of concern. "Still?"

After several seconds, she nodded.

They had discovered it when she was barely five years old. Altaf had taken Firdaus with him to the Wazir Khan mosque one Friday, and leaving her in the studio while performing the jummah prayer, he had returned with a perfectly blossomed rose. They had been strewn across the mosque courtyard and, selecting the most beautiful one, Altaf had carried it to his daughter. She had held it up to her nose in excitement, but almost instantly declared that it smelled of nothing.

"What do you mean?" he asked her, puzzled. It was sweet, full, and deeply evocative. Once again, he held it out to her, and once again, she shook her head.

"Abbu, I cannot smell it."

Altaf sat up straighter, now alarmed. "Can't you smell . . . the sweetness?"

Young Firdaus shook her head vigorously. From then on, Altaf made his daughter smell many things, living and nonliving, to understand the nature of her condition. It was an altogether absurd endeavor, according to Zainab, who could not understand why the girl couldn't just smell a rose, and dismissed it as mere theatrics. She refused to have some doctor examine, let alone diagnose, a condition that sounded this ridiculous. And anyway, *what would people say?*

But Altaf persisted, offering foods and stones and tree barks and paper and leather for the child to smell. In those early years, he would even stop walking in the middle of the street, point to a puddle or a mossy patch of green or a cat, and have Firdaus sniff at it. He would take her to the mango orchards, to the dairy farms, to the horse stables and to the ghats where washermen beat their clothes clean, in order to gauge her nose. He would have her inhale the smoky tendrils of incense sticks, or the ubtan paste that Zainab applied onto the child's face each night. He would watch as she smelled the morning dew, the evening rain, the mutton curry, the calligraphy inks, and even the dirty dishwater.

At the end, he arrived at the conclusion that, for reasons unknown, his daughter could not discern the smell of certain flowers. A rare and oddly particular kind of hyposmia—smell blindness—toward the scents of heady, intensely sweet flowers like rose, jasmine, and tuberose. She simply could not smell them, no matter how hard she tried.

"Do you believe *me*?" Altaf had finally asked. "Do you believe me when I describe a smell?"

Firdaus slowly nodded. It was difficult for her to understand why she couldn't smell certain kinds of beauty, but the exploration had been enough to convince the child that something about her anatomy was amiss.

"Well"—Altaf embraced her—"if you *believe* in the smell I describe, then the smell exists."

That day, to compensate for the splendor that would evade her senses in the years to come, he encouraged a new hobby in his daughter—the collecting and pressing of leaves. A distraction of sorts, to concentrate on a different kind of floral beauty, which inevitably found its way into her artwork, the borders of her manuscripts always bearing leaves and hardly ever flowers. And because this olfactive handicap barely affected her daily life or chores, it remained a well-concealed secret within the Khan household. Until, of course, Firdaus met Samir.

"I never told him, Abba jaan," Firdaus began, tears now pouring down her face. Not a single tear had been shed for her mother, and yet the mere sight of a rose had made her weep. Altaf led her to the bed, where she crumpled. "I never told him," she repeated. She couldn't understand why, after so many years of being married to Fahad, the thought of Samir refused to leave her.

Altaf rubbed his daughter's shoulders and breathed a sigh of relief. Time had made the distance between them so vast. Each day away from her had been spent in agony. But now, two decades later, under circumstances hardly believable, she had finally been returned to him.

She looked at him now. "I could never properly smell anything he composed. When I was seventeen, he presented me an ittar in the most magnificent golden bottle I had ever seen. He said he'd spent years dreaming and making it, and I brought it up to my nose, thinking that enough time had passed, that I'd been cursed for long enough. I *wanted* to love it, Abba. But I could not even smell it, because its heart was the tuberose. A flower that is supposed to be heady and romantic, but to me, it smelled of . . . nothing." Her words slurred into tears now. "For Samir, *everything* began and ended in the nose, and that is the sole organ I cannot trust. So many times, I wished I didn't have this condition, that I simply hated the smell of flowers. That way I could have forced myself to like what he made me, and not have to lie altogether. Samir's talent was wasted on me . . . and perhaps even his love."

And then, suddenly, the tears stopped. She wiped her face and sat up straighter. "I would have never understood him completely. You were right to banish him, you were right to separate us. *Aapne bilkul sahi kara.*"

Maybe these twenty years had been necessary for him to understand what profound sadness she must have endured while watching him leave. How it felt when a piece of your heart, a part of yourself, was severed.

He looked at his daughter, held her face in his hands, and kissed her forehead. "Don't ever say that again. Listen to me when I tell you what happened was wrong. *I was wrong.*"

Holding back tears, he looked out the window at the glistening Sunehri Masjid, and remembered the days after the Shahalmi fire. Lahore was burning; everywhere one looked, Lahore was burning. The Hindus and Sikhs who had managed to escape the fire fled for their lives. During those days, Altaf had set out to look for Samir. To right his wrong, to prevent a marriage that could leave Firdaus forever unhappy, he searched for the man his daughter loved. In his pursuit, the guilt-ridden calligrapher traversed the entire city, watching the wrath of Partition consume the land, but the young perfumer was nowhere to be found.

It became impossible to discern even a shadow of old Lahore in this independent land of Muslims. In the months following, Altaf would try to recognize the street corners and voices, the hawkers and shopkeepers who had come to inhabit this new Lahore, but he recognized nothing and no one. And in the end, he considered himself as much to blame as any politician or angrez Raj, for he had been just as complicit in obliterating the culture of the city he loved.

He returned now to his daughter, and taking her small, cold hands in his, he whispered, "Whenever the story of Firdaus is written, it will not be without her Samir."

# 45

# Les Jardins De L'inde

In 1970, forty-three-year-old Samir returned to Paris. Having apprenticed with the deRoses for an entire decade, he now set up a perfumery of his own in the city of lights and lovers. In his will, Rose sahib had bequeathed him a residence and shop in vibrant Saint-Germain-des-Prés. On the fourth floor of a historic building on rue Visconti were two apartments facing one another, separated by the building's staircase. The one on the right was Samir's living quarters, and the one on the left was set up as an atelier. Sunshine streamed generously into both at different times of the day, his home overlooking the Église Saint-Germain-des-Prés, and the atelier looking out at the quaint garden on rue Visconti.

The shop, an out-of-business perfumery once owned by an old friend of Rose sahib's during the war, was a five-minute walk, on the corner of rue Bonaparte and rue de l'Abbaye. Though dusty and old, it still held the enchanting remnants of a perfumistic world—glass bottles half filled with bespoke fragrances, ornate vintage atomizers, sculptures of civets and musk deer, and a remarkable olfactory atlas lined up on an organ in the back room. For the few months after his arrival, the perfumer devoted his days to reconstructing the shop he had left behind in Lahore. The black-and-white photograph of the Vij men found its place behind the counter, and on opening day, like his great-grandfather, grandfather, and uncle once had, he, too, proudly hung up an iconic black-and-white sign painted in French and English, at the entryway: LES JARDINS DE L'INDE, ESTD 1970, PARIS. The gardens of India.

The deRoses, more family than competition, often recommended Samir's shop to friends and acquaintances in Paris, for he occupied a unique place in the world of modern perfumery. Situated at the cusp of East and West, he witnessed firsthand how his fragrances took people *somewhere else*. How they provided a momentary refuge from the bustle and noise of the city, away from any lingering memory of war, death, or grief, away from France, far away, across the waters to the sublime gardens of India. From the jasmine fields of Madurai to the saffron pastures of Pampore, from the cinnamon estates of Ceylon to the fragrant woods of Assam, Samir distilled, bottled, and sold refuge.

Morning to evening, he'd be surrounded by customers gently daubing perfumes on their wrists, the dazzling sun illuminating the glass bottles, the spritz of an atomizer, noses rising and falling in satisfaction, a laugh, a sniff, a sigh. But every gesture, every dream, every image they described took Samir instantly back to the shop in Lahore. And if days were spent in the chaos of tending shop, then nights were spent in composition. The nocturnal stillness evoked images that the busyness of the day was unable to conjure. It happened often that just as he was about to fall asleep, Samir would have a vision, a memory, a brilliant scene that would compel him to crawl out of bed and walk across the hallway to the atelier.

꧁

In the years after he returned to Paris, Samir experimented with the world of synthetic ingredients, enjoying the diverse palette they offered. Though he still preferred the familiarity of naturals, the evolution in science offered combinations he could have only dreamed of. He made fruity notes fleshy, and manipulated musk to the point that it smelled of shaving cream. He became a forager of chemically composed notes like gunpowder, hard-boiled eggs, sweaty palms, hot caramel, and the smell of a newborn baby's scalp. The olfactory atlas of the entire modern world was now held in laboratory vials of clear liquid.

He often studied his uncle's formula journals from Lahore, and one day, tucked between the fraying pages, discovered Khushboo Lal's address in Kannauj. He wondered whether the business still existed. In an attempt to start building the landscape of home, Samir took a chance and wrote to the late perfumer's descendants to procure bottles of the same ingredients that he had grown up with. If the shelves of Les Jardins de l'Inde were to hold the same perfumes that the Anarkali shop once held, then they would be composed with ingredients insperable from that history.

Encouraged by Gaspard, he also began reading about the great perfumers of the world, poring over books, formulas, and journals. He read about the legendary French perfumer Jean Carles, who toward the end of his life became nearly anosmic, losing his sense of smell. But he soon developed a Beethoven-like imagination for aroma, wherein he continued to compose from memory. Samir read on the perfumes that had been composed following the Second World War, and in doing so, he thought not only of Vivek's opulent *Ab-e-zar*, but also of Rose sahib's immortal words on how, in moments of great trauma, artists and perfumers became the transporters to a world absolved from grief.

He found comfort in music, unintentionally gravitating to pieces composed by those who had died tragically premature deaths—George Butterworth's compositions on the idyllic English countryside, written before he died from sniper fire during the Battle of the Somme in 1916, or the Spanish pianist Enrique Granados's *Goyescas,* inspired by the paintings of Francisco Goya, composed before he died of drowning. He grew fond of the *Gymnopédies* of Erik Satie, who died suddenly due to illness of the liver, and the early Romantic Austrian composer Franz Schubert, who, in the course of his three-decades-short life, wrote over a thousand pieces of music. But Samir's heart was, without doubt, most taken by the work of Czech composer Antonín Dvořák, who—apart from writing music that Samir could physically smell—apprenticed as a butcher and, as self-critical as a perfumer, burned most of his early works.

But where Samir found true clarity was in returning to Vivek's war journals. Had he not discovered them, he might have continued to commit himself to a life devoid of perfume, as penance. As he read them now, devoid of haste, guilt, or disbelief, moving from document to document like a conservator, turning the frail pages, unfolding corners, laying flat the sheets that had buckled with moisture, and studying the tangible traces of his history, he began to return to the days flanked by family and love, the perfume shop and the calligraphy studio. As a decades-older Samir made his way through the chronicled years, he began to feel the presence of two distinct days, two distinct years, two distinct lives being lived one atop another. Where there was a wound, there had to be a way to heal it, and it began with a liquid language encompassing both lived and inherited memory.

Many evenings in his atelier were spent imagining two pelagic voyages, separated by decades of history. For months, Samir considered the depths of briny and salty water to be the bridge between Vivek and him, changing the course of each of their lives. The waves, the wind, the breeze, the tide, the cloudless sky, the sense of stillness and escape, he allowed these sensations to flood his imagination and composed a saltwater accord. Bergamot, basil, mandarin, rosemary, sandalwood, the wild-smelling indole, a touch of damask rose, sweet ylang-ylang, vanilla-like benzoin, and the minty, sweeping sensation of wintergreen oil found their place in a composition that linked together generations, lending it the name *Silsila*.

Thereafter, whenever he returned to the journals, it was with a sense of equilibrium. Memory could no longer serve as an assault: it had to become companion or catalyst to his compositions. The success of *Silsila* at the perfume shop only bolstered his belief that the separation from Léa had not been in vain, that there was something far greater, more significant, and necessary to preserve than the relationship he had discarded.

⚶

When her father had first left for Grasse, Sophie was only four, and remembering snippets from his stories of war, she liked to imagine him fighting on far-off battlefields. It was only when she saw him at work that she replaced the battlefield with a flower field, telling friends at school that her father was a soldier of perfume. And though she saw him often enough, it was the periods of his absence that stayed with her, periods that she tried to fill with her imagination. Sometimes after school, while her mother was still at work, Sophie would show Madame Blanchet drawings she had made of Samir in his flower fields.

Every few weeks, a letter would arrive from Grasse, sometimes accompanied by stems of jasmine or iris, pale rosebuds or violets, other times with vials of perfume that her mother dutifully arranged on her vanity. On the days these letters arrived, her mother would weep into the night when she thought Sophie was asleep. She remembered Léa sitting her down every few months, promising that they would soon live together again. But those promises became less frequent as the years passed, and stopped completely when they moved to Marseilles. By the time her parents' marriage dissolved, eleven-year-old Sophie had learned to have a relationship with each of them separately.

She grew up to be independent and introverted, finding company in books and art. As soon as she was old enough to take the train by herself, she'd begun visiting her father in Grasse every month. There, she spent the days reading or drawing, but would sometimes assist him in the atelier, even though, despite his many efforts, she showed no technical talent for perfumery.

The year Sophie entered high school, Léa moved them back to Paris, where she found work at a hospital and a small apartment on the Left Bank. The year after that, Samir returned as well, and with the opening of the perfume shop, Sophie began to see her father almost every day after school. She would help him arrange ornate flacons on the shelves or tend to customers, but that was the extent of her interaction with the world of perfume. The hours she loved the most were the ones they spent in museums or walking the city together.

One day, Samir took her back to the apartment building where she'd lived the first few years of her life. They boarded the metro toward the 9th arrondissement, sitting side by side. Over the last few years, the one trait Samir had been surprised to discover in his daughter was her sense of restraint. Perhaps she and Léa openly spoke about the past, but not once had Samir been interrogated on his departure to Grasse, or his reasons for the divorce, or even about his life before France. At times, her habits reminded him of Firdaus's, in the way her fingers grasped a pencil with intention, or how they moved across a blank sheet, effortlessly rendering the figures of flower-pickers and lush trees. On such days, he was tempted to tell her everything, but he feared complicating her life. Or maybe he just didn't know the words to say.

That morning, as they walked to rue Chaptal, he recalled to her those early years of fatherhood. "On weekends, we picnicked under the sun, or fed the pigeons along the Seine. You used to bake cakes with Madame Blanchet, and sometimes, we would read together." He wondered if she remembered the journals, but quickly moved on. "Your *most* favorite thing to do was ride the old Sacré-Coeur carousel, with its painted Venetian ceilings, bobbing horses, spinning teacups. We must have ridden it hundreds of times!"

"I remember that, Papa!" Sophie laughed, her hazel eyes glistening in the sunlight.

He led her to their old building, which seemed to have received a fresh cleaning, restoring it to its cream-colored glory. But inside, father and daughter learned that Madame Blanchet had passed away and the property had gained new ownership. Samir knew that for a while Léa had written to her from Marseilles, but he felt ashamed for not having kept in touch at all. Walking back outside, the pair stood facing the facade, hand in hand, wistful smiles on their faces.

"That window—" Samir pointed up to the window with white shutters, now framed by a lush growth of ivy. "It was by that window that I used to sing you to sleep."

# 46

# The Longest Distance

Seventeen-year-old Sophie paid for her coffee and crammed her books back into her bag. Now in her final year of school, she had walked straight to a café after classes, and as the evening drew to a close, it was time to meet her parents for dinner. Buttoning up her coat, she wrapped a scarf around her neck as she walked down rue Bonaparte, bookbag on her shoulder and a file tucked under her arm. When she crossed her father's perfumery just minutes later, the shutter was drawn and the lights were out, so she walked on, taking the next right onto rue Visconti.

File still firmly under her arm, she unlocked the door of the apartment building to find the downstairs neighbor checking his mailbox, a little dog waiting patiently by the door.

"Bonjour, Monsieur Dupont," Sophie chimed. "Salut, Babette." She reached down to scratch the dog's ears. "*Ça va?*"

After a few minutes of conversation, she walked across the stone court-yard and climbed four flights, until she reached her father's floor. Catching her breath, she held the file tighter to her chest. Next year, she'd be off to university. She had her heart set on studying art history, and her teachers had recommended La Sorbonne as a natural progression. But if

Sophie stayed in Paris, then she would forever remain lodged in between her parents' strange relationship. They were so different that at times she wondered what had ever brought them together. As far back as memory served, they'd lived separately, with Sophie shuttling between homes and cities. She remembered being put on a train by her mother in Marseilles, where the air smelled like fish and salt, and arriving hours later in Grasse, where the air was saturated with rose and lavender, as she was received by her father.

When Sophie was younger, people barely believed that she was her father's daughter, for they looked nothing alike. She knew his passport stated that he was born in a place called Lahore, which to him was an entire sensation, but to her was just a sound. *Lahore.* She had once looked it up in an atlas and, tracing her fingers across the page, had found it at the border of a country called Pakistan. But when her mother walked into the room, she had hastily turned to another page, pretending to work on geography homework. Beyond that, Sophie had never asked anything, despite perhaps wanting to, and her father had never offered to tell.

In any case, he was always preoccupied with formulas of flowers and herbs, pages of old manuscripts and vials of liquid. Like an alchemist, he would spend his days smelling and perfecting formulas. Everyone she knew loved his creations; there was something magical about the stories his perfumes told. But Sophie always felt that she had remained at the borders of her father's life, at the threshold of something deeper. He was always kind, but always formal.

She now stood in the thickly carpeted hallway, contemplating the decision she would announce to her parents that evening at dinner. Yes, she would leave the following year, live in a different country, far away from her father's obsessions and her mother's loneliness. Oxford it would be, she had decided, patting the file protectively.

Earlier that afternoon, on his daily walk, Samir had strolled into a little square with stone benches and beautiful autumnal trees. He sat down, adjusting his scarf as a lone leaf fell down beside him. It was perfectly almond-shaped and brilliantly burgundy, a unique shade he had only seen once before—in Firdaus's collection. As he picked it up, brought it to his face, and closer still to his nose, Samir felt convinced that this arbitrary leaf would somehow fold back time, and transport him to the studio where Firdaus used to draw vines of red leaves across the borders of illuminated manuscripts. But when he inhaled the waxy surface, it smelled of nothing and took him nowhere. Even so, he had pocketed the leaf.

Half an hour later, he sat in his atelier, waiting for Sophie to arrive. At their daughter's insistence, both Léa and Samir had agreed to a family dinner that evening. Picking up a bottle of *Noor,* he held it tightly within his palm, and closed his eyes. A shower of sparkling white tuberoses flooded his memory.

He thought of Standard Restaurant. The summer of 1946. The exquisite golden bottle. The white shalwar kameez, pink dupatta, and kohl-rimmed pistachio eyes. The sparkling diamond pierced through the nose, an inky-black beauty spot on the chin. The wild laughter ringing in the wind, the empty lengths of Lahore's Mall Road. The tender touch, the warm crevasse, the smooth island of skin.

Even at a continent's distance, the tenderness that Samir had once felt for Firdaus had only deepened with the passing years. He didn't know whether she had married, whether she was happy, or even whether she was alive. But what he felt in his heart had remained unchanged. The arc of life and death had nothing to do with love, then. Love continued on, if left to its devices.

Samir opened his eyes, and then opened the bottle of perfume. He smelled it once from afar and then closer and closer, until the tip of his nose hung inside the rim. Liquid touched the barely visible hair of his nose. He wanted to get as physically close to the smell as he could, until he felt it sink into him. A few minutes later, he placed the bottle back on the table. From his wallet, he retrieved the passport photo. Folded and discolored, a teenage Firdaus looked up at Samir.

Traveling over land and water, across a distance of 7,313 kilometers, Samir's nose carried him back to the Lahore of his youth. And then, upon hearing Sophie knock on the door, Samir hurriedly snuck the photograph back into his wallet, closed the perfume bottle, walked ten steps to the door and into the present.

⚖

Léa smelled it the moment Samir entered the restaurant with Sophie, a waft of tuberose following him to their booth. Immediately she recognized the smell, wishing that she hadn't. *Noor.* All those years ago in Grasse, she had envied how the mere memory of his former beloved had continued to seduce Samir, and now Léa felt that feeling return. Twelve years had passed since she'd first heard the story of this perfume, seven since they'd divorced, and yet the flicker of jealousy still persisted. Samir had left Léa to spend the better part of a decade feeling unloved and abandoned, and despite that, she couldn't help how devastated she still felt in his presence. Heartbroken, she turned her attention back to the table, where Sophie was talking to them about her future, yet all Léa could think about was the past.

⚖

"Ammi, you will stop wearing black now, won't you? Abbu would have wanted you to," Aayat asked Firdaus as they rolled up the thick Persian carpet and dragged it against the wall by the windows. Suitcases had been packed and placed by the door, curtains had been removed, bedspreads folded and stored, furniture sold, dishes and crockery emptied out from the kitchen and cupboards, an entire household packed up and ready to be moved. Now only an echo occupied the otherwise empty rooms.

It was the spring of 1980, but Lahoris were already drenched in sweat. Aayat threw open the wooden windows and fanned herself with the ends of her dupatta, as Firdaus remained seated on the rolled-up carpet. Studying her mother's face, Aayat reached out and patted down her unmade hair. Firdaus was fifty-one years old, and until recently, could have passed as an older sister to thirty-one-year-old Aayat. But the last few months had changed her. White had begun to streak her long braid, fine lines had appeared on her face, and confined to the four walls of this flat, her skin looked paler than ever, only the singular dark beauty spot on her chin standing out.

Taking her daughter's hand, Firdaus nodded. No more black, she agreed.

The pair walked to her bedroom and began packing the collection of books. From the vanity, Firdaus picked up the diamond nose pin and put it back in place. Her wedding band—slim, solid, gleaming golden—remained on the shelf, and she stared at it. She recalled her grief the day Fahad had slipped it on her finger, wishing the ring had been from another. But as the years passed, that wish dimmed, for by his side, she learned that there were many kinds of love. That it was possible to entrust a part of her heart to the past, and still have enough to offer to another in the present. He was a good man, respectful, kind, attentive—even when she might have been underserving of it, even in those moments that her heart had been elsewhere. She had been lucky to spend her life with him, no matter how the alliance had begun. As she looked around the bare room now, she could feel the shape of his absence. With a deep sigh, she picked up the ring from the shelf, placed it in a velvet pouch and into the box of her favorite books.

In the last four months and ten days of her iddat period after Fahad's death, she had routinely worn only dark, black, or completely unembellished clothes. She hadn't adorned herself with any kohl or jewelry. She had not stepped foot beyond the threshold of the house, as was custom, and was dependent on her daughter for even the smallest of her needs from the outside world. Vegetables, meat, salt, sugar, flour, and even soap—Aayat came by every evening bearing the necessities. It had been six years since her own marriage, and some days she was accompanied by her two daughters—Mariam, four, and Yasmin, barely a few months old.

During the mourning period, Firdaus had spent a considerable amount of time thinking about the remainder of her life. And now, on the very first day after, she began afresh. Her in-laws had moved to Karachi several years ago, where both Saira and Sitara were married, leaving Firdaus and Fahad alone in the two-story building in Bhati Gate. Now Firdaus, too, was abandoning this marital house and moving back in with her father. She had lost her mother to a heart attack and her husband to cancer within a span of twelve years, and with half her life already lived on the terms of others, she had decided to live the remainder for herself.

Over the next few days, with Aayat's help, she packed up the premises and took a tanga to her childhood neighborhood, smiling as soon as she caught sight of the beautiful golden mosque. Despite the circumstances in which she had returned, Altaf could not have been happier to welcome his daughter back, for it seemed like a long-awaited homecoming.

On that first night back, Firdaus walked to the balcony and stared at the moon-soaked night. Dabbi Bazaar was still teeming with customers, and the Sunehri Masjid had been lit up like a bride. This was a good night, she thought to herself. Tonight, her heart was light.

For a few moments, she felt seventeen again. Partition had not yet happened, and any minute now, Samir would ride up on his bicycle with a folded letter in his hands. He would deposit it in the woven basket, and she would pull it up and devour his words of affection. There would be no riots and no violence. No fires would dot the Lahori landscape, and no exodus of friends and neighbors would occur. There would be no border and no war. She would still be able to go to Standard Restaurant with Samir, still be able to work at the studio, still laugh and write and draw and study in college. She would still be free.

A cool breeze blew the dupatta off her head and her braid fluttered. *Samir,* this was what the word meant, a gust of gentle wind. And then, for the first time in decades, her face broke into a wide grin and she found herself laughing. She had no idea where in the world Samir was, but she knew, in that moment, he was there with her. Smiling into the night, she pulled up the length of rope that still held a vegetable basket at the end of it. The basket was new, as was the world around it, but the old secrets it had once carried still endured.

# 47

# The Heirs

In 1985, Samir was returned to Firdaus.

In the hospital ward where Aayat had given birth to her third child, Firdaus held a baby boy in her arms. His eyes were pistachio-colored, like the long line of Khans who had come before him. Eighty-one-year-old Altaf stood beside Aayat's bed and patted her forehead lovingly. Mariam and Yasmin tickled their new brother's toes, touching his chubby cheeks and tugging on his blanket. Aayat's husband's family collected around them, eager to meet the baby. Meanwhile, he cooed in Firdaus's arms as she cradled him lovingly, whispering to him in a language he would not comprehend till much later. He would be her companion, her favorite, her green-eyed boy, she could already tell.

"Samir," she announced to the room full of people, her voice buoyant and hopeful. "He will be called Samir Khan."

"Oh, Ammi!" Aayat beamed, innocently unaware of his namesake. "Yasmin, Mariam, isn't that a beautiful name? Meet your baby brother, Samir."

Within minutes, the name was on everyone's tongue, fluttering around the room, acquainting itself with its new family. Firdaus smiled, as the name she had imprisoned in her heart for years resounded loud and clear.

It was as unrestrained as the day she had first uttered it in the studio of Wazir Khan mosque. She closed her eyes and the years came flooding back—books full of pressed leaves, sixteen beauty marks across a sandy face, stolen glances in a calligrapher's studio, paper boats made with secret letters.

She opened her eyes as Altaf reached out for her hand and squeezed it. Perhaps he already knew that in the years to come, the secret that he and his daughter had so devoutly protected would one day be bequeathed to Samir Khan.

⁂

When Samir Vij saw Léa Clement again, a decade had passed. Sophie had graduated Oxford, where she'd not only trained as an aspiring art historian but also met her future husband, an Englishman named Mark Adams. When the perfumer had encountered his ex-wife at the wedding in London, she greeted him with the formality of someone who had never shared his days. And while she was escorted by a gentleman, Samir attended alone. During the service, he watched her—joyous, content, buoyant, as if she had secrets and history with her new partner—and he felt relieved. It was a sad realization, though, to acknowledge that they had never truly given each other the power to hurt or destroy one another. That took either deep love or deep hate, neither of which had managed to fill the depths between them.

Then a few years later, in 1987, Sophie gave birth to a baby girl. When Samir held his granddaughter—somehow already a part of his heart—for the very first time, bringing his hands to her soft, rose-colored cheeks, she grabbed onto his index finger and led it to her nose. A deep inhale followed, and Samir knew in that moment that this child would become a perfumer. His legacy had somehow remained unbroken, even if it had bypassed a generation. Awash with emotion, he offered Sophie and Mark the name that Vivek and Ambrette had once reserved for their unborn child: Anouk.

◦ ᷎ ◦

In 1992, upon turning seven years old, quiet, demure Samir would be left with his grandmother Firdaus while the remainder of Aayat's family moved to Islamabad. Altaf had passed away a few years ago, but Firdaus had continued to live by herself in the Delhi Gate house. Many times, Aayat had suggested that she move northward with them, but resistant to change, and unable to be separated from yet another Samir, Firdaus requested that her daughter leave the boy in her care instead. He grew up to be his grandmother's shadow. And just as Altaf had bequeathed the art of calligraphy to her, she passed it on to her grandson. They became inseparable to a point that no topic remained undiscussed, apart from one.

He was in middle school when he asked about it for the first time. Prompted by the celebrations at school for the fiftieth anniversary of the Partition of British India and independence of Pakistan, Samir had asked, *What was this Partition, Nani? Did you live through it?*

He had looked at her so innocently, it broke her heart. But there were some things that would need to remain unspoken. *I cannot remember it, beta,* she had responded.

◦ ᷎ ◦

Anouk, meanwhile, would grow up in London, far from her French roots and even farther from her Hindustani ones. But her talent undoubtedly lay in her nose, for whenever she visited her grandfather in Paris, the pair would spend hours in the atelier or the shop, blending, smelling, experimenting. They shared a bond that often made Sophie secretly wish that she, too, had been perfumistically gifted. Her daughter greedily inhaled the world, living, breathing, dreaming of fragrance in a way that Sophie had known only her father to do. But in many ways, Anouk wasn't that much different from her mother, for she, too, accepted her grandfather just as he was, curious about nothing else beyond tutorials of the nose. And so, for much of yet another generation, history remained unrevealed.

In the year 2000, when thirteen-year-old Anouk requested to move to Paris so she could begin her official training as a perfumer's apprentice, Sophie agreed. In this way, Anouk came to occupy the second bedroom in the apartment on rue Visconti, and her mother's old position at the perfumery.

⚘

Born two years apart, at opposite ends of the world, the lives of Samir Khan and Anouk Adams would take on parallel trajectories, tethered to their respective grandparent. And over the course of their youths, they would each inherit one half of a secret.

# PART FIVE

# 48

# A Pakistani in Paris

The earliest hours of their morning were reserved for smelling. If composition was a solitary process, smelling was a shared pleasure for Samir and Anouk. The old perfumer enjoyed the rhythm of his granddaughter's thoughts, the clever associations she made, even the deliberateness of her silence as she deciphered a particular scent.

As the sun rose that day, the fragrance of bergamot filled the atelier. Its five-month-long production, from October to February, resulted in different kinds of bergamot essences, from intense and green to floral and sensual. The desk was littered with dozens of bottles, blotters, smell strips, and notebooks of formulas. Quietly, seventeen-year-old Anouk meandered through the bottles, dipping a smell strip in each and bringing it delicately to her nose. She would inhale, pause, set it on the table, write down her impressions, and then repeat the process with another sample, as her grandfather observed.

"Of all our senses, smell is the most fragile," he said as they concluded the day's lesson. "It is the least understood and also most secretive."

Inching close to eighteen, having just graduated from high school, Anouk had decided to not go to perfumery school but to learn the art from her grandfather instead. Many aspiring perfumers her age enrolled in the schools at Grasse and Versailles, highly competitive and intense programs. But these years with her grandfather were precious. Now that he was in his late seventies, age was fast consuming his nose, but there was still much Anouk could learn from him. She wanted her creations to transport, like her grandfather's did. She wanted to follow in the Vij tradition, for her work to outlive her.

A few hours later, as afternoon light poured into the shop, a distinguished-looking gentleman approached the counter. "Bonjour, monsieur," Samir greeted him. The customer was dressed in a well-tailored suit and woolen scarf, his hair was graying, and his beard was neatly trimmed, and in his hand was a bottle of *Ambrette*.

"*Ah, puis-je vous aider?*" Samir gestured to the perfume, but the man merely studied his face the way people did when trying to recognize a distant acquaintance.

"Pardon, monsieur, do you speak English, maybe?" he tried again.

The customer opened his mouth a few times to speak, but said nothing. And then, just before Samir could say anything else, he uttered a greeting so familiar yet foreign that it left the perfumer speechless.

"*As-salaam-alaikum.*"

It had been so long since Samir had heard it in the warm, full-bodied accent of undivided Punjab that it left him momentarily paralyzed. He looked back into the gentleman's eyes, trying to recognize someone familiar.

"*Wa-alaikum-salaam,*" Samir finally returned, slowly enunciating every syllable, the words emerging from somewhere deep inside him.

"*Tussi . . .*" the gentleman began hesitantly, addressing him in the informal way one spoke to friends or family, "*tussi Lahore de ho?*"

Often, customers would ask Samir whether he was from India, l'Inde, inferring from the name of the shop. They would expect exotic stories, magical tales, and oriental fables. But this stranger had simply walked in, picked up a bottle of *Ambrette* as if he knew of it, and spoken to him directly in the language of the unspeakable past, asking whether he was from Lahore.

Samir didn't know how to answer, remaining silent for so long that he thought he might have actually forgotten his own language. He looked toward the storeroom, where Anouk was taking inventory, before turning his attention back to this mysterious customer. How much more courage would it take for him to claim a homeland that already belonged to him?

⁂

From the storeroom, Anouk heard laughter and peeked out past the curtain, into the shop. Her grandfather stood at the counter with a tall gentleman, conversing in a language she didn't understand. They spoke quickly and animatedly, but if she listened very closely, she could make out some English words peppered throughout. Every now and then, her grandfather looked back toward the storeroom, causing Anouk to hide behind the curtain.

Many years ago, on a visit to her grandfather from London, she remembered prying open the door to his atelier and standing at the threshold, watching him from behind, assuming he was immersed in a composition. The air was heavily perfumed—with jasmine, she still remembered—and in a soft timbre, her grandfather's voice rose above it all, speaking the same foreign language she now heard.

He had been reading from a handwritten book, and for the longest time, Anouk considered it a language that he had simply made up. She never had the chance to ask him about it because she never heard it again. But it was obvious: what he spoke then and what he was speaking now was a *real language*. A language he was adept and comfortable in; one that poured from his tongue in a smoother manner than French or English ever had. It sounded old and faraway, melodious, and like nothing she had heard before.

Suddenly, her grandfather called out for her.

"*Eh meri dothi.*" In the foreign tongue, he introduced her to his new acquaintance, Yusuf Ahmed.

"Bonjour," she said, and he smiled warmly in return.

"Ma chérie." Samir held her hand. "We are going to go for a walk. Do lock up if it gets late and I will meet you back at the apartment. I'll pick up dinner on the way."

She nodded slowly as the two old men walked out the door.

⚘

"It is a thing of great comfort to know that at least perfume cannot be restricted by borders," Yusuf Ahmed said, finally breaking the long silence between him and Samir. The pair had walked from the perfumery to the Luxembourg Gardens, where they now sat in front of the Medici Fountain. Thick layers of moss enveloped the sculptures, and Yusuf followed Samir's gaze to the pool of water beneath. There was much to talk about, but it was difficult to begin.

From his coat, he extracted the bottle of *Ambrette* he had purchased, and repeated his statement, this time in their private tongue, "*Kabhi kisi ne khushboo ka watan socha hai?*"

Samir looked up at him, visibly moved. "How did you know of this perfume?" he asked, and Yusuf led him down the lanes of Lohari Gate, until all borders vanished into a single mass of shared history. He was candid in a way that one could perhaps only be with a complete stranger. But in his tone, Samir sensed great melancholy.

In the summer leading up to Partition, Yusuf had been eleven years old, living on a street nestled between Lohari and Shahalmi Gate, which had six Hindu and Sikh houses and two Muslim ones. His family was one of the two, and had found themselves at the epicenter of religious riots. As he recalled that summer, he could never have known just how close he was veering to Samir's own history, narrating the days of the riots, arriving finally at the Shahalmi fire of June 1947.

"You asked me how I know this perfume," Yusuf continued. "I know it because of my mother. She used to visit your shop in Anarkali, and wore this ittar every single day. After the fire, the riots only became worse. The remaining Hindus and Sikhs of Lahore took their revenge, attacking Muslim neighborhoods and shops. The Muslims would then retaliate, and this cycle continued on until Partition in August, when most of the non-Muslims fled, either to refugee camps or across the border. But between June and August, so many unthinkable things had already been done that life as we once knew it could never be the same again."

Samir wanted to say that he had fled right after the fire, but Yusuf's story wasn't finished yet.

"Many women were abducted during those months. Hindus, Sikhs, Muslims, Christians, even recent converts, it didn't matter. They were abducted, raped, murdered, sometimes never to be seen again . . ." His voice quavered. "She was so beautiful, my mother. I can see her even now with her long, river-like hair and gray eyes. One evening, when my father was still at work, she went out into the back courtyard to feed the goats, and never returned. That was the last time I saw her."

Then Yusuf broke down completely, and it was clear that, like Samir, he had buried things inside himself for long years. Perhaps this was the implicit side effect of living through Partition—that everyone eventually became a site of excavation.

"Yusuf bhai . . ." Samir began, but did not know what to say.

Yusuf clutched the bottle of perfume tightly. "We searched for her everywhere—in the neighborhood, in the city, on the outskirts, we even tried to locate her *across* the border. And the same thought kept playing in my mind . . ." He closed his eyes and tears fell down his cheeks. "Given the riots and violence, I should have fed the goats that day, but I just let her go . . ."

Had Samir not thought the same about the night the fire had taken place? Had he not blamed himself, too?

After a pause, Yusuf continued. "My father lost hope, and eventually, he remarried. He barely spoke to me after that. He threw out all of my walida's things—her clothes, her burqas, her kohl, her bangles, and even her ittar—as if he wanted to erase any trace of her. Maybe it was too painful to remember, so he tried to forget her completely. But I could never forget, and have held her in my heart all these years." He caressed the bottle of perfume. "When I smelled *this* today, I felt like I was a child again, and she was still here. So much that had been lost was returned to me in the most unexpected way. We were destined to meet."

Samir nodded, and then, unable to help himself, he asked, "What happened to the perfumery after Partition?"

"Destroyed," Yusuf responded without missing a breath, "along with half the market."

He went on to recall the curfew that shadowed the city for weeks, the rationing of food, schools being converted into refugee camps, trains arriving laden with corpses, mobs looting the vacant homes, until gradually the Lahore of old times had become unrecognizable. By mid-October, Partition had been normalized, accepted, and one nation had officially assumed the divided shape of two.

Then Yusuf smiled sadly. "Apart from the disappearance of my mother, there are some things I still remember. Seemingly trivial things that lodged themselves in my memory. Back then, I had no Hindu or Sikh friends, even though we lived on the same street. But during the festival of Diwali, their homes used to be lit in celebration, clusters of earthen lamps twinkling like fireflies. This is a sight I will never forget, for after Partition, the taaqs of these Hindu and Sikh homes lay bare . . ." His voice trailed into the late afternoon.

Partition was a double-edged sword, and if Yusuf had borne one half of the wound, the other half had been borne by Samir. For the next hour, he told his tale of life and death, beginning with the creation of the perfume *Amrit,* now *Ambrette,* and ending with the fire. Then again, there was silence, filled only by the rustle of trees above them.

⚘

"*Kadi yaad aandi hai,* do you ever remember it, Lahore?" Yusuf asked Samir later.

Turning to face his new acquaintance, Samir admitted, "One can leave a place completely, and yet the place can refuse to leave you. For so many years after Partition, everything real seemed to slip so easily out of my fingers; I had no grasp on the ground beneath my feet or the sky above my head . . ." And then it was difficult for Samir to stop the whole truth from tumbling out. "I was married for a while. Léa, her name is Léa. And if I think about it now, she discovered my greatest weakness—that I was, *am,* longing for something that no longer exists and cannot be retrieved."

"For your family, you mean?" Yusuf asked, the memory of the fire still blazing bright.

"Yes, for them, and . . ." He paused, then took out his wallet and retrieved something from the innermost fold.

Yusuf took the black-and-white passport photograph in his palm and stared at it.

"Firdaus," Samir said quietly. "Her name is Firdaus Khan."

"Where is she now? In Lahore?"

Samir shrugged. "I don't know . . ."

"Haven't you ever looked for her, or wondered whether she is looking for you?"

The perfumer shook his head and narrated his last hours in Lahore. The dupatta, the tears, the separation, the suffering. So far away it all seemed, and yet somehow Samir could still feel the heat of soot on his body, the sense of betrayal in his heart.

"Given the way we parted, Yusuf bhai, it is unlikely that she is looking for me. And I don't think I ever had the courage to look for her. No, it seems rather pathetic even for me to be talking this way, all these years later, as an old man. To want to be remembered by someone. To want to matter. To want to know, to *need* to know, that no matter how long it's been—days or months or years—someone could still be thinking of you. It makes me sad."

"But this is love," Yusuf insisted. "This is love."

Samir took a sharp breath in. "Tell me, Yusuf bhai, do calligraphers still sit in Wazir Khan?"

"Not anymore, not for a while. Why do you ask?"

"She . . ." Samir began, and then stopped abruptly. "No reason, I was only wondering about my ustad sahib, who used to own one of the studios."

Samir said nothing more, but Yusuf had been given his first clue.

As darkness set in, Yusuf checked his watch. His daughter would be home from work soon, and he needed to take the métro back all the way to her apartment on the Right Bank, where he was visiting. He cleared his throat and gestured to Samir. "Shall we leave?"

Samir nodded, and a strong gust of wind suddenly blew a shower of leaves down onto them. He laughed as he stood up from the bench, catching a few. They were that perfectly rare end-of-summer, start-of-autumn color, partly green, partly yellow, with watercolor-like washes of orange. Samir twirled a leaf in his hand. It was five-lobed with three main veins running through. As expected, it had no smell, but that didn't stop Samir from bringing it up to his nose, anyway.

"Firdaus had this habit of collecting and pressing leaves. It was never flowers, always leaves, and I never asked why that was. But for a long time after I arrived in France, I wished to have perished in the fire with my family, mixing in with the soil of Lahore, so that maybe one day I could have been reborn as a stem or a root or a leaf to be picked up and cared for by her."

As the pair buttoned up coats and wrapped scarves around their necks, Yusuf bent down to find the most perfect plane leaf. Without Samir noticing, he wiped it clean of dirt and water, and deposited it carefully within

the inner breast pocket of his coat. It would accompany him back to Lahore, where he had a role still to play.

_&_

That evening, when Samir returned to the apartment, bearing containers of dumpling soup, steamed jasmine rice, and chicken with bok choy,
Anouk felt him to be a completely different person. All through dinner,
she surveyed her grandfather as one would a stranger. Then, unable to
bear it any longer, she pushed her plate away.

"What was that language? Where are you from?"

In the seventeen years that Anouk had been alive, she had never felt
odder asking a question whose answer she ought to have already known.
*Where are you from?* She had asked in a way that made it sound like an
accusation. But her grandfather had only smiled, polished off his bowl of
rice and said, "Tomorrow. There are many things you should know, ma
chérie. But tomorrow."

# 49

# This Is How It Happened

When Anouk awoke the next morning, her grandfather was already prepared. Dressed in crisply ironed pants and a thick cardigan, he was sitting at the dining table with a cup of tea for himself and a freshly brewed pot of coffee for her. Clearing her throat, Anouk poured herself a cup, tied up her hair, and focused on the slim book her grandfather had placed on the table. It was an atlas, opened to Asia.

"Here." He pointed to a tiny dot within a large landmass. "I am from here."

Anouk leaned in and followed his fingertip to a city called Lahore. "You are from Pakistan? We are Pakistani? But the perfume shop is called . . ."

She was so naively unaware that it almost hurt him. "No, my darling, I *am* Indian," he clarified. "*Je suis indien.*"

A fold appeared on her forehead. "So . . . we are from India?"

"Well, I only lived in India, this present India, for a few months." Samir leaned back in his chair and rested a palm against his jaw. Then he began again. "Actually, in a way, I am from both India and Pakistan, from a time when they were one, undivided. Back then, we called it Hindustan. So I am from Hindustan, but above all, I am from a city called Lahore."

That morning, Samir Vij took his granddaughter back to a time when two lands had been one, when neither republic nor democracy existed, but only colony. He spoke about the rearing of silk, about the illness that took his grandmother, about the river Ravi and the smell of monsoon, about Anarkali Bazaar and the perfume shop, and about his family. He spoke about a time when belonging to a land was more important than belonging to a religion. He spoke of his flight to Delhi and journey to Bombay, his vow to never return to Lahore, his voyage across the oceans, and his emigration to France.

"I have spent more years now thinking about the past than the number of years when the past actually happened," he concluded.

"Didn't you ever want to go back?" was her first question.

"I'm afraid there is no place for someone like me who refused to accept a divided Hindustan. I do not feel Indian enough, nor am I Pakistani. Exile from both seemed more suitable than any kind of half-life in either. You see, rejection from a person or a group of people is one thing, but rejection from one's own land is incomprehensible. The soil rejects you, the air banishes you, and when the elements desert, then you know you are unwelcome. I was forced out of my home, and every day, I am weighed down by its memory; sometimes, I am obliterated by it. But I have had to find ways to balance what has been lost with what has been lived, for this is self-exile. An exile of choice."

He reached out and held Anouk's hand.

"Perfume is the only normalcy," he continued, "the way to remain connected to Lahore."

"Did you ever tell Mum?" she whispered.

*Sophie. Sophie with hazel eyes like her mother, with the Parisian accent, his little assistant at the shop standing at the edge of his world. Sophie at a distance.*

"No," he spoke slowly and with remorse. "She never asked about this and I never offered."

He looked into Anouk's eyes, knowing full well that secrets changed the way we loved, that today would change them. He chose his next words carefully, taking time, filling his speech with pauses. There was little he could say to justify his actions, but the truth had to be told.

"When I was younger, the past was a confusing place, and I felt I always had to choose between *here* and *there.* It was difficult to begin life in this country again, and even more difficult to raise a child who would unfairly inherit her father's tumultuous history."

Minutes passed in silence as the smell of coffee overpowered the room and the winter sun spilled in broad rays across the floor. Grief was an arduous yet invisible process. There were no prescribed remedies, no predetermined time for mourning, no boundaries. One simply had to grieve through grief, whether for a person or a place.

"So . . . why now, why me?" she asked. "Why are you telling me all this?"

Samir watched as his granddaughter's fingers traced the deeply entrenched Radcliffe Line between India and Pakistan in the atlas.

"Because everything I can still recall is now yours. It is time."

The next day, he was waiting for her again. There was more; there was still so much more that needed to be revealed. Anouk was to Samir what Samir had been to Vivek; *she would become his lightness.* On the stove that morning, no coffee brewed, but Samir stood boiling a pot of whole milk. On the counter were several pieces of de-seeded dates—the fat, sticky, fleshy kind. When Anouk emerged, he dropped them into the glass of frothy milk, mixed in their sweetness and handed it to her, but she pulled a face.

"Oho, it's something my mother used to make in Lahore. Khajoor-doodh, dates in milk," he said.

Any hesitation Anouk felt vanished at the mention of her great-grandmother. *Savitri,* she silently repeated the name to herself. *Saavitrrri.* An elongated *a,* a dull *t,* a rolling *r.* Her grandfather had described her to Anouk. Daughter of a medicine man, she was the keeper of natural cures—sandalwood to lessen stress, lemon oil for varicose veins, jasmine for skin ailments, marigold extract for stubborn wounds, and rose to lighten the heart. Her name, *Savitri,* meant "a ray of light." Anouk had looked it up in a Sanskrit dictionary in the library last evening.

"Tell me more about Lahore, Grandpa . . . your house, the streets, the city." She sipped on the frothy, sweet milk.

"Nanu, you can call me Nanu. In my language, it means maternal grandfather."

"*Naanoo,*" she enunciated, trying to imitate his accent.

"Lahore . . ." He now sat back. "What shall I tell you about Lahore except that when we were young, we could have never predicted what the city would endure. Lahore is ancient, and its stories, myths, and legends are endless. Like any city of its age, it is a place where the past and the present often meet. Lahore boasts of Hindu, Muslim, Sikh, Afghan, Mughal, Persian, British influence, all at once. There is no place quite like it in the world."

In a faraway voice, Samir transported Anouk to the city of his birth and now the city of her dreams. Where a large ancestral home no longer existed, where the lanes he had run through were destroyed by a fire in the summer of 1947, where even the remnants of the neighborhood gate called Shahalmi Darwaza had now likely been razed to the ground. He spoke foreign words she had never heard of but readily accepted as her own—*phool,* flower; *lassi,* frothed milk; *aam,* mango; *pyaaz,* onions; *patang,* kites; *kucha,* lane; *ittar,* perfume. He talked of places that she could assign no images to—Machi Hatta Bazaar, Papar Mandi Bazaar, Sua Bazaar, the hakims in Wachowali gali, a mausoleum for a dancer named Anarkali who was entombed alive, a great bore cannon called Zamzamah made with the melted utensils from the homes of the people of Lahore, the tanga-wallahs, the festivals of basant and Holi, Eid and Lohri. No matter how much time had passed, her grandfather remained an encyclopedia of the city she had never even wondered about. And now all she had were questions.

The morning extended into afternoon, which extended so far into the past, that at the end, she almost *felt* Lahori. She was struck by how quickly the sense of belonging to a previously unknown place could be formed, how seamlessly the oceans could be traversed through mere words, and how little she knew about her own family.

Soon, Anouk began to read books on the history of India and Pakistan—conjoined twins, two halves of a whole, whose children had been born on the same soil and under the same sky, having together endured two hundred years of slavery and British rule only to be cleaved apart at the bosom. At Partition, Hindus and Sikhs had migrated to India, and Muslims to Pakistan; India became a secular republic, and Pakistan, an Islamic one. When her grandfather spoke of the loss of Lahore, he considered it a loss of breath, a loss of blood, a loss of all those things that kept a person alive. Since Partition, India and Pakistan had fought four wars and lived now as mirror images, with shared history but also shared hate. The tall customer who had inspired her grandfather's recollections had been Pakistani, but if Anouk had not known this, she'd have barely been able to tell the difference between the two men.

In reading about the oppression Indians had faced under foreign rule, Anouk felt flattened by the entire weight of her genealogy. She might have been one-fourth Indian and one-fourth French from her mother's side, but from her father's, she was half British, thus inheriting both sides of colonial legacy.

☙

What brought Sophie the most joy in her adulthood was witnessing the bond between her father and daughter develop through their shared language of perfume. Every few weekends, she would take the train from London to Paris, and watch as Anouk learned all those things that Sophie wished she had. But it was the year she turned fifty that Samir invited Sophie into the nucleus of his life.

On the weekend of his seventy-eighth birthday, the perfumer brought

his daughter and granddaughter to the atelier. One by one, Samir unwrapped all of the heirlooms he had kept hidden over the years. Savitri's
broken green bangle, Som Nath's charred book, the corner of that railing
from Vij Bhawan that had refused to burn in the fire, the bundle of heirloom jewels—he offered these to his descendants. Only Firdaus's maroon
dupatta and photograph remained a secret. There had been no mention
of her yet.

While Sophie held her father's hand, Anouk approached the aged
items, running her fingertips tenderly over each object. She bent down
to smell—of course she smelled everything—but she also wished that
she'd been more curious as a child, had asked about the secret language
the first time she'd heard him speak it, had asked about the color of her
grandfather's skin, the mixed accent he spoke in, his hands, his eyes, the
inspirations for his perfumes, the land of his birth. By now, she would
have collected so much more. Nestling then into her mother's body, she
drew tears for people she had never known, but whose stories she now
cradled—

A great-great-grandfather named Som Nath, besotted with a great-
great-grandmother, Leela, who smelled only of sandalwood and died too
early in life. A great-grandfather named Mohan, reserved yet wise, and a
great-grandmother named Savitri, the ally of the sun, the stirrer of dates
into hot milk. A great-granduncle named Vivek, the origin of her nose,
the first keeper of smell. They were all hers, as she was theirs.

"Do you know why I suggested the name Anouk?" Samir finally
asked Sophie. When she shook her head, he presented them with the
greatest love story he had known, of Vivek and his Ambrette. That her
daughter carried part of their ancestry in her very name overwhelmed
Sophie.

Samir showed the girls the wedding photograph of his uncle and aunt.
Sophie held it up, tracing their smiling faces.

"How do you know about her?" she asked.

"From the dead," he said. "The dead told me about the dead."

It was then that the journals were offered, as was the misery of war, the shame of flight, the tale of Grasse, and the strength of heartbreak.

"This is why you chose France . . ." Sophie wondered out loud, "and why you lived in Grasse."

"It was the farthest place I knew that would still feel like home," he answered.

Sophie knew nothing about the Great War, let alone those from Hindustan who had fought in it. The fact that she was a descendant of a man who was a descendant of a soldier turned perfumer filled her with all sorts of questions she never imagined herself asking. Turning the wedding photograph, she read the inscription, *Ambrette & Vivek Vij, 13 Avril 1918. Grasse, France.* Vivek, her granduncle Vivek, whose face she had memorized from the 1937 black-and-white photograph hanging in the perfumery. But here, nearly twenty years earlier, as a younger man, he bore a remarkable resemblance to her father.

"Why do you think he wrote in these journals, Nanu?" Anouk now surveyed the tall pile. She skimmed through the pages of faded handwriting, tracing the shapes of the words. She couldn't read the script, but that wouldn't always be the case. With the passage of years, Anouk would learn many new things.

"I don't know, puttar, I have also wondered this, many times. Why did he enlist? Why did he write in the journals? Was it to remember the days, or to forget them by depositing them onto the page? Maybe it was to have a record of witnessing history, fighting on those great battlefields. Or perhaps he had hoped to pass the memories on to his own children one day . . . I cannot say. But my uncle has taught me many things—in life and in death—and one of those things is how time and circumstance stretch us to live multiple lives, sometimes simultaneously, sometimes without choice. You see, he died holding on to *so many* secrets, and only by accidentally reading these journals have I discovered the many shades of him, especially the ones he chose to bury or forget. They told me every-thing he may never have been able to."

Then, meeting Sophie's gaze, swallowing the lump that had formed in his throat, he concluded, "But that will not be my fate. I want to tell my story, in my own words, to those whom I love."

# 50

# The Emissary

"Oho, Ayaaz, look carefully at how my hands move across the page, how they hold the qalam," Firdaus instructed her newest student, the neighbors' thirteen-year-old son. She tucked her dupatta behind her ears, placed her thumb and forefinger on the bamboo reed pen, holding it in place with the middle finger. She then dipped it into a dish of sooty ink and demonstrated. After rendering a few alphabets, she held the page out to the boy. Then, using the nib—the qatt of the qalam—she measured each alphabet.

"The rules of calligraphy are essential, and every khattat, even an aspiring one, must follow them. See, *alif* is three qatt, and *be* is eleven qatt, and so on . . . *na ek qatt zyada, na ek qatt kamm,* not a single centimeter here nor there. If you do not learn this properly, you will never be a decent khattat, and then what will I tell your walid sahib and walida, hmm?"

With a thud, she placed Mir Ali Tabrezi's fourteenth-century manual on how to render perfect alphabets in front of young Ayaaz. Famously known as Qodwat-al-Kottab, the chief of the scribes, Tabrezi had invented the elegant and popular nastaliq style, by combining the earlier styles of naskh and taliq, in a way that letters, deep and hook-like, floated across the page.

"Ji, ustani sahiba." Eyes downcast, Ayaaz accepted the book and began practicing.

Ustani, that was what Firdaus's students called her. If her father had been known as ustad sahib, then after his death, continuing in his footsteps, Firdaus had been bestowed with the title *ustani*. When the calligrapher's bazaar at Wazir Khan mosque had shut down several years ago, Firdaus restarted classes in the baithak of her home. This was the only way she could protect her legacy. She couldn't allow such an intimate and graceful form of art to fade into oblivion, and so she persisted.

A female calligrapher was a rare thing, and female students were even rarer, and so over the years, Firdaus had made special efforts to recruit girls who had talent but lacked formal training or attention. In the same way her father had nurtured her, she, too, instructed them on their technique and artistry. Now, at the age of seventy-six, she taught a weekend class to five students—three boys, two girls.

"Ustani sahiba," ten-year-old Noori called out from near the window, placing her wooden slate on the ground, "*Nastaliq kya sabse asaan hai?*" She asked whether Tabrezi's script was the easiest one to learn, eager to become adept at it.

"*Uff badmaash,* nothing is easy, *kuch asaan nahi hai!* Back to work, all of you!"

As her students returned to their handiwork, she chuckled to herself. The old radio Altaf had loved, that he had carried home from the ittar shop in Anarkali after the legendary fire, played faintly in the background.

Between classes and taking care of the house, Firdaus barely had any time to continue her own artwork. Every once in a while, she would begin a piece—a wreath of leaves, a garden, a rendition of the Sunehri Masjid, an image from memory—painstakingly crushing her dyes and sharpening her qalams. But soon enough, it would be time to cook dinner, or hang up the clothes, or check her students' work, or read over her grandson's essays. Samir was twenty and a student of journalism at the Government College, Lahore. As her life inched toward its end, her world became smaller and smaller—it was now just the two of them, grandmother and grandson, with matching pistachio eyes and a hunger for poetry and art.

Samir walked out of his room into the baithak and was greeted by his grandmother's students in unison. "*Wa-alaikum-salaam, wa-alaikum-salaam,*" he responded animatedly, and then, to his grandmother, "Nani jaan, I'm going to the library."

"On a weekend?" She clicked her tongue. "Stay home, I'll make aloo paratha for breakfast!"

Samir laughed. He would have loved to stay and devour his grandmother's parathas, but the final exams of his second year were barely a month away.

"I'll be back soon after lunch, *khuda hafiz.*"

"Beta, please don't be late," Firdaus called after him. "He will come this afternoon."

⚘

At 3 p.m., Yusuf Ahmed left his home in Gulberg and traveled across Lahore to the old city. His driver parked the car outside Delhi Gate; he would wait there, as the inner streets were much too narrow to drive through. Address in his hands, a dehydrated leaf in his pocket, Yusuf climbed onto a rickshaw and rode it toward Sunehri Masjid. He was sweating, even in March—the beautiful spring breeze drifted by, as the semal flowers were only just opening up their silky red petals, as the bustle of Dabbi Bazaar enveloped him.

Ever since his return from Paris last autumn, he had spent months searching for a woman named Firdaus. He was equipped with no details apart from the fact that she would have been around the same age as Samir, and had some connection to the calligraphy studios at Wazir Khan. Yusuf had discreetly asked around, but the efforts had been in vain, until two weeks ago, when an old classmate's ninety-seven-year-old father—at one point the leading Urdu publisher of Lahore—had recalled with clarity the name Firdaus Khan.

The girl he knew had been a young illuminator of manuscripts, working alongside her father in the studio, a rarity in a world otherwise occupied by men. Firdaus's father, Yusuf learned, had been a beloved khattat whose perfumed manuscripts were praised and remembered by all those who had frequented a pre-Partition Wazir Khan. The moment this fact emerged, Yusuf knew he had found her.

Now, two weeks later, Yusuf rode to Firdaus Khan's home in the late afternoon, under the guise of bringing a manuscript for restoration. *Those were the days,* the old publisher had told him, *the days of exquisite skill and artistry. Her dyes had been bluer than the open sky, silver like twinkling stars, gold as warm as sunshine, and indigo deeper than the ocean. Those were the days.*

Yusuf closed his eyes, and pictured Samir Vij by the Medici Fountain, passport photo in hand, heart on his sleeve, and prayed that he had found his Firdaus. When the rickshaw-wallah stopped in front of Sunehri Masjid, he paid and, asking around for ustad sahib's house, was directed to a two-story building just across the street. Patting down the creases in his kurta, he walked to the door, took a deep breath, and rang the doorbell.

⚘

Samir Khan was in the storeroom on the roof when the bell rang, taking down the trunks of old clothes that his grandmother had been meaning to give away. Firdaus was in the kitchen, fingers deep in a bowl, mixing besan with water and spices to make pakoras. Sliced vegetables sat on the counter, waiting to be battered and fried. On the stove, water was ready to be boiled for tea, clusters of tulsi, cardamom, and ginger floating around.

Their guest was early, she noted looking at the clock, all of fifteen minutes early. A rather un-Pakistani trait.

She called out to her grandson, but he barely would have been able to hear anything over the bustle of the market traffic below. Washing her hands, she tried again, but no answer. Sighing, she walked out into the balcony and looked down. It was the stranger.

"*As-salaam-alaikum*," she called out, and he looked up, shielding himself from the sun.

He could barely see her. Did she have pistachio eyes? Was she holding a qalam?

"*Wa-alaikum-salaam*," he replied and paused, wondering how to correctly address her. But before he could say anything, she yelled out again.

"Please come up."

While she might have felt uncomfortable receiving the stranger herself, she could not have let him wait downstairs in the sweltering heat, least of all because of who had organized this meeting. The previous week, she'd received a phone call from an old and dear acquaintance of her late father, a publisher she had known since she was old enough to hold a qalam. In his frail voice, he spoke about an old manuscript that needed restoration, and out of respect, Firdaus has agreed to take a look. Ordinarily, she would have received the guest at the studio, but since there was a studio no longer, she had agreed to hold the meeting at home, in Samir's presence. And now, the boy could barely hear her.

Looking at her reflection in the hallway mirror, Firdaus tucked her hair under the dupatta, and using the voluminous cloth, covered her head and torso with it.

*

When Firdaus opened the door, Yusuf knew he was staring at an older version of the passport photograph. The likeness was so unmistakable that he almost gasped. She wore a light green cotton suit with a white dupatta. Fine wrinkles decorated her face, on her chin sat the distinct beauty mark, and the diamond of her nose pin sparkled. She wore no makeup, not even kohl. Yusuf checked for a wedding band, but he found none. Had she never married?

The air smelled like gram flour and coriander, salty potatoes and onions. Eyes downcast, she led him into the baithak, and he had barely begun to introduce himself when they heard footsteps.

"We are in here! I've been calling out to you for so long." Firdaus now smiled at Yusuf. "My grandson, he was just upstairs in the storeroom."

Yusuf nodded and smiled back. *So, she* had *married.*

"*Maaf karein, Nani jaan,* it took longer than I expected to bring down all the trunks."

A tall young man walked into the room, wiping his hands against one another, his clothes covered in dust. In the shape of his face and the color of his eyes, his grandmother could be clearly discerned. A sprinkling of light brown freckles dotted his nose and his longish brown hair stuck up in places. Using a cloth from the kitchen, he wiped down his hands and clothes, and then greeted their guest.

"Samir beta," Firdaus began to introduce the stranger, but was interrupted.

"S-Samir," Yusuf said. With wide eyes, he leaned forward, now focusing all his attention on the young man. "Your . . . name . . . is . . . Samir?" he asked, enunciating every word.

"It is, yes," the young man responded, confused by the manner of questioning.

Firdaus shuffled in her seat uncomfortably. She had been told that this meeting was about a manuscript, and yet the stranger bore no documents or papers. She cleared her throat, prepared to ask him to leave.

"*Samir?*" Yusuf clarified, shifting his gaze to the old woman seated next to him.

And it was in this moment that Firdaus knew he knew. Simply by the way he had said the name Samir, with such familiarity and intimacy, making it sound less like a person and more like a place of refuge, a sanctuary, a haven. *He knew.* She did not understand what was happening or how, but in that moment, in her heart, in every breath that escaped her lips, in every tiny cell of her body, she knew that they shared a person. *Her person.* Excusing herself abruptly, she went to make the tea and pakoras.

⁓

There had never been a stranger evening. The tea had gone untouched; the pakoras had been wasted. Only two things emerged.

The first was a completely dry, perfectly pointed leaf. The stranger had extracted it from the front pocked of his kurta and offered it to Samir's grandmother. Surprised—but not nearly as much as Samir—she had accepted it in a way that one accepted a blessing on Eid. Her hands cradled the leaf like a treasure.

"From . . . from Paris, for your collection."

Samir had turned to her, bewildered, almost ready to laugh at the absurdity, but for the first time, he couldn't read her. All the lines on her face, all the soft folds of her skin, all the light in her eyes reflected a time he had never seen. For a moment, he barely recognized the grandmother who had raised him.

The second thing to emerge was a single, folded piece of paper. It was placed on the table with great intention, and when his grandmother reached out to open it, the room became so quiet that Samir could have heard a spider spinning its web in the corner. A few minutes later, the stranger cleared his throat, cutting through the silence.

"Aapa," he said calmly, "in case you are looking, *this* is where you will find him."

# 51

# This Love, Older than I

For weeks, his grandmother held on to the mysterious piece of paper, hardly letting it out of her sight. Even while sleeping, she tied it tightly into the end of her dupatta, protecting it the same way that she had protected Samir all these years—fiercely and with purpose. The few times that Samir had tried to question her, she would respond with sentences that hovered in the air, with no beginning and no end, her voice emerging from the trail of a deep thought and dissolving right back into it. At times, he would find her crying, yet she barely noticed the tears, always allowing them to trickle down. Some days, she would dress in vibrant blues, teals and lapis, as if she were a young girl, open her braid to let her long hair flow, and line her eyes with kohl. On these days, he felt that she even said his name differently, pronouncing it in a tone that made him seem like someone else.

More than once, Samir had considered mentioning the change in his grandmother's demeanor to his mother, or perhaps tracking down the stranger himself to ask what the visit had really meant. But something always stopped him. It was the unaccustomed look in his grandmother's eyes—partly melancholic, partly wistful, but also entirely euphoric—that made him pause. Whatever this was, whatever this visit had meant, had done or undone, would be told to Samir in due time. He could feel it.

⁊

In the summer of the same year, Firdaus awoke with an unusual desire. She waited all morning for her grandson to leave for summer classes at the college, and then, locking the front door, she walked barefoot across the house into her bedroom and sat down on the floor. It wasn't easy anymore—she was seventy-seven—but gently, she descended her wiry frame to the ground and reached underneath her bed. There it was, the memento of old years. Pulling it out, she studied it.

"Oh, Samir . . . So many years later, and here you still are." She was speaking to the box of letters he had written to her, but at the same time, her hands were undoing the knot at the end of her dupatta, revealing the piece of folded paper.

*Samir Vij*, it said, followed by a string of words she couldn't pronounce, and then, *Paris*. She wondered how far that was from Lahore.

"Paris," she said out loud, making it sound more like *Peyris*, but still, she liked the way it rolled off her tongue, unfamiliar yet holding within it the most familiar part of her. He was alive, and he was there.

She had been so startled by the reason for Yusuf Ahmed's visit that she barely had the presence of mind ask him the most crucial questions—the whys, hows, and whens. Even after he left, she had just stared at the folded piece of paper in her hands, not understanding what had happened or what to do next. Only when her grandson reheated the untouched cup of tea and brought it to her did her muscles relax.

Now, months after the visit, she sat before an unopened box of love, collecting her courage. In a single, swift motion, she removed the lid, selected an envelope, and opened it before she could change her mind. It was written in the autumn from the year she turned fifteen.

October 12, 1944

 Firdaus, I am writing to you from the crown of our Hindustan, the village of Pampore in Kashmir. The air is purer here than it will ever be in Lahore, and if one stands on the topmost hill, the entire landscape is dotted with saffron fields. The sight is dazzling, and one that I can see being painted in the borders of your manuscripts . . . endless pastures of purple, dotted with specks of orange. Someday, I will bring you here, so that—

Firdaus stopped reading. What was it about Samir's words that had kept them alive even now, so many years later? They ran from right to left across the page in careful penmanship, and as she ran her fingers over them, she was certain that each alphabet had the ability to reach out and touch her. The *shin* and *qaf* would unfurl over her skin, the *mim* and *nun* would trace the wrinkles on her face, and the shikara-shaped *be* would swim in her hair the way she had heard the boats floated across the Jhelum.

The letter went on to describe the smell of saffron, earthy, leathery, and sometimes like the air of the sea, and then, he asked her—

 Have you ever seen the sea? They say if you travel to the edge of Karachi and stand with your arms outstretched at the port, you can meet the endless sea. The air from its water kisses your skin and the smell is divine. Taya ji told me about it, its smell is divine. Before we are both old, Firdaus, we will visit the sea.

She was now old, and had still never met the sea. In fact, the only way that she had ever traveled anywhere was through the shapes of leaves and the text of manuscripts, through poetry and the accounts of travelers, and, vicariously, through Samir's excursions with his uncle to procure ingredients for their perfumes. *That* was the sum total of her travels. She folded the letter and placed it back into its envelope, and then her gaze fell on the gold bottle of ittar. She grazed the filigree engraving that had oxidized over the last many decades, and cautiously raised her nose to the room and inhaled. It smelled like nothing out of the ordinary. Then, with nervous hands, she picked up the bottle and uncorked it, releasing the aged elixir to the air. But she still smelled nothing, and brought the bottle even closer to her nose.

Fifty-nine years ago, at Standard Restaurant, Samir had described this as the heart of the tuberose, rajnigandha. She recalled the exact expression on his face when he had presented her with the exquisite gold bottle, and how his face fell when she'd pushed it aside. She hadn't been able to smell it, after all. At least not in the way it was supposed to be smelled. Then, fifty-seven years ago, the ittar had irrefutably drawn her late husband to her, but even then, she hadn't been able to smell what he had.

Taking deep and deliberate inhales, she now rubbed a small drop of liquid onto her wrist as she had once seen her mother do, gently, tenderly. Still, she discerned no sweetness. She inhaled again, deeper, and a tear appeared. But she persisted, taking an even larger drop and depositing it onto her collarbone, nestling her nose into the skin. Yet again, no fragrance emerged, but her tears became as large as raindrops. She removed her dupatta and then, head naked, hair in tangles, she rubbed a dollop of the oily film behind her ear and took a purposeful inhale of the air around her. Nothing, still nothing. Nothing beautiful, at least. Tears ran down her cheeks. Forcefully now, she massaged the liquid liberally into the crook of her elbow, the patch of skin that Samir had once kissed. She inhaled from her gut, drawing her stomach in concavely. She rubbed it onto her ankles, her fingers, the bones of her feet, and the nape of her neck. Nothing, nothing, nothing, nothing. Only tears.

Growing hysterical, Firdaus now deposited nearly the entire bottle onto herself, dousing her skin and clothes. But there was no Samir to be found within that bottle, no Samir to be found upon her body. The box of letters lay open on the bed, the bottle of ittar clutched tightly within her hands.

⚮

When Samir Khan returned from college that evening, he unlocked the door to find the house alarmingly quiet and flooded with sweetness. A honey-like, warm, waxy aroma trailed down the stairs.

Puzzled, he walked in and called out to his grandmother. "*As-salaam-alaikum, Nani jaan.*"

Then walking directly to her room, he knocked on the door. "Nani?" he called out again, now worried. Maybe she had fallen; maybe she was unwell. Panic rose within him, and he knocked louder. There was no answer, but this was certainly the source of the smell. When many seconds passed and she did not answer, he opened the door and walked into a room that smelled like a field of tuberoses. His grandmother was lying on the floor at the foot of her bed, dupatta discarded. Her eyes were closed, as if she was sleeping, and her long gray hair was in disarray. Alarmed, he rushed to her side, picked her frail body off the ground, and placed her on the bed. Then he covered her torso with the dupatta. It was difficult not to gag, though, for every inch of her skin smelled like it had been saturated with the honeyed smell.

"Nani jaan . . . Nani!" He shook her, and she opened her eyes slowly.

"*Beta, aap aa gaye,* how was your day?" She spoke with such normalcy, as if nothing was wrong.

Inhaling sharply, he looked around the room. A box of envelopes, an antique gold perfume bottle, and the stranger's folded note lay strewn across the floor. "What happened here?" he asked.

Firdaus's smile faded and, lifting her body up, she looked directly into her grandson's eyes.

"I'm afraid," she said, "I haven't been completely honest with you."

꠶

She began with the facts, things that she was certain about, things that had not been in her control. She began with Partition. She described what she remembered from the summer of 1947. Disorder, death, fire, and flight. It was strange, but after middle school, Samir had never once asked about Partition again, taking his grandmother's word that she did not remember it. And now that a whole world of memory was being revealed to him, he hardly knew what to say or how to feel.

Evening light cascaded into the room, but there was no respite from the summer heat. After Samir had calmed his grandmother, he'd gone into the kitchen and prepared two glasses of cold lemonade, which they now sipped.

"See, when I was younger," she said, "there was an ittar-kadā in Anarkali run by the Vij family and they—"

"Vij?" he interrupted her, having never heard that name before.

"Hindu. They were Hindu."

"Hmm . . ." Samir nodded. Of course, in school he had briefly read about how much of Anarkali Bazaar was once owned by Hindus and Sikhs. And despite the ban, he'd rented pirated video cassettes of Bollywood films with his friends, watching *Sholay* multiple times purely for the hero that was Amitabh Bachchan. But he had never actually met a Hindu before, and certainly wasn't well acquainted with their names.

"The family had a son, not much older than me," Firdaus continued. Her voice was resolute and confident, but throughout the conversation, her eyes never met her grandson's. She knew what she was about to tell him could change everything about their relationship, and if not that, then certainly his perception of her. Still, it was now or never.

"We met in 1938, and I can't say what, but something powerful drew me to him. There I was, in this shop filled with all kinds of old and new smells, and . . . there he was . . ."

She let her voice linger and Samir cleared his throat. He didn't know if he wanted to hear the rest. Quickly, in his mind, he calculated how old she would have been in 1938.

"Nine!" he exclaimed. "You were nine years old then."

"I know, but it was a different time. Girls were married off at twelve, thirteen . . . At least my father had the foresight to educate me, give me skills that were mostly forbidden to other girls."

Samir was astonished at the honesty and directness in her every syllable, as if she had made up her mind that this needed to be done *today*.

"For the next ten years, he mixed with me," she continued.

Her words were chosen carefully, spoken slowly, drawn from memory. But the image of one human mixing into another was something Samir was wholly unfamiliar with.

"But . . . Nani, he was Hindu?" It was supposed to be a comment, but it came out sounding more like a question, as if he was making sure that what she had said was what she had meant.

"Oh, yes, I know!" She laughed. Her first uninhibited laugh since their conversation began. "But it wasn't imprinted on his head, beta. In our day, things were not the way they are now. Lahore was a different kind of city. Musalmaan, Hindu, Sikh—at the end, everyone was Punjabi with little obvious difference. It didn't matter so much, actually . . . until it did, and it did quite suddenly." Her voice turned grave. "His family died in the riots in the summer before Partition, all of them in a single night, and then he just disappeared . . . well, I made . . ."

His grandmother was still talking, but he was not really listening anymore. Along with all of the questions that had crammed into his mind, one thought emerged.

*The tall stranger's visit. The folded piece of paper. The "he."*

His next words were no louder than a whisper, his own name sounding like something he had no ownership over.

"Was his name . . . Samir?"

"It is."

֊ჟ֊

For many weeks, Samir didn't know how to speak to his grandmother about his namesake. He tiptoed around the subject, just as he did around her, and soon, a distance grew between them for the first time. Over chapatis at the lunch table, during her weekend classes with the students, over the bowls of dye and folios of paper, in the kitchen while slicing potatoes and chopping coriander, Samir would stare at his grandmother, wondering about her life in a pre-Partition Hindustan. He thought of her as a young girl—laughing, reading, drawing illuminated borders on manuscripts, and being in love. Mostly, he thought of her being in love.

From his mother, Samir had heard that his grandmother had been devoted to her husband, who happened to be her cousin and who had died before Samir was born. A few years ago, Aayat had shown him some photographs from her childhood, where her parents were always either smiling stiffly into the camera, or cradling her as a baby, or posing in gardens on family outings. They had made a handsome couple, and his mother had always stressed how content they had been together. But *had* she been happy, he now wondered. She was his grandmother. It made him uneasy to think of her as a young woman once in love with a man who was not his grandfather. Could he really hold a grudge against something that happened before he was born, though?

When he finally approached her, his inquiry was simple.

"Tell me about him, Nani jaan."

At once, she put down her cup of tea and nodded at her grandson. She brought out the box of letters. And then, from the cupboard in her room, she retrieved hundreds and hundreds of drawings, placing them before him like an offering. Eyes, ears, fingers, faces, strands of hair, and noses, many noses. There he was, her Samir.

That same night, the summer wind blew Firdaus's wooden window open.

"Samir," she whispered to the night, "is that you?" She turned on the light and rushed to the window, but there was no one. "Can you hear me?" she asked the silence again.

Then, shutting the window, she slowly walked back to bed and switched off the light. As the room once again flooded with darkness, she allowed her tears to soak the pillowcase. Firdaus knew just where he was, so unreachably far from her, and yet she helplessly repeated, "Are you there? Can you hear me?"

# 52

# I Have Known Her Heart

In the summer of 2007, Samir Vij made a trip to Grasse. Though he might not have shown it, age was catching up, and he had no intention of departing the world without paying homage to the flower fields once more. Anouk offered to travel with her grandfather, even to drive him, but Samir insisted on taking the train. He gestured to his walking stick, adamant on it being his only companion.

"I need some time there by myself," he said to her, "with Vivek, with Ambrette."

By now, he was older than his family members had ever been, and found himself no longer referring to Mohan as Baba or Savitri as Ma or Vivek as Taya ji. Each of them had become characters in his story, fictional almost, ghosts whom he spoke with and listened to, in waking and in dreams.

⚘

For the week that her grandfather was away, Anouk managed the shop and spent time with her friends. They never understood why or how, at the age of twenty, she still lived with her grandfather. She knew they found it strange, but could never explain how her grandfather's candid disclosure of the past introduced her to a world she now craved. She needed him as much as he needed her.

As usual, her evenings were spent at the Bibliothèque Mazarine, in their oriental section. For two years now, Anouk had remained perhaps the most devout member of the library, devouring everything she could find on Lahore and the Partition. Day after day, the librarian Pascal, a bald, bespectacled, middle-aged man who had a large and vibrant collection of bow ties, would note her presence. Intrigued by the young perfumer's apprentice who came to the library not out of university requirement but her own personal interest, he would ask from time to time about whatever she was reading.

That week, Pascal walked to her table and whispered for her to follow him to the back. Anouk followed, curious.

"There is something new that came in two weeks ago, donated by a Franco-German family who were traders in India in the early 1900s. The moment I saw it, I thought of you." His hands gently removed the archival tissue to reveal a beautiful lithograph, nearly two feet by three feet in size, printed in vibrant browns, blues, and black. It was a map of a city by a river, built in the shape of a parallelogram with a dense network of lanes.

Anouk bent lower and inhaled. It smelled like musty books and worn-out jute—humid and earthy. Despite the years, she could still discern the grittiness of printing ink. Peering closely, she followed the cluster of alleys and boulevards, but they were labeled in a language unreadable.

Looking up at Pascal, she shrugged.

"Yes, I can't read it either," Pascal said. "But—" He pointed to the key and the signature below the map. *Wagner & Debes' Geogr. Establ., Leipzig,* it read, and right above that was the magical word *LAHORE.*

She gasped, and he smiled in return. "They were once very famous German cartographers; the press was established in 1841 and lasted for over a hundred years, terminating sometime during the Second World War. We have quite a few maps and atlases by them, though rarely any in the local languages, particular Eastern languages. When I asked the family how or why they acquired it, they said it had been a gift from one of the traders their great-grandfather had worked with. While I was digitizing it last week, I thought . . . perhaps you would like to print a copy of it for your grandfather?"

That evening, Anouk left the library with a treasure.

Two days later, she prepared a stew for dinner and then went to Gare de Lyon to pick up her grandfather. The journey was long, he would be tired, and though she wanted him to have a quiet, comfortable night, she also couldn't wait to show him the map. Over dinner, they opened a bottle of red wine, and he told her about his week amidst the jasmine fields. He had spent hours every day at Ambrette's grave, reading out her husband's journals and telling her about his life in Paris.

After they had cleaned up, she told him to close his eyes and laid the map across the table. When he opened them, he could hardly believe that his Lahore was staring up at him. For a few minutes, he was speechless, just like Anouk had been at the library. Then, he began to speak.

"This is where I was born, yahaan, this is where my house was—Vij Bhawan, it was called. Right here, inside the Shahalmi Gate. Oh, you can see all of Lahore's thirteen gates in this map, *wah!* Here, here, the old bazaar, and the majestic mosque and gurdwara right next to it, and see, we used to play in this old water well!" He laughed jovially and clapped. "This is where my uncle went to college before the war. And here is where my mother was born, in the neighborhood of doctors. You can even see her exact street!"

Unable to contain himself, he told Anouk to get his magnifying glass and, using it, peered at the tiny, nearly illegible text. Murmuring under his breath, he moved his gaze from mohalla to mohalla, marketplace to city, river to fort, and then to Anouk. With one hand, he touched her cheek, for he had no words to thank her with.

"Is it in . . . Urdu?" she asked, and he nodded. "Do you still remember how to write it?"

Samir smiled mischievously, and asked his granddaughter whether she thought time was strong enough to erase things that had once been second nature. "*Apni zubaan toh apni zubaan hoti hai,*" he said, and then said to Anouk, "The mother tongue will always remain imprinted upon us."

Placing paper and pen in front of him, she gestured with her eyes. *Let's see then.*

He was hesitant at first—as images of Firdaus, the studio, his old qalams, the sooty ink, Wazir Khan mosque, all flooded into his mind—and he observed the pen, as if he were almost unsure of how to place the nib on the page. He brought it to the paper several times before actually beginning, and despite what he had said, he wondered if he had, in fact, forgotten.

But then, with Anouk watching closely, Samir took a deep breath and allowed not logic but muscle memory to lead him. Softly, as his hands moved from right to left, he narrated, "*Alif . . . be . . . pe . . . te . . .* this is how we learned the language. These are my alphabets."

꿎

With Anouk, Samir began, once again, to think of perfume with passion, and not merely technique. A new form of instruction emerged in his final years, one that resided both in the nose and the heart. Perfumery became about land and soil, *his land and soil,* as much as it was about air.

One afternoon in October, the perfumer hobbled to the cupboard of ingredients. Lovely autumn light trickled in through the atelier windows and outside; the plane trees had turned a lush golden-orange. He returned to Anouk with an ornate silver box, inside which sat a cloth pouch. Undoing it, he emptied the contents onto his palm.

"Zafran," he exclaimed, "the saffron from Pampore village in Kashmir."
It had been sent by Khushboo Lal's grandson just two weeks ago.

Anouk picked up a single thread and held it to the light. It was perfect, more perfect than any raw ingredient she had ever seen. It was the shade of fire, and smelled of an earth she had not yet inhabited.

"When I was young," Samir continued, "there were certain ingredients that were sacred to all ittar-saaz; they were the most coveted items from across India. Jasmine from Madurai, musk from Leh, rose from Kannauj, and this zafran from Pampore. It was the women who picked the saffron, spending hours collecting the vibrant purple flowers in their sacks. Then, day after day, they painstakingly broke the brilliant orange stigmas off. It took hundreds and thousands of stigmas to make a single kilogram of saffron. Depending on the kind, it can smell from anything like paprika to smoked pepper, to sweet prunes or cranberries, or even like the hibiscus flower. The Kashmiri saffron smells woody, whereas the Iranian variety is floral."

Anouk smelled the thread again.

"The Persians used to dissolve saffron and sandalwood into water to use as bodywash, because of its medicinal qualities. It was used for coughs, colds, stomach ailments, heart trouble, and even insomnia. Alexander the Great, who invaded India in the fourth century, was known to take long saffron baths as a treatment for war wounds."

Anouk looked down at the delicate thread resting on her palm. To weave the story of the world through conquest and war was one thing, but to do it through the frail yellow-tinted wisps of a spice was a rare gift she knew only her grandfather to possess.

"In fact, during the plague in the fourteenth century, the demand for saffron soared as people began using it as an effort to cure the disease. In an attempt to gain wealth and control, a large shipment of saffron heading to Basel was seized, sparking the fourteen-week-long Saffron War, ending only when the shipment was returned."

Anouk gasped.

"Oh, there is more!" Samir's eyes sparkled with excitement. "Many began selling adulterated saffron as well, soaking it in honey or mixing in marigold petals, which led the authorities of Nuremberg to pass what was known as the Safranschou Code, making such adulteration punishable by death. Spices are powerful, they can change the course of life in their own unique way." Samir smiled. "In our day, it was said that the fragrance of saffron was so irresistible that it could even make people fall in love."

Anouk burst out laughing. "You don't actually believe *that*, do you, Nanu?"

"Why not?" he asked his granddaughter. "A whiff of something intoxicating on someone intoxicating . . . someone's own scent, their skin and sweat, can make you fall in love in an instant."

It was the way in which her grandfather admitted the instantaneous nature of love that had made Anouk ask whether he was speaking about her grandmother. They had long separated, but perhaps when there had been love, it had been of this nature. But instead, another secret spilled out, one for which she was wholly unprepared.

At first, Anouk was lost for words.

"I don't understand," she began.

He had returned to the Partition, and spoken a great deal about Hindus and Muslims and a calligrapher in an old mosque and a manuscript illuminator with pistachio eyes. He had talked about writing letters and making portraits, and riots and curfew and the fire. *The fire.* It all sounded like a very dramatic film to her, and she stared at him, unable to understand.

"What are you saying? Did you not love Grandma Léa when you married her?"

A simple yes-or-no question.

"Did you love someone else, even then?"

Anouk could hardly believe that this was her tone, that she was so close to shouting, that she was speaking to the grandfather who had raised her and cooked for her and washed her clothes and trained her as a perfumer and lied to her and kept so many secrets from her.

"Tell me the truth now, all of it . . ." She was close to breaking down, and, holding her face in her hands, she appealed, "Please, Nanu."

Samir nodded. After years of self-restraint, he had no patience for such discipline any longer. And no need for it either. He was eighty—what did he have to lose? What more, anyway? He took his granddaughter's hand.

"This is the truth. I don't know if your grandmother and I ever really loved one another. Well, I don't think *I* allowed love a real chance to grow. Yes, when we met, the time was right, we fit together, we held each other up through our lows. But she rose, and I remained. I don't know what it was, but it was never . . . love," he admitted in a small voice.

"Does Mum know?" Anouk asked, the skin on her face now taut.

Samir shook his head, looking down at their entwined hands, "Only your grandmother knew. She saw my past consume me, watched my memories swallow our reality."

Her grandparents had separated well before Anouk was born. She had never known them together, but had assumed that her family had begun from happiness. Only now did she truly realize that her biggest inheritance was a secret.

"This woman in Lahore . . . Fir-doss?" she said the name bitterly. "Did you . . . do you . . . do you love her?"

"I would write her letters—week after week, year after year, I wrote her letters. But in all the time we knew one another, the word *love* was never uttered. We never said it, neither she nor I. It was simply understood."

And so, it settled into the atelier; it took up all the empty room, painted itself across the walls, was suspended in the air, *the love*. Anouk even felt it in her heart, the love he spoke about. It was heavy and cumbersome. The kind of love that had been flung against the tide, against the wind, against the escaping time, and had emerged, gasping for breath, still alive.

The kind of love that happened to a person once, if at all.

She loosened her grip on his hand and looked at his gray hair, the wrinkles on his cheeks, his nose. She looked into his eyes, warm, buttery, a shade of roasted almond. In them, she saw release.

"I do hate to break your heart, my darling, but you asked me for the truth. And you deserve to know it. You may think I am selfish and unjust, and even undeserving of your compassion, and I will understand if you do. I know I have not always done the right thing, but I have sacrificed too much, lived too long in sadness and pain to obscure this part of my life any longer. This is the truth then, all of it." With his wrinkled hands, he squeezed her slim fingers. "For as long as I shall live, and perhaps in every life after this, there will only be Firdaus . . .

"I have known her heart," he concluded, matter-of-factly.

# 53

# Dvořák in the Atelier

Two years had passed since her grandfather told her about Firdaus, and though she had eventually listened, Anouk had never asked any more questions. He had divulged the information and she had accepted it. After memorizing the most fragile corners of their relationship, and learning to steer clear of them, the pair had gone back to their normal routine. But every now and then, Anouk found her thoughts returning to the young girl with pistachio eyes, and wondered why, if the past was so opaque and unchangeable, she was resisting it this much. She wondered why she was being so unforgiving of her grandfather, for the relationships he had once built and broken changed little between them.

Now, closing her eyes, she distracted herself with her current composition. The world of fragrance Anouk inhabited was quite different from her grandfather's, for hers was almost entirely made of synthetics, where perfumery surpassed the conventions of mere beauty and embellishment, and could become an abstract artistic medium. The most recent object of her affection was the peony, and she imagined hundreds of feathery, cloudlike gauzy-pink peonies suspended midair.

The peony was an unusual note to include in a perfume. It was rare, voluptuous, futuristic, and the potential it offered enthralled her. She opened her eyes, chewed on the end of her pen, and tried to imagine what peonies smelled like in zero gravity. It was a fantastical thought, evoking an image of the full-faced flower floating in an atmosphere where nothing else survived. Armed with this inspiration, Anouk rushed across the hall-way to the atelier, to discuss the concept with her grandfather.

At the threshold of the atelier, she paused, listening. Antonín Dvořák's Humoresque no. 7.

Smiling, she began to sway. The peonies melted away. Dvořák's sono-rous world, having nothing to do with England and everything to do with Bohemia, always took Anouk back to her mother's study in London. She pictured Sophie in the white-walled room, bespectacled, carefully study-ing a print with a photographer's loupe, books perched on every available surface and a large oil canvas on the wall behind her. In truth, the hu-moresques always swept Anouk into the colors of that oil painting—lapis, cerulean, sea green, dark teal, jade, gold—hues of the beach, where the setting sky met the silent water. She knocked on the door and walked in.

Samir lifted his fingers to the light, in the same way he imagined a pia-nist would have, and played an invisible score. Listening to Dvořák made Samir want to be young again. He wanted to live as boundlessly as the wind in his name. He wanted to love just as boundlessly. The humoresque unfurled across the room, like a kite in the sky. But so sublime it was and so lost Samir was within it that he barely heard Anouk walk into the atelier. Only when the piece finished did he open his eyes to find her before him.

"Every single time," she said, smiling.

"I dissolve into it," he admitted happily.

And then, from the full-bodied piano cycle whose first traces were for-aged in the lush green pastures of Bohemian paradise, the record began to play Dvořák's lighter, folkier *Slavonic Dances*. Immediately, Samir's foot began tapping to the music. He got up, discarding his walking stick by the desk, and held out his hand to his granddaughter.

"May I haf zees daans, mademoiselle?"

Giggling uncontrollably, Anouk obliged.

As the music moved, they moved with it. Samir leaned on his grand-daughter, and they circled the room like a typhoon in slow motion. Lus-cious and rich, the music fell like warm sunshine on the floor, like butter melting on his mother's stuffed parathas, like the sandalwood paste lath-ered across his grandmother's arms, like vetiver rubbed into the hands of his father, like coconut oil massaged into the aging scalp of his grandfa-ther. The marvelous sounds of piccolos, bassoons, and flutes reverberated. The ache of the violin, the penetrating cello, the trumpets, the trombones.

As they twirled to the *Slavonic Dances,* Anouk laughed, throwing her head back with delight. Samir, too, was happy, but his heart was very sore. Oh, how he would have loved to dance this way with his Firdaus. How he would have loved to hold her.

Abruptly, he stopped dancing, crumpling in the middle of the room. Anouk stared at him, confused by his tears. Breathing heavily, she reached out to wipe them from his soft cheeks. She had no idea why her grandfa-ther was crying, but his tears were mirrored in her eyes. She sat him down on the chair, brought a glass of water, and removed the needle from the record. Then she sat down at her grandfather's feet.

"What is it?" she whispered. "What happened?"

"It's nothing." He wished not to burden her any further. "It's nothing."

"What is it?" she asked again.

"It's just that I wish . . . I wish sometimes that I could have grown old with her. I wish she wouldn't have let me go easily, I wish I could have held her and we could have danced and laughed and felt light and continued to be in love . . .

"Firdaus," he finally whispered, "Firdaus."

Anouk had never felt as small as she did then. She cursed her hardened heart, her sharp edges, her jaded youth, for being so judgmental of a love she had not even tried to understand. Immediately, she knew she had to rectify whatever it was that she had broken. She needed to put the pieces back, however impossible it seemed.

"I–I will find her." Her words tumbled out. "I will find her for you. We will find her, Nanu, I promise. I'm sorry, please don't cry."

"My darling, there is no need to be sorry . . . or even to find her. See, in my dreams, we are together and anything is possible. This is the beauty and hopelessness of dreams. But it is not the truth, and . . . I just don't want to be reminded of what is."

"But it's not difficult to find people anymore." She gestured to her phone enthusiastically. "I can search for her. Look, look, Nanu, we can search for almost anyone on the internet now. I can even teach you how to do it . . ."

But even before she had begun typing the name into Google, Samir placed his palm firmly on the screen. His heart was beating fast, and he felt the muscles on his face tighten. He couldn't deny that part of him wanted Anouk to search and find Firdaus, for them to be somehow reunited. But there was also a part that wouldn't be able to bear it if she found nothing. Or, worse still, found something that would confirm that Firdaus had lived a blissfully happy life all these years without him. If he learned he had been forgotten, that would shatter him.

With the cell phone still sandwiched between both their hands, Samir spoke in a tone of seriousness that Anouk had never heard before. "Promise me that you will not search for her."

"But . . . we may actually find her, Nanu," she protested.

"But she is not your person to find."

At that, Anouk let out a small and helpless sigh. She nodded, but her heart still did not agree.

"Well, why don't we . . . find her through fragrance? Compose her?" She had said it softly, a whisper almost, for she feared how her grandfather would react.

Samir folded his arms over his chest, contemplating the suggestion. He had wanted to tell her that the last time he became obsessed with a composition, *Firaq,* it had ruined his family and nearly driven him to madness. But he stopped himself because he knew this time was different. This time he was different.

"Do you know," he asked her, "what Dvořák wrote to his publisher while composing the second set of *Slavonic Dances*?"

Anouk shook her head.

"For a long time, Dvořák was a relatively unknown composer, before he won a large fellowship, catching the attention of none other than the master composer Johannes Brahms, who introduced Dvořák to his own publisher. The publisher took a chance on the novice and commissioned him to write something light and dance-like, for the public to enjoy. Hence, the first set of *Slavonic Dances*."

Anouk didn't understand where this was going.

"The sheet music for all eight dances sold out in a single day, and from then on, Dvořák gained international repute. As the years passed, he wanted to do larger-scale orchestral pieces—which he did—until nearly ten years later, when his publisher requested him to write yet another set of dances."

"Okay . . ."

"It was then that Dvořák said that to do the same thing twice was devilishly difficult, and as long as he was not in the right mood, he could not do it. One must have the proper enthusiasm for things, in order to embark on them wholeheartedly." Samir now paused. "What I am trying to say, in a very roundabout way, is that . . . now the time is right. You are right. For many years, I had not the right mood nor the courage to compose a perfume inspired by her. But now, the time is right. And we will work on it together, you and me."

When Anouk lay in her bed that night, she took out her phone and stared at the screen. At the end of the afternoon, her grandfather had taken out a faded photograph from his wallet and showed it to her, hesitantly. Anouk had placed it on the table and studied it for many minutes.

"Is this . . . her?" she had asked and he had nodded.

For the first time, Anouk uttered the name with a desire to know more. "Firdaus."

And when her grandfather had gotten up to put on a new record, she had taken out her phone and clicked an image of the photograph. Her own secret. She might never understand her grandfather's wishes, but she knew she had to respect them. Now, as she flipped onto her stomach, chin resting on her pillow, Anouk stared at the image on the screen and understood this to be the moment when all boundaries between her and her grandfather dissolved, cultural and generational.

# 54

# Three Hundred
# and Eighty-Eight Letters

Across the world, Samir Khan had lived each day searching for his
namesake, or at least remnants of him. He wished desperately
to know what was written on the note he had left behind, but
because his grandmother guarded the paper with her life, the young man
was forced to begin an investigation of his own.

Throughout his final year at Government College—one year since the
stranger had visited—Samir had pored over books on the Walled City,
hoping to find something on the businesses that had prospered before
Partition that would lead him to his namesake. The most famous book
that brought the old city to life was written in the early '90s by a retired
Indian diplomat born in Lahore. Another, *Tareek-e-Lahore,* written in
1884, by Kanhaiya Lal well before the creation of the border, gave a com-
prehensive history of the Anarkali area, but made no mention of shops or
shop owners. Then one day, in the rare books section, Samir came across
a frail pamphlet on the bazaar, published in 1940 by the Government
Printing Press, Lahore. The author had been a lecturer of history at the
Government College, and had detailed, shop by shop, the inhabitants
of the famed marketplace. There, nestled between the Lahore Stationery

Mart on the left and the chemist Beli Ram and Sons on the right, Samir Khan found what he'd been looking for: the mention of an ittar shop named Vij & Sons, established in 1921, Lahore. His heart was racing, but thrilled at the discover, he broke into soft laughter, causing students all around him to look up from their books in irritation. Packing up his things, he brought the pamphlet to the librarian to ask where he might find the author now, only to learn that he'd passed away a few years ago, at the grand age of ninety.

Unable to borrow a rare book from the library, he took a photograph of the document, and followed it to Anarkali. Walking the same streets he had walked so many times before, looking at them now with fresh eyes, Samir tried to find any traces of a world that had paused at Partition. He asked shopkeepers and passersby, but finding not a single shop that matched the descriptions or names in the pamphlet, he left the bazaar, disheartened.

This quest to search for his namesake, however, led Samir to apply for a journalist position at *Dawn* newspaper after graduating college the following year. There, he wrote on the history, culture, and heritage of the Walled City and, using his column, sought out the city's oldest residents for stories and secrets. He wrote on Mughal monuments and English legacy, on the great Sikh kingdom and the remnants of Partition, on the earliest papermakers and Urdu publishers, on food and literature and gardens and hamams, documenting, above all, the everydayness of Lahori life. Samir had perfected the art of documentary, of seeing that which not everyone could see, of recording the beauty in banality. But more often than not, inspired by his grandmother's memories, he would seek out the Lahore she had grown up in. Camera around his neck, recorder in hand, he'd roam the narrow lanes where his grandmother had once loved a man who was not his grandfather, hoping to hear a story about a Hindu family of perfumers.

Samir would often find himself in the Shahalmi area, where, in lieu of the once-dominating Mughal gate, there hung lengths of messy electrical wires. One afternoon in 2007, the twenty-two-year-old ventured deep into the labyrinthine neighborhood, trying to locate where his namesake's home had once stood. He peered carefully at name plates and stone plaques, but the fire of 1947 had obliterated the entire landscape. The area had been reconstructed and was now unrecognizable, even to the oldest residents of the city.

Leaving the cluster of lanes behind, Samir found himself in the Papar Mandi Bazaar, where a pocket of perfumeries had sprouted over the last few years. Taking a deep breath, Samir approached the least crowded shop, where an elderly gentleman with a henna-colored beard, who looked in his seventies, was filling small glass bottles with essential oils.

"*As-salaam-alaikum, chacha*," Samir began hesitantly. "Uh . . . before Partition, there used to live a family of perfumers in this area. Hindu perfumers. Vij was their name."

"Hmm," came the response as the old man slowly looked up, his hands lathered with jasmine. "*Suna hai,* I have heard of them. They had a shop in Anarkali, my father told me once. But I was only a child then."

Samir eyes widened with hope as he turned on his recorder.

"But you are wasting your time," the old man continued. "There is nothing left of them or their Lahore anymore. That world exists now only in memory."

Back at the office, the journalist sat at his desk in frustration. On the table before him was the photograph of the pamphlet from 1940. He stared at the blank computer screen for several seconds, and then suddenly sat upright, opened the browser, and typed in "Vij & Sons 1921." Nothing came up, so he tried different combinations of the words "Vij," "Perfume," "Ittar," and "Lahore." After a few tries, he replaced the word "Lahore" with the word "India," deducing that if his namesake had made it across the border, he likely would have established another perfumery there. After another moment of thought, he added the name "Samir" to the search, and then clicked enter. He scrolled down the page, ignoring the many ads for perfume that had popped up, until a string of words on a French website caught his eye, and he brought his hand up to his mouth in disbelief.

"Paris," Samir announced at dinner that evening, causing Firdaus's heart to sink.

She knew, even when she had relayed the past to her grandson, that it was only a matter of time before he found out more on his own. When she said nothing, he handed her a printout in a language she didn't understand. On the top was a photograph from inside a perfume shop, glistening bottles arranged across shelves in the same way that they had been in Anarkali.

Placing the printout back on the table, she heaved a sigh and walked to her room. When she returned to the dining table, it was with the stranger's note.

"Paris," she concurred, eyes glistening with tears.

Before she could say anything else, he spoke. "I will write to him, Nani." Samir couldn't believe that two years had passed with the address in her possession. So much time had been wasted, time that could have been spent in each other's company. "We will write to him tonight."

Sadly, she shook her head from side to side. "I should have written to him a long time ago. But despite knowing exactly where he was, I just couldn't. I was scared, I was . . . embarrassed. What would I have said? What *could* I have said? How would I ever explain this to your mother? All those years with your nana jaan, and now this . . ." Tears now rolled down her face. "Letting Samir go has been the greatest regret of my life. I wish things had been different then. I wish I'd been braver, but . . ."

"But you still can, you have another chance now," Samir urged.

"I cannot."

Her grandson stared at her, waiting for an explanation, but she had none. Firdaus had no words to explain why the guilt of history would not allow her this reunion, how she had convinced herself that she did not deserve it. Perhaps this was her greatest punishment. Her father's words returned to her then, having served more as a prophecy than a warning. *Not all love stories are meant to end in happiness.*

"I cannot and neither will you," she said to Samir.

꙳

In the years that passed, Samir tried many times to bring up the topic of the perfumer, until one day, his grandmother lost her temper in a way that he had never seen before. The episode caused her blood pressure to increase, and a doctor had to be called. From that moment on, Samir never spoke of his namesake again, but in secret, he continued to read whatever he could find.

In the summer of 2014, eighty-five-year-old Firdaus contracted an illness of the lungs, making it hard for her to breathe. She coughed frequently and wheezed throughout the day. Panicked, Samir took his grandmother to the hospital for a series of tests, only to learn there was no cure for this kind of chronic illness. The cause was likely environmental, for the growing pollution of Lahore easily affected someone her age. Armed with a strong prescription, he brought her back home and explained that she needed a better living situation, cleaner air, outside the Walled City in an area less congested. With his mother on the phone, they even tried to persuade her to move to Islamabad, where Aayat could care for her. But Firdaus had merely laughed, amused that now, at the very end of her life, they expected her to leave the city that had built her.

"I will die in this house, Samir beta," she declared, as if she could foresee it.

A few days after her diagnosis, when her grandson was at work, Firdaus sat down to compose a letter, while she still could. It would be the first and last one she'd ever write. She could no longer sit on the ground, nor go through the laborious task of using the qalam, nor making the ink from scratch. So she used the next best thing—a fountain pen. Sitting by her desk at the window, she rolled up her kurta sleeves to reveal her bony forearms. After thinking for a moment, she began to write.

"Samir, I wonder if you will remember me . . ."

Immediately, she crumpled the paper into a ball. *No, this won't do.* Suppressing a cough with her palm, she began again.

"Samir, I am writing to you from the window overlooking Sunehri—"

*It is better to make no mention of this window. He was banished from this very window! Why is this so hard? How did Samir do this hundreds of times?* She looked at the box of letters beside her on the table and grazed their surface. *What did he write about, week after week?* She picked one, dated May 1947, and began reading.

It was from the time when Firdaus's family had temporarily moved to Badami Bagh, on the outskirts of Lahore. Riots and subsequent curfew had blanketed the city for nearly twenty-four hours a day, and from the confines of his home, Samir had written with great despair about being separated from her. He had ended the letter with a secret, a phrase that belonged only to them, to remind her that no matter when she returned to the city, he would be there, waiting for her.

She folded the letter and smiled to herself. His laughter, the shape of his hands, the perfect slant of his nose. Firdaus reminded herself of what it meant to be young and in love and careless to the world's demands. If this would be the only letter Samir would ever receive from her, then she would have to find a way to inscribe her heart into it.

⁂

Through the course of the year, her condition deteriorated. Her cough was always accompanied by sickly colored phlegm, and she suffered from terrible fatigue. She complained so often of tightness in her chest that it alarmed Samir into putting in an application to work remotely. He had a weekly column to write at *Dawn*, an assignment he could easily complete anywhere. Systematically then, he created a schedule where he'd venture out into the city for field research a few hours each day, and spend the remaining time caring for his grandmother.

Incidentally, during this time, many of Firdaus's childhood memories resurfaced, most naturally. She remembered her days at the Calligraphic Bazaar, what the secrets of the oldest Lahori bookbinders were, the pre-Partition travel routes poets and scholars had taken from Central Asia to Delhi via Lahore, and endless stories of how the city had transformed before her eyes. All these intimate recollections found a home in Samir's column, giving it an unexpectedly personal tone.

And other things that hadn't been given much importance till then, like Samir's consistent bachelor status, were also brought up. Bedridden, reluctantly dependent on him for her every need, Firdaus would joke that after she was gone, her grandson would need a lovely bride to keep him company.

"Tch, uff, enough, Nani jaan . . . not this again."

"Beta, you cannot remain alone forever, *kunware rahoge? Umar ho rahi hai . . .*" She would remind him that at twenty-nine years of age, he was no longer young. Sighing dramatically, she would wish for freshly hennaed hands to make biryani and kheer, and massage oil into her hair.

For a whole year, they continued that way, following a routine of X-rays, tests, and medication. Firdaus held no more calligraphy classes at home; she could barely lift a qalam, let alone raise her voice high enough to instruct anyone. Her skin and lips developed a ghostly bluish tinge. Her legs and ankles swelled, fevers came and went, and the tightness in her chest remained.

One day, when Samir was in the kitchen, he heard his grandmother cough. A slight cough was normal, so he continued to pour out tea into two cups, straining the ginger and cardamom. But seconds passed and the cough intensified, so, abandoning the dripping strainer on the counter, he ran to her room to find her curled on her side, coughing uncontrollably.

Half her body was hanging off the bed, as if she'd been trying to reach for something. Holding back tears, he helped her up and brought her a glass of lukewarm water. He couldn't believe how anemic she looked, from the silver in her hair to the pale flesh of her arms. The only thing that reminded Samir of the woman his grandmother used to be were the pistachio eyes that still continued, somehow, to gleam.

She lifted an arm toward the cupboard and asked Samir to open it.

"The box . . . take out the box," she whispered.

He did as instructed, extracting it from the lowest shelf and placing it on the bed. The box of old letters from his namesake. She opened its lid and, drawing out a new envelope from underneath the pillow, she added her own letter to the pile.

"We can still write to him, Nani jaan," he whispered back. "There is still time."

"Now there is no more time, the end is almost here." Tears rolled down her face, and Samir motioned for her to stop talking, that they could continue this later.

Instinctively reaching for her hand, he tried to quiet her. "*Shh . . . ab bass.*"

But Firdaus persisted, bringing her hand to his face, she stroked his cheek lovingly, "Samir, my Samir beta. Promise me that when I am gone, and *only* when I gone, you will return these letters to him."

He stared at her and shook his head from side to side. He couldn't let her go this way.

She repeated it. "Promise me."

Again, he said nothing, and so she begged, "Promise me, please."

To refuse would be an act of cruelty Samir could never bear to commit. Holding her hands softly between his, he nodded.

# 55

# A Rose Can Never Hide

In Paris, Samir and Anouk had been working on their new perfume. At the age of eighty-eight, Samir's nose was deceiving him, and so he needed his granddaughter more than ever. He needed her to be his nose.

The heart of the new perfume, it was decided, would be the rose. Before they began, Samir had retrieved a completely dry, pressed flower and offered it to Anouk, in the same reverential way that Som Nath had once offered it to him. And like he had as a child in Lahore, Anouk, too, had brought it to her nose. It smelled nothing like a rose and everything like a piece of aging paper, musty, acidic, and almost vanilla-like, due to the presence of lignin within it. With her fingertips, she had gently traced its brown veins and hardened edges.

"My grandfather plucked this very rose in 1927, the year I was born. It is a rose as old as me." Samir then repeated Som Nath's words, "Go on then, take it. Now it belongs to you."

Carefully, Anouk inserted the rose into a book of Rilke's poetry.

"The rose is a classical flower," Samir had stated matter-of-factly. "It's been adorned across cultures for thousands of years, but now, it is an obsolete flower. In a perfume shop, no one gravitates to the rose anymore, not because they don't like it, but because they regard it as too ordinary. But there are more than five hundred molecules in the smell of a rose, and we need to find a way to reinvent it, provoke it."

Anouk had nodded. "But why the rose?"

Immediately, Samir had thought back to how Firdaus's skin always smelled of the roses from her ubtan, or how their very first meeting had been because of a rose ittar her father had commissioned for a manuscript, or how each week, when he went to the Wazir Khan mosque, a young Samir walked through a sprinkling of rosewater at its entrance. From everything that had ever touched Firdaus, it was the rose that had remained emblematic. It was the most definitive and elegant aroma, akin to her persona.

"Because"—Samir had merely smiled at his granddaughter—"a rose can never hide."

⚘

Over the last many years, Samir and Anouk had composed many likenesses of a rose. In the span of a single day, it was possible for the pair to create up to ten trials, stored in miniature bottles and placed in a separate cabinet. As his apprentice, it was Anouk's responsibility to properly label these drafts and, over the course of time, record any changes. Upon smelling them—either minutes, hours, or days later—she would notice transformations, for time had swept through the compositions, either lifting notes or strengthening them. These details she transcribed and presented to her grandfather.

"The reason why we compose these various sketches is to be able to see what remains as time passes, and what dilutes," he explained. "We are trying to create something that does not yet exist, and discover the direction our rose perfume will take."

And they did, for one day, lined up on the table before Anouk, was a sea of roses. Quietly, she meandered through the various mouillettes, or smell strips, trying her best not to read the numbers or formulas written, nor recount the ingredients they contained. Seated across from her, Samir did the same. A gentle sniff, a satisfied exhale, the scribble of a note, a chuckle, a sigh, grandfather and granddaughter luxuriated in the pleasure of smelling with purpose.

"The citrus note in this is lovely," Anouk finally said of the smell strip in her hand. Returning her nose to it, she added, "And mixed with the patchouli, it evokes this sensation of endlessness."

Samir nodded, encouraging her to continue.

"This one"—an intense, dark, sweet smell wafted up from the blotter she held out to Samir—"reminds me of a trampled rose, actually . . ."

"How interesting." He took it from her and smelled.

"It is not a foul smell, but a dark one. There's something sharp to it, much sharper than the centifolia rose from Grasse," she concluded and moved on to the next. "This is a bouquet of green notes, rose scented with henna."

"What else do you smell in it?"

Anouk inhaled again. "There is . . . labdanum, a woody note, and loban." And then, meeting her grandfather's gaze, she smiled, overwhelmed by the wonders of their shared world. To compose a unique rose was one thing, but to compose a unique rose four or five different ways with different ingredients was another art altogether. But this was what a perfumer did; this was the world she would forever inhabit. The world of boundless imagination.

"This one has a paper-like note in it," she continued, placing several smell strips between her fingers like a Japanese fan, deftly moving from one to the next. Her face was pensive, and Samir could tell that she wasn't necessarily only discerning the ingredients, but also experiencing the sensation evoked by each rose note. Like him, Anouk smelled with her nose, her heart, her body, and her mind.

"This is slightly waxy, which is a texture I don't enjoy. And this one has a watery quality, it's petal-like." She lingered on it for a while. "It's pillowy, no, it's creamy . . . perhaps too creamy?"

"Mm," he agreed, "it reminds me of luxury face creams from the twenties."

Moving on to the final bottle, Anouk dipped two smell strips into the composition and offered one to her grandfather.

Samir held out his arm and smelled the inside crook of his elbow to clear his nose. Then, with eyes closed, he plunged into the rose. The world slowed. A glimmer of sun spilled in. This was the smell of the calligraphy bazaar at dawn, the river Ravi on weekends, the Pattoki fields in spring; the smell of stillness and serenity, dreams and dalliances.

"*This* has real beauty," he whispered.

⚘

By the beginning of 2017, Samir Vij had become obsessed with the rose. Samir knew this would be the last perfume he would ever compose, and so he would make it his magnus opus, his collected works, the story of his life and a manifestation of his only love. There would be beauty—the rose would make sure of that—but it would not be devoid of tragedy. And so, day after day, he smelled, tweaked, wrote, and dreamed, and Anouk now observed from a distance. This was not her territory any longer.

She watched as he offered himself to his craft, summoning every dormant and concealed memory as raw material for distillation. Memory was to a perfumer what words were to a writer, what an image was to a painter. And a portrait was not to be taken lightly, for this final one was as much of Samir Vij as it would be of Firdaus Khan.

One day, Anouk asked the question that had long burdened her.

"Why did it take you so long to begin this composition, Nanu?"

It caught Samir off guard, and he turned to face Anouk. "Why do you ask?"

"Well, you left Lahore in 1947, and now we are in 2017. Seventy years have passed . . ."

"Well," he began, unsure of what words he could string together to explain the distance he had deliberately drawn from everything beloved, "I suppose I felt a composer's block. If you can't accept a memory, then how can you distill it into perfume? A perfume does not arrive like an idea, fully formed and flawless; it needs persistence and dedication and, well, time. It has taken its time, but it has kept me alive."

A few months later in spring, as Samir sat alone in his atelier, he took out Firdaus's photograph from his wallet and held it up to his face. He had wanted to tell her about the rose perfume, but immediately, he felt self-conscious, fearing she might not recognize him as an old man. His hands reached for his cheeks, feeling the constellation of wrinkles that had appeared over the years. Then, chuckling, he reminded himself that this was just a photograph. That she was on the other side of the world, living her life in their Lahore, breathing the air he craved to breathe.

Still smiling, he stroked her paper-like face with his thumb, blissfully unaware that Firdaus had already passed away.

# 56

# The Namesake

A week after his grandmother's death, thirty-two-year-old Samir Khan emptied out her closets with his mother. His sisters, Mariam and Yasmin, who had spent the last few days helping, had finally left to go back to their homes and families. A heartbroken Aayat stood at the window overlooking Sunehri Masjid, a half-folded shawl in her hands.

"She loved this window, you know . . ." she whispered.

"She loved this house, Ammi."

Aayat held back tears and looked at her son as he folded kurta after kurta with a precision that only his nani jaan could have taught him. She felt guilty that she hadn't been there when her mother had passed, guilty that Samir had been all by himself when it happened. He seemed so unexpectedly mature that sometimes Aayat barely recognized her youngest child.

"I never thought she would go so suddenly," she said.

"She'd been holding on for three years." He looked around the empty room, the ghost of his grandmother lurking in every corner. "And on the last day, she . . ." He stopped mid-sentence, for one thing would surely lead to another, and secrets that were not his to disclose would cascade out.

"What happened on the last day?"

"Well . . . she was in a very bad state, that's all."

"I never even got a chance to say goodbye."

*No one did, not even Samir.*

He walked over to his mother and wrapped her in an embrace. Together, by the evening light of the golden mosque, they wept for her who
was no more. And when they parted, she ran her fingers through his long
hair, taming it, patting it down. She wiped the tears from his eyes—
indistinguishable from Firdaus's eyes, from Altaf's eyes—and kissed his
forehead.

"What will you do now?" Aayat asked. In her will, Firdaus had left the
Delhi Gate house to her grandson. "You can sell it . . . and move home
to Islamabad?"

"But Lahore is my home," he reminded her.

"I know, beta, but this is too big a house for one person. Not to mention it's right in the middle of the old city. Everything around you is
dilapidated. And the noise, the hawkers, the sounds, the smells . . . Samir,
Islamabad is quieter, you will like it."

"Nahi, Ammi, Lahore is Lahore. I like the sounds and smells and even
the half-broken buildings. These are the things I write about, all the history that continues to survive. But I *was* thinking of taking a sabbatical
from the newspaper, maybe for a year or so."

"What do you mean? But your column is so popular . . . what will you
do if not that?"

Under the bed, the rectangular box containing three hundred and
eighty-eight letters sat unseen.

"Mmm . . ." He scratched his head. "I want to write something for
myself. A book, maybe?"

Aayat was not convinced. "Yes, beta, you write your book-shook, but
don't give up the column. You need to still earn a living."

"I can manage comfortably for a year or two, Ammi. I have some savings. And anyway, there is somewhere I need to go, some things I need to find out, before I even begin writing."

Later that night, he took out the box from under the bed and studied the sea of paper. Hesitantly, he fished out the earliest letter and held it up with both hands. *Firdaus Khan,* it read. *Firdaus Khan,* he repeated voicelessly. Samir looked out at the mosque and up at the moon, and then spoke to the room. "*Mujhe maaf karein, Nani,* please forgive me."

Before her ghost could change his mind, he opened the envelope and extracted a note. For many seconds, he simply stared at it, studying its corners and creases. Then he unfolded it and read. Tears stung his eyes upon meeting the untidy scrawl—

*Tumhari yaad ki kashti iss dil ki darya mein doob gayi hai.*
The paper boat of your memory has drowned in the river of this heart.

Helpless, he began to weep. Tears fell down his cheeks and onto the paper, before he quickly folded it, stuck it back into the envelope, and into the box. He couldn't do this; it was too private, too intimate, *too much.* So instead, he opened his laptop and checked for the most affordable flight to Paris.

⚘

Across the world, Samir Vij turned ninety years old. It rained all day and all night, as expected, and somewhere in the middle, Sophie arrived from London to spend the day with her father. In her suitcase was a parcel wrapped in brown paper, a book that Anouk had found and ordered to her mother's address in London, as a surprise present for her grandfather. It was a book of letters, the first of its kind, written over a century ago by Indian soldiers during the First World War, and compiled by a professor in England. Letters that had been translated from the many Indian languages into English by the British censors during wartime.

Anouk had immediately thought of Vivek—the ancestor with the nose, with the secret love; the one she never knew but who had come to define her grandfather's, and in some ways her, existence. The ancestor who had made the Great War theirs.

And as Samir unwrapped it now, warmed by the gesture, astonished that such an archive even existed beyond the rectangular confines of his uncle's private journal, thirty-year-old Anouk wondered whether any of Vivek's letters, too, might have found their way into this book.

Over the next few days, the perfumer pored over the pages. He obsessed over names and villages, comparing the dates in the book to the dates in Vivek's journals. To aid his reading further, Anouk and Sophie had found a map of the Western Front, and he meandered his frail fingers through the lands swallowed by trenches and time.

"They came to Paris, too, did you know? The sipahis . . ." he called out one evening from the living room. Anouk was in the kitchen, blending tomatoes for a sauce. Peeking her head out, she asked what the Indians had done in her city of lights, over a hundred years ago.

Samir pushed his spectacles up. "Well, this is what Mahomed Firoz Din, a Punjabi Muslim from the Sialkot Cavalry Brigade wrote to Firoz Khan from the 19th Lancers, on 7th March 1915—'I went to Paris for seven days. What is Paris? It is heaven!'" Samir clapped his hands jovially.

"*Mais c'est vrai*," Anouk agreed. "It *is* heaven!"

On other days, the letters weren't as buoyant. On June 27, 1915, an Afridi Pathan from the same regiment as Vivek wrote a letter to his brother in India. Samir had read out the letter in a manner so intimate that Anouk felt he could have written the words himself. "In Pashtu, he writes—'Oh, happy paper, how I envy your lot. We shall be here, but you will go see India . . .'" He let his voice trail off.

Anouk watched from across the room, realizing that there were some things she might never be able to repair. Fractures that would outlive her grandfather.

"How I envy your lot, indeed," he agreed.

⅃

In the first week of September, Samir Khan locked up his grandmother's house in Delhi Gate and took a taxi from the old city to the airport. Having put in an application for a few months' sabbatical at *Dawn,* he boarded the only direct flight, which flew once per week from Lahore to Paris. Suspended midair, Samir's thoughts invariably kept returning to the fact that his grandmother's death had made things so final, so unalterable. And it was this finality that saddened him—perhaps even more than death itself—for now there wasn't even a possibility of reunion between her and the perfumer.

Eight hours and ten minutes later, he arrived at the Charles de Gaulle Airport, a suitcase by his side and a folded piece of paper in his pocket.

"Roo Bo-na-part," he read out the address to the taxi driver. "Saint . . . Gerrmain . . ."

"Saint-Germain-des-Prés? *D'accord!*"

As they drove through the city, it began raining, and the golden day turned suddenly cold and blue. Samir took a deep breath in, and opened his suitcase to retrieve the rectangular box of letters. He had carried it just as it was—letters, perfume bottle, dried leaves and all—too afraid to disturb anything. He placed it in his lap and then turned to the window to catch his watery reflection staring back. Boulevards lined with trees, buildings more decorative than he had ever seen, ornate fountains carved out of stone, and centuries of history, all shone in his pistachio eyes.

He held on tightly to the box.

⅃

Meanwhile, slowly lifting himself from his perch at the back of the shop, Samir Vij made his way to the window, walking stick in hand, to watch the drowning world. There were days when he felt as though the rain belonged only to him. Days like today. He smiled, thinking of paper boats floating in Lahore's puddles, the flooded Shahalmi area, the peacocks near Mughal tombs and gardens spreading out their jewel-feathered wings in dance, young men in crisp white dhoti-kurtas carrying black umbrellas through Anarkali, and the monsoon swell of the river Ravi.

Lifting his palm to the glass, he traced the falling drops and began singing to himself, "*Rabba rabba meenh vasain . . . saadi kothi daaney paaein . . .*"

From behind the counter, Anouk looked up. "Mmm?" she asked, unsure of whether she had, in fact, heard her grandfather singing.

"It's just a song we used to sing as children . . . a song about the rain." His fingers floated midair in a slow-moving dance.

"Sing it for me, Nanu."

"Well, it is just an old folk song," he said, and then began singing, with long pauses between each word, sung almost to the tune of a lullaby, "*Rabba rabba meenh vasain, Saadi kothi daaney paaein, Khakharian, kharbooze laain, Auran di kothi daddu vasain.*"

Anouk's fingers drummed to the rhythm on the countertop. "What does it mean?"

"God give us rain so our granary is full, so that we have cucumbers and melons. And in the homes of our enemies, let there be no rain but only frogs!"

Anouk applauded and Samir erupted into laughter, the wrinkles by his eyes filling with tears of joy. Still smiling, Anouk walked to the row of glass bell jars at the center of the shop. The most popular perfumes were sprayed onto knots of thick fabric and placed inside the jars, for customers to lift and smell, just as they had been in the Anarkali shop. One by one, she refreshed the samples by spraying the fabric with perfume. The world of Les Jardins de l'Inde came to life once more, with the olfactive poems of jasmine and tuberose, honey and holy basil dispersing through the air. Still humming the folk tune, Anouk heard the door open behind her.

The old perfumer looked up from his perch and his apprentice turned on her heels to greet a half-soaked young man holding a suitcase in one hand and a rectangular box in the other. He scanned the room, nervous and unsure, as if he'd suddenly chanced upon a place he hadn't expected to find. When his gaze finally fell on the perfumer, the young man wiped the rainwater off his face. Anouk stood motionless as he walked right past her.

"V-Vij sahib?" The question emerged as a stammer.

The old perfumer looked at the customer curiously.

"*Aapka naam Samir Vij hai? Lahore . . . Lahore shehr se?*" the young man asked.

"*Ji.*" The perfumer was now worried. This was the second time he'd been caught unaware by his own mother tongue. But he beckoned the young man to come closer. "*Aur aap kaun?*"

Anouk, not yet fluent in Punjabi or Urdu, understood the word *Lahore,* and deduced that the young man had come looking for him. Twelve long years had passed since Yusuf Ahmed had come into the shop with an eerily similar query. But this encounter felt different to Anouk. She watched as the visitor slowly dropped to his knees by her grandfather's feet, eyes lowered. She leaped forward to help, but the perfumer stopped her.

Placing his hand on the young man's shoulders, he inquired again, "Who are you?"

And when he looked up, Samir Vij knew the answer.

*It was in his eyes. The answer was in his eyes.*

They were the same eyes that had stared at him through the rows of perfume bottles in the ittar shop in Lahore, the same eyes that had lowered their gaze in the studio at Wazir Khan, the shy eyes from Standard Restaurant, the sad eyes from the window by the Sunehri Masjid, the eyes from his dreams, the eyes from his nightmares. *He knew these eyes.* Samir stared at the young man, bending toward him until he nearly lost his balance. These were, without a doubt, Firdaus's eyes.

✌

The young man looked up at his namesake. He studied his aged face, the deep lines on his neck and hands, the elegant slant of his nose, and tried to remain composed. He thought back to the very first time his grandmother had mentioned the perfumer, he thought of the very last time she had uttered his name, he thought of her shroud, he thought of the letters in his hands.

"My name is Samir Khan," he said finally, handing over the box, "and I've come to return these to you."

# 57

# The Book of Everlasting Things

With trembling hands, the perfumer opened the box to find three hundred and eighty-eight letters of love that a boy named Samir Vij had once written, in an undivided Hindustan, to a girl named Firdaus Khan. Frail and yellowing, torn at the edges, they bore his hesitant Urdu script, freshly learned in the studio of the calligrapher Altaf Khan.

After the box was presented, he had remained seated, paralyzed by what was now in his possession. His granddaughter had rushed to his side, touching his face, his shoulders, his lips, trying to get him to answer her, but he'd remained as still as stone. She had looked at Samir Khan helplessly, and despite never having met her before, he knew exactly how she was feeling.

Now, one hour later, he was seated in their apartment, which was a few minutes' walk from the shop. As the perfumer sat cradling the box, his granddaughter brought three cups of ginger tea and passed them around. She also put out a plate of biscuits, which Samir gratefully accepted. The silence was momentarily broken by the metallic sound of spoons stirring in honey and milk. And then they waited for the perfumer to say something, *anything.*

When it became clear that he wasn't going to speak, Samir cleared his throat.

"She died this spring."

Still nothing, so he continued.

"It happened suddenly one night. I heard a voice in my sleep, and when I awoke, I realized it was Nani jaan. She was very weak at the end of her life, the disease in her lungs made it hard to breathe normally. Her voice was feeble, lighter than a whisper. So despite the fact that I was sleeping on the floor of her room, I heard her only after she'd been calling out for a while."

The perfumer lifted his head.

"*Samir* . . . she was saying my name, over and over again, *Samir* . . ."

The perfumer's gaze fixed onto the young man.

"It was soft at first, but then it became louder and louder. *Samir, Samiiir,* she was calling out, as if she were in pain or–or–or something was happening deep inside her body. When I got to her side, it was as if she couldn't even see me. She just kept calling out, *Samir Samir Samir.* The arms she could have barely lifted that same evening were held out toward the window, up toward the sky. *Samir Samir Samir.* She kept repeating it, the most painful, gut-wrenching sound. My name, my own name, sounded like it didn't belong to me at all. Like it was being projected elsewhere, to a place very far away. That night, her voice took on the most vulnerable, defenseless, distant tone that I'd ever heard. As if she was possessed . . ."

He used his sleeve to wipe the tears that ran down his face.

The perfumer hadn't moved a single inch, nor had his hands loosened their grip on the box.

Samir continued, "She fell asleep after that, holding my hand. And when I awoke in the morning, she was gone."

Anouk swallowed hard.

"It took me a while to realize this . . ." he said, looking straight at the perfumer. "It wasn't until I opened the box of letters that I fully understood it."

"Understood what?" Anouk whispered on behalf of her mute grandfather.

"That in her last moments, she wasn't calling out to me." Samir got up from his seat now and walked up to his namesake, prying his hands off the box and cradling them within his own. "She was calling out to you."

That night, Anouk heard soft wails emerging from her grandfather's room—similar to the kind the young man had described. Painful, tender, urgent. She had leaped out of her bed to comfort her grandfather, who was, no doubt, going through the box of his old letters. But she stopped in her tracks, her heart tightening, realizing that he needed this, needed to endure this, needed to emerge from this. She crawled back into bed and looked toward the moon hanging outside her window. The quietest, most private person she had known, who had swallowed grief and tragedy in monastic silence, had finally reached the limits of his suffering.

Meanwhile, Samir Khan, for whom a bed had been set up in the study, thought back to how the day had unfolded. Lying on his back, he shut his eyes to the world, finding a strange comfort in the sounds of sadness that floated out of the perfumer's room.

The next morning, Samir Khan got up early, jet-lagged, and wandered to the kitchen. Making himself a cup of tea, he walked around the house. In the last few years, Anouk had transformed the minimalist apartment into a gallery of Lahore. Now Samir wandered along the brightly painted walls, tracing his fingers over framed maps and vintage watercolors of his city.

Suddenly, a beam of light burst into the living room behind him, and he turned to find the perfumer drawing open the thick curtains, one by one. Slowly, his hands reached for the drawstrings and pulled, welcoming the flood of sunshine as it fell onto the wooden floor. Samir greeted him hesitantly.

"*As-salaam-alaikum, Vij sahib.*"

"*Wa-alaikum-salaam.*"

Walking to the kitchen, the old man began preparing breakfast— measuring the oatmeal, pouring out milk into a saucepan—but Samir insisted on making it, leading him to the table. He put the kettle to boil for tea, and picked up an apple from the fruit basket to slice over the oatmeal. The perfumer watched in amusement, and meeting his eye, Samir laughed. "Well, if we were in Lahore, I would have made you a fine aloo paratha. But this will have to do for now." Minutes later, he carried his breakfast over to the table.

The perfumer ate slowly, taking his time with every bite, saving his tea for the end until it was nearly cold. Then, finally, he asked the young man, "So, your name is Samir, too?"

"After you. My nani jaan named me."

The perfumer nodded slowly and then retrieved the gold bottle of *Noor* ittar from his front pocket. The one from Standard Restaurant, that Firdaus kept safe all these years in her box of letters. For a while, he kept it enclosed within his fist and then placed it on the table with intention. There was barely any liquid left in the bottle, but a wave of tuberose still washed over the room, overpowering and irresistible.

"Did you know," he said, "I made this for your grandmother when I was a teenager. It was the first perfume I ever composed. Tuberose is very difficult to work with, tenacious, temperamental, like she had been." He chuckled. "It took years, but I made it for her."

Samir knew this story; he knew it well. He picked up the bottle and held it to the light. How much more pain would he have to bestow upon an already devastated man?

"She couldn't smell it, you know . . ."

The perfumer inhaled sharply. "What do you mean she couldn't smell it? She could, she told me that it wasn't to her liking, but surely she smelled it."

Samir shook his head. *This,* this insignificant little detail, would cause more sorrow than anything else.

"She could smell, but just not certain flowers . . . the kind of sweet-smelling flowers that are used in perfumes, *your* perfumes. The jasmine, tuberose, rose . . . I tried to get her to go to see a doctor so many times, but she always brushed it off, saying it no longer mattered."

The perfumer thought back to the very first time he had met Firdaus in the ittar shop. Drawing apart the dense curtain of aroma, he concentrated only on her image, on the shape of her face and the movement of her nose. He remembered noticing how she barely inhaled anything. Her nostrils had remained alarmingly still, as if she had been holding her breath, and now, eight long decades later, he felt foolish for never asking, for never knowing.

Exhaling in frustration, he said, "She was mysterious in life, and she's remained mysterious in death, it seems." Now, facing Samir, he asked sadly, "Tell me, can you be angry at the dead?"

Feeling any formality fade away, Samir nodded with equal sadness. "Yes, yes, I think that's allowed."

Holding the near-empty bottle in his hands, the old perfumer sat with his eyes closed. Samir watched as the sun shone behind him, outlining his silhouette.

"How long will you stay?" he asked, finally opening his eyes.

Samir shrugged.

"If you can, stay a while."

Samir nodded.

"And now, I have something for you . . ." Gesturing for the young man to wait, the perfumer walked slowly out of the apartment and across the hall into the atelier. Minutes later, he returned with a cloth bundle tucked under his arm and a journal in his hand.

"Here." He held out the bundle to Samir, who undid the knots carefully, to reveal a bamboo reed pen. Its nib was half dipped in ink, dully blackened at the very top. He picked it up and began studying it from all angles, wondering whether it had once belonged to his grandmother. Meanwhile, the perfumer opened the journal to a particular page and held it out, tapping his forefinger on a section of text. It was a neatly handwritten page, dated to April 1915. Samir began reading through the Urdu passages, mumbling each word under his breath, and then looked up at the perfumer, confused.

"Iqbal Khan?"

"He would have been your great-grandfather's cousin," he said and then reached out to touch the young man's face. "Puttar, it's all in the eyes, he had the same eyes as you do. He served with my uncle in the First World War, and this qalam belongs to him."

꙳

Samir stayed on for longer than he thought he would. Days turned to weeks. He began to spend time with his namesake, observing him as he worked on his final perfume, helping him rearrange and catalog his library and records, and, most enjoyable of all, cooking for him and his granddaughter. Samir Khan cooked all the things his nani jaan had taught him—dumm biryani on one day and gosht-aloo with chapati on another, chicken in tangy tamatar curry and lamb marinated in mint. The smells of Lahore filled the Vij household once again. And the perfumer felt the layers of his childhood reveal themselves, one by one, with every day that the young man spent by his side. It was a strange relationship—two Samirs connected by a Firdaus—but one they both craved and cherished.

The perfumer had noticed, though, that whatever the young man did, wherever he went, a notebook accompanied him. And one night, as they sat down to dinner, he asked about it.

"A journalist?"

Samir explained the kind of pieces he wrote for *Dawn*.

"And now"—the perfumer took a heap of fragrant chana pulao— "Anouk tells me that you are working on a book. Is that right?"

"Well, I have some ideas."

"A book about what?"

Samir looked around the room, at the perfumer's attentive gaze and Anouk's supportive smile, and wiped his hands on his napkin. "Actually, a book about *this*. About the unspoken, intimate parts of family history. A book about Lahore, Partition, Nani jaan, and . . . you. A book about love."

"Love?" the perfumer probed further.

"Love, and other intangible things that are passed down from generation to generation, like memory or myth. Things that are not eclipsed by life or death. Everlasting things."

The perfumer drummed his fingers against the table and smiled widely. "The book of everlasting things."

# 58

# The Grandchildren of Partition

A few weeks later, in November, the old perfumer, Anouk, and Samir spent the day cleaning the atelier. Vials in different shapes, sizes, and colors, bearing all sorts of ordinary and extraordinary aromas, were clustered on various tables. Winter had arrived, the city outside was blanketed with snow—the first snowfall Samir had ever seen—and a blue-golden sunshine kissed every surface of the room. Dvořák played on the record player, further painting the room in his splendor. Over the past few months, with the exception of the hours the perfumer spent working on the rose, this atelier had become Anouk's domain, as the natural heir to the perfumery.

"Vij sahib," Samir called out from across the room, "may I ask you something . . . personal?"

The perfumer chuckled, as if everything hadn't already been personal. He nodded.

"Well, ever since Nani jaan mentioned you, I have wanted to know about—" Samir paused. He felt awkward even thinking about it, let alone attempting to voice it. Clearing his throat, he chose his words carefully. "After the incident in 1947, did you continue to . . . love Nani jaan?"

The perfumer nodded, though taken aback by the young man's directness.

"And now, do you still love her now?"

The perfumer's eyes widened, Anouk stood motionless by the organ, and Samir wondered whether this was the line he had feared crossing.

But the old perfumer ruminated on the question and, minutes later, spoke. "What does it mean to be in love? I have thought about this many times—particularly after you asked me about your grandmother, Anouk. What does it mean to be in love? It isn't the most original question, nor is it the most unusual one. Many have asked it, and many will continue to. But what does it mean to be in love with someone who is no longer around, no longer available, no longer alive? Is it still love? Does love die when the beloved dies?"

While he hadn't offered an answer, he had raised many questions of his own.

"But do you wish that things would have been different, Nanu?" Anouk now asked.

"Do I wish I could go back and change the course of history?" The perfumer sighed. "Do I wish that I could have prevented the Shahalmi fire, and saved my family from perishing? Do I wish that Firdaus had never done what she did, that we'd never have parted the way we did? Yes, on days, I wish this deeply. I wish she would have fought for me, and I for her. But I have lived too long holding on to this wish. And now, all I can say is this: There are things we are expected to do for the people we love. Things that are, at times, beyond our understanding, but we do them anyway, out of duty. Maybe this is what Firdaus had to do . . ."

He turned to look at her grandson, and he nodded, unable to forget how his grandmother had once described the morning of the fire, the evening by the window; the day of separation, the night of regret.

"But how did it happen? The fire, the riots . . . Partition?" Samir now ventured into other unspoken territories. Anouk, too, abandoned the organ and sat down on the chair, legs folded and pulled up against her chest.

"How did it happen." The perfumer repeated the words gravely, amazed at the innocence and simplicity of the question. How *did* it happen? How was one to explain the word *Partition*? He brought his palms together, folded in front of his chest.

"Can you imagine a heart, a single beating heart?"

Samir and Anouk nodded, and the perfumer drew his palms suddenly and abruptly apart.

"Well, divide the heart into two pieces. That is how it happened."

Silence.

"With a single incision, Hindustan became India and Pakistan."

The grandchildren of Partition, one half each of the undivided heart, looked at each other.

"Each moment, each event, is so unique to its context that we can understand it only through the lens of its unfolding. The question, then, may not be *how* did the Partition happen, but *why* did the Partition happen, and how could we have done this to one another?"

Through the silence, Samir Khan's pen scratched across the page of his notebook. The book of everlasting things had begun.

"What do you remember from that time?"

"I remember that no single person could have understood all that was happening, all that would happen. Truth, even reality, had so many versions, and they were all being lived simultaneously. Religion quickly became the root of all misfortune. *Us or them.* And who was them, who was the other? It was us. We had created *the other* ourselves, for we were all *the other* to someone."

He paused for a few seconds.

"But I still don't understand it. Despite having lived through it, I cannot explain what exactly happened during the Partition. It was as though some poisonous nightmare had descended like a dark cloud over us all. What happened, how it happened, who started it, who retaliated? I don't remember clearly. But these things no longer matter because everyone lost something. And Hindu, Muslim, Sikh, the blood of all was equally red."

"Nanu, weren't you scared?" Anouk asked.

"I was twenty years old, and in a single day, I had lost my entire family, the woman I loved, and the land I called home. Of course I was scared."

Partition was no ordinary wound. It cut deeper, far deeper than all the layers of skin, deeper even than muscle and farther still, to the bone. And as Anouk and Samir listened to the perfumer—accepting part of that anatomy as theirs—they understood that the past would be renewed with each retelling, for every generation.

"People in Lahore don't generally talk about this period of Partition much," Samir said. "They speak with nostalgia about the glory of the time before it and the pride of independence after it, but Partition—the riots, the violence, the exodus—remains dark."

"Perhaps it is too painful. I felt that way for many years . . ." the perfumer offered, meeting Anouk's eyes. He was quiet for a few moments before adding, "It's just the way traumatic events happen. They unfold differently for different people, leaving different scars. See, at the time, there were no journalists, no writers like you, Samir, who went around cities or villages or refugee camps, recording what people had felt. There was no time to think about what had happened, what had been lost, *who* had been lost. Those realizations would come much later. But during the days of Partition, survival became of utmost importance, and then, I suppose, over time, people just normalized the new way of life. They had to move on, because . . . well, because life went on."

"And then they just . . . forgot?"

"Oh, no, puttar," the perfumer said, shaking his head slowly from side to side. "It is difficult to forget, but it is even harder to keep remembering."

# 59

# Khazin-E-Firdaus,
# the Keeper of Paradise

"So, a perfume is composed with memories?" Samir asked.

"Well, they are as fundamental as flowers or herbs, woods or resins. Before we compose, we imagine a smell, and that imagination is inspired by our memory," Anouk explained.

"So, the rose perfume . . ."

". . . is inspired by your grandmother," she finished.

Samir looked over at her smiling face, the sky reflected in her light brown eyes, and smiled back. Over the last few months, he had observed the perfumer working on what would be his final creation and had smelled traces of the rose all over the apartment and atelier. But only recently had he learned that the muse for this final masterpiece was his grandmother. Spraying it first on a smell strip and then on his wrists, Samir had sniffed and inhaled with concentration, trying to find her traces in a flower that she would not have been able to smell.

"It is hypnotic," Anouk concluded. "The rose is hypnotic."

This was the first perfume Anouk had witnessed her grandfather compose in its entirety. And there was something so extraordinary about this composition—nostalgic, beloved, even familiar—that, despite never having visited Lahore, Anouk began to dream about its streets and skies.

She now ran across the street, and Samir followed her through an ornate wrought-iron and stone entrance into a flood of golden sun. Pausing to take in the glass roof, the semicircled arches above, and the mosaic floor below, he asked, "What is this place?"

"*Bienvenue à la* Galerie Vivienne!" She opened her arms to either side. "This is one of my favorite places in Paris. In the 1800s, when Paris still lacked sewers and footpaths, and the roads were crowded with carriages or mud on a rainy day, these passages were built as temporary refuge. They were lined with shops on either side—tailors, cobblers, bookshops, cafés— and because they were covered, they attracted all kinds of passersby and flâneurs. The city is full of secret passages, but *this*, Galerie Vivienne, is the queen of all arcades!"

Samir could see why, for the glory of every inch of the passage drew him in. He walked slowly—glided, almost—across the tiled floor, the circular patterns of gold, brown, gray, and blue sparkling like fragmented reflections of the sun. Arch after arch suspended from the roof gave the impression of a never-ending hallway to heaven. Since it was nearly Christmastime, the shops on either side had covered their front windows in twinkling lights, creating an even more magical aura. They walked by a rare bookshop with gilded leather hardcovers arranged neatly in the front window, and Anouk paused, looking in with longing.

"This place always takes me back to an era with gaslight and horse-drawn carriages, perfumed gloves and gorgeous bustle dresses!"

Samir chuckled. "Well, it may not be as fashionable, but parts of old Lahore can do that too. Walking into Wazir Khan mosque, and letting your fingers trail over the beautiful kashi-kari tilework in cobalt blue and firoza, vibrant green, orange, and deep golden yellow . . ."

They sat down at A Priori Thé and ordered two cups of hot chocolate.

"Don't you want to see what Lahore is like?" he asked.

"More than anything. But he won't come with me and I can't leave him . . ."

Samir nodded.

"There are so many things I don't know about India and Pakistan. It's been over a decade since I learned about my grandfather's past, and I've read a lot about Partition. But books don't really . . ." She paused, searching for the right words.

". . . tell ordinary people's histories?" Samir offered.

"Exactly. I wanted to know whether other people experienced what my grandfather had, whether other families perished or how they survived. But I couldn't find the voices. The books were all very official, the governance and politics of Partition, but there was nothing . . . human in them. I wanted to know how these people had felt, or what they had hoped, or even feared . . ." She thought for a moment before adding, "But we seem to assign very little value to memory."

"And yet," Samir responded, "it is memory that brought me here."

Something both Anouk and her grandfather were grateful for.

"But I do think that when it comes to history, the more we search for it, the deeper we descend. Like sedimentary rock," he continued. "There are many things even I don't know, despite being born and raised in Pakistan. Did you know that your great-granduncle and mine fought together in the First World War? Apparently, they were friends. Vij sahib gave me a pen that belonged to Iqbal Khan, but before that, I had never even heard of him, let alone knew that Indian sipahis had fought in the war."

Anouk nodded. "Over the last few years, my grandfather has brought the ghosts of so many people into our lives. I can't ever forget the warmth with which he summons them, the tenderness in his voice, his conversations with the dead. Sometimes, my grandfather forgets who he is speaking to, and I become Fir— . . . your grandmother, or my mother, or my grandmother . . . It reveals just how easily he is held prisoner by memory. It always breaks my heart."

After spending months in her company, Samir was comfortable opening up to Anouk about things he might never have even with his family, for she innately understood them.

"At the end of my grandmother's life," he revealed, "it seemed that her memories existed entirely separately from her. They adopted qualities and textures of their own, they expanded and contracted, and they were constantly tangled. At times, her own child—my mother—became a stranger; her home—the one I shared with her—became unfamiliar.

"And then," he continued, "just as you described, there were days she wouldn't recognize me. At times, she spoke so formally, and other times, with childish abandon. When I learned of your grandfather, some things began to make sense. But the illness, though not in her mind, seemed to confuse her. As I would massage her feet, she would ask me about the perfumery in Anarkali, your family's perfumery. Her eyes would sparkle, but I had not the heart to tell her that it was no longer there, that it hadn't been there for decades. That Partition had happened . . ."

"What would you tell her, then?" Anouk asked, "when she would ask you about the past?"

"I would tell her that everyone is well, *sab khairiyat hai.* I would tell her that I had been at the perfumery just that afternoon. I would play along, even enjoy the theatricality from time to time."

"But that's cruel!"

"Oh, I know. *I know.* I felt cruel, but in those last few months, it was one of the only ways to make her happy."

Anouk sighed.

"See, this is what I have come to understand. Firdaus Khan's memory was full of darkness. But at the end, she wished for there to be a light, no matter how false it was. And that light was always Samir Vij."

"But that meant that she was always somewhere else," Anouk reflected.

He smiled at her in such a way that she already knew what he would say next.

"Yes, she was always with us, but she was also always in a place of the past." He paused for a few seconds and then added, "Don't you also know what that's like?"

While Anouk and Samir were away, the old perfumer locked the door to his room and unfolded the only letter he had ever received from his beloved. *Samir Vij,* the envelope read in her ornate Urdu script. The paper smelled of dense tuberose ittar, having lived in the same box for many months. Over the last few weeks, he had read and reread this parting note so many times that by now, he had begun treating it as a conversation, responding to her words.

"*Salaam, Firdaus jaan,*" he addressed the letter.

June 2014

Samir, I know it has taken me long to write to you, but now time is no longer on my side. I hope this reaches you before it is too late. There are so many things I want to say that mean so much more than any words I would attempt to write.

He sighed. "But I wish you would have written something, *anything.*" Removing his spectacles, he wiped his moist eyes and continued.

I feel sometimes that our youth was unkind to us, that it happened at a time when it could be easily seized and swallowed by the violent ongoings of the world. And at such a time, when I should have revolted, I chose duty over desire. This has remained my biggest regret. I would ask you to forgive me, but I know the time for that has long passed. Now there is nothing I can surrender but my heart, for I am bereft of all else. I may have lived my years in regret, but not without the company of a singular truth—that I was once in love with you, that I will always be in love with you. And this truth has nothing to do with country, family, religion, life, or even death. This truth is endless. When you read this, look to the sky. That is where I shall be. Now we will only meet at the place where the winds touch the edges of paradise. That is where I will wait for you. Keep me in your heart, keep me there until we meet again.

Yours, forever yours,

Firdaus

He folded the letter and placed it back into the envelope. Looking up to the darkening sky, he whispered, "Until we meet again."

A few days later, Samir Vij stood by the window of his bedroom after dinner, watching the snow blanket the world outside. Another Christmas had come and gone, and the year was drawing to a close. Through his parted curtains, the dull yellow light of the streetlamps illuminated the room and he smiled to himself, remembering the first time he'd ever seen snow.

Opening his mouth to the sky, a twenty-one-year-old Samir had collected the flurries on his tongue as Madame Blanchet had watched amusedly. It had been a moment of great comfort, to realize that there were still joys to experience in the world. And now, as the snow fell heavily on the roof of the Église Saint-Germain, Samir walked over to his desk and rummaged through the pile of journals. Opening one to November 1914, he read of the first snowfall in the battlefields of France.

Very fine flakes have fluttered down and fallen in a heavy sheet across the camp and I am reminded of the windblown cotton from the fields near the Railway Colony in Lahore. The weather is cold, but it is very beautiful. For the first time since we arrived in this land, we have felt ageless.

Vivek had died containing so many secrets, so many burdens. And with his death, with the fire, these had all risen up into the blazing air— soot-like, fumes of memory—and settled onto, *into*, Samir. Out of the ninety long years of his life, seventy had been spent here, in France, in self-inflicted exile, following the impulses of his nose. Now, in chronological order, he arranged the pile of his and his uncle's journals.

He was about to turn his attention to the single bottle of perfume on his desk when he heard voices outside. Pausing, he wondered what Anouk and the young man were talking about. The young had so much to discuss, particularly when they had inherited all the heaviness of the old. Samir had been in their lives for four months now, and the perfumer hoped he would stay for longer.

With this thought, he picked up the bottle of perfume. Generously dousing a knot of linen cloth in the liquid, he placed a bell jar over it, to be able to smell it tomorrow. Despite how cold it was outside, Samir Vij felt cocooned in the aroma. All the warmth of his life had returned. Everything was now complete. Letting out a triumphant sigh, he rose to draw the curtains. He walked over to his bed, removed his spectacles, and fell into a deep and unburdened sleep.

᭝

The next morning, Anouk decided to make crepes with strawberry compote for breakfast. She began whipping the batter and brewing the coffee, and designated Samir to chop the strawberries. Holding up the fruit grudgingly, he teased her by saying that *real* Lahori breakfasts were halwa-puri from Capri's or Waris's spicy nihari-naan. Aiming her whisk at him, she told him to continue chopping.

Her grandfather's door remained closed, and though that was unusual, she decided to let him sleep in. But forty-five minutes later, when the warm smell of honey crepes and sugary berries had filled the apartment, and the perfumer still had not emerged, she looked over at Samir, concerned.

She walked to her grandfather's door and knocked. "Nanu? Breakfast is ready."

When he said nothing, she placed her ear over the door and listened. Not a single sound emerged from the room. Opening the door in haste, she found the curtains still drawn and her grandfather still soundly curled up in bed. Smiling to herself, she walked over to his bedside and nudged his shoulder gently.

"Nanu, wake up . . ."

When he still didn't rouse, she nudged harder. Then, finally, she called out to Samir, her voice fraught with panic. He rushed into the room to find her sitting on the bed, holding on to her grandfather's arm.

The perfumer had passed into the night.

Samir's year had been bookended by quiet deaths. Breathing in, he walked to Anouk and embraced her. He knew how this felt; he knew it all too well. She leaned into him, tears running down her cheeks and onto his shirt.

"Light," she exclaimed with urgency, after a few minutes. "I need light. I need to see him."

Swiftly, Samir drew the curtains, and sunlight poured into the room, mixing into the sweet aroma of roses already lingering in every corner. Anouk began to shake the perfumer's face, his shoulders, his hands, his nose, but there was no life left in him. Samir pulled her away and she staggered toward the desk and into her grandfather's chair. Anouk began running her hands over the objects scattered on the desk, wanting to touch anything that still held his warmth. She opened notebook after notebook, until a note fell out. Unfolding it, she looked at her grandfather, her body full of equal amounts of anger and sorrow.

My darling Anouk,
   Do not be sad. You know this had to happen sometime soon.
Know that I am leaving everything to you. All that was once
mine is now yours. Take care of yourself and do not be afraid of

love, as I was. My father once told me that I should not allow the hostile world to erode my gift of smell, that I should never disrespect or belittle it. I offer the same advice to you, but with an addition—celebrate the gift that nature has given you, use it, wield it, ma chérie. But do not ever let it consume you or dictate the actions of your life. You are so much more than your nose.

Your nanu

She handed the note to Samir as her gaze fell on the bell jar placed at the edge of the desk, by the window. A single perfume bottle stood next to it, indicating that the final composition of Samir Vij's life was complete. With trembling hands, Anouk lifted the bell jar to release a deluge of roses into the room. The smell was exquisite, more sublime than anything she could have dreamed of, and she raised her arms to touch the invisible curtain of perfume that had dispersed all around. A masterpiece composed as an homage, a tribute, a eulogy, a memory, a desire, a longing, a love.

She glanced back at the bed, at the perfumer peacefully departed, and felt her body deflate. Then, picking up the bottle from the desk, she noticed that it bore a label. *He had finally named the perfume.* Anouk tried to read it, half knowing what to expect, but she was slow, and her tears impaired her. She turned to Samir, who bent down to get a better look.

Upon reading, he felt a warmth course through his body. He rose slowly, straightening his back.

"What does it say?" Anouk asked.

Samir Khan turned to face Anouk Adams. One half inheritor of the history they shared, he looked into her brown eyes. "*Khazin-e-Firdaus,* the keeper of paradise."

# Notes on the Text

**Composed by Jahnvi Lakhota Nandan of *The Perfume Library***

*Ibtida*, inspired by Madame deRose's historic formula in Grasse and composed by Vivek Nath Vij as his first perfume in Lahore, is based on *Brown, Yellowish, Golden, Tanned, Blonde and Bisque*.

The Lahore series, composed by Vivek Nath Vij in Grasse between 1918 and 1920, inspired by the mimosa flower offered to him by Ambrette in the distillery, is based on *Mimosa 25*.

*Amrit*, composed by Vivek Nath Vij in Lahore as homage to his late wife, Ambrette, and modernized by Samir Vij in Paris during the 1970s, is based on *Ambrette Accord*.

*Ab-e-zar*, composed by Vivek Nath Vij in Lahore during World War II, is based on *Guggulu*.

The accords *Gauhar, Shafaq, Sahil, Nargis, Parwaz*, and *Sapna* are based on unnamed accords created by Nandan.

*Noor*, composed by Samir Vij in Lahore and presented to Firdaus at Standard Restaurant in 1946 and then remade in Paris, is based on *Sutra*, also known as *That's Why I Wear The Hats to Keep Everyone Away From Me* or *Issieblow* or *Bedouin* or *Freida*.

*Arzoo*, composed by Samir Vij in Grasse, in memory of Vivek and Ambrette's first meeting in the jasmine fields, is based on *Aphtoori Absolut* and *Kama*. His composition of the original jasmine note is based on Nandan's own composition from perfumery school.

*Firaq,* composed by Samir Vij in Grasse using tulsi, or holy basil, as the heart, is based on *This Space in Between You and Me,* co-created by Nandan and the late artist Hema Upadhyay, as a scent-translation of her 2002 artwork by the same name.

The smells of Rose sahib's library, when Samir first meets him at Villa deRose in 1959, are based on notes from *The Delighter of Shiva.*

*Silsila,* composed by Samir Vij in Paris in the mid- to late 1970s, inspired by the pelagic landscape he shared with his uncle, is based on the saltwater accord *Baji.*

*What Do Peonies Smell Like in Zero Gravity,* envisioned by Anouk Adams, is based on the *Fusun C23* accord.

*Khazin-e-Firdaus,* the final perfume of Samir Vij's life, composed with his granddaughter Anouk in Paris, is based on *Firdaus.*

### ADDITIONAL NOTES ON THE TEXT

In Chapter 19, the perfumer Khushboo Lal is based on Mr. Vijay Narain Kapoor, from M. L. Ramnarain Perfumers, Kannauj, India.

In Chapter 32, the Russian artist mentioned by Vivek is Massia Bibikoff, who spent time with the Indian soldiers at their camp in September 1914 and published her drawings and observations in the book *Our Indians at Marseilles.* In the same chapter, the janral sahib mentioned is General Sir James Willcocks (GCB, GCMG, KCSI, DSO), who was given command of the Indian Corps in France in 1914.

In Chapter 35, the Afridi jemadar is based on Mir Dast (IOM, OBI) of the 55th Coke's Rifles, who received the Victoria Cross for his services during the Second Battle of Ypres in April–May 1915.

In Chapter 41, the bottles of perfume that American soldiers took back home following the First World War were by François Coty, who soon after began to distribute his products in the United States. In early June 1940, during the Second World War, the people of Menton and the border villages along the Upper Tinée, Vésubie, Bévéra, and Roya Valleys were evacuated to Grasse, Cannes, Antibes, Barjols (Var), Annot, Saint-André-les-Alpes, Barrême, and Castellane (Basses-Alpes).

In Chapter 54, the book written by the retired Indian diplomat is Pran Nevile's *Lahore: A Sentimental Journey* (Allied Publishers, 1993). Samir Khan's column in *Dawn* newspaper is inspired by the work of Mayank Austen Soofi, also known as the Delhi Walla.

In Chapter 56, the book of letters from Indian soldiers is Professor David

Omissi's *Indian Voices of the Great War: Soldiers' Letters, 1914–18* (Palgrave Macmillan, 1999).

The title of this novel is borrowed from a book of collected poems published in 1914 that I discovered while interviewing art historian and professor Partha Mitter at his home in Oxford. It belonged to his mother, Pushpa Lata De, and its story can be read in my first book, *Remnants of Partition: 21 Objects from a Continent Divided* (Hurst Publishers, 2019).

# Acknowledgments

Quite like the protagonists of this novel, the germ of my idea began with vials of perfume. My maternal grandfather, who worked as a chemist at the Indian pharmaceutical company Dabur, used to often receive fragrance samples to use in soaps and shampoos. They had names as basic as flowers or fruits and as flamboyant as Arabian Dreams, Meadow-Mist, Rambo, and Dream Girl. He would bring these samples home and, as my mother recalled fondly from her childhood, mix them into the water of the air cooler during summertime, so that the whole house would eventually be doused in perfume. If it were rose one day, then it would be apricot on another and lemongrass on the third. And when my mother told this story, it was with such simple, childish delight and made me wish I'd been there. This singular memory of hers became the anchor upon which this story began to take shape.

The precious smell memory of the air cooler was enhanced by time spent with the gifted perfumer Jahnvi Lakhota Nandan, founder of The Perfume Library. When I began thinking about this book, it was not with any natural talent, but mere curiosity for perfume. However, the more you smell, the better you smell, and over the last five years, I have learned from, observed, and interviewed Jahnvi extensively across India and France, in a way that her vocabulary, gestures, and perfumistic atlas have been folded into *The Book of Everlasting Things*. Every perfume in the story is an already-existing composition created by her, making this text an homage to the highly secretive and esoteric realm of smell that she invited me to temporarily inhabit.

I am also grateful to other perfumers who have shared their knowledge over the years: Pranjal Kapoor and his father, Vijay Narain Kapoor, of ML Ramnarain Perfumers, my hosts in the perfume city of Kannauj who demonstrated the ancient techniques of ittar distillation passed down the generations of their family. Gulabsingh Johrimal in Old Delhi's Dariba Kalan, where I would often go searching for samples of the ingredients I was writing about—from rajnigandha to kewra, bergamot to ambrette seed oil. Berket & Sons Perfumers in Mozamjahi Market and the shops around the Charminar in Hyderabad that introduced me to ittars like kashish and safa marwa.

Chroniclers of smell who have taken out time from their schedules to indulge my oddly specific questions: Cynthia Barnett, for her profound observations and research on rain, Dr. Rachel Herz on the psychology of smell, Christopher Kemp on ambergris, and Victoria Frolova, writer of the olfactive blog *Bois de Jasmin*, which quickly became a treasured resource. Perfumers and scientists whose writings and research, provocations, scent experiments, and techniques of composition have nourished this text: Jean-Claude Ellena, Edmond Roudnitska, Jean Carles, Luca Turin, and Mandy Aftel. Texts exploring the relationship to smell that I returned to often during the writing process are *Sandalwood and Carrion: Smell in Indian Religion and Culture* by James McHugh, "The Ittar Wallahs of Hyderabad" in *The Lost Generation: Chronicling India's Dying Professions* by Nidhi Dugar Kundalia, *Nimmatanama* translated as *The Sultan's Book of Delights* by Norah M. Tiley, *The Emperor of Scent* by Chandler Burr, *A Scented Palace: The Secret History of Marie Antoinette's Perfumer* by Elisabeth de Feydeau, and the work of Elena Vosnaki, fragrance historian and founder of *The Perfume Shrine*, on the smell of war.

I have to admit, I never imagined I would write fiction. Having begun my literary career as an oral historian of the 1947 Partition, I've spent the better part of the last decade writing about migration routes, divided families, unspoken histories, objects and memory. Thus, the sections pertaining to Partition came most naturally. In writing about Lahore, I drew from the trips I'd been fortunate enough to make in 2014 and '18, and the pre-Partition memories of my mother's family—the Vijs, who can trace their history to Choona Mandi, and the Berys, who lived in Machhi Hatta Bazar—in particular, my grandaunt Jiwan Vohra (née Bery), who recalls the fire that tore through Shahalmi Gate in the summer before Partition.

I want to thank Kanza Javed, for introducing me to the magnificent Wazir Khan mosque, where part of this book is set; Air Commodore Kaiser Tufail, for information on the calligraphy bazaar inside the mosque compound and for providing a copy of Yasmeen Lari's Guide to the Walled City; Seher Ali Shah, for taking time to discuss the history of female calligraphers and for her thesis, *A History of Traditional Calligraphy in Post-Partition Lahore* (University of Redlands, 2013). For conversations on Lahore, I thank Farhan Ahmed Shah, F. S. Aijazuddin, Haroon Khalid, Iqbal Qaiser, Majid Sheikh, Harleen Singh, and the late Pran Nevile. Dr. Ishtiaq Ahmed's seminal work *The Punjab: Bloodied, Partitioned, and Cleansed* and Fikr Taunsvi's *Chhata Darya,* translated as *The Sixth River* by Maaz Bin Bilal, played key roles in constructing the landscape of immediately pre- and post-Partition Lahore. I also thank Hussain Zaidi sahib in Old Delhi's Chitli Qabar, for his knowledge on the art of calligraphy, and Aamir Wani, who helped in the translation of Urdu texts.

The Great War arrived through the military testimonies I'd recorded during my Partition fieldwork. Men and women who had served in World War II narrated stories of their forefathers who had served across the black waters in World War I. My interest, thus, grew in the experiences, desires, sacrifices, loyalties, and longings of the 1.5 million Indians who fought in the war, and how their extraordinary contributions had been relegated to mere footnotes until very recently. I've had the opportunity to learn about this remarkable army from experts in the field, and I thank them for their time and generosity: Jasdeep Singh, Squadron Leader Rana Chhina, Adil Rana Chhina, Parmjit Singh, Amandeep Madra, Santanu Das, David Omissi, and George Morton Jack, who read early drafts and provided editorial notes. I am grateful also to the National Army Museum, India Office Records and Private Papers at the British Library, Imperial War Museum, Victoria & Albert Museum, Royal Brighton Pavilion, Centre for Armed Forces Historical Research of the United Service Institution of India, and the Archeological Survey of India, for allowing me to access and draw from their archives. The chapters set during the war use details from the thousands of letters that Indian soldiers wrote home—available to us only because they were censored—and the daily movements of troops is based loosely on the *Great War Diaries: 57th (Wilde's) Rifles (Frontier Force)*. I have also drawn from the memoirs of General Sir James Willcocks, Captain Roland "Roly" Grimshaw, and Massia Bibikoff.

To my agent, David Godwin, who, years ago, listened to a winding tale of uncles and nephews, perfume and war, letters, journals, partition lines, and unrequited love, thank you for believing in this novel. To Philippa Sitters and Amandine Riche at DGA, and Becky Wearmouth, Lisette Verhagen, and Lucy Barry at PFD, thank you for your unending support. In America—my editor, Caroline Bleeke, who created a novelist out of a historian and read every single draft with exceptional attentiveness and foresight; Sydney Jeon, who carefully considered the arc of each character and brought a fresh set of eyes to the manuscript; Mary Beth Constant, for thoughtful suggestions while copyediting the text; Jeremy Pink, for overseeing final proofs; Michelle McMillian, Keith Hayes, and Kelly Gatesman, for the elegant interior and luxe cover design, and the entire team at Flatiron Books. In India—Sohini Basak and Udayan Mitra, for having faith every step of the way, and Ananth Padmanabhan, for always creating a home for my work at HarperCollins.

For five long years, this story has lived with me, which means it has also lived with those who populate my world. I am grateful to everyone who has read pages, trudged through archives on my behalf, accompanied me on field research, or given advice on various sections of this text: my father, Anuj Bahri, siblings Aashna and Aaditya, Sharvani Pandit, Shruti Brahmbhatt, Navdha Malhotra, Priyanka Pathania, Laura Emoke Gabor, Pranav Misra, Kumail Hasan, Yunus Lasania, Karuna Ezara Parikh, Kavita Puri, Jassa Ahluwalia, and Naveen Kishore. To my mother, Rajni Malhotra, and aunt, Mona Mehra—thank you for your stories.

Lastly, it is to my grandparents, Vishwa Nath Vij and Amrit Bery, that I dedicate this novel.

# About the Author

Aanchal Malhotra is a writer and oral historian from New Delhi, India. A cofounder of the Museum of Material Memory, Malhotra has written two nonfiction books on the human history and generational impact of the 1947 Partition, titled *Remnants of Partition* and *In the Language of Remembering*. *The Book of Everlasting Things* is her debut novel.

aanchalmalhotra.com